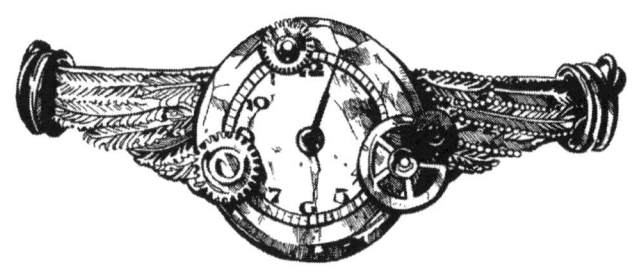

Clouds of War

Book Two of the Aether Saga

by

Melissa Ann Conroy

CLOUDS OF WAR

Cover art and book design by Brent Schreiber
www.brentschreiber.com

SteamyGirl Publishing

11261 Martin Ave.

Omaha, NE 68164

ISBN 978-0-9895043-3-1

Printed in the United States of America

Acknowledgments

This book is dedicated to the pilots and crews of Mercy Air. It has been a privilege and delight to be your dispatcher over this past year. I am deeply grateful for what you have taught me about flight, patient transport, contrary engines, weather conditions, and other elements that have made their way into my writing. Your dedication, courage, and cheerful spirits have helped lighten the workload during trauma season and times of high volume flight requests. Your work is both critical and high-risk, and I am glad to assist in bringing you all back to base safely.

Special thanks to Gary Lange for his inspiration for Grey Wulfe and the aether flyer *Horus*. Gary, thanks for many fun steampunk cons, a lot of laughs, and your endless support.

To Kevin Breem, my wonderful editor, a million thanks for your hard work, advice, and patience in this endeavor. Your attention to detail and commitment to historical accuracy are most appreciated.

Again, I warmly thank those who contributed to my Indiegogo fundraiser during August 2012. Thanks to Mark Arnold, Joe and Miriam B., Jason Burns, Heather Carouth, Barret Dent, Dustin Fickle, Theresa Frankovsky, Molly Ketchum, Scot Klinger, Gary Lange, John LeVan, Matt Manning, Luna Meschiari, Merinda Peterson, Daniel Moreau, Stephen Ormsby, Adam Reiff, Kenneth Robertson, Jenna Tomlin, Thomas Werner, and Dave West.

Aether Saga

Steam on the Horizon

Clouds of War

Clouds of War

Chapter One

The gargantuan rock roared up from the foaming seas, reaching past wisps of white clouds and skimming the sky. Lofty and majestic, it surveyed the warm waters of the Mediterranean with magnificent grandeur. Seagulls wheeled and cried in the air currents, their voices mingling with the hissing roar of airships gliding through the clear blue sky. Below, marine ships rode the white-capped waves, their sails shining in the warm sunlight.

On topdeck of the airship *Horizon*, Captain Gavin Roberts soaked in the heat and let it scour away some of the fatigue dragging him down. It was August 7th, and the *Horizon* had flown non-stop for thirty-six hours following her hasty retreat from London. Leaving the smoldering remains of Halloway's workshop behind her, the *Horizon* had turned her prow towards Gibraltar in the quest for friendlier skies and fresh opportunities for her captain and crew.

Fighting the weariness in his legs, Roberts stamped his feet and examined his surroundings, particularly the dozen or so airships circling the rocky fortress of stone that was Gibraltar. He counted at least six military airships, two transport vessels, and several merchant flyers, none of which carried a Smothers crest. After the events in London a few days ago, Roberts did not want the *Horizon* near an airship belonging to his enemy.

His most pressing concern was fuel. The *Horizon* was almost down to her two hour fuel reserve when she landed at Gibraltar, and Roberts did not know if he would find anthracite at port. The airship had been forced to leave London with whatever supplies she had on board, and her coal hoppers were half-empty upon departure.

Even with the question of coal, Gibraltar was a logical destination choice. It was within reasonable flying distance of London, and the flight path was across Spain's well-patrolled airspace. Gibraltar was a bustling port and offered a reasonable chance at fuel and work. At the very least, it would give the crew a chance to catch their breaths while Roberts made plans for the future.

Gibraltar's public wharf was embedded in the side of the cliff and jutted out into the open air. Immense piles held up dozens of airship berths, stacks of cargo, and gantry cranes growling in the salty air. At the waterline, marine ships, both military and merchant, lined the docks and jockeyed for a position to unload their cargo and take on fresh supplies.

The crew set the *Horizon* down carefully on an empty berth and prepared for a full shutdown. Roberts moved among his men, supervising their work and observing them carefully. They were all tense, exhausted, and overstrained, deeply worried about the future and entirely uncertain about what was ahead. The stress of their hasty departure and sudden change in fortune had been compounded by the addition of five new crew members on board. Tempers had flared during their flight to Gibraltar and tension ran high as the older crew struggled to incorporate the new.

However, considering the circumstances, Roberts was fairly pleased with how the new crew members had settled into the *Horizon*. Barking Jack had quickly proven to be an excellent pilot and the *Horizon* responded well to his hand. Big Tom silently stalked the catwalks, vigilant for leaks and alert for any problems in the envelope. With Halloway wrapped in a morphine-induced sleep during the journey, Sparrowman assisted Jenkins in the engine room and the pair kept the *Horizon* moving forward.

Long Tom passed Roberts and gave a negligent nod. Roberts returned the nod coolly, not quite finished with his assessment of the new able airman. Long Tom was competent in his duties but he carried an undertone of belligerence that Roberts had noted more than once. He had kept Long Tom under careful surveillance during the journey and would continue to do so until the airman proved his worth.

A movement off to the right and Roberts saw Bloomberg trudge across the deck, clear exhaustion etched in his face. The few days on board the *Horizon* had not been easy for the former postman: already his excess flesh was melting away and his pale skin was disappearing under a rapidly deepening suntan. Bloomberg had done his best, but he was on the receiving end of a crash course in airship piloting, and the sensitive, responsive *Horizon* was not the easiest airship for such lessons. Yet he fought determinedly to learn the ins and outs of an airship and voiced no complaints.

As the crew went about their duties, Roberts' attention shifted to the senior members, especially Farrington. The bosun had remained quiet and uncharacteristically somber during the flight to Gibraltar, his thoughts no doubt consumed with the family he had left behind and his infected wound. Harding had attended Farrington carefully, using his store of leeches to eat away the dead, infected tissue.

Already patches of healthy flesh were beginning to replace the green, fetid rot that had patchworked Farrington's injured arm. "He's looking better," Harding had said just that morning. "Gangrene is devilishly tricky to completely eradicate, and it can lurk in the body when you think it's gone. I'll monitor it closely and we'll...just have to see what happens." If not, it would fall on Harding to remove the offending limb and Halloway to fashion a construct arm out of whatever parts he could find.

The crew had borne up stoically during their flight to Gibraltar, but with an unclear future awaiting them, morale was grim. Roberts knew that if he couldn't find work quickly and formulate a plan for the upcoming months, he would risk a mass exodus once the airship landed. He was nearly out of money and the *Horizon* was currently doing nothing to earn anything. Every flight hour an airship took was costly, and the next time the *Horizon* lifted, it needed to be for a job.

Once the airship was fully landed and shut down at Gibraltar, Roberts paid for two days of docking fees and released the crew. Barking Jack was already speculating about what Mediterranean beauties awaited the men in town. "When the ladies see a construct leg, they always want to know how far up it goes," he announced with a lecherous wink. "And what's missing under the trousers. Matter of scientific inquiry, it is. So I shows them."

This brought on a few laughs, but grim worry still filled the airship and the crew departed with little enthusiasm.

Gibraltar was an expensive port, and some of the more thrifty-minded men were watching their coppers too closely to have a wild spree in port.

Harding stayed on board the *Horizon*. "I'm an old man and the pleasures of the flesh are less pleasurable these days. Besides, someone has to look after that fool Halloway."

In the fire that had destroyed his workshop, Halloway had breathed in too much smoke: it had damaged his lungs and dimmed his eyes. Harding had kept him sedated with opiates during the journey, and Halloway had slept the sleep of the dead, rising fitfully only a few times to eat and drink before sinking back into troubled oblivion.

With no crew to supervise, Roberts was free to turn his attention to the pressing matter of their next transport job. He was wrestling with this problem topdeck, cool salt air on his face and sun on his shoulders, when the sound of hesitant feet approached. He looked over to see Halloway stumbling from below decks: eyes glassy, lank hair mussed, feet bare, legs moving as if they were in no mood to cooperate.

With painful effort, Halloway made his way to the railing and blinked owlishly at his surroundings. "Where are we?" he questioned hesitantly.

"Gibraltar," Roberts answered. "Southern part of Spain. Gibraltar's under British control," he added in case Halloway did not know.

Halloway absentmindedly scratched his head. "How long was I out?"

"Almost three days," Roberts grunted, watching him carefully. "You alright?"

More scratching was the answer. Halloway said nothing for several seconds, then tentatively asked, as if not entirely sure about the words, "That...happened, right? I mean...my shop."

"Yes, Jacob," Roberts sighed. "It happened, and I'm damned sorry about it."

Silence fell over them as Halloway continued to look out over the foaming sea. Finally he said in the same hesitant voice, "So what happens next?"

"We coal up, fix what needs to be fixed, let the crew rest a bit," Roberts responded. "I let the men off for two days. I'll look for work here. If there's none, we'll head to Tangier."

Other footsteps sounded, and Harding appeared with a bowl and handed it to Halloway. "Eat, man," he commanded. "You'll blow away in the wind if we don't get some weight on you. You barely ate anything on the flight here."

Halloway nodded in mute obedience and downed whatever was in the bowl without a fuss. His abrupt, high-energy arrogance and confidence had abandoned him and what was left was strangely human. Shock and grief had ripped most of Halloway away, stripping him down to the essential humanity.

Halloway continued to eat mechanically, gazing blearily into the distance as thoughts began to tick to life behind his clouded eyes. Roberts watched quietly, noting that with each spoonful, his old friend gained a little more color. Finally, the spoon clattered in the empty wooden bowl. Halloway wiped a dirty hand over his lips and questioned, "Did Jenkins finish the patch job?"

"He did a seam and seal that held us over," Roberts responded. "We kept between twenty and twenty-five knots during the flight."

"Oh. That was good," Halloway said absentmindedly, then made a movement as if to leave. "I'd best go see to the boiler." With, that he padded carefully across the deck and disappeared below as Roberts watched him, a tight frown creasing his face. Shock had rendered Halloway meek, but eventually he'd recover his habitual belligerence and tensions would rise on board. Halloway would fare ill as a permanent crew member, and what was to be done with him was a deeply troubling question.

Roberts scanned the ocean again, noting the marine ships sailing the waters, some filled with soldiers. Others bore cargo from all corners of the world, some of it legal and much of it covert. Gibraltar had earned a name not only as a major shipping port but also as a hub of enthusiastic smuggling, much appreciated by captains eager to avoid Spain's sharp tariffs. When she had arrived at the wharf, the *Horizon* had received only the most cursory of inspections. The bored official who had glanced briefly below deck was not interested in seeing anything worth official documentation.

The remembrance made Roberts smile wryly. There was work in Gibraltar for the asking. Honest work, he was less sure of. But it was honest work he would find for his airship; he would not have her sink lower, nor put her or the crew in more danger. Her captain would have to keep her in the sky through legal means.

Harding reappeared topdeck, juggling the last of the bread and two bowls of surprisingly good potato and leek soup. After a few mouthfuls, Roberts commented, "The boy's learning fast."

Harding snorted. "I may be a chronic bachelor, Gavin, but I am capable of making potato and leek soup. I am also proficient in making leek and potato soup."

They ate in companionable silence, each man intent on his own thoughts. However, Harding was not long before he drove home the point. "What is it that you plan to do next?" The words were blunt but not couched as a challenge and Roberts didn't take them as such.

"I can't keep flying her unarmed," he responded.

"Well, yes, that would be a good starting point," Harding stated dryly. "This rock is a military base. There is armament to be found here." He fought down a tough bite of bread before continuing. "She's a good ship, Gavin," Harding said in almost gentle tones. "She'll carry you through this."

"It's not her I doubt," Roberts responded darkly.

Harding paused. "Well, it's not you I doubt." His candor was expressed with unaccustomed kindness and the moment was particularly poignant. But Harding broke it almost as soon as it had materialized.

"You're addled with fatigue, man," he switched topics neatly, scooping up their discarded bowls. "You can't think properly like this. Get some rest. It can wait until morning." With that, he disappeared below, leaving Roberts with the fresh blowing wind and his own troubled thoughts for company.

Chapter Two

The streets of Gibraltar were narrow, steeply angled cobblestone streets gouged between gaunt buildings, and choked with bodies. The babble of several tongues filled the air as civilians and soldiers went about their business. Roberts stalked the streets moodily, his mind preoccupied with the task ahead but also noting changes throughout the city. He had last visited three years ago, and he had seen the skeletal beginnings of a massive pumpworks station which promised to distill sea water into fresh, solving Gibraltar's chronic water shortage.

Roberts had passed the completed pumpworks station on his way into town and paused for a few minutes to observe. Massive piping half visible in the waves ran well out to sea and drew from the blue waters of the Mediterranean. Machines blasted the saline waters into steam that was then condensed into potable liquid for the thirsty city.

With a steady supply of drinking water, Gibraltar had grown and improved. Roberts saw few signs of disease and filth, and he guessed that the population had significantly expanded. The upturn in good fortune had made the famous port even more desirable to passing airships and marine vessels, and the smuggling trade, already a staple force in Gibraltar, had increased considerably.

It was to this end that Roberts moved through Gibraltar, leaving behind the more orderly main streets to delve into the underground market that, while hidden away, lingered just under the surface. He disliked turning to smuggled goods, but he didn't have much choice. The *Horizon* needed armament and Roberts had very little money left. Illicit weaponry was the only way Roberts could protect his airship and crew.

A guard at the entrance of the narrow cave glanced Roberts over with the glazed, detached expression of one who had orders not to detain anyone who looked like a paying customer. Roberts rolled past him unchecked and entered the cave. Inside was a low ceiling of stone and a space fitfully lit by a collection of sputtering candles, all the better to shade the furtive souls inside. Business was brisk, and a steady line of customers made their way inside and out.

Nonchalantly, Roberts strolled through the dim cavern, taking his time as he perused the goods. He was running his hands casually over a gun barrel when he sensed rather than heard a presence at his side.

"Beautiful, isn't she, sir?" a voice ingratiated in his ear. Roberts kept his gaze forward as he subtly examined the speaker out of the corner of his eye. Short, bandy, and smoking a cheap cut of tobacco, the man had the voice and demeanour of a born salesman.

"That's a Vandenberg volley gun, that is, sir," the salesman began limbering up his sales pitch. "Brand new from London and top-of-the-line. It has one hundred and twenty-one barrels inside the cannon, and each one shoots out a fifty caliber bullet. Aim it where you please, sir, it'll shred anything in its path with one shot."

The salesman moved an inch closer. "Light as a feather, weighs just four hundred pounds, and only needs three men to run it. Good airship needs a light gun that won't fill up your hull, sir, or take too many men away from the airbags. You won't find a better weapon than this Vandenberg to protect your ship and your crew."

He's good, Roberts thought, impressed despite himself. Roberts had been master of the *Horizon* for four months now, but had yet to look the part. His nondescript attire was part parsimony, part a deeply abiding conviction that he'd be damned if he was going to wear stockings every day. As first mate of the *Lucky Lady*, Roberts had reluctantly donned a formal uniform on occasions, but Captain Albert was usually too drunk to much care what his first officer was wearing. As a result, Roberts had long preferred workman's clothing and he wasn't eager to give them up for breeches and epaulettes. Yet, somehow the salesman had picked up enough subtle signs to identify his potential customer and tailor his sales pitch appropriately.

"Has a range of over two thousand yards, sir," the salesman pressed. "Long enough to blow an airship out of the sky before she has a chance to do a mischief to your vessel." Roberts grunted noncommittally, but he was surprised at the news. As the *Lucky Lady*, the airship had carried two twelve-pounder carronade cannon with a range of three hundred yards, effectively useless for anything but point-blank firing. In the few skirmishes she had encountered with Roberts on board, she had peppered the attacking airship with grapeshot, then fled, receiving no casualties aside from Captain Albert, who had been a hysterical mess. Two thousand yards of range coupled with the *Horizon's* exceptional fleetness would be a strong guard against anything in the sky that wished her ill.

The salesman moved in for the kill. "Make a beggar of myself, I will, sir, but I'm prepared to see this little beauty walk out of here for just five hundred pounds."

Roberts whistled through his teeth. He was expecting a steep price for a good weapon, but the named price was more than he expected and far more than he could afford. "That's a pretty penny," he stated dryly.

Roberts gave the muzzle a final pat and straightened up, giving the salesman a quick but thorough glance. As he suspected, there was a set of corporal stripes hanging from the man's unbuttoned jacket, marking him an enterprising soldier who had an uncanny knack for finding things. The cave's interior was filled with items no doubt reassigned from their original posts or fallen off the back of an airship. However, such men could be useful.

The salesman's face took on a particularly rat-like expression as he leaned negligently against the gun's breech and stared into the distance. Neither man said anything for a moment. Roberts bided his time until the salesman spoke again. "Pity about the *Santa Maria*," he stated conversationally.

"Hmm?" Roberts responded mildly, moving to a rifle next to the Vandenberg gun. It was good steel, and the stock fitted his shoulder well as he lifted it to his eyes and sighted along the barrel.

"Little Spanish militia flyer that was doing some night training around Gibraltar last week," the salesman stated nonchalantly. "She wasn't well lit and she got herself smashed against the rock, taking all hands with her. This Vandenberg here was on board with a twin, and the other one's damned near stuck in the mud up off of Hangman's Cliff. The Spaniards want it back, but the *Santa Maria* wasn't cleared to fly and she wasn't where she was supposed to be. Since she crashed on Gibraltar, our navy says the Vandenberg's ours by rights."

He lit a rollup, filling the air with acrid smoke. "The Vandenberg is well stuck in the mud, and shifting it out will be a chore." The salesman shrugged with exaggerated casualness. "It could be damned near stuck there for weeks while there's a squabble over salvage rights."

Roberts still made no comment, but the salesman looked pointedly at him. Dirty fingers waggled expectantly, and Roberts dug for his money pouch. Furtive coins crossed palms and the salesman sidled off to another customer, but not without offering a few more words in parting.

"Dangerous winds around Hangman's Cliff," he warned quietly. "A captain sailing that high up the rock best mind his airship and his pilot."

The caution echoed in Roberts' mind as he headed towards the mouth of the cave. There were others poking around inside the cave, but all were intent on their own errands. None paid Roberts any attention as he ducked under the low entrance and stepped back into sunshine, grimly pondering his next course of action.

***   ***   ***   ***

"Anthracite?" the black-streaked foreman repeated in puzzlement. "I've got stores of it for the ironworks, but damned good it will do an airship, Captain."

Roberts had to strain to hear the foreman's words in the hellish din of the coal mine where great beasts of steel and wire burrowed deep into the earth. Grim human figures, many of them just children, trudged wearily amidst the mechanical boring arms and whirling shearing plates, but it was obvious that the machinery made up most of the labor force. Blasts of steam and heat from overworked metal parts turned the air warm and humid and the smell of hot oil, sweat, and coal dust was pervasive.

"If you want bituminous, I've got the best coking coal you'll find in the Mediterranean," the foreman continued, still visibly puzzled. "Twenty-five pounds a ton, Captain, to load on our dock or twenty-seven pounds delivered."

The foreman's confusion wasn't misplaced. Practically all airships and steam-powered marine ships ran on bituminous coal. Virtually none of them relied on anthracite for fuel. Halloway had stated that the *Horizon's* new boiler would run on regular bituminous if no other option presented itself but with diminished efficiency and speed. Roberts would have none of that.

"I want anthracite," he insisted. "I'll pay twenty-five pounds a ton for ten tons, but I want it pulverized before pickup." It was less than what Roberts had paid for anthracite in London, but the foreman didn't protest. From his expression, anthracite was in low demand in Gibraltar.

"Okay, Captain," the foreman responded with a shrug. "Your airship. Your funeral. I'll have it for you by morning."

They shook hands on it and Roberts left the mine, accompanied by the brilliant blue sun and his own internal calculations. The *Horizon* had only logged about seventy-five flight hours since her rebirth under Halloway's renovations, and her crew was still learning her whims and moods. So far, she had burned through an average of seventy-five pounds of coal per hour of flight time at minimum load capacity. Fully loaded during her flight to Larne, she had taken in under one hundred pounds an hour. Ten tons of coal would give her about ten days of flight time. A pitiful amount, he knew, for a long-range airship, particularly when reliable sources of anthracite were few and far between.

Scowling, Roberts remembered the words Halloway had uttered only a few months ago. *"When I'm done with her, she'll fly to Canton and back."* Roberts had not believed it when the *Horizon* was a broken wreck in Halloway's shop, and he did not believe it now. Their flight to Gibraltar had been impressive enough but fraught with difficulty. Bringing the *Horizon* beyond the borders of Europe was an exceedingly difficult challenge and a frankly fantastical proposition.

The immediate problem weighing on Roberts' mind was not his airship's destination but her defense. No one would give her cargo to carry if she couldn't protect it. Like it or not, the contested Vandenberg gun stuck in the mud on Hangman's Cliff was currently the only financially feasible option. Stealing a valuable weapon from the British military was an extraordinarily risky prospect. Attempting it would take careful planning, along with more luck than one airship captain could rightly commandeer.

Lost in thought, Roberts found his way to a seedy tavern that nevertheless offered a grand, glorious view of the Mediterranean from several hundred feet of elevation. He sat down, planted his weary feet on an empty chair, and gazed out over the vast expanse of blue sky and even bluer waters. Airships sailed to and fro in the dancing winds while marine vessels plowed sedately though the brilliant ocean. The magnificent scenery lifted some of the blackness out of his mood, but the weight of the half-finished letter in his pocket tugged his thoughts towards domestic concerns.

Dear Susan...

Roberts scrutinized the page etched with his decisive, carefully formed writing. His letters to his sister usually erred on the prosaic and brief but they were consistent, and he usually wrote a few times a month. A letter posted in London and air-delivered to Bombay could arrive in a month, and Roberts had always paid for air mail rather than waiting months for marine-delivered mail.

Pondering over a sentence, Roberts rummaged in his pocket for a stained, folded picture and gazed at it longingly. Susan, her beauty beginning to soften under the march of time, motherhood, and the fierce climate of India, stared back at him. Roberts felt sharp longing tear at him. It had been five years since Susan had followed her husband Graham to the mission field in India. For the first three years, Roberts had flown on the long-flight *African Queen* which had routinely made port calls in India. He had been able to see Susan and her family regularly. But the *Lucky Lady* had never ventured far from London and Roberts had not seen his sister in over two years.

The three boys Gavin, Trevor, and Peter were slightly blurred in the picture, and Roberts knew that Susan had been hard-pressed to keep them still long enough for the camera exposure to take hold.

Gerald, the patriarch of the tribe, stood with his hand on Susan's shoulder, and Roberts' glance lingered on his brother-in-law. He would have paid dearly for a few hours of Gerald's time and the council his brother-in-law could give.

Roberts ordered coffee and called for ink and pen from the serving girl. When the items were delivered, he turned his attention back to the letter to his sister, the words stumbling in his mind before ever reaching the page. As he struggled with the letter, a monkey suddenly scurried across the deck and snatched something off a customer's plate undetected. By the time the man noticed his absent food, the monkey was safely in the bushes. Roberts laughed and described the scene in his letter, knowing the boys would find it humorous. He stayed quiet about anything that might possibly worry Susan. He had written to her twice since acquiring the *Horizon* but had been vague on the details. She didn't need to be worrying herself, especially since she was prone to fretfulness.

In his pocket was a finished and much more candid letter to Gerald, and Roberts had spared no bones about outlining his new ownership of the *Horizon* and the terms surrounding it. Roberts confided in few men, and it was a relief to share his secrets with someone who would both keep them and know what to say in return.

Finished with his correspondence, Roberts left the tavern. His means no longer extended to air postal services, but he would find the money somehow instead of waiting months to hear back from his family. If Halloway's predictions miraculously came to fruition, perhaps, just perhaps, the *Horizon* might bring her captain to reunite with his sister and her family in India one day.

All was quiet on board the *Horizon* when Roberts thumped across the boards. Harding was dozing in the sun and Halloway, unsurprisingly, was holed up in the boiler room. He glanced up briefly as Roberts entered but said nothing. Roberts examined his old friend critically and didn't like what he saw: Halloway seemed greatly diminished, both body and spirit, and shock was still etched on his frame. It did not escape Roberts that Halloway had suffered more loss than anyone on board and was the person least suited to deal with change.

Without preamble, Roberts announced, "I think I've found us a weapon, a Vandenberg gun. She'll need a mounting system." Halloway nodded mutely and Roberts' brow furrowed. There was no challenge in Halloway, and his deeply ingrained belligerence and arrogance had vanished. While Roberts welcomed the lack of opposition, it seemed that all the fire had died in Halloway just when Roberts most needed him to be at his best. From experience, Roberts knew that Halloway occasionally sank into fits of depression, avoiding work and doing little but moping and brooding.

More loudly, Roberts continued, "It will be just one gun, but I want firing on both sides. You'll need to figure out a way to swing it to both sides to get us maximum firing range. She'll need a mounting system that absorbs recoil. I won't have a loose cannon rolling around or have the *Horizon* knocked off course because she can't stay level with the shot."

Halloway nodded again but now Roberts detected the slightest glimmer of interest in the inventor's eyes before it died. "Don't have much to work with," Halloway mumbled.

"Then you'll have to make do," Roberts snapped, trying to provoke Halloway into an argument. "I don't want any excuses from you."

Halloway flushed with anger which Roberts was glad to see. Continuing, he announced, "You'll have the gun in a few days. I want a working mounting system a week after that."

Something complicated settled over Halloway's face as Roberts turned to leave, his feet thumping against the wood, back up into the sunlight to plot and brood and worry about his next course of action.

Chapter Three
FULL RETRACTION FROM LONDON GUARDIAN

The headline screamed in bold letters, hovering above a clear picture of none other than Miss Pickens, looking rather crestfallen and defensive. Behind her, Jules stood with one massive hand covering her shoulder protectively.

Roberts picked up the discarded newspaper and scanned it with interest. *I'll be damned*, he thought, shooting a glance at the date in the header. August 6th, two days after Miss Pickens' article had hit the presses. Smothers didn't habitually let any grass grow under his feet, and he had clearly reacted with swift, crushing action to counter the embarrassing smear against his name.

A serving girl gave Roberts a saucy wink in passing and he winked back, but for the moment, another woman had captured his attention in a much less pleasant way. Sitting back in his chair at the pub, he scanned the newspaper carefully. Gibraltar was filled with London's newspapers, thanks to airships filling the skies, and the newspaper in Roberts' hands was only four days old.

Harvey Whiteside, Editor of the London Guardian, gave his full apology to the Smothers family. "I deeply regret the embarrassment and shame the London Guardian has brought upon Sir Cornelius Smothers and his family," Whiteside said in an official press statement. "The article was written by a young female reporter who, most tragically, let sensation and hysteria truncate good reporting skills and fact. The article she presented for my approval was drastically different than the one sent to the press. I regret that I did not uncover this deception until it was too late. I never would have authorized the printing of such poorly written slander."

Roberts was unconvinced. He suspected that Whiteside hadn't been able to resist such a juicy story and had supported Miss Pickens' efforts up to the moment the lawyers arrived. It was entirely possible that Whiteside had encouraged her efforts, knowing that her gender provided an automatic safety net in the event the situation backfired. Backed into a corner, Whiteside could cast blame on a woman's hysterics and deceitfulness and escape censure.

Roberts continued reading. *"I sincerely regret that I did not more carefully supervise Miss Pickens. She is no longer on staff at the London Guardian, and I can assure my readers that the London Guardian will never again employ a woman reporter."*

A nearly nonexistent stab of pity fluttered in Roberts' breast. Despite his fury over Miss Pickens' actions, he suspected that she had fared badly in the aftermath of the blowup. Whiteside likely had profited from the event: Miss Pickens' article had sold out copies of the *London Guardian*, and Whiteside was no doubt seeing massive sales increases. If he could avoid having his publication shut down and redirect wrath by offering Miss Pickens as a scapegoat, the publicity and sensation from the fallout just might work in his favor.

Further down the page was a picture of Sir Smothers, stern and resolute. The article continued.

Sir Cornelius Smothers spoke out publicly against the article, stating, "There was nothing in that article but lies and sensation during a time of great grief for my family. As I have previously reported, four months ago my beloved son, Albert Melvin Smothers, tragically perished in a boiler explosion on board the airship Lucky Lady *which he commanded. The source of the explosion was traced to a malfunctioning boiler from the manufacturers Marks & Smith. My son had this boiler installed at the insistence of his first mate Gavin Roberts and against his own better judgment. Marks & Smith has been indicted for several safety violations, and I am vigorously pursuing a wrongful death action lawsuit against the company.*

"After my son was killed, I agreed to sell the Lucky Lady *to Gavin Roberts for an undisclosed sum. The airship was badly damaged yet he insisted on purchasing it. I let myself be persuaded against my better judgment and responsibility for the airship was transferred to Gavin Roberts. However, if I had known that this agreement would be rewarded with such scurrilous accusations and slander, I would never have allowed the transaction."*

With something like humor, Roberts kept reading to see what further sins would be placed on his shoulders.

"I will clearly state that any report of an airship named Horizon *making any sort of historic flight and breaking speed records is utter nonsense. Dock officials at Larne report that on August the first, an airship named* Horizon *flew from London to Ireland in just*

under twenty hours, an impressive timing to be sure, but hardly record-setting. I have official witnesses and paperwork to document that this flight time is accurate."

"Of course you do," Roberts muttered dryly. "And damned be the man that breathes a word different." His eyes continued down the page. There was no further mention of Miss Pickens or her brother. For their own sakes, Roberts hoped that the pair had taken his advice and left London before Smothers' anger hit the press.

The article continued with more recants and protestations and threats of impending legal action before Roberts finally pushed it away. While an ignoble part of him was bitterly pleased to see Miss Pickens' downfall, it was a Pyrrhic victory at best. He knew that the retraction would in no way placate Smothers. The *Horizon* was still a marked vessel, and Europe's skies would continue to be unfriendly for her.

In disgust, Roberts abandoned the paper in favor of another cup of coffee. It was *good* coffee too, although he'd practically had to restrain the serving girl from adding hot milk to it. He had won in the end and the full-bodied, fragrant beverage had went unadulterated by either milk or sugar. As Roberts raised the coffee cup to his lips, the quiet of the morning was utterly shattered by a painfully familiar voice.

"Captain Roberts! How fortuitous!"

Roberts went rigid, every muscle clenching as he forced himself to turn around. Coming at him was none other than Miss Pickens, gliding elegantly while Jules plodded in her wake. Even at the distance, he could see that her eyes were bright and determined, and her lips were curving with the full force of her charm and appeal.

Social niceties may have demanded that Roberts rise to greet her, but his boots remained firmly planted on the chair in front of him. He watched Miss Pickens minced her way towards him, noting the well-cut suit coat neatly showing off the curves underneath, the waterfall of brown curls, the creamy white skin. But Roberts was far too irate to be enticed with her charms. He fixed Miss Pickens with a cold stare that did not waver and crossed his arms over his chest.

Miss Pickens seemed to pause a bit, then push forward determinedly under Roberts' hard eyes. "Captain Roberts," she said, a trifle breathlessly. "We just arrived in Gibraltar, and I *knew* I saw the *Horizon* at port when we landed..."

Roberts cut her off abruptly. "What are you doing here, Miss Pickens?" he demanded.

Her hand fluttered like a bird as she responded, "Our grandfather is a naval commander who was stationed at Gibraltar. Jules and I usually spent our winters here. Our father is a widow, and our grandparents practically raised the two of us. When you suggested Jules and I leave town for awhile, we, ah, considered it prudent to follow your advice."

Her smile returned in all its beaming charisma as her head cocked coyly to the side. Bending a little towards Roberts, she cooed, "And how fortunate I am to have found you here."

Irritably, Roberts pushed back his chair and stood abruptly, noting with cruel pleasure how Miss Pickens' eyes opened a little wider and Jules stepped forward protectively. "Miss Pickens," he stated bluntly. "Thanks to you, my name is ruined from London to back and wherever airships fly. My men too are blacklisted because they've stayed loyal, and my oldest friend just saw his entire workshop blazing before his eyes, courtesy of Smothers. Can you name me, *Madam*, any reason why I should exchange one more word with you?"

Miss Pickens' pretty mouth fell open in a moue of shock as Roberts glared at her coldly, then turned to leave, tossing a coin on the table. "Wait!" Miss Pickens called out as Roberts took two angry strides off the patio.

"I can help you!" A soft hand caught his right bicep and held on with surprising strength. Roberts tried to shake her off, but Miss Pickens clung like grim death as she struggled to match his pace. He was frankly surprised that Jules wasn't taking control of the situation, but the enormous man seemed content to trail a few steps behind his sister and let her manage negotiations on her own. Granted, if Roberts acted roughly, he suspected a fist would fly his way in a heartbeat. He resisted the urge to harshly pry Miss Pickens' clinging fingers from his arm and tried to increase his pace.

"I can make it right, Captain Roberts, I can!" she insisted, the other hand coming around to meet the first one and forming a lock on his arm. Roberts could have broken free but he might have hurt her in the process and in his current state, he did not trust himself to be gentle. Instead, he gave a bitter laugh.

"Ma'am, the best help you can give me is hightailing it out of here and never letting me see your face again," he growled angrily.

"No, I *can* help you," Miss Pickens repeated. "My grandfather is a Navy commander. He has a great deal of influence and contacts..."

"Miss Pickens, there is not enough gold in India to erase the harm that was done by your article," Roberts cut her off. "Your grandfather may be a commander, but Smothers rules the air and you know it." With more force than he intended, Roberts pulled his arm free and thundered angrily into the street, the two reporters hot on his tail.

Miss Pickens was hampered by a long skirt and heeled boots as well as a sizeable hat, and she fought to keep pace with Roberts who was as equally determined to remove himself from her presence as quickly as possible. His long, angry stride soon left Miss Pickens and her silent brother in his wake and her protests were drowned in the babble of the streets. Now free, Roberts immersed himself in the massed throng and rolled heavily towards the *Horizon*, anger blazing white hot in his gut. The crowds of people on the street, sensing Roberts' dark mood, parted silently to let him pass through the twisting streets of Gibraltar down to the airship wharf.

Roberts' anger had not dimmed by the time his feet hit the decks of the *Horizon*. He was already bellowing William's name as he approached. The young lad was catching a nap topdeck and at the sound of Roberts' approach, he woke blearily and fumbled off a hasty salute.

Roberts was in no mood to tolerate slackness. "You've got three hours to find the crew and get them back on the airship," Roberts commanded harshly. "Ground leave is suspended as of now. We're leaving tonight."

"But..." William looked suddenly frantic. "Sir, how do I find them?"

"I gave you an order, boy," Roberts thundered. "I expect you to fulfill it. *Dismissed.*" With that, he pounded down the ladder towards the boiler room where he fully expected to find Halloway. He wasn't disappointed but to his consternation and alarm, Halloway was sitting with his back against a wall and a vague, vacant look on his face.

Roberts slammed the door shut but Halloway didn't react. His scowl deepening, Roberts barked out, "Get her back up in the air, Halloway. We're taking off tonight."

Halloway didn't move. *Dammit,* Roberts thought as he glared at the inventor's immobile form, squelching the urge to kick him into liveliness. "On your feet, Halloway," he ordered.

"I'm not one of your crew, Roberts," Halloway replied dully, only the barest skim of insolence in his voice.

"That so?" Roberts snarled back as he towered over the inventor's recumbent frame. "We'll you're on my damn airship and unless you intend to ride on her as a paying passenger, you *will* earn your keep and you *will* take orders."

His words had zero effect for Halloway continued to stare listlessly at the floor. With mounting frustration, Roberts stated heavily, "You're the only one this airship that can get the most out of her, and I need her at full strength."

Less harshly, he added, "Halloway, the *Horizon*'s got a mark on her as big as China. I need everything you've got to keep her afloat and the men inside her alive. Right now she's staying afloat by luck. Luck eventually runs out. I need more than just chance to keep her going."

Halloway did not move for several moments, then reluctantly pulled himself to his feet. He still refused to meet Roberts' eyes but dully turned his attention to the boiler with heavy, labored movements. As Halloway set woodenly to work, Roberts watched for a few minutes, glad to see the inventor back on his feet but still worried about Halloway's lack of energy and drive.

After several moments of observation, Roberts left Halloway and turned his face to the topdeck. Dark anger still rolled through him in waves, but he strangled back the raging emotion. The task at hand was hazardous, and emotion only made for careless mistakes. By the time the *Horizon's* crew reentered the airship, clearly peeved that their ground leave had been cut short, Roberts had mastered his rage and moved back into calm purposefulness.

He observed his men carefully as they stepped on deck. Signs of hangovers were present, and Bloomberg was clearly worse for wear after his first ground leave as an airman. However, Roberts' attention was drawn to Farrington. The quartermaster's face was tight and dark, his thoughts no doubt consumed with his still-infected arm and the family he had left behind, including the child due any day.

"Captain on deck!" Oboe called out firmly.

Roberts nodded at them and then barked out, "Fall in! Now!" The crew scrambled over each other to obey his command, getting in each other's way in their haste. In the upheaval following Roberts' new ownership of the *Horizon*, he had been a trifle lax about formality: putting her back together had taken precedent over discipline and structure. It was past time for Roberts to start demanding proper order.

He paced the rank, measuring each man carefully. *William, Carter, Long Tom*, he counted, eying the three he had chosen for this particular task. William and Carter he knew he could trust. Long Tom had yet to earn that trust, and the evening's activities would go a long way towards establishing whether Roberts could depend on him.

Finished with his inspection, Roberts stepped back a pace, taking in his crew as a whole and letting the silence settle for a few minutes. The men fidgeted, waiting to hear why their captain had dragged them in from ground leave a day early.

Finally he spoke. "We've got a job to do."

    ***   ***   ***   ***

Sun baked the ground and made the air shimmer. Roberts dashed away the sweat on his brow with a swipe of his hand as he glanced quickly at his men. At his side, Carter moved steadily through the hot air while William panted quietly, his feet scrambling several paces behind. Long Tom brought up the rear, the four picking their way up the steep hill. Underfoot, the ground was crumbly with loose shale and generously garnished with pointy vegetation that snagged their clothes and poked them with brambles.

Hangman's Cliff was dead ahead. Roberts had gleaned some general directions by dropping a few choice questions into casual conversations with locals. Their course was hindered by patrolling soldiers, and it took stealth and cunning to move through the hills. An hour or two of careful searching, and they found their destination.

Hangman's Cliff well lived up to its name: a generous chunk of rock jutting out from the side of the mountain into the salty air. As Roberts suspected, there were guards posted on the scene, but the watchmen were two young soldiers, barely older than William, and clearly bored. Roberts drew his men back into the shadows where they crouched under a thick line of bushes and surveyed the situation carefully. Carter tripped over his feet as he backed away, but the guards didn't notice and the four men went undetected.

Roberts hushed Carter with a look, then turned his attention back to their surroundings. At the base of Hangman's Cliff was a steep basin lined with shaggy trees and surrounded by boulders, through which a thin stream of water trickled. It did little but feed the muddy bog of the basin. At the heart of this was a nearly submerged Vandenberg gun, only its muzzle and part of the chassis showing. It would be a job pulling it free, even for the *Horizon*.

Wreckage from the doomed Spanish airship littered the ground, but there had been some salvage work done. There were fresh skid marks around the Vandenberg, indicating someone had tried to wrestle it loose from the mud without success. Much of the wreckage was useless, broken beyond redemption, and the Vandenberg were stuck fast. The guards were little more than a formality, likely two privates listlessly watching over something they knew wouldn't be stolen.

Intent on the situation, Roberts crouched motionless, and he was pleased to see that his men were quiet in their turn. Carter was flat against the scree, unmoving and silent, and

Long Tom blended seamlessly into the shadows. William was breathing loudly but Roberts doubted the two guards could hear or would even pay attention to any odd noise. Both had their jackets off and one was lounging idly in the sun while the other intently probed the interior of his nostrils as if seeking buried treasure. They would be laughably easy to disarm.

Roberts and his men watched the scene for several minutes before, at a silent hand movement from their captain, they slipped away for a hasty conference at a safe distance. They clustered together, voices hushed, as Roberts doled out rapid-fire commands. William was dispatched to bring orders back to the *Horizon*. As he was preparing to leave, he cast a fearful look at Roberts. "Sir, what do I do if I get caught?" he questioned worriedly.

"Don't get caught," Roberts intoned darkly. "This all rides on you, William." This was a heavy responsibility: William had to make his way back down the mountain, dodging any patrols he might encounter. It was growing late and the *Horizon* was waiting for orders and the cover of dark. It was all in William's hands.

The young steward gulped with trepidation, but Roberts was pleased to see William set his jaw and nod. "I won't sir," he said bravely.

"Go now," Roberts ordered and watched the boy hurry away, head down and frantic movement in every limb. It was a risk sending the lad on his own, but Roberts knew that William was more likely to escape suspicion. There were boys in the city, and surely plenty of them roamed around the mountain looking for adventure. Patrols were less likely to suspect a boy than a man.

Long Tom, however, seemed less than convinced. "The boy will get caught, Captain," he muttered.

"He'll make it," Roberts growled back.

Long Tom frowned. "And if he doesn't?" he demanded.

"That's enough from you," Roberts snapped, almost too loudly. "Keep your mind on the job."

Long Tom retreated a pace. The air hung chilly and the three men settled down for a prolonged wait. It was still a few hours before dark, and there was nothing to do but hold their position and wait for the cover of night while evading detection. The latter proved to be almost laughably easy as the two guards were paying only the slightest attention to their post and barely strayed a dozen feet from the Vandenberg.

Long minutes slogged by with painful slowness. The sun seemed permanently adhered to the sky with no inclination towards dropping to the ground. At Roberts' side, Carter fidgeted restlessly, not enough to rouse detection but enough to express his general boredom and level of anxiety. Once or twice, Roberts had to throw a sharp word at his bosun to stop the twitching. Long Tom stayed frozen, eyes dark and shoulders tense. For himself, Roberts fought to keep still as his mind twisted with worry.

As night fell, a fire crackled to life and smoke rose in the warm air. Relaxing by the fire, the guards began settling in for the evening. Now closer to their goal, Roberts' small band tensed for action. Darkness began to throw shadows across the trees and rocks, and Roberts' ears strained to catch sound of his airship approaching.

As luck would have it, the moon rose sullen and dull, lurking behind a light veil of clouds. Dim visibility would hide their actions better, but it would make it more hazardous for the *Horizon*. It would take meticulous care to direct the airship up the face of the mountain without an accident, and it galled Roberts that he was not on board directing operations. Oboe could have led the expedition to Hangman's Cliff, leaving Roberts to captain the *Horizon* up the mountain. But the ground mission was too hazardous for Roberts to allow anyone else to lead. If they were caught, he would take the full blame.

As thick blackness fell across the Mediterranean, Roberts caught the faint sound of engines in the air, and the blood quickened in his veins. From the distance, it was impossible to tell if the approaching vessel was the *Horizon*. He waited impatiently, straining to catch sound of the oncoming aircraft as Carter and Long Tom lifted their heads skyward.

"It's her, Captain," Carter stated with hushed urgency. His knack for identifying aircraft by the sound of their engines rarely failed him, and his word was all Roberts needed. It was time to move out. Hissing a few words to his men, Roberts dropped to all fours and crawled through the sharp-edged vegetation, Carter and Long Tom following closely.

One of the young guards was openly snoring when Roberts stepped abruptly into the clearing, both pistols aimed. The other guard yelped and scrambled for his rifle, but the sound of a hammer cocking froze him in place.

"Let's not be stupid, lad," Roberts warned. The guard gulped and elbowed his compatriot who blearily opened his eyes, then flailed in surprise. With their eyes fixed on Roberts, they didn't notice Long Tom creeping up behind them.

Long Tom moved swiftly. The butt of his knife hit both heads with expert precision, swiftly knocking out the guards before either could object. He paused over the guards, knife poised to deliver further blows, but he had done his work entirely well. Both guards were out cold, slumped against the log where they had been resting.

Sorry lads, Roberts thought with genuine remorse, but it was done. "Tie them up," he ordered harshly as he stepped forward to assess the wounded. Both guards were breathing but one was bleeding slightly from the head. Long Tom obeyed the order, seemingly indifferent to the damages he had inflicted, but Carter's jaw was tight with worry.

The two men worked quickly and Long Tom soon finished his last knot. Carter lit three of Halloway's lanterns and threw a long coil of rope over his shoulder. Overhead, the sound of engines grew closer, and Roberts knew for a certainty that it was the *Horizon*. They had to move fast. If the *Horizon* spent too much time hovering around the mountain, she would quickly attract attention.

She moved closer, steadily rising up the face of the mountain. As she approached, Long Tom signaled three quick flashes, opening and shutting the door of a lantern to identify their location. The *Horizon* moved in and Roberts knew that it was taking every ounce of Barking Jack's skill to bring her close to the jagged rock without a crash. Thankfully, there was no wind and she held steady in the sky.

Roberts lifted up a lantern to cast its illumination on the Vandenberg. Eying the steep angle of the basin, he said to Long Tom, "We'll get in and out quick. Don't get stuck."

With that, Roberts and Long Tom slid down the basin toward the weapon. It was only about ten feet down, but the mud was thick and heavy. When Roberts' feet hit the bottom with a dull thud, his boots quickly began sinking. With some effort, he pulled his feet free with a sucking sound and worked his way over to the gun where Long Tom was already tying one of the ropes to it.

Up on the lip of the basin, Carter was signaling to the *Horizon* which shimmied into place. Two ropes dropped overboard, and Carter seized them. He fed them down into the basin where Roberts and Long Tom were lashing rope around the Vandenberg. That task completed, they took the tie ropes, knotting them around the rigging while the mud sucked at their boots and hindered their efforts.

Elbow to elbow with Roberts, Long Tom called to him over the sound of the *Horizon*'s engines. "It's not going to come loose, Captain. It's too damned stuck."

"She'll manage," Roberts shouted back. Long Tom shook his head and made to say something but Roberts cut him off. "Mind your knots!"

That earned him a dark look from Long Tom which he returned sharply as they struggled to finish their knots. In his gut, Roberts knew that Long Tom had a point: the *Horizon* wasn't fashioned to be a tugboat and the gun was all but rooted to the earth. But it was coming out, hell or high water.

The second their task was finished, Roberts and Long Tom pulled themselves out of the basin. Roberts signaled the *Horizon* and three quick drop lines fell to earth. He was already barking orders before he reached topdeck. Oboe hauled him aboard and Roberts hurried to the com device, rapping out commands to the boiler room and calling out orders to the rest of the men.

The *Horizon* surged forward, power pouring into her engines. She bucked and swayed in the air, straining to wrestle the Vandenberg from the mud. Carter and Long Tom fell on board as the airship fishtailed under them, straining mightily against the gun which anchored her to the ground. Boards shuddered as the airship strained in the darkness.

"HALLOWAY! JENKINS!" Roberts thundered into the com device, "FULL POWER NOW!" The engines squealed louder and a tang of acrid smoke hung in the air, hinting at potential mechanical trouble.

"CAPTAIN!" Farrington called out, pointing at the ground. Roberts followed his line of sight and saw, to his consternation, a relay of lights flickering in the distance and heading towards them with purposefulness. The *Horizon*'s activities had not gone unnoticed.

Dammit, Roberts thought with alarm, quickly weighing the distance between his airship and the oncoming patrol. If the *Horizon* couldn't pull the gun loose in the next few minutes, he would be forced to abandon the attempt and hightail his airship out of Gibraltar. The crew redoubled their efforts and shivers of movement started to hum on the tow lines as the Vandenberg began to pull loose. Calling exhortations to his men and keeping his eyes on everything at once, Roberts felt his airship winning the battle over mud. Finally and with a juddering shiver, the Vandenberg came free.

"Hard right and full speed!" Roberts commanded sharply. The *Horizon* obeyed his order, spinning elegantly and turning from Gibraltar with the Vandenberg dangling from her belly. For one brief but happy moment, Roberts felt confident that his airship would escape with her prize undetected. A blast of distant cannon fire soon corrected his misplaced optimism. Turning to the railing, Roberts saw an airship in the distance, closing in on the *Horizon*.

The *Horizon* was well beyond range, but the other airship was intent on closing the gap. At Roberts' word, the *Horizon* surged ahead, her engines roaring fiercely as her speed gauge raced to thirty knots. Worry gripped Roberts as he examined the airship following them. If the *Horizon* was identified, her flying days were over. Between Smothers and the British Air Force, she wouldn't last a week in the skies, no matter what airspace she flew through.

The moon obliged the *Horizon* in her plight by hiding behind a bank of clouds. They were enveloped in black, the waters below only a pale shimmer. The military airship was fast, but she was no match for the *Horizon* who quickly exceeded thirty-five knots, making good use of the darkness and her exceptional speed. The Vandenburg still swung from her gondola and Roberts hoped the knots would hold; otherwise, their purloined prize would slip into the waters of the Mediterranean.

Only when the lights of Gibraltar started to fade behind them did Roberts' heartbeat ease. He was still intently watchful, but they had left their pursuers well behind. There was a risk the *Horizon* had been identified but with the veiled moon and the dark night stretched over the sky, she likely had escaped with her anonymity.

With the initial excitement over, the crew settled down as Roberts took hasty stock of his men and airship. The Vandenberg was hauled up onto topdeck where it sat in a sticky pool of mud, ignored for now. Tangier was ahead, a bustling hub of profiteering, smuggling, business, and crime. It was a wild port but one where the *Horizon* could rest while her crew took stock of their new acquisition.

As he strode the deck of his airship, preparing his crew for the landing in Tangier, Roberts' glance fell on two rifles shoved into a corner. He picked one up, knowing exactly where it had come from. Turning to Long Tom, he stated sharply, "I don't recall giving orders about taking the guards' weapons."

Long Tom shrugged. "We needed them."

He was right, of course. They had already stolen a valuable weapon from a fortified military outpost. Taking the guards rifles was a mere petty offense, and the *Horizon* needed all the weapons she could commandeer. Yet, Roberts knew the two guards would face serious punishment for failing their posts and allowing their weapons to be stolen.

With some yammering of his conscience, he set the rifle down and turned his attention towards the glittering lights of Tangier. Morocco awaited.

Chapter Four

Tangier blazed like a thousand diamonds on black velvet as the *Horizon* touched down at port, squeezing into a narrow berth between a sizable medium-flight German airship and a ragged Corsair vessel. A cluster of men was dragging a trio of belligerent camels onto the German airship, the beasts filling the air with their indignant grunts. An overworked gantry crane, precariously overloaded, lifted and swung heavy loads on and off airships. Gunshots rang out unexpectedly but few paid heed; gunfire at Tangier's air wharf was apparently not uncommon.

The crew swiftly shut down the *Horizon* and turned their attention to the Vandenberg. It was late but the excitement surrounding their new weapon and the thrill of spiriting it away from Gibraltar kept the men awake far into the night. Loud conversations and semi-serious arguments rose up as the crew clustered around the weapon, speculating about how to mount it and who would form the gunnery crew. William, Carter, and Farrington were soon hard at work cleaning mud off the muzzle and digging it out of the thin barrels lining the inside. They worked for hours before exhaustion drove the crew to bed.

Cleaning and arguing resumed in the morning, and Roberts was pleased to see Halloway observing the squabble with mild interest, although the inventor offered no comments. Roberts left the men to bicker amongst themselves while he took a walk along the jammed wharf to keep his eyes and ears open for potential work. He needed to find it, and fast: fueling the *Horizon* had taken almost every last farthing he had, and they were down to ten days of flight time before being involuntarily grounded for lack of fuel.

Roberts' feet brought him to the marine wharf which was larger and even more crowded than the air wharf. Everything from Bulgarian windjammers to Dutch fluyts filled the waters encircling Tangier. He watched the ships come and go until he caught sight of a fine steamer gliding through the harbor towards the wharf. She was a beautiful sight and deftly handled, sliding smoothly into port with the grace of a dancer.

As Roberts eyed the marine ship, his eyes quickly picked up on the signs: merchant marine by her looks and a certainly heaviness in her keel indicating she was fully loaded. She had no airships sailing overhead, Roberts noted with satisfaction. It was common for marine vessels, particularly merchant, to join ranks with airships during a voyage. In such partnerships, the marine vessel carried the bulk of the cargo and fuel and the airship served as a scout and navigator and helped carry cargo ashore if needed. Marine ships typically welcomed aerial assistance and paid a fat price for the privilege of an airship escort.

Roberts stood on the wharf, carefully observing the merchant steamer and liking what he saw. Her crew was brisk and skilled and the ship was handled with care. Finally finished with his examination, he nodded in satisfaction, then turned to leave. He'd give the ship a few hours to settle into port, then return for a talk with her captain.

  ***   ***   ***   ***

"Ahoy, *Morning Star!*" Roberts bellowed over the noise of hundreds of voices all vying mightily to make themselves heard. He'd been at busy ports before, but Tangier took the prize. Night time had brought no ease from the constant bustle of activity and sound, and the cacophony of night blended seamlessly into the dawn of the next day.

Roberts' hail was quickly answered by an officer whose handsome features were scarred and weather-beaten. An elaborate scar ran across his face and a complicated construction of brass and lenses covered his left eye like a patch. The eyeball underneath was livid and bloodshot, and the lenses magnified the damage.

The officer assessed Roberts quickly, then grinned. "Morning to you, sir, and welcome to the *Morning Star*," he greeted heartily. "John Arterbury, First Mate." He saluted.

Roberts returned it. "Captain Gavin Roberts of the airship *Horizon*," he began.

Arterbury reacted visibly, his grin increasing as he gestured for Roberts to step aboard. Roberts noted the reaction, caution nagging at him, and he paused carefully.

"Captain Gavin Robert of the airship *Horizon*," Arterbury repeated with emphasis and obvious delight. "Pleasure to meet you, sir. You and your good airship's been the talk of the air and the water."

Roberts kept his expression neutral while a growl of anger snarled in his belly. Arterbury continued cheerfully. "Sailing men gossip like fishwives, Captain, and there's not an English airman or sailor what hasn't heard about you from the *London Gazette*. It may have been a skirt what wrote it, but the truth's the truth, sir, and the truth's damned impressive."

Roberts' eyes darkened as Arterbury gleefully pounded a fist against an open hand. "Forty knots an hour! That's a number to be impressed with, sir! Not an airship in the sky or clipper ship in the water can come close to matching that, Captain Roberts!"

Neither verifying nor denying the claim, but wanting to change topics, Roberts got to the heart of the matter. "Has your ship contracted out an airship?" he questioned.

Audible scorn was Arterbury's answer. "Aye, she had the *White Raven* as an escort, a damned lazy captain and a crew of drunkards. We left her in Gibraltar and good riddance to her, I say. Captain Fosselweight said he'd damned well rather travel alone than sail with the likes of her again."

He paused, an edge of keenness to his voice. "I don't speak for my captain, sir, but if your fine airship would be inclined to sail with the *Morning Star*, well, I'm thinking arrangements could be made." He grinned, a gold tooth flashing in the upper deck.

"What's the cargo?" Roberts questioned.

"Military supplies," Arterbury responded. "She's carrying three hundred tons of food, two hundred tons of armament, and a hundred tons of clothing, medical supplies, plus tents and equipment.

"There's more than twenty thousand soldiers up in that damned wasteland and they're already starving out," Arterbury said soberly. "From what we've heard, sir, Crimea's a hell of a port to sail to, and that's if you can get through the Bosporus and up the Black Sea. You make bay in Calamita and by all accounts, it's damned difficult to navigate. If you can get cargo into port, headquarters camp is several miles away and the roads they've got are all but useless. Airships are about the only thing that can transport inland."

"There many airships up there?" Roberts asked.

"A few, sir, but there's hardly anywhere to land and barely a scrap of coal." He paused and looked at Roberts significantly. "Any airship captain willing to operate in Crimea can name his price."

Roberts nodded as Arterbury continued, "There's damned few airship captains willing to risk Crimea. Shame, really. An airship that can fly supplies from the bay to headquarters camp is worth her weight in gold. A fast airship, one that can do a quick drop and run before cannon start firing, that's what's needed."

"Have you heard any report of air activity?" Roberts questioned slowly, already weighing the risk.

Arterbury shrugged. "From what we've heard, there's not much air activity going on in Crimea, nor has been. Those damned Cossacks can't touch England for airship technology, and it's little but ground troops up there. What airships the Russians have, they've been sending elsewhere.

"'Course I can't make a formal offer, sir," Arterbury spread his hands. "But, I have a feeling my captain would like to talk to you, if you please. He's not on the ship now, but with your permission, Captain Roberts, I'll pass word on to him and let him know your fine airship might be inclined to join us."

Arterbury saluted Roberts, who left the *Morning Star* feeling more optimistic than he had in days. His lighter spirits were heightened even further when he stepped on board the *Horizon* to the tune of Halloway having a blazing fit below deck. Roberts went down to find the newly cleaned Vandenberg in the middle of a knot of arguing men, Halloway's voice ringing out the loudest.

"You damned idiots, do you want to send this cannon punching through the keel?" Halloway barked out.

"How the hell are we supposed to load...?" Farrington barked back but Halloway cut him off.

"That's your problem, not mine!" Halloway yelled sharply. "Your captain's the one who said he wanted firepower on both sides and..."

"That's *enough*." Roberts thundered heavily, watching with concealed approval as his men, save Halloway, sprang to attention. Halloway, meanwhile, had been caught mid-rant and was restraining himself only with extreme difficulty. Roberts shot him a hard look, secretly pleased to see Halloway on his feet and punching back.

About damned time. While a subdued Halloway made for a calmer airship, they had work to do. Halloway performed best when he had something to bitch about.

Halloway shoved his hands deep in his pockets and scowled at Roberts. "Not that it makes a damned difference, there's barely any tools on board..."

"That's enough, Halloway," Roberts growled, watching as the inventor stiffened in anger. *Good*, he thought. He'd keep aggravating Halloway for as long as it took to keep the dark moods away and get the inventor back to his normal self.

To the room in general, Roberts announced, "I'll be talking to the captain of the merchant marine *Morning Star*. If all goes well, we'll join with them and make for Crimea."

Most of the crew, save for William and Harding, were clustered around the Vandenberg, and their captain's announcement met with everything from surprise to interest to dismay. Roberts' attention was diverted to Farrington, who received the news quietly but clearly did not like the idea of ranging so far from London.

Halloway, however, had quickly returned his focus to the gun, already at work on a movable mounting system. Currently the hull was empty of cargo and Halloway was making lavish use of the space inside. A handful of tools were scattered about the floor and Roberts cast his eyes up to see a network of scribbles etched in chalk on the ceiling. He frowned in puzzlement.

Carter, catching Roberts' expression, crossed his arms over his chest. "Someone has the brilliant idea to suspend the gun from the ceiling, Captain," the bosun stated sarcastically.

Halloway stiffened in indignation but Roberts cut him off with a look and flashed a frown at Carter, who shrunk under the penetrating stare. Silence reigned heavily for a long moment before Roberts turned his attention back to Halloway.

"You have a plan?" he questioned, jerking his head at the chalk marks.

Halloway nodded impatiently. "If this lot would stop bitching and get out of the way," he snapped curtly.

Roberts surveyed his men, most of whom were clearly eager to tip Halloway overboard to the sharks at the earliest opportunity. "Halloway is in charge of mounting the gun," he announced to a general consensus of dismay. "I have no reason to mistrust his judgment and neither should any of you. You'll all do what he says." Sullen acquiescence followed Roberts' words but the men resignedly set to work under Halloway's barked commands.

Roberts, meanwhile, strategically retreated, knowing that the Vandenberg was safe in Halloway's hands. As he left, he towed Farrington along with him up into the fresh sea air and all-encompassing noise of the wharf.

"Let's see that arm," Roberts stated. Farrington extended his right arm without hesitation. There was only a light bandage wrapped around the wound and Roberts was pleased to see pink, healthy tissue closing up the gaps. Harding and his leeches had done their work well. The wound wasn't fully healed and a few troublesome patches remained, but Farrington was clearly on the road to full recovery.

As he examined the arm, Roberts said, "Best write to Grace and tell her we'll likely be away for several months."

Farrington smiled sadly at the mention of his wife's name. "I wrote to her in Gibraltar, Captain. I'll send another letter from Tangier." He cast his eyes out to sea in thought, then stated a trifle wistfully, "I'd just like to know if it's a boy or girl and if it got here safely."

"Could be twins," Roberts attempted a joke, watching as Farrington blanched heavily.

"In that case, sir, we can stay in Crimea till they start walking and are past the crying stage."

Roberts laughed as he rewrapped Farrington's arm, fussing over the nearly healed wounds. It was a few moments before either man spoke again.

"Grace's father was an airman, Captain," Farrington said, shrugging one shoulder. "She'll understand." He pushed a strand of dark hair out of his eyes as Roberts finished with the bandage, then gave Farrington a firm thump on the shoulder.

That task completed, Roberts moved across topdeck, taking in the air and keeping his eyes alert for anything out of place as the unholy cacophony of the wharf poured across the deck. Every berth on the airship wharf was full, and several more airships circled overhead in vain hope of a landing spot. Marine ships choked the waters. and every airman, sailor, and wharf worker available was busily attending their vessels. Great clouds of black smoke and billows of steam filled the air and canvas sails flapped in the wind.

A hail at the gangplank caught his attention, and Roberts turned to see Arterbury, his glass and metal eye contraption gleaming in the sun. He towered over a tiny whippet of a man at his side. The shorter man sported an elaborate captain's hat perched jauntily on his head and was all but hiding behind a monumental walrus mustache.

"Ahoy, Captain Roberts!" Arterbury called out. "Permission to come aboard, sir!"

"Permission granted," Roberts rumbled, trying not to laugh as the jockey-sized captain marched briskly on board with Arterbury looming over him. They saluted Roberts, Arterbury with a grin and the captain with perfect crispness.

"Pleasure to meet you, Captain Roberts," the other captain thundered in a surprisingly voluminous voice for one so diminutive. Although the hand he offered Roberts was woman-sized, it had strength to spare and was lined with calluses. "Captain Archibald Fosselweight of the merchant marine *Morning Star*."

"Glad to have you on board, Captain Fosselweight," Roberts said, nodding at Arterbury.

Captain Fosselweight's hand pumped Roberts' several times. "A fine airship, Captain Roberts, a fine airship indeed.

I've heard nothing but good reports of her. It will be a pleasure sailing with you, sir, if you would be so inclined."

Roberts rather took a shine to the man. Fosselweight looked small enough to blow away in a moderate wind, but he had charisma and his brisk manner was bracing. Granted, with nearly empty coffers, Roberts was inclined to be charitably disposed towards anyone offering him employment, but he had a hunch that this was the start of a profitable and enjoyable business venture.

"Now then," Fosselweight said, slapping his hands together. "What say we get over these tedious business matters and get our respective ships in the air and water, shall we?"

   ***   ***   ***   ***

"Well, that should do it, Captain Roberts," Fosselweight stated briskly, tapping a sheaf of papers together to line them up neatly. He and Roberts were crammed inside Roberts' small cabin with Arterbury and Oboe, four pairs of shoulders filling up the small room considerably.

It was a fairly straightforward arrangement: the *Horizon* would follow the *Morning Star* to Crimea while serving as a scouting and reconnaissance vessel. Each ship would come to the assistance of the other if attacked. The *Morning Star* would carry all the cargo and much of the fuel for both vessels, significantly lessening the *Horizon*'s weight ratio and lending her speed. Once they reached Calamita Bay, the *Horizon* would move supplies to the British camp.

"We will be in Constantinople in three to four weeks," Fosselweight stated. "The *Morning Star* runs at ten knots comfortable and fourteen under full speed. However, with both ships' boilers to feed, we will need to stop for coal at least twice, if not more than that."

"Fuel may be a problem," Roberts cautioned. "The *Horizon* runs on anthracite."

"Anthracite?" Fosselweight goggled at Roberts. "It burns clean but is devilishly tricky to light. How on earth did you manage that, Captain Roberts?"

Roberts merely smiled. "One of my engineers has a knack with engines."

Arterbury whistled as he shook his head in discouragement. "Anthracite's not easy to find, Captain Roberts. The *Morning Star* best take on the coal stores you need here in Tangier. I don't think we can count on finding much anthracite, not where we're going."

"She can run on bituminous if needs be but she flies best on anthracite," Roberts pronounced. "We'll coal her up before leaving Gibraltar and carry what we can, but if your ship can take on a store of anthracite, I'd be obliged. "

He mentally ran calculations and tried not to frown in worry. Following the *Morning Star* would easily quadruple the *Horizon*'s average flight time, and the extra time in the air would burn through her coal stores. Fuel was always a pressing concern on an airship, and the benefits of anthracite were almost outweighed by the aggravations of using it as a fuel source. It was typical of Halloway to completely ignore the fact that anthracite wasn't readily available. The fastest airship in the world would do Roberts little good if she was stuck in a port out of coal and with no prospects of getting more.

Fosselweight nodded. "The *Morning Star* has room in her belly. She'll manage both our coal stores nicely, Captain."

"My thanks, Captain Fosselweight," Roberts stated, but worry continued to eat at him. Quietly, he suspected his airship's trip to Crimea would be her last. From the sound of it, there was hardly any infrastructure available. The *Morning Star* could bring up what the *Horizon* needed to complete this mission but the airship couldn't stay in Crimea without a consistent source of fuel and a place to land safely.

Roberts kept these thoughts to himself and focused on the business at hand. Finally, Fosselweight briskly tapped the stack of papers into a perfect rectangle."Well, I think that all is in order. Sign, if you would be so kind, sir."

Roberts dipped a pen into the inkwell and carefully inscribed his name across the contract in big, visible letters. It seemed the more his name was dragged through the mud, the more careful he was about making sure the world saw his signature in print. It was a small defiance, a sign that Gavin Roberts was not going down without a fight.

While the ink dried, Roberts glanced at the numbers again. The *Horizon* would earn forty pounds a day escorting the *Morning Star* to Crimea and thirty-two pounds a ton transporting cargo from the merchant ship to the British camp once they reached port. On paper, the fees looked generous, but the airship needed considerable resupplying before she was ready to travel and her captain was nearly penniless.

Much to Roberts' deep relief, Fosselweight handed over partial payment up front. "If your ship is in need of supplies, I would find them in Tangier, Captain Roberts. You'll find better prices than in Rome or Constantinople."

He smiled, but there was the barest hint of knowing in his eyes. Roberts took the money quietly, realizing that Fosselweight probably suspected the *Horizon* had beat a hasty retreat out of London, scantily provisioned and not precisely flush with money. What he had just handed over to Roberts would get the *Horizon* needed supplies and pay for a mounting system and shot for the new Vandenberg.

With gracious tact, Fosselweight stated, "The *Morning Star* is at your complete disposal, Captain Roberts. If there are any supplies or equipment you would like to make use of..."

"You blazing idiots!" Halloway's yowl of rage cut effortlessly through the cabin door as his feet pounded the deck. "No! I said put it..." His bark of impatient anger faded away as he stomped toward the other end of the airship, freely spreading chaos and ire in his wake.

Fosselweight looked a little taken aback, but Roberts merely smiled. "My chief engineer is a bit of a hothead but a brilliant man. If your crew can stand him on board, I'm sure he'd be happy to raid your stores for any tools he could use."

"Of course, Captain Roberts," Fosselweight said, still a bit surprised but covering it gamely.

Soon after that, Fosselweight and Arterbury took their leave. Roberts stood on the sunny topdeck, nearly buoyant with relief and optimism. He had money in his pocket, some weapons on board, and a job for his airship. The Black Sea was far beyond London, and although the *Horizon* would be sailing directly into a war zone, she would be far away from Smothers' reach. Roberts could start to work on the debt he owed on her and begin rebuilding his name and reputation. If his luck held out, he just might be able to keep the *Horizon* in Crimea and demand fat fees for her services.

Below deck, Halloway had commandeered most of the crew to help him with the Vandenberg, and a fine squabble was in full force. Roberts waded into the mess to shout things into order and dispense new commands. Farrington and William were dispatched with a full money sack to buy provisions for the upcoming journey while Carter and Long Tom were sent on their way with more money and another list of supplies. Halloway, Roberts was pleased to see, was in top form, manic with energy, feverishly intent on the project at hand, and driving everyone crazy with his demands.

Leaving Oboe to keep a lid on Halloway's temper, Roberts left the airship to attend to his own task: arranging for shot and powder for the Vandenberg. While he was exceedingly grateful to have armament at last, the new weapon had unique considerations. Although he could see the value inherent in its design, each individual barrel would require breech loading by hand, a tedious and slow process. Halloway had muttered something about creating a cartridge, and Roberts had reason to hope that they could devise a quicker and easier way to reload.

The munitions dealer in the crowded bazaar was a tall, dark-skinned man who spoke nearly perfect trade English. He listened to Roberts intently before handing over a fifty caliber bullet tapered at both ends. Roberts examined it before placing an order for as much powder and shot as his limited resources could handle. The *Morning Star* was equipped with fourteen carronade cannon that fired cannonballs or grapeshot as desired, but neither were ammunition the Vandenberg could handle. Still, with enough lead on board, the *Horizon* could make her own bullets if needed. And powder was powder.

They concluded their business with the dealer promising delivery by the end of the day. Roberts left the bazaar and immersed himself back in the choked streets of the city until he reached the airship wharf, which was even more crowded and noisy that before. A small bag of coffee beans was carefully tucked away in his jacket, and the rich aroma reached his nose through the stink of garbage and smoke. With money still in his pocket, he hadn't been able to resist when he passed a coffee vendor on the street. William's cooking skills had improved to the point that Roberts was just about willing to trust him with a coffee grinder.

With a rather light step, Roberts pushed his way through the teeming crowds towards the *Horizon*, until the sight of a parasol stopped him dead in his tracks. *No*, he thought with a growl of fury and dread. *Not her.*

It was. Dainty and elegant and dressed in immaculate yellow and white despite the wharf's grime and with Jules looming protectively at her side.

No. Not again.

"Captain Roberts!" a bright voice cut through the air. Roberts paused for one long second, clenching and unclenching his hands and mustering up every last ounce of self-control.

Miss Pickens didn't move from her spot at the foot of the *Horizon*'s gangplank, one hand grasping her parasol and the other one elegantly fluttering a lace fan. They were delicate objects but Roberts saw fan and parasol as weapons in the hands of a master marksman, and both were turning their sites in his direction.

Fortunately, he was far too irate to fall under the gunshot of feminine weapons. Not trusting himself to avoid saying or doing anything he would later regret, Roberts settled for giving the reporter pair a blank look, then thundered towards the gangplank, studiously avoiding them.

As he roared past Miss Pickens, trying to keep the scent of her perfume out of his nose, she did not shrink from his approach. Instead, her light, feminine voice reached out to his ear. "I owe you an apology, Captain Roberts," she said quietly.

Roberts stiffened. "An apology is not enough, Miss Pickens," he stated icily, his back to her. "And following my airship from port to port won't help."

"I offered you a proposition, Captain," Miss Pickens stated. "I told you, my grandfather is a high-ranking military commander. The Crimean War is in desperate need of supplying. A good airship that can bring supplies to the troops will earn much fame and recognition."

Roberts still had his back to her but her words reached him effortlessly. "Fame enough to overcome any notoriety, with the right backing..."

Roberts' words were dark. "Miss Pickens, I will manage my own airship and my own situation. My best advice, *madam*, is to go back to Gibraltar. There is no place for you in Tangier."

"Take me to my grandfather," Miss Pickens stated doggedly. "He sails on the *HMS Dante* in the Black Sea. He can help you..."

"I don't need your help," Roberts growled out darkly. "I'd advise you to leave now, Miss Pickens." Roberts took two angry strides forward on the gangplank, resolutely keeping his back turned to Miss Pickens. Her next words froze his blood.

"That is a lovely new weapon you have on board, Captain Roberts," Miss Pickens stated mildly. Roberts paused, one heel not even touching the gangplank as the repercussions of what she just said filled his brain. He was dimly aware of Miss Pickens tripping up the gangplank after him. She gestured towards the rear of the *Horizon* where a porthole had opened up to the air, the muzzle of the new weapon sticking through it.

"A Vandenberg gun, if I am not mistaken," Miss Pickens continued in the same light tones as each word rang with meaning. "Why, interestingly enough, there was just such a weapon causing a great deal of fuss back in Gibraltar a few days ago," she stated breezily. "Jules heard that a Spanish airship had crashed on Gibraltar with two Vandenbergs on board. One became quite stuck in the mud and the Navy was unable to recover it." Her tone was light but Roberts heard every unspoken word and the promises they brought.

Roberts was still fighting valiantly to control his temper. His voice was barely level as he responded tightly, "Are you trying to blackmail me, Miss Pickens?"

A dainty glove appeared on his forearm and the scent of perfume filled his nostrils. "Not blackmail, Captain Roberts," Miss Pickens stated in a rather husky voice that played along his spine like a harp. Despite his fury, he could not deny that she was an exceedingly attractive woman.

"Persuasion, yes, but not blackmail," she said in a more businesslike manner. "War is news, Captain, and there will be much of both in Crimea."

Roberts' bark cut her off. "War's no place for a woman, Miss Pickens," he stated bluntly.

"Jules and I have both sailed on the *Dante* before," Miss Pickens replied confidently. "There are more women in battle than you hear about, Captain."

Roberts opened his mouth for a rebuttal but Miss Pickens quickly changed tactics. "I can offer you three hundred pounds to take Jules and me to my grandfather. Cash up front," she added, seeing Roberts' eyes narrow.

Against his much better judgment, he considered the offer. It was a generous sum, more than what an airship passenger would spend to fly the same distance. His conscience argued that it was far too risky a trip for a lady to make and his common sense yowled that it had no interest in being forced to endure Miss Pickens company, much less allow her on board the *Horizon*. In the end, his wallet won the debate.

"Four hundred pounds," Roberts growled. "In cash up front." Miss Pickens frowned in protest as Roberts added, "And you'd best make good on that promise, Miss Pickens. The *Horizon*'s not a passenger ship, and you've caused me quite enough damage as it is. I expect a return on my investment, and not just in transport fees."

"My grandfather will be able to help you, Captain Roberts," Miss Pickens stated, but Roberts cut her a black look.

"I don't want your grandfather's help," he said bluntly. "I'd *like* to see him turn you over his knee and teach you the lessons he should have taught you years ago, but I'll *settle* for him taking responsibility for his granddaughter's actions and righting some of the wrongs she caused."

Miss Pickens flushed, and there was a subtle shift from Jules that told Roberts he better watch for a vindictive fist coming his way. In his current irate state, he would have returned the punch gladly.

Ignoring the looming slopes of Mount Jules, Roberts turned his back resolutely to the two reporters. "We'll be leaving port in three days," he announced. "You're to be on the wharf at daylight with four hundred in cash, Miss Pickens, or you can find your own way to your grandfather." With that, he pushed off his back foot and stomped aboard the *Horizon*, leaving Miss Pickens and her silent bodyguard behind.

His former good mood now completely vaporized, Roberts thundered onto the *Horizon*. He was intent on taking out his anger on the first hapless crew member that made a wrong movement, such as breathing, but to his consternation, everyone was either busy or absent. Even the movement around the Vandenberg was oddly cooperative. Halloway was elbow-deep in a network of metallic odds and ends he had scrounged from around the airship and wasn't currently yelling at Sparrowman or Jenkins. Seeing nothing to aggravate his already blazing temper, Roberts stalked from one end of the *Horizon* to the other, fighting to calm himself down. The rest of the crew quickly scuttled out of his way until he had walked off the worst of the temper.

It's four hundred pounds in cash up front, Roberts reminded himself several times. *You can put up with her for a few weeks, then drop her off at her grandfather's and rid the airship of her.* Yet something deep inside warned him that shaking Miss Pickens off his tail wouldn't be nearly that simple.

Chapter Five

Three days at port in Tangier passed in a blur of activity, most of it centered on the Vandenberg. Halloway had no qualms about gleefully raiding the *Morning Star* for any tool or supply he needed, and Captain Fosselweight graciously opened his stores for the crew of the *Horizon*. With an abundance of equipment and parts at his disposal, Halloway set to work in a fury, building a carriage for the new weapon and filling the airship with chaos.

Carter and William were busy stocking the *Horizon* with everything she needed for the journey. Some of the supplies went into the airship's belly and others were rerouted to the *Morning Star* which would function as the warehouse for most of the trip. Roberts became increasingly more grateful for the new partnership with the merchant marine; with the *Morning Star*'s generous storeholds, the *Horizon* could drop a significant amount of weight and not worry about running out of coal in the middle of the Mediterranean.

Coal was a pressing concern for both vessels. With two boilers to stoke, fuel was a major discussion point during the long planning sessions Roberts and Fosselweight held.

"Greek coal is exclusively lignite," Fosselweight sniffed in disapproval as the two captains stood on the *Horizon*'s topdeck. There were maps spread out in front of them and a sextant, telescope, and compass joining them. "Devilish to transport and has a tendency to spontaneously explode," Fosselweight added. "It'll do in a pinch, but I'm not going to let it on board the *Morning Star*. The Greeks may have anthracite, but I would advise you not to trust it."

He rustled a map and jabbed it with a small finger. "We can stop in Cagliari and Sicily for fuel and that should last us nicely until Constantinople." He frowned through the mustache. "Though I'm not certain what stores of anthracite there are to be found in Crimea."

"We'll make do," Roberts rumbled evenly, masking the worry chewing at his gut. Fuel was a pressing issue for any airship, but the former *Lucky Lady* had only flown within England where coal supplies were abundant. The frozen wasteland of Crimea would be an entirely different matter. Although the *Horizon* would be light on cargo, she would also have the weight of the two unwanted passengers and their baggage, another factor to consider.

Remembering this, Roberts tightened his jaw. "The *Horizon* is taking on two passengers," he said evenly. "A Miss Pickens and her brother Jules. She says she is the granddaughter of a commander whose fleet is sailing the Black Sea." He huffed a little. "She wants me to bring them to him."

"Pickens? Surely you don't mean Commander Horace Pickens?" Fosselweight frowned, then looked astonished. "His granddaughter will board the *Horizon*? And fly to the Black Sea? But that...that simply won't do, Captain, to take a lady into a war zone."

Roberts was sorely tempted to express his exact thoughts on the matter. Instead, he shrugged indifferently. "She paid well for passage. I aim to see them both delivered safely."

Fosselweight's mustache quivered. "What on earth could a lady want in a war zone?" he said in a bewildered tone.

"They're reporters," Roberts shrugged. "They have their own intentions, I suppose." He could have been honest with Fosselweight but decided to spare him the sordid details. The professional relationship between the two captains was progressing nicely, and Roberts didn't want to spoil it by dragging Miss Pickens-related drama into the open.

"A woman reporter?" Fosselweight said in wonder. "My heavens, what are these young ladies getting up to these days?" he trailed off as Farrington stepped forward with a question and the captains turned their minds to other matters.

Roberts, however, did not put the matter of the unwanted passengers so easily out of his mind. Ever since yesterday when Miss Pickens and her recalcitrant brother had showed up at the *Horizon*'s gangplank, he had kept the issue to himself, his anger too great to give the news to the crew. However, everyone needed to know about the two extra souls on board in order to prepare accordingly. A woman on the airship would mean extra accommodations and the presence of this particular woman would cause no end of tension.

That afternoon, Roberts called for an inspection and the men fell into place, with even Halloway standing in line with something that looked dangerously like compliance. Roberts paced the ranks, looking the men over, then announced flatly, "We're taking on two passengers, a Mister Jules Pickens and a Miss Pickens." Faces wrinkled in confusion as the crew digested the news about passengers, then eyes widened in shock when the names were mentioned.

Roberts continued, "Yes, these are the two reporters who wrote that article about the *Horizon*. It was against my better judgment to take them on, but they're paying well and they've promised work contacts."

"You all are to keep well clear of them both," he stated sternly. "Do not forget that they are reporters. Don't speak to them any more than necessary. Even so," he added, "You're to treat them with respect. Neither reporter is a friend of the *Horizon* but I'll drop like an anvil on any man who gives a woman any grief in my presence."

Halloway stiffened visibly, and Roberts looked at him thoughtfully. He had been so consumed with his own rage that he had scarcely considered how difficult it would be for Halloway to have the two reporters on board.

I'll talk to him later, Roberts thought. Aloud, he called, "Dismissed!" and the neat line disintegrated as men quickly moved back to their former tasks. Roberts strode to his own cabin and entered it, still irritated. Like it or not, he'd have to stow Miss Pickens in it; there was no other place on board for her. He and Jules could bunk down with the crew.

It would be a long trip, even more so with the reporters on board. Despite the benefits to partnering with the *Morning Star*, it would take weeks for the merchant marine to chug its way across the Mediterranean, dodge around Italy and Greece, and trudge into Constantinople. In the weeks that passed in the air, stuck with Miss Pickens as a constant presence, Roberts wasn't entirely sure he would reach Constantinople with a sane mind. He wondered if he could possibly convince her to sail on board the *Morning Star* for a spell and then conveniently forget to pick her up until they reached Constantinople.

It was an idea worth considering, and Roberts sifted through his meager possessions in a thoughtful frame of mind. Finishing with his task, he looked over at the narrow bunk that was his. It occurred to him quite forcefully that there would soon be a beautiful woman in his bed: normally a most delightful and intriguing prospect.

Shaking his head wryly, Roberts left his fantasies behind him, shutting the cabin door firmly and forcing his mind towards mundane matters. There wasn't much time for him to dwell further on women. With the departure date for their long voyage fast approaching, there was scarcely any room for him to breathe, let alone think.

Within three days at Tangier, Halloway had a prototype mounting carriage for the Vandenberg assembled. Once the two ships left Tangier, they could try it over open water. A small powder room grew to life in the hold, far away from the boiler and carefully guarded from flame. A barrage of supplies rolled towards the *Horizon*, some to enter the airship and others to be carried by the *Morning Star*.

At dawn on the day of departure, Fosselweight and Arterbury were standing with Roberts in the middle of a sea of organized chaos as they worked out a few last-minute issues. Fosselweight was clearly preoccupied with the needs of his own ship waiting for him, and he edged slowly down the wharf as he offered some last-minute advice to Roberts.

"Sicily is a tricky port, Captain, and be mindful of docking fees, they'll...eh..." Fosselweight trailed off as his attention was firmly diverted elsewhere.

"There you are, Captain Roberts!" a female voice sailed out gaily. Roberts sighed heavily and resolutely turned to face Miss Pickens, who was heading his way. She was nattily attired in a jacket and skirt of sapphire blue, white lace at her cuffs and collar, and her tiny waistline curving to the roundness of her hips. A jewel or two flashed in the sunlight and a rather daring hat sloped enchantingly over her brow and rested enticingly over her right eye, plumes waving. A little behind her was Jules, loaded down with an assortment of suitcases and hatboxes and wearing a look of weary resignation.

The moment his eyes fell upon Miss Pickens, Roberts forgot momentarily exactly why he was so furious with her, and ire melted away for a moment of genuine appreciation. It was with some difficulty that common sense wrested back the controls and metaphorically kicked Roberts sharply in the posterior. Shaking his head a little, he reluctantly pulled himself back to reality. As he did so, he heard Fosselweight inhale sharply.

Having suddenly remembered why he was not pleased to have the two reporters on board, Roberts nodded at the pair slowly. "Miss Pickens," he said heavily. "Mister Pickens." He eyed the luggage, silently calculating its weight and how much fuel he would burn transporting it and the two passengers.

Miss Pickens bustled forward. "Oh, tosh, Captain Roberts," she cooed, her eyes peeping winsomely from under the brim of her hat. "There is no need for formalities, not when we will be traveling together. Please, call me Victoria and my brother answers to Jules."

She stepped lightly across the well-scrubbed boards to stand just a few feet from Roberts. He could smell an intoxicating perfume wrapping around her like a silken cloak, drowning out the honest smells of sweat, coal dust, and engine oil that was the normal bouquet on board the *Horizon*. With her perfume in his nostrils, Roberts could honestly state that he preferred the regular odor of the airship; it didn't make his stomach dance a jig across his lower intestines.

A strangled sound drew Roberts' eyes to Fosselweight. The man was obviously dazzled. He stood riveted in place, his mouth dropping open as Miss Pickens flashed a lovely smile at Roberts, then turned to the other captain.

"And who might you be, sir?" she beamed.

A whip of motion and Fosselweight's hat was firmly in his hands, exposing a bald spot as he popped off an elaborate bow. "Ma'am," he said, the word coming out in a high-pitched squeak. He cleared his throat and tried again. "I am Captain Archibald Fosselweight of the merchant marine *Morning Star*. May I say that it is truly a great honor to meet the granddaughter of Commander Horace Pickens."

Miss Pickens laughed coyly, "Come, Captain Fosselweight, we will all be traveling together. Surely there is no need for such formalities. Please, call me Victoria."

A deep blush crept around the boundaries of Fosselweight's mustache and spread to the exposed parts of his cheeks. Miss Pickens was a good three or four inches taller than Fosselweight, even subtracting the extra height gained by her heeled boots and the feather tipped hat on her head. But he was clearly entranced, even more so as Miss Pickens minced her way forward and took him by the arm.

"Now, Captain Fosselweight, do tell me where it is we are going," she said gaily. "All I know is that we are heading toward Constantinople. Tell me, what route can we expect to take?" Miss Pickens deftly steered Fosselweight forward, her head inclined enchantingly in his direction. Roberts watched in amusement as Fosselweight visibly inflated, his skinny chest sticking out and his chin rising up like a sail being hoisted.

"Well Miss...*Miss Victoria*, I can tell you that we will make our first port in..."

The pair stepped away as Roberts, grateful that the reporter was occupied, swung his attention back to the *Horizon*, but not before Arterbury gave a low whistle. "*That* is one fine woman," he said admiringly.

"Tell your captain he's welcome to her with my blessings," Roberts replied dryly.

Arterbury's grin was wolfish. "I'd be glad to take over if my captain feels he is not up to the task, sir."

Roberts allowed himself a snort of amusement, then turned his head back to business. The *Horizon*'s envelope was almost taut, her boiler churning vigorously, and her engines sputtering to life. The crew was nearly finished with their preparations, and the warm Mediterranean air was tangy with salt and brisk with fresh winds, practically begging the airship to break loose from her tethers and soar into the atmosphere.

Fosselweight finally reluctantly parted ways with Miss Pickens who merrily entered the *Horizon* with Jules at her side. With chilly courtesy, Roberts directed Miss Pickens into his cabin, watching as she sauntered into it and made herself right at home. Jules set down the suitcases and Roberts left the pair to unpack, shutting the door behind him and hoping they would stay out of the way while the *Horizon* lifted.

With the reporters out of sight, Roberts' good mood crept back. Feeling some lightness move back into his spirits, Roberts turned to the wheel and interrupted a flying lesson between Barking Jack and Bloomberg.

Shooing them away from the helm, he said, "I'll take her for now." It was good weather for flying and he felt like taking a turn at the wheel.

With full-voiced shouts and excitement rising in their voices, the crew of the *Horizon* directed the airship up into the sun-soaked heavens, leaving Tangier behind for adventure and battle ahead.

Chapter Six

The sky was clear but dull, the winds still as the *Horizon* sailed limply through the sea air, her chronometer clocking in at a sluggish ten knots. Roberts scanned the heavens, noting the shapes of far-off airships legging their way through the sky. Marine ships dotted the water, some accompanied by airships and others on their own. However, all other ships were several miles away, and the *Horizon* and *Morning Star* had plenty of space to stretch out their wings.

Tangier was two days behind them, and the two ships were working their way along the coast of Spain, moving towards the Balearic Islands and steering clear of Africa's coast, whose waters and skies were notoriously thick with pirates. Roberts anticipated a skirmish at some point on their voyage, but was not overly worried. The *Morning Star* moved easily through the waves, and her fourteen cannon would help guard her in an attack. The *Horizon* was fleet and was preparing to test out her new weapon on the open seas. With it in operation, both vessels would be able to put up a strong defense.

Noise below decks drew Roberts' attention away from the skies ahead. Halloway was below with anyone he could bully into helping him test the Vandenberg. The rest of the crew was nervously tying down anything that might knock loose, should Halloway's spring-loaded carriage absorb less recoil that promised. Roberts would have preferred first trying out the gun on shore, but there wasn't time. They'd have to make do with a field demonstration. He knew that there were massive amounts of tinkering and several dangerous test runs ahead before they had a properly working system and the Vandenberg could be put in full operation.

Moving among the men, Roberts eyed everything on board for its potential to cause a disaster, dispensing instructions and encouragement where needed. The most hazardous thing on board, however, was walking toward him just now, staggering a trifle.

Roberts sighed darkly as he stepped forward, eying the reporter warily. "You should be inside the cabin, Miss Pickens," he said gruffly, noting as the reporter wobbled, not having quite mastered her air legs yet. "We'll be running some practice shots and it could shake the whole airship."

"How exciting!" Miss Pickens trilled and smiled winsomely at him. He did not return the smile. Briefly, he wondered if she had any idea how much difficulty she had brought on board his ship. Although the crew had heeded Roberts' commands and displayed tolerable courtesy to the reporters, resentment and anger were palpable. Halloway, in particular, stayed below decks and avoided all eye contact with Miss Pickens if their paths happened to meet. There was very little room for avoidance on an airship, and uncomfortable collisions were regular.

To Roberts' relief, the two reporters spent much of their time writing in his cabin. Miss Pickens had brought a newfangled typewriter on board and the clicking of its keys continued day and night. Roberts had put an edict on any further articles about the *Horizon*, but he had no assurance that his orders were being heeded.

Miss Pickens clutched her elaborate hat, which flapped in the wind as she increased the magnitude of her smile. Against his better judgment, Roberts found the corners of his mouth twitching upwards before he wrestled them back into a more appropriate stern gaze. "It will be noisy on deck," he warned her.

"Never you mind, Captain Roberts," Miss Pickens replied airily. "I'll tuck myself away in the cabin and won't be a bother." Somewhat to his surprise, she did just that. She shut the cabin door, leaving Roberts to finish supervising while the entire airship braced for a test run of the Vandenberg.

Below decks was a welter of activity. Halloway was in fine form and yelled at everyone while several crew members moved about under his orders. At the heart of the action was the Vandenberg gun, suspended from a ceiling-mounted carriage. Carter and Farrington were carefully sliding wadding and shot into the gun's numerous barrels while Halloway fussed, making last-minute adjustments and even more noise. More quietly but no less resolute, Long Tom was directing Bloomberg and William about with purposeful action.

Surprisingly, Jules had stoically inserted himself into the action. The enormous man had barely said three words while on board, but when his sister wasn't demanding his time, he added his considerable strength to the crew's efforts unasked. Right now, he was holding up the barrel of the gun and meekly obeying Halloway's demands.

"Captain," Barking Jack's voice broke over the babble of voices. "Click from the *Morning Star*. She'll stay her course seventy-five degrees so she's well out of the range of fire."

Roberts nodded sharply. Ever since the two ships had left port two days ago, communication had flowed steadily back and forth between their signal clickers, which transmitted coded flashes of light. Bloomberg, in addition to his increasing skills as a pilot, was developing quite a knack for deciphering clicker code. He claimed it was due to years of translating bad handwriting on envelopes and letters.

"Signal back that we're holding at one-eighty at half a mile," Roberts ordered. This would give them room to move but be close enough for the *Morning Star* to come to their aid if the *Horizon* ran into trouble.

Bloomberg relayed the message to the *Morning Star*, and the merchant marine signaled back understanding. The *Horizon* banked sharply to the right and cut a wide arc through the air, moving away from the merchant marine but still keeping her in her sights. Barking Jack held the *Horizon* steady, her engines growling as he pulled her into a tight idle, pulling her rear out to face one-eighty degrees into the open sea.

The Vandenberg screeched as Jules and Big Tom wrestled the nose of the gun forward towards the starboard side cannon porthole. The ceiling-mounted carriage was centered in the middle of the airship and suspended from a retractable chassis that allowed the Vandenberg to be pulled forward when in use, then retracted back. This kept the weight of the gun located in the center of the airship at all times and allowed the gun to fire from several positions. Yet the retracting chassis was clearly not as effective as promised and Jules and Big Tom were wrestling mightily to pull it forward, under fire from Halloway's frenzied commands.

Finally the muzzle of the Vandenberg was coaxed through the cannon porthole and the breech was loaded with shot and powder. Excitement and trepidation grew in the crew as last-minute adjustments were made and Long Tom stepped forward to man the lanyard. Poised for action and potential danger, the crew of the *Horizon* tensed themselves and waited for orders. Finally, Roberts gave the command and Long Tom ripped the lanyard free.

What happened next was an almighty bang as a hundred and fifty-two rounds of fifty caliber balls tore across the sky and obliterated a passing seabird. The Vandenberg shot backwards, slamming into the spring-mounted carriage, and crunched hard on the retractable chassis. The *Horizon* juddered heavily in the sky, sending William and Long Tom to their knees and the rest of the crew flailing to grab hold of any nearby uprights.

Roberts barely managed to keep his footing. He surged forward, his voice cutting through the yells of his crew. A few minutes of shouting and a battalion of orders soon established that the *Horizon* and crew was jarred but unhurt. There were some broken crates and cracked crockery but damages appeared to be minimal.

Halloway's retractable chassis and spring-mounted carriage, however, were another story. The inventor hovered over his creation with barely-contained frustration, saying nothing as Roberts settled his crew down. It was clear that more shooting practice was not going to happen until Halloway worked out some of the issues with the Vandenberg. Roberts dismissed the crew to check the airship for any possible problems and turned his attention to the inventor.

Angrily, Halloway kicked objects out of his way as he stormed over to snatch up some tools from a box. Roberts watched him carefully, then stuck his head out the porthole to see a white dot floating down to the waves, a few feathers marking all that was left of the unfortunate bird that had strayed in the Vandenberg's path.

"Well, it did a hell of a number on that seagull," he commented with quiet humor. An icy silence was Halloway's response, but Roberts' mood was buoyant. Once properly mounted, the Vandenberg would be an excellent weapon. One hundred and fifty-two rounds of lead shot would punch through a ship's airbags and hull like paper. The shot had been tightly contained and hadn't spread out like grapeshot, but a hit in the right place would do more devastation than several cannonballs. A shot like that with a range of over two thousand yards, and the Vandenberg could hold off anything.

Turning his attention back to the weapon, Roberts examined the twisted metal of the damaged chassis. "You need supplies off the *Morning Star?*"

Halloway gave a barely perceptible nod, and Roberts hoped that Captain Fosselweight's generosity would continue. "I'll have a click sent. You and I can take the lift basket down. I have some things to discuss with Captain Fosselweight."

Towing a grumbling Halloway with him, Roberts returned to topdeck and called out orders. At his command, the *Horizon* swung around to intercept the *Morning Star.* Her engines surged forward, briefly moving the airship past ten knots as she had not done since leaving Tangier, and within a few minutes, the *Horizon* was dropping to hover over the merchant marine.

Roberts would have preferred taking a quick drop line since it was faster and more efficient than the lift basket. However, Halloway didn't know how to use one and would put up a fuss. Instead, the two men entered the lift basket and let the crew lower them to the *Morning Star's* deck.

Captain Fosselweight graciously welcomed them on board and invited Halloway to further plunder the *Morning Star* for what he wanted. The two captains left Halloway to his pillaging and repaired to Fosselweight's cabin.

"Most delighted to have you on board again, Captain Roberts," Fosselweight stated as a steward placed tea in front of the two. Roberts awkwardly cradled a thin china cup in his massive paw, hoping he wouldn't break it. Taking a sip, he glanced around Fosselweight's well-appointed cabin, from the polished silver setting to the books neatly lined on a shelf. In contrast, Roberts' own cabin was a study in austerity.

"We have made excellent time," Fosselweight continued. Roberts kept his own opinions to himself, that being that the *Horizon* was just barely crawling through the air. While the slower pace was easier on the engines, it made for tedious days. Fosselweight, however, could not hope to coax anything like forty knots out of his vessel, and their current pace was more than adequate for a marine ship.

Fosselweight cleared his throat. "Miss Pickens is keeping well, I trust?" he questioned in a too-casual voice.

"Well enough," Roberts responded neutrally. The other captain was looking a tad wistful, clearly disappointed that the female reporter hadn't made an appearance on the *Morning Star*. However, Roberts wasn't keen on continuing the topic so he switched directions. Pulling a map over to him, he tapped it. "We're traveling a bit too northeast for my liking," he said.

"Yes, but it wouldn't do to hug too close to the coastline, Captain Roberts," Fosselweight responded as the conversation turned away from women and towards less perilous topics such as open seas and the high likelihood of encountering an enemy ship.

The two captains concluded their business before Halloway had finished his, and Roberts had to drag his chief engineer up from the bowels of the *Morning Star*. He was dismayed at the amount of supplies Halloway had freely looted, but Fosselweight waved them on generously. "Take what you need, Captain. I want to see that gun of yours in action!" It took two basketfuls to move everything up to the *Horizon*, and Roberts tried not to think about the extra weight this was adding to the airship. However, much of what Halloway had pilfered were tools that Roberts would see back on the *Morning Star*, no matter Halloway's protestations.

As the airship pulled away from the *Morning Star* and resumed her course in the sky, Halloway got to work below deck while the airship continued her slow pace. Despite the low speed, she flew well and the men were kept busy attending her needs. As the afternoon progressed, Roberts noted a growing downturn in morale that had settled on the airship ever since they had lifted from Tangier. There was still some tension as the new crew learned to mesh with the old and become adjusted to the *Horizon*. Their harried flight from London and the uncertainty about the future sharpened tempers and darkened moods. The presence of the two reporters on board, as well as the distraction of pretty female in what was typically a staunchly male environment, only exaggerated complications.

Oboe, however, had further bad news. "Captain," he said later that afternoon as he took Roberts aside. "A few of the men have reported missing items. Trinkets mainly, but accusations have been made."

"I couldn't find my compass this morning," Roberts commented. He was certain he had set it down on his coat the previous night before clambering into a hammock, but it had failed to make an appearance the following morning. He initially dismissed the incident; the berthing area was crowded, especially since he and Jules were sleeping among the men, and it was easy for things to go missing. Other accusations of theft, however, pointed to a pickpocket on board.

"We'll search the berthing. There's not many places on the ship to hide anything," Roberts said. "Get the men together. I want a fair search so no man is accused without proof."

While the rest of the crew ran the airship, Bloomberg, Jenkins, William, Long Tom, and Carter were pulled from their duties and ordered to turn their bags out, shake out their bedding and clothing, and lay out all their possessions. Roberts and Oboe watched carefully as they moved through the berthing area - on the hunt for the missing items.

Something screeched like a banshee and Carter hollered with surprise, recoiling away from a small pile of clothing bags. A dark, furry shape skittered across the floor and shot out the open door, chittering to itself. Carter was after it in a flash, and the rest of the men abandoned their search and followed him.

"Come back here, you bloody imp!" Carter bellowed in fury, shaking his fist up at a small monkey dangling from one of the envelope ropes. It cocked its head to the side, then swung easily to another rope which offered a better perch. Roberts had to laugh as he gazed up at the simian dangling from one foot and one hand, its bright eyes fixed on him intently. It was small, still a baby, but nevertheless, a monkey, and very much unwanted on board. It looked at him full in the face, then dropped excrement on the scrubbed decks of the *Horizon*.

No longer amused, Roberts eyed it, wondering how they would coax it down from its perch. The monkey was in its element among the suspension ropes holding the envelope to the gondola. It flitted lightly from rope to rope, unaware or uncaring that it was several hundred feet in the air with a long, fatal drop to the waters below.

Carter came panting up to Roberts. "The bastard bit me, Captain!" he reported angrily, holding up a hand to show the clear impression of teeth and a drop or two of blood. He wiped the blood on his trousers and growled. "I'll get a rifle and shoot the bastard off the ship."

"No," Roberts said curtly. "You're not getting a bullet anywhere near the envelope."

Coming to his senses, Carter cleared his throat. "Right. Er, sorry, Captain," he responded, then added hesitantly. "How do we get the bugger down then?"

"We'll have to lure it down," Roberts responded, and then frowned as Bloomberg and Long Tom pressed forward to get a good look at the creature. "Easy," he said in a low tone. "It's not going to come down unless it's quiet on deck. Make a fuss, and it will stay where it is."

The men watched as the monkey dangled well above reach, observing them impishly. Baby or no, it looked strong and mischievous, and Roberts could easily imagine it chewing through an airbag or biting ropes. They needed to get it down, and quickly.

Heels clicked and Miss Pickens hurried onto the scene, her gray skirt and white blouse fluttering in the wind. William trailed behind her with a stirring spoon in his hand which he held like a weapon.

"It's a Barbary macaque!" Miss Pickens called out, gazing up at the monkey which swung lightly between several ropes. "It must have climbed on board at port," she commented, and her eyes brightened. "There are packs of them all over Gibraltar, Captain. I saw them many times when I was a girl." The monkey chittered at her, and she visibly melted. "Oh, he is just a baby! How darling."

"It could tear the ship apart," Roberts grunted. "We need to get it down."

"Give me some time. I'm sure I can lure it down," Miss Pickens stated confidently. "They're quite used to humans, you know, and will take food from your hand. If your men pay it no mind, it will feel safe enough to come down and eat. Let me get something it will like." She hurried off to the galley. The men returned to their duties while the monkey observed the processes as if waiting to see what would happen next.

Miss Pickens soon returned with a dish of cut up vegetables and fruit. She put it down on the deck and began calling to the climbing pest as it gamboled among the ropes. After only a few minutes, the macaque slipped down the ropes and scurried across the deck to the dish. Miss Pickens allowed it a few bites before she pulled the dish away, an action which caused the macaque to shoot backwards a few paces. Coaxing, she tossed a piece of potato at the macaque which it ate and looked for more. Bit by bit, it moved forward until it was taking food from Miss Pickens' hand.

Piece after piece disappeared down the macaque's gullet while Roberts watched carefully, worried it would scratch or bite Miss Pickens. It ate avidly for several long minutes, then boldly ran up her arm to twirl around her head, disturbing her carefully arranged hair.

She laughed. "See there, Captain, it's quite tame. I used to feed the monkeys when I lived in Gibraltar. They can be a bit vicious in packs, but this one is not even an adolescent yet. He won't harm anyone."

Roberts decided not to mention Carter's bleeding hand, not when the macaque was letting him take one step after another towards it. He slowly picked up a piece of apple from the dish and handed it to the macaque. It sniffed the fruit curiously, then stuffed the entire piece in its mouth, regarding Roberts. Gently, he extended his hand to it and after a moment of consideration, the macaque scrambled up his arm.

Roberts lifted a finger and stroked the animal on the top of its downy head. Miss Pickens smiled and said, "There, Captain, it's just a little monkey, that's..."

With lightening speed, Roberts' thumb and two fingers clamped down on the macaque's neck, encircling it like a steel collar. It immediately fought back, kicking and clawing as Roberts held it at arm's length. The macaque was stronger than he expected, and its long fingernails raked at his skin as he twisted his arm, preparing to hurl the pest into the open air and well away from his airship.

"STOP!" Miss Pickens screamed, throwing herself at Roberts and planting her hands on his chest. "Don't throw it!" she pleaded desperately.

Roberts tried to edge around her without putting her in danger of the macaque's flailing limbs. "It's a dangerous pest, Miss Pickens," he spoke rationally. "It'll tear the ship apart, spread disease, might even bite open an airbag."

But Miss Pickens refused to be moved. "It's just a baby!" she wailed. "You can't kill it! It's cruel!"

Roberts fought for patience. "Miss Pickens, I've got my airship and my crew to consider. It could put us all in danger."

Miss Pickens was on the brink of hysteria, her eyes glassy and her lip trembling. "Please!" she begged. "Please don't kill it! I'll watch it, you can tie it up, I'll even pay for anything it damages. Don't kill it, please!"

She took a step closer and Roberts could smell her perfume eroding away his resistance as surely as Miss Pickens' agony-wracked face and heaving bosom were doing. The macaque gasped for air, weakening by the second as its tiny body shook painfully.

A moment or two of tension passed. Roberts huffed, then yanked loose a burlap sack from a net and stuffed the macaque inside. The second it hit the inside of the bag, it began kicking and yowling. Roberts bellowed, "Carter!"

"Yes, sir!" The bosun hurried to his captain's side, still nursing his hand.

Roberts handed over the kicking burlap sack. "Take it to Halloway and have it fitted for a chain. Not a rope or it might chew through it. Secure it somewhere out of my sight."

He turned slightly to the trembling woman. "Miss Pickens, I entrust you with its care."

"Thank you, Captain Roberts," she responded, eyes still glistening with tears.

"If it does escape, I will throw it overboard," Roberts warned her quietly. "I can't risk the safety of my airship or anyone on board. Is that clear?"

Miss Pickens nodded, but Roberts added another edict. "The second we reach port, I want it off my ship. Do we have an agreement, Miss Pickens?"

Miss Pickens nodded again. "Yes, thank you, Captain," she said softly. She moved forward to join Carter who was holding the agitated bag. A ripping sound warned that the monkey was hell-bent on escaping.

Carter looked distinctly unenthusiastic about his new task, and Roberts barked at him, "What are you waiting for, man? Get it chained up before it escapes."

Carter snapped to attention and disappeared below deck, Miss Pickens trailing after him, fretting and clasping her hands. Calmness settled back over the airship, except for occasional outraged monkey shrieks echoing from the bowels of the ship. After a time, Carter tramped heavily up the ladder, fresh blood trickling down his right arm, and presented himself to his captain.

"The monkey is secure, sir," he reported tersely. "Miss Pickens is attending it."

"Good," Roberts said, looking down at Carter's arm.

Carter's jaw was tense. "Permission to report to Mister Harding?" Roberts granted it and as Carter turned his back, a section of pallid buttock showed through a good-sized tear in his trouser bottom. Roberts stifled a laugh but let Carter go without comment. As the bosun stomped away, Long Tom and Farrington snickered behind his back. Now that the worst was over and the macaque safely chained, Roberts had to admit the situation was rather funny. As long as the bloody thing stayed below deck and didn't cause any further damage, he would grant it some clemency.

Miss Pickens kept her promise and the macaque stayed below. Occasionally it filled the airship with ungodly shrieks, but Miss Pickens kept it well-fed and occupied so that it was only a minor nuisance. The next day, Oboe found a hidden stash of missing items surrounded by scraps of food, all fingering the Barbary macaque as the thief. Roberts' compass and the pilfered trinkets were returned to their respective owners and the mood on the airship lightened considerably as suspicions were lifted and accusations died away. The next day, dawn broke in a riot of Mediterranean sunshine, filling the gondola with heat and light and chasing away the gray sullenness of the past few days.

They reached Cagliari, capitol of Sardinia, in seven days, a distance the *Horizon* could have reached in little over a day of flight time. But Roberts did not begrudge the time: the *Morning Star* was paying well and her coal storage was crammed full with far more anthracite than the *Horizon* could carry on her own. The port in Cagliari was crowded with steam-powered ships, both air and marine, jockeying for a position to feed greedily on its ample coal seams. The *Morning Star* was quickly filled with several dozen tons of bituminous coal, but the *Horizon* had a longer wait before the coal workers tracked down and pulverized twenty tons of anthracite. Most of anthracite found its way on board the *Morning Star* as a safeguard against uncertain coal sources ahead.

The docks of Cagliari were overloaded with men, machinery, and cargo. Roberts, standing right next to Fosselweight, had to shout to make himself heard over the noise. It was just a quick stop in Cagliari, enough to pick up fuel and water, and Roberts was intent on lifting as soon as possible. He was distracted by operations on board his airship and only just heard Fosselweight announce crisply, "A very good morning to you, Miss Pickens!"

Roberts turned to see Miss Pickens stepping their way, her blue dress immaculate, her hat riding the crest of her elegantly arranged hair, and the macaque wrapped in her arms. A chain ran from Miss Pickens' hands to the collar around its neck, and its arms were entwined around her left arm.

Roberts intercepted the pair. "I thought I said I didn't want to see that thing above deck, Miss Pickens," he said quietly, but forcefully.

Miss Pickens merely beamed at him. "But Captain, the poor thing has been locked below for days without a bit of sunshine. I have him chained still, he won't escape." Giggling a little, she lowered her chin to the monkey's head, cooing to it softly. It was curled against her breast, its bright eyes gazing curiously yet smugly at the men.

Fosselweight cleared his throat, transfixed. Miss Pickens lifted her adoring eyes to the smaller captain and smiled at him under her long lashes. Roberts watched the silent interchange with wry amusement, but he was surprised when a hint of something sharp and jolting welled up in his stomach. He examined the sensation critically before forcing it down with some difficulty.

"I say, that's a rather jolly chap," Fosselweight offered, looking at the macaque. "Is he your pet, Miss Pickens?"

Miss Pickens laughed again, that little coo that rippled off her lips like silk. "Oh, this naughty boy snuck aboard the *Horizon*." The monkey snuggled its head under her chin and wrapped its small fingers around her thumb. It was a rather enchanting scene, Roberts had to admit, and Fosselweight's eyes were almost misty as he looked at the two.

Miss Pickens continued. "Captain Roberts wanted to throw the poor little thing off the airship, but I begged him to reconsider." She pouted her lips at Roberts in disapproval which he stoically ignored.

Fosselweight snorted in indignation. "Throw him overboard? The very thought, Madam!" he said, his mustache quivering with outrage. Although his comment was directed at Miss Pickens, Roberts well knew it was for his ears.

"I know. He's just a baby, can you see harming him?" Miss Pickens responded coyly.

Roberts snorted. "It's a dammed, disease-carrying nuisance that left several bite marks on my bosun."

"Captain Roberts," Fosselweight said coldly. "I'll thank you not to use strong language in front of a lady." That captured Roberts' attention and he looked up to see Fosselweight beginning to inflate with affronted chivalry. Miss Pickens smiled coyly, and Roberts suspected that she was pitting the two captains against each other, most likely for her own amusement.

Roberts had no intention of falling for the ruse, but he didn't want to get Fosselweight worked up needlessly. Swallowing his pride, he responded evenly, "My apologies, Miss Pickens, Captain Fosselweight. This monkey, while it has its charms, also has a pair of very sharp teeth, long nails, and a tendency towards biting when provoked. I've had it chained to prevent it causing damage or disease, and it is in Miss Pickens' very tender care."

The answer seemed to mollify Fosselweight somewhat, and he reached out a hand to the macaque. "Hello there, old chap," he said tentatively. The macaque sniffed his fingers curiously, observed the captain for several moments, then adroitly scrambled up his arm and began playing with the plumes decorating his hat. Fosselweight laughed uneasily. "Rather endearing little thing isn't it?" he commented.

Roberts said nothing. His lack of response seemed to buck up Fosselweight who cleared his throat and pronounced with a soupcon of bravado, "Well, Miss Pickens, since Captain Roberts doesn't seem entirely keen on your new traveling companion, I wonder if I might convince you to sail a spell on the *Morning Star*? That is," Fosselweight added dutifully, "if Captain Roberts can spare your company."

It took some force of will for Roberts to bite back exactly what he thought of Miss Pickens' company. He kept his tongue and shifted his eyes to the lady. Aggravating or not, Miss Pickens and her brother had paid well to travel on the *Horizon*. If they left the airship prematurely, they likely would demand some of their money back.

Miss Pickens smiled gently at Fosselweight. "I am afraid that I have always had a touch of seasickness, Captain Fosselweight. Flying is less agitating on my poor nerves. I was told that we can expect choppy seas ahead, and I believe for now, it is best I stay on the *Horizon* until Constantinople. But I do appreciate your offer. I hope to take advantage of your hospitality in the future."

Roberts was both disappointed and oddly pleased at her answer, and the alluring flutter of lashes aimed in his direction did nothing to help mend the confusion. Fosselweight's disappointment was visible but he recovered quickly and the matter was settled. Monkey in her arms, Miss Pickens disappeared back on board the *Horizon*, leaving the captains to get their ships out of Cagliari, prows bent towards Constantinople.

Chapter Seven

"READY!" Roberts bellowed, ears ringing and eyes trained on the steam-filled canvas balloon drifting a few hundred yards from the *Horizon*. It was a floating target for the Vandenberg gun, whose chassis and carriage Halloway had finally hammered into working order. That accomplished, the crew now needed to learn how to use their new weapon.

"AIM!" Below decks, Long Tom, Carter, and Farrington wrestled with the Vandenberg, training its nose on the floating target. Roberts had chosen his gunnery crew carefully, but operations around the Vandenberg were far from smooth. Long Tom had shown unprecedented initiative and quickly taken over command of the weapon. His orders to Carter and Farrington were abrupt and demanding, and it was tense below decks as the three men struggled to learn their new weapon.

"FIRE!" Gunshot roared, bullets arcing their way across the sky. The balloon shuddered in the air, quivered for a moment, then nosed downward towards the waves. Through his spyglass, Roberts watched it fall and saw that they had just winged it. A direct hit would have shredded the balloon into fragments. Frowning, he called down below decks, "That clipped it, but not dead on."

"We hit it, Captain," Carter objected, traces of gunpowder settling into the lines on his face.

Roberts moved tiredly down the ladder towards the sweating trio of men. For two hours, shots from the Vandenberg had filled the air with noise and gunpowder smoke. The Vandenberg was an unusual weapon, and its mounting system was entirely of Halloway's design, making it challenging for the gunnery crew to master. Everything from loading the gun to aiming and firing was different from the carronade cannon airships normally carried. Practice was the only remedy, but each discharge expelled a great deal of bullets and powder into the air. After two hours of firing, the *Horizon* was nearly out of both.

Facing the gunners, Roberts examined them, knowing they were tired and irate. "Winging an airship is better than nothing," he said evenly. "But we don't have the shot to waste on anything but a direct hit. One good shot, and we can take out anything in the skies at two thousand yards." He cast a glance at the open crates at their feet. "How many more shots do we have left?"

"Six more cartridges," Long Tom replied, wiping sweat from his brow.

Roberts nodded. "Two more shots, then," he ordered. "We'll save four until we get more bullets and powder off the *Morning Star*."

The gunnery crew set to work reloading the Vandenberg. Halloway had quickened that task by creating cartridges and a loading frame. Each cartridge held one hundred and fifty-two bullets. The loading frame perforated the cartridge and pushed a bullet into each barrel in one movement, eliminating the need to load each barrel one by one.

At a command from Roberts, Bloomberg loosed another target. It drifted several hundred yards away from the airship. Roberts watched it float in the breeze, measuring its height and distance before calling the gunnery crew to aim.

"FIRE!" Roberts commanded but instead of instant compliance, only silence met his order. Perched on the ladder halfway through the opening onto the main deck, Roberts glared at the gunnery crew and gave the order again, this time more emphatically. Long Tom didn't move from his position at the muzzle of the Vandenberg, hunched over it and peering intently down the length of the muzzle.

"LONG TOM!" Roberts barked loudly, to no effect. Long Tom held his position, frozen over the Vandenberg and making slight adjustments. Roberts stepped forward, intent on stamping out the insubordination, but as he moved toward the men, Long Tom ripped the lanyard from the gun, sending powder and noise roaring through the *Horizon*.

Roberts' head jerked above deck, his spyglass pointing out into the open air and encountering nothing but clear skies. The balloon had been at least eight hundred yards from the *Horizon* when the shot had gone off and exploded it into a thousand pieces. There was nothing left but a few strings spiraling down to the waves below.

Yells of triumph echoed around the airship as Roberts tramped down the ladder to the gunnery crew. "Fine work," he praised. "Now, one more shot like that."

The success seemed to put heart in the men. They tackled the Vandenberg with fresh fervor. As the gunnery crew loaded the last cartridge and prepared to fire on the new target, Roberts commanded, "Long Tom!" The able airman lifted his eyes as Roberts continued, "On your mark."

Long Tom nodded and turned his attention to Carter and Farrington, giving terse orders as they moved the weapon into position, training on the last target. Seconds ticked by as the gunnery crew sighted on their target and calculated the trajectory. Finally Long Tom yanked the lanyard and the explosion roared across the sky, shredding the target at six hundred yards and leaving nothing behind.

With that, target practice was concluded for the day. Pleased with the gunnery crew's work, Roberts ordered extra grog for them, which they received gladly. By the smells emanating from the galley, William was hard at work cooking something tasty, which further heightened morale. Jokes, boasting, and good-natured insults bounced around the airship. The successful gunnery practice had put everyone in high spirits.

As the sun set, the mood on board the *Horizon* was convivial and celebratory. Carter and Farrington dug out musical instruments that had been gathering dust, and the *Horizon* began to fill with music and laughter. Even Halloway was coaxed out of the engine room to join the crew for a short spell of coerced socialization.

Miss Pickens and Jules sat a pace or two from the festivities, observing them quietly but making no intrusions. The macaque was back in Miss Pickens' arms, but it minded its manners and didn't make a noise. In a jovial mood, Roberts felt moved to speak with the two reporters. He had avoided them as much as he could during the journey, and Miss Pickens had obliged by keeping herself out of the way. Courtesy nagged at Roberts, and he stepped forward to speak some pleasantries to the pair.

"I apologize for the noise of the gun work earlier today, Miss Pickens," Roberts said, approaching her.

"Nothing to worry about, Captain," she responded, stroking the monkey. "Jules and I have sailed with my grandfather's fleet before. Eighteen cannon practicing at once will wake the dead."

As she spoke, the *Horizon* hit an air pocket, and Jules braced himself against the airship's railing with one massive hand while steadying his sister with the other hand. He said nothing, but Roberts observed the gesture keenly. He suddenly suspected that it was Jules, not Miss Pickens, who was prone to seasickness. His suspicion grew when she placed a comforting hand on her brother's knee and patted gently.

Odd, Roberts thought. The brother and sister were a baffling pair. *The sooner I see the back of them, the better*, he snorted, then dipped his head in respect and returned to his crew, strangely thoughtful.

***　　　***　　　***　　　***

It was August 31st when the *Horizon* and *Morning Star* finally reached Constantinople, and the headwaters of the Bosporus were abundantly packed with marine vessels. Many of them flew French and British flags, heralding the movement of Allied troops up to Crimea, but a panoply of other colors fluttered in the stiff winds: Spanish galleons, German windjammers, Scottish steamers, Grecian schooners, and many more vessels.

In the air, the *Horizon* had more than ample company. Dozens of airships crisscrossed the skies, many of them military and others partnered with marine ships below. At the helm, Barking Jack wore a scowl of unhappy tension as he directed the *Horizon* through the crowd of airships. The rest of the crew was just as edgy and alert as Roberts paced the airship, exhorting his men and issuing sharp commands.

Constantinople's marine and air wharfs were bursting with vessels, and it was hours before the *Horizon* and *Morning Star* secured berthing. The airship wharf was poorly managed by a small collection of ragged dockworkers who nevertheless demanded a staggering docking fee for the privilege of landing.

Roberts ordered the *Horizon* shut down for the night and her airbags deflated in the humid air. Halloway set to work at once recalibrating Engine One, which had manifested signs of internal stress. The rest of the crew, mindful of the upcoming journey across the Black Sea, scoured the airship for other signs of potential trouble.

Miss Pickens and Jules left the *Horizon* soon after the airship touched down in port. "We're off to the *Constantinople Times*, Captain Roberts," Miss Pickens announced brightly. "It is the only British-produced newspaper published in the city, and the chief editor is an old friend of my father. We have much to discuss with him."

The pair quickly took their leave, the damned macaque perched on Miss Pickens' shoulder and Jules carrying two of his sister's suitcases. Roberts, his thoughts consumed with other matters, didn't register the sparse amount of luggage leaving the *Horizon* until he walked into his cabin. Normally bare, the room was now liberally strewn with female garments and knickknacks and the air was heavily scented with perfume. Briefly examining the room, Roberts retreated with a heavy sigh and shut the door. It was a relief to have Miss Pickens off the airship, but, judging by the elaborate nest she had left behind, she had full intentions of returning.

Four days in Constantinople passed while the *Horizon* and *Morning Star* rested in port and their captains fell victim to a serious case of bureaucracy. Wearily trudging through one strata of military hierarchy after the other, Roberts and Fosselweight finally shook loose marching orders for the next leg of their journey. As luck would have it, their path neatly coincided with Miss Pickens' desire to find her grandfather. Commander Pickens was master of a fleet of six warships cruising the Black Sea, and a casual mention of his name was enough to open doors for Roberts and Fosselweight.

"We've had no contact with Commander Pickens' fleet for almost two months," stated the harried, flushed-looking major over the top of his disorganized desk as he glanced at Roberts and Fosselweight. Roberts' patience was steadily eroding after two days of being bounced from one office to the other in a vain attempt to wrestle orders from someone. Fosselweight was more familiar with military procedure, and he maintained a calmer demeanor than Roberts himself felt.

"There's orders and messages for the commander and he himself is most likely in need of fresh supplies," the major continued. "Our scouting airships have had little success locating the fleet. The airship *Countess* believes that it spotted the fleet five days ago a hundred miles southeast of Odessa, but it was forced to turn back due to a storm." He looked at Roberts directly. "There are few airships that we send over the Black Sea, Captain Roberts. It is vast with unpredictable winds, and this time of year, storms can erupt without warning. There have been few reports of enemy action in the skies, but it is a war zone and is not without risk."

He paused significantly while Roberts waited, knowing what was coming next. "I have read of your airship, Captain Roberts. Her speed is impressive," the major said. "You sail with a merchant marine bound for Crimea, so clearly you are not a man adverse to risk."

Roberts' expression was stoic as the major continued. "If you would put your airship to use as a search vessel to assist us with locating Commander Pickens' fleet, I can offer you special Class Five certification for the duration of six months. This would, of course, entitle you to whatever resources and equipment you require for the search efforts as well as your fee for your airship's efforts. You would be granted special flight privileges as well."

"And if we don't locate the fleet?" Roberts questioned flatly, looking the major directly in the eye.

The major cleared his throat. "The terms are subject to the successful location of Commander Pickens' fleet, of course."

It wasn't an unreasonable demand and the offer was tempting but dangerous as well as logistically demanding. The Black Sea was indeed vast, and the *Horizon* could scour it for months without locating her target. If she failed, all her efforts would be a waste of time and coal. The *Morning Star* was waiting to take her load into Crimea, and the search efforts would be a huge delay.

Fosselweight glanced sideways at Roberts. "I wonder if you might leave us for a moment to speak in private, Major Billings," he requested courteously. The major complied, leaving the two captains alone.

"It is an offer worth considering, Captain Roberts," Fosselweight assessed carefully.

"My ship is contracted with yours through to Crimea," Roberts reminded him.

"My ship is not ready for the Black Sea," Fosselweight frowned. "She has taken on too much water these past four days and we can't keep her bilge emptied, mainly because a pump needs replacing. Besides, our entire cargo will have to be assessed and docketed before I bring it to Crimea. We are likely to be in Constantinople for a minimum of two weeks." He smiled. "Though it would grieve us, my ship could part company with yours if you choose to take this mission."

In two weeks at port, Roberts' men would grow fat and lazy and the airship wouldn't earn a penny. It was a risk taking on the search, but each day the *Horizon* didn't work was costly. Class Five certification was not easily earned, especially by an airship with no prior record as a military transport flyer. Such a certification would open up many more work opportunities once Roberts' contract with Fosselweight ended.

When the major returned to his office a few minutes later, Roberts had an answer. "My airship will find the fleet."

"Excellent," the major looked relieved and began unearthing stacks of official documents. He and Roberts negotiated their way through the terms of their agreement, and Roberts left the meeting pleased yet deeply preoccupied with the upcoming mission. Fosselweight was tactfully silent as the two strode away from the military headquarters and towards the wharf, intent on their own ships.

When Roberts returned to the *Horizon*, he discovered that most of the crew was back on the airship, having voluntarily cut their ground leave short and clearly displeased with what they had found in Constantinople.

"Damned boys in uniforms crawling everywhere you look," Jenkins complained loudly.

"A man wants a pint and they charge him for a barrel," groused Big Tom.

"Too damned many men and not enough women," Barking Jack added.

Roberts mustered the men who seemed pleased that they were not going to be stuck in Constantinople for much longer. The crew tackled their work with vigor. Tracking down the fleet demanded a light load, and the airship needed to be stripped of all non-essentials. Every pound they could remove would allow for a little more fuel on board, and Roberts was intent on cramming her as full of anthracite as possible. They could be out at sea for days with no coal sources available. The *Horizon* needed as much fuel as she could carry.

The rest of the crew returned to the airship that evening when their ground leave was up, and the *Horizon* was busy with preparation. Non-essential cargo and equipment was moved from the *Horizon* to the *Morning Star*, which would guard the items until the airship returned from her mission. Speed was her imperative, and Roberts scoured his airship with his crew, eyes alert for anything that could possibly hinder them in their search efforts.

Morning rose early, and the *Horizon*'s boiler steamed afresh, the airship preparing to take to the air again. Roberts was intent on logistics, maps, and weather, but his attentions were wholly commandeered when, as if summoned by some dread god of chaos, Miss Pickens and Jules appeared on the *Horizon*'s gangplank and clambered aboard uninvited.

"Hello, Captain Roberts," Miss Pickens gaily hailed a surprised Roberts. "Word is, your fine ship will be seeking out my grandfather's fleet."

"She will," Roberts stated. "Without the two of you in tow, I may add, Miss Pickens."

"Oh come, Captain, may I remind you that you promised to bring me to my grandfather?" Miss Pickens smiled but there was an edge of steel to her lips. "I do believe that I paid you well for that promise."

"Ma'am, the *Horizon* is leaving on a reconnaissance mission. She's got several hundred square miles of open sea to search for your grandfather's fleet in the middle of a war. We will be flying hard and fast and I've no room on board for passengers, not when I'm counting every pound I put on the ship. When the *Horizon* locates the fleet, we'll return to Constantinople. Then, and only then, Miss Pickens, will I bring you to your grandfather."

Miss Pickens smiled coyly. Roberts' senses twanged in alarm as they recognized the warning signs of a lovely woman marshalling her best powers of manipulation and charm. Before she could loose the first volley, Roberts stiffened his resolve and drew his shoulders up. "Let me repeat, Miss Pickens," he said harshly, his dark tones rolling across the gangplank. "You will not board the *Horizon* without my permission. and that will not be until after I have located your grandfather's fleet. That's final."

Miss Pickens bristled, the flirtatious look gone and her eyes flashing with anger. She opened her mouth to speak, when both of their attentions were caught by someone calling over the noise of the wharf. It was Captain Fosselweight, and he hurried forward eagerly, his eyes fastened on Miss Pickens. Roberts watched narrowly as the reporter's irate expression smoothed away, her sights now set on a more affable target.

"Captain Fosselweight! What a pleasant surprise!" Miss Pickens trilled out as she minced forward to greet the diminutive captain. He gallantly doffed his hat, clearly delighted to encounter the reporter.

"Miss Pickens! I am most honored and delighted to find your lovely presence on the wharf," Fosselweight sounded in a carrying voice. Roberts watched the interaction. *Get rid of her. Now,* he silently telegraphed at the other captain, who paid him not the slightest attention. After a few pleasantries exchanged between Fosselweight and Miss Pickens, he offered his arm to the lady and the two set off down the wharf without a glance back at Roberts.

Threat averted, Roberts snorted with wry amusement. Fosselweight had obviously come to the *Horizon* with some clear purpose in mind, which he had abandoned instantly in favor of courting Miss Pickens' favor. Now the pernicious reporter was on Fosselweight's arm, Jules trailing behind obediently, and, more importantly, both walking in the opposite direction of airship wharf. *Good riddance*, Roberts thought, yet a curl of jealousy growled in his innards at the sight of Fosselweight proudly escorting Miss Pickens. Shaking his head, he scoffed at the passing wisp of emotion, kicking it to the wayside before turning his attention back to his airship.

When the *Horizon* lifted off the berth to begin her mission, she had to dodge her way around a few dozen airships that crowded the skies above the wharf. One airship darted quickly forward to take the *Horizon*'s now-empty berth. The rest hovered impatiently in the air and made no move to clear the way for the *Horizon*, much to Barking Jack's frustration. The Bosporus ahead was crowded with marine ships, and Roberts directed the *Horizon* to swing around the strait and avoid most of the air traffic.

Once the Bosporus was behind them and the open sea under their hull, Roberts could turn his attention to their mission. They were flying into unknown airspace: not a man on board the *Horizon* had traversed the Black Sea before. However, Major Billings had provided a set of excellent maps and had arranged a meeting with Captain Bluestone of the *Countess* who had provided what help he could. The *Countess* was grounded for maintenance, unable to retrace her steps back to where her crew had caught glimpses of Commander Pickens' fleet. The information Captain Bluestone had provided was invaluable but the *Horizon* was searching for a tiny needle in an enormous haystack. Roberts was consumed with endless worry over how much risk he was taking.

As the *Horizon* left the coast of Turkey behind her and sailed out over the waters of the Black Sea, Roberts was marginally encouraged by the high visibility and clear skies ahead. With her crew working briskly, the *Horizon* was soon a thousand feet in the air and racing forward at a brisk thirty-five knots. She was frisky and relaxed after her time at port and listened obediently to her handlers who encouraged her forward. A stiff tailwind boosted her speed, and she was moving at an excellent pace.

A few ships dotted the waves in the distance, but Roberts ignored them. The *Horizon* was nowhere near the search zone radius where Commander Pickens' fleet had allegedly last been spotted. Captain Bluestone and Captain Fosselweight had meticulously plotted out a search zone for the *Horizon*, calculating a number of factors. The resulting area was decidedly smaller than the whole of the Black Sea but still contained hundreds of miles of open water.

Three days passed as the *Horizon* reached the search zone and crisscrossed it, searching intently for the fleet. Their efforts were limited to daylight hours, their nights spend hovering purposelessly in the air waiting for light as the boiler consumed fuel and their coal stores depleted. At first light, four men were posted to scan the waters for the fleet, and the crew had lookout duties added to their considerable workload. They all slept little and ate less, Roberts fighting day and night to keep his airship flying well and his men's courage up as the long, tedious hours of searching passed.

The fourth day dawned chilly and grey, with dropping visibility hindering their search efforts. The crew, already growing restless with the monotony of their search, was riding hard on tempers worn thin from lack of sleep. Roberts was preoccupied with the weather and kept one eye fixed worriedly on the skies around them. Storms at sea could erupt with little warning, and the *Horizon* was well away from land, surrounded by nothing but open water. Romania's coastline was roughly a hundred miles to the west, but the country's ports would little welcome a British vessel.

As the morning wore on, the weather was uncooperative but stable. Roberts felt in his bones that trouble was brewing in the skies, but his surroundings offered no concrete proof. He was weighing his options, his eyes tilted towards the heavens, when Long Tom called out, "Captain, there's a fleet of five marine ships to starboard four o'clock."

Roberts strode over to the side of the airship and trained his spyglass on the distant specks, adjusting the lens carefully to capture as much detail as possible. There was precious little to see, even with the magnification of the telescope. He could make out that there was a fleet of what looked like five ships. However, he could not identify any distinguishing characteristics, nor determine if they were allies or Russian. Unless Long Tom had far better eyesight than Roberts possessed, it was impossible to determine whether the ships were even on their side, let alone their quarry.

After several minutes of intense scrutiny, Robert let the spyglass drop, thinking hard. He estimated that at top speed, they would reach the ships in less than an hour of flying. However, they could reach the vessels only to discover a fishing fleet or a host of Russian warships. Then there was the matter of weather: sailing towards the ships would put the *Horizon* even farther from land. She just might find herself in the heart of a monster storm at sea for her troubles. Roberts' experience with overwater flight was not as rich as he would have liked, and he was wholly unfamiliar with the Black Sea.

Skies to the east were marginally lighter, and instinct told Roberts that turning east toward the fleet would put them into smoother skies. His decision made, he shouted orders.

"Target is sighted! All hands to stations!" Roberts roared as he thundered towards the helm. Reaching the com device, he bellowed into it, "Engine room, full steam now. I want forty knots. We've got a fleet to find!"

The airship burst into action as crew members rushed to their stations, the boiler already demanding more anthracite. Roberts hurried to where Barking Jack stood, grimly gripping the wheel. He glanced up to see his captain approaching, and tightened his jaw.

"Steady at the wheel, Barking Jack," Roberts ordered. "We're keeping her high as we can until we get in closer range. I'm not having her nose down until we're certain those are allied ships we are flying towards. We'll not drop in flight unless the clouds force us down."

Barking Jack nodded mutely and Roberts examined him critically. Exhaustion was evident in the pilot's limbs, both metal and flesh. The long days of searching and Bloomberg's inexperience had kept Barking Jack at the wheel for hours at a time, and fatigue was clearly evident.

"I'll take over if you need," Roberts frowned. "You've been at the wheel too long."

Barking Jack shook his head. "I'm fine, sir. You're needed elsewhere."

Roberts was unconvinced. "If you can't keep your eyes open, you're..."

"*Captain.*" The pilot's words were sharp with tension, as were his rigid shoulders. His metal fingers were digging into the wheel, indenting the tough wood. Roberts took the reproach quietly and stepped back a pace. Barking Jack clearly wanted to be left alone to work in peace. His movements were deliberate and mechanical as he manipulated the steam valves and the *Horizon* pushed forward.

"Thirty-four knots, Captain," Barking Jack announced tiredly, rolling his shoulders back.

"I want forty knots. Make the call," Roberts ordered.

Woodenly, Barking Jack called down to the engine room, "Forty knots. Captain's orders. On my mark."

Halloway's voice snarled through the speaker box. "Tell the captain he can bloody well wait. We're doing what we can." Jenkins yelled something indistinguishable and Halloway's voice trailed off, to be replaced by Sparrowman.

"Stand by at steam divert," Sparrowman called out. Barking Jack pulled the lever, loosing more steam into the engines and increasing the *Horizon*'s speed until she reached forty knots. Exhausted but determined, the crew paid scrupulous heed to their duties, aware of the airship's slightest whims and constantly alert for the first sign of danger. Roberts looped endlessly from topdeck to below decks, consumed with the needs of his airship and his men and acutely attuned to every flutter of wind.

The *Horizon* was running eagerly, her speed holding steady despite the tug of the winds beginning to buffet her. She charged ahead through the vast expanse of gray skies. The weather held steady for her, overcast but stable and offering only a subtle hint at a possible storm. For nearly thirty minutes they flew at just under forty knots, holding pace in the brisk wind. Just as Roberts began to hope they had left the worst of the weather behind them, the sky suddenly dropped to an angry gray and a sharp crack of thunder shook the deck boards, reverberations rising up through the crew's feet and sending all eyes scanning the heavens.

As shadows fell over the skies, the marine ships ahead disappeared, leaving the *Horizon* with nothing but coordinates to draw on, if any navigational signs could be surmised in the thick clouds. The sun was blotted out in darkness, and the *Horizon* shivered in the press of winds buffeting her. The fleet was dead ahead, and if the *Horizon* dropped altitude and held her course, they might reach their target. But with visibility falling and the storm growing, it would be easy to miss what they were aiming for and leave the airship blundering around helplessly in the clouds, burning up fuel and risking the lightning. Behind them was angry darkness and ahead were the unfathomable seas. Like it or not, they were in the thick of a storm, and there was nothing to it but to battle through.

Shaking his head, Roberts barked into the com device. "Hold your positions, men! It will be a rough ride, but we're moving forward."

Motion on the ship increased to a fever pitch as orders and yells for assistance raced across the decks. A crack of lightning briefly illuminated the sky, chasing away the darkness for a brilliant moment. The men winced at the sound, then glanced up at the taut peak of the envelope. The *Horizon* was the highest point for dozens of miles, a perfect target for any lightning bolt seeking contact. They were too high, sailing among the dark clouds and lightning. Diving lower to ride underneath the worst of the storm was their only option.

"Barking Jack!" Roberts ordered sharply through the air. "Take us down to five hundred feet! All hands, prepare for sharp descent!"

The airship dropped to five hundred feet, bucking and kicking in the wind, to dive under the worst of the clouds. Rain was flying nearly horizontal, soaking everyone on the main deck and drenching the canvas envelope. Below them, the storm-tossed sea rolled in angry dark waves occasionally illuminated by flashes of jagged lightning.

Roberts, barking commands with every step, fought his way to the com device. "Engine room, report!"

"Holding steady! She's doing as well as she can with this damned storm," Jenkins yelled back, and Roberts' eyes flickered to the speed gauge. The *Horizon* was flying at twenty-seven knots, her engines running at their full strength and her speed hampered by the driving winds beating at her. But she was holding steady at five hundred feet, her engines strong and her envelope taut and full.

Minutes crawled past like centuries in an angry world of driving rain, bellowed orders, and flashes of lightning. The decks of the airship pitched and rolled in the forceful winds. Roberts was in the thick of it, raging across the *Horizon*, shouting instructions and commands, when Big Tom's voice ripped through the com device. "BURST VALVE IN MAIN STEAMLINE F!"

Dammit, Roberts thought with furious alarm. Steam valve ruptures could be catastrophic, especially to any catwalk man unfortunate enough to be near the breech, and every second was precious. Boiling hot steam could rush out of the breech at any moment, deflating airbags, unbalancing the airship and filling the interior of the envelope with choking steam. Roberts fought his way to the com device and barked into it, "DAMAGE REPORT!"

"NO INJURIES!" Big Tom's thick voice came pouring out. "BUT I CAN'T GET CLOSE TO THE DAMNED THING!"

"Keep your shirt on, I've got this," Halloway's voice cut in, calmer than Big Tom's but sharp with tension. Words followed actions, and Halloway came stumbling up the ladder to the main deck. Half shoving, half helping the inventor, Roberts pushed him along the deck towards the catwalk ladder. Halloway had little balance and no air legs even after weeks of flying, and the *Horizon* was juddering violently under his feet. At the catwalk ladder, Halloway paused and was about to climb up before Roberts barked, "SUIT UP THE SECOND YOU REACH THE ENVELOPE!"

Every airship kept emergency suits in the envelope for disasters: oiled leather jackets and overalls that would resist heat burns as well as glass and leather helmets to protect the head. Big Tom was wearing his emergency gear, and his helmet was now visible at the apex of the catwalk ladder, where he waited to help Halloway into the envelope.

"NOT ENOUGH TIME TO SUIT UP!" Halloway shouted back.

"GOD DAMN YOU, THAT'S AN ORDER!" Roberts roared. "YOU'RE NO DAMNED GOOD TO ANYONE BOILED!" Up the ladder, he barked into the envelope, "BIG TOM, YOU'RE NOT TO LET ANYONE ENTER THE SECTOR WITHOUT SAFETY EQUIPMENT!"

Frustrated, Halloway gave up the argument and began awkwardly climbing the ladder to the envelope as the airship tossed and bucked in the strong winds. Once or twice, he slipped on the wet rungs, but the second his head entered the envelope, Big Tom reached out an arm and bodily lifted Halloway onto the lower level catwalk. As the men disappeared from view, Roberts turned his attention back to his airship fighting for her life in the violent storm.

"TWENTY-THREE KNOTS AND DROPPING, CAPTAIN!" Barking Jack yelled over the screaming of engines, and Roberts staggered his way forward to the helm.

"ALTITUDE?" he demanded.

"HOLDING AT FIVE HUNDRED, BUT IT'S A FIGHT, CAPTAIN."

Steamline F was one of the six pipes chuting boiling hot steam into the envelope where it routed to ten individual airbags that were now losing steam due to the rupture. The angry waves roaring below them were only a few hundred feet from the *Horizon*'s hull, which was far from watertight. If they hit the waves, they would quickly take on water and sink.

The skies above, around, and below them raged, the storm holding its intensity and the winds throwing the *Horizon* around like a dog worrying a stick. "FOUR HUNDRED FEET AND FALLING, CAPTAIN!" Barking Jack yelled across the deck. Roberts turned his attention back to the helm. Despite the drop in altitude, the *Horizon*'s decks held steady and Roberts was able to run, not stagger, up to the helm.

He growled a low rumble of anger, then barked into the com device, "ENVELOPE, REPORT! HALLOWAY, WHAT'S YOUR STATUS?"

Nothing sounded over the device for several long seconds, and Roberts repeated his words, cranking up the intensity. Several hisses of steam and some clanging was his only answer until Big Tom's voice came in. "HALLOWAY SAID GIVE HIM FIVE MINUTES, SIR!" the catwalk man yelled back, his words slightly distorted.

Roberts swept the skies briefly. The situation was dire, but the storm was starting to abate a trifle. The driving rain was slowing to a brisk patter, and the lightning blasts were less frequent and more distant. The *Horizon's* engines were roaring loudly with the strain of keeping the airship moving forward against the strong winds. But the darkness was starting to lift, and there was a suggestion of light gray in the distance.

The *Horizon* continued to plow though the storm, struggling to keep her altitude and speed. Halloway wrestled with the burst valve, fighting clouds of choking steam and screaming orders at Big Tom. Below, Roberts raged across the decks of the airship, shouting commands and exhorting his crew as they struggled to keep the airship flying forward. Erratic bolts of lightning still scorched the skies, filling the damp air with brilliant light, and the *Horizon* was still dropping air, sending her keel nudging even closer to the waves below.

At last, Halloway's voice ripped through the com device. "RUPTURE FIXED!" he bellowed. "ENGINE ROOM, DIVERT ALL AUXILIARY STEAM TO STEAMLINE F!"

A burst of even more frenetic activity broke out as the crew rushed to their tasks with renewed vigor. The *Horizon's* envelope, which had been growing slack, began to tighten once again as the ten airbags refilled slowly. Minutes ticked by as the crew held their breath, praying that Halloway's hasty repair would hold. It did, and the *Horizon* began gaining altitude and kicking up her speed.

With the storm still pressing down on them, Roberts held her to five hundred feet. There was nothing above them but angry rain-soaked clouds and scattered sheets of lightning.

However, the healed rupture gave the airship strength and she moved forward at a brisk pace, charging steadily through the still-strong storm.

Then, like a cork popping loose from a champagne bottle, the *Horizon* shot out of the towering bank of storm clouds and into a world of calmer skies once again, leaving the raging storm at her back. And, miracle of miracles, practically under the *Horizon*'s hull was a fleet of five marine ships, British flags fluttering in the sea air.

Roberts leaned heavily over the side of the *Horizon*, intently scrutinizing the fleet below. The ships had clearly suffered the worst of the storm: two were missing masts and the main deck of each ship was a beehive of activity that indicated significant damages incurred. The largest of the vessels was sporting a hole carved out of her hull. As Roberts scanned her carefully, he caught the words *HMS Dante* painted on her side.

Around him the crew of the *Horizon* let loose a collective cheer of elation, both in relief from having escaped the storm and excitement at finding the fleet. Heads below lifted skyward at the sound of the *Horizon*'s churning engines, and hands waved eagerly, welcoming the airship forward as she sailed into clearer skies to hover directly over her target.

Chapter Eight

The battleships below were equipped with anti-aircraft cannon, and Roberts watched them carefully as the *Horizon* lowered to the fleet. Her appearance was sudden and she had not been cleared to approach, all of which could mean a volley flying her way. Still, the British flag and the blue and gold colors of a merchant ship that fluttered from the *Horizon's* bowsprit were clear signs that she was an ally. As she dropped to three hundred feet, cheers and shouts echoed from the marine ships below. Roberts could see that all five ships had sustained damage, and he guessed the fleet had recently been under heavy fire. If the dozens of waving arms were any indication, the *Horizon* was eagerly welcomed.

Light flashed from the *Dante* in a rhythmic pattern and Bloomberg called out, "Captain! The commander of the fleet invites you aboard."

"Tell them I'm coming down," Roberts ordered. As the message flashed across the sky, the crew maneuvered the *Horizon* directly above the *Dante*. When the airship drew closer, Roberts slid overboard on a quick drop line to the *Dante*. A respectful landing zone opened topdeck as sailors scurried out of the way. No sooner had Roberts touched down than a collection of officers hurried his direction.

An older man with the insignia of a Navy commander stepped forward, and Roberts acknowledged him quickly. "Captain Gavin Roberts of the merchant airship *Horizon*," he announced with firm intent. "She's a Class Five merchant airship and is charged with locating the fleet of Commander Horace Pickens."

The other man gave a visible sigh of relief. "Your ship and crew are most welcome," he said with frank honesty. "I am Commander Pickens." The man was unkempt and haggard, with stubble clinging to his cheeks, his white hair greasy and stringy, and his uniform disheveled. A white bandage was wrapped around his left leg, and his face was flushed as if he had either undergone exertion or was running a fever. However, there was no mistaking the determined resolution in the commander's face.

"What have you for me?" he demanded as assorted officers and sailors listened eagerly to the conversation. Out of the corner of his eye, Roberts saw signs of injury, disease, and desperation written on the faces of the men.

"Commander, I have nothing on board for you save orders and information," Roberts spoke bluntly. "We left Constantinople three days ago with an empty hold and orders to locate your fleet."

Roberts undid the thick leather satchel hanging from his shoulder and handed it to the commander. Pickens opened it and sighed wearily as he uncovered a bundle of sealed documents, no doubt official military orders for the beleaguered fleet. His men stirred restlessly around him, their faces hungry and anxious as they watched him. Pickens gave the documents only a brief glance before refocusing his attention on Roberts and the hovering *Horizon*.

"Come with me, Captain Roberts," he ordered. His men parted to let them through as Pickens led Roberts into a spacious cabin. "Sit down," he gestured at a chair while collapsing in his own with a creak of worn leather.

"We've seen nothing but action the past three weeks and we're the worse for it," the commander stated wearily. "We lost the *Cassandra* a week ago, and I've lost almost half my crew to battle and disease. The five ships I have left are half-crippled and running on skeleton crews. The *Intrepid*'s on quarantine for a measles outbreak, and the *Falcon* is taking on water as we speak. With the right supplies, we might be able to save her but that wild squall did us no favors."

"My airship can top forty knots, Commander Pickens," Roberts stated confidently. "She can be in Constantinople by daybreak. If you hold position, I'll bring a supply ship back to you as soon as I can." Such promise would mean a long, sleepless night for the entire crew, but it was clear that the fleet's current predicament was dire indeed.

"Forty knots?" Commander Pickens repeated incredulously. As an answer, Roberts presented his certification to the commander who read it carefully, his furrowed brow lifting in surprise.

"Well, Captain Roberts, that is quite a name you have made for yourself and your airship," Commander Pickens pronounced, handing the certification back. Roberts reached out to take the document, but the commander held his grip for a moment, looking Roberts firmly in the eye. "I've men dying as we speak and a ship sinking," he stated frankly. "Get a supply ship back to me, Captain Roberts."

"I will, sir," Roberts responded but with concern clenching in his gut. The *Horizon* had been battered about aplenty by the violent storm. It was sheer dumb luck that she had come out of it intact and with the fleet practically under her nose. It would take some calculating to fix on their exact point, but as best Robert could tell, the *Horizon* could return to Constantinople by daybreak. However, she could easily encounter another storm or an irate Russian airship determined to blow the *Horizon* out of the sky.

Even reaching Constantinople quickly, the *Horizon* had no guarantee of getting a supply ship back to the fleet in time. A marine ship would need to be prepped for the voyage and would travel far more slowly than the *Horizon*. Right now, the *Falcon* was listing heavily in the water, disease and injury were rife on the ships, and Commander Pickens was clearly running on his last reservoirs of strength and determination.

A pen began scratching across parchment. Pickens bent over the sheet with a frown of concentration. "I will give you a letter. See it delivered to Lord Creagan in Constantinople. He will authorize anything your airship requires to complete this mission and bring a supply ship back to my fleet."

He paused for a moment, still intent on the page. "You sustained damages in the storm?"

"A blown valve," Roberts shrugged. "Nothing serious."

Pickens huffed. "By all rights, your airship should be at the bottom of the ocean. You were God's own fool to fly through that storm."

Roberts' eyes narrowed but the commander lifted his head with a smile of approval. "Bring me a supply ship back and you can name your price and your terms on any military contract you desire. Well done, Captain Roberts."

He finished scrawling the last of the letter, then closed the still-damp page with a blob of wax. A thump of a seal and it was finished. Handing it over, Pickens stood to his feet, Roberts following suit. As Roberts' hand closed on the letter, Pickens did not let go for a moment, locking eyes with him.

"Fair winds at your back, Captain Roberts," Commander Pickens said bracingly. "And speed to your engines. Get back with a ship as quick as you can."

"I will, sir," Roberts promised. A nod and he left the commander's cabin, treading across the crowded deck to his own airship which waited for him.

Back on board the *Horizon*, Roberts touched down to find the crew in active motion, Oboe dispensing orders with the calm urgency of one who had anticipated the next series of events. Roberts eyed the sky, sensing out what potential dangers awaited them in the long, high-speed flight back to Constantinople. The sun was almost completely submerged under the sea and the storm had roared forward, disappearing into the darkness of night, treacherous and unseen.

Roberts turned back to his crew and gave his orders. "We'll make Constantinople by daybreak," he pronounced to the general dismay of the crew who knew that meant a sleepless night full of constant peril. "There's men dying on the fleet. They need everything the *Morning Star* is carrying."

A few grumbles echoed around the airship but the crew resignedly set themselves to their tasks as the *Horizon*'s engines churned, banking the airship sharply and winging her forward into the dark night, dead set for Constantinople.

The long hours of the night passed in a mind-numbing parade of engines crashing, tired bodies moving forward, and orders roaring. Yet luck sailed on the *Horizon*'s bowsprit. Halloway's emergency patch job held true, and the airship kept forward at just under thirty-five knots. Even more welcome was the full, glorious moon that rose in the heavens, illuminating clear skies ahead and not a sign of bad weather to trouble the airship as she hurried forward.

Dawn was just breaking over the skyline as the *Horizon* sighted on Constantinople and jostled her way into a berth on the airship wharf. In their few days' absence from the city, the air wharf had grown even more heavily populated, and the *Horizon* had plenty of company in the sky. Barking Jack kept up a colorful stream of criticism directed at the skill level of the other airship pilots who hindered the *Horizon*'s path.

Once the *Horizon* had settled into a berth, the crew had barely enough strength to shut her down. Tasks finished at last, sleep was their only objective. Carter and William fell asleep on topdeck, in full sun and oblivious to their surroundings. The rest of the crew practically crawled to their hammocks where they lay like dead men. Roberts himself was swaying on his feet, his vision blurring and fatigue dragging like chains, but the urgency of his mission goaded him forward. He had to deliver Commander Pickens' letter.

With Oboe at his side, Roberts left his airship in the hands of sleeping men, Halloway the only person still awake. The engineer was at work on his patch job, transforming it into something more substantial. Roberts hailed a surprisingly modern and well-fitted steam cab which carried him and Oboe through the teaming streets of Constantinople. Oboe's head nodded throughout the journey as he repeatedly shook himself awake, at one point almost falling asleep against his captain's shoulder. Roberts fared little better, and when the cab pulled up to the Naval headquarters, it took supreme effort to step out of the cab and deliver Commander Pickens' message.

The visit to headquarters passed in a blur for Roberts; he remembered little beyond a parade of uniforms. Major Billings appeared, fussing and worried and made an effort to relieve Roberts of the message, but he clung to it woodenly, determined to deliver it to Lord Creagan in person. He had to wait to do so, and both he and Oboe were in danger of falling asleep on their feet when they were finally ushered into Lord Creagan's presence.

The lord was imperious and obviously displeased with two unkempt airmen sullying the perfumed interior of his office. However, his attitude changed dramatically when he broke the seal of Commander Pickens' message and scanned its contents. He quickly called to his orderlies and Roberts and

Oboe soon found themselves in the middle of a cluster of solicitous and impressed concern. Orders and busyness happened, which Roberts was only vaguely aware of, and the two were quickly ushered back to the cab with orders to return to the *Horizon* in preparation for flight.

Oboe was soon fast asleep, his head tipped back while he muttered strange words in his native language. Roberts clung to vestiges of consciousness, enough to see them back to the *Horizon*. Once onboard, Oboe found a shady spot topdeck and was asleep instantly. Roberts did the same, not caring where he fell. The berthing area was crowded and his own cabin had been colonized by Miss Pickens' abandoned possessions. However, it was pleasantly warm and sleeping topside was no hardship. Unconsciousness was instantaneous.

Voices on deck woke Roberts midafternoon as his men stirred to life and began moving about the airship. Grudgingly, he rose to his feet. They were all still exhausted from their efforts, but Commander Pickens' fleet desperately needed them. The airship herself had been battered around by the storm and needed to be checked for damage. There was too much work to do and very little time to accomplish it.

Groggy and vaguely befuddled, Roberts sought out the *Morning Star* to discover her crawling with activity. He had to fight his way through sweating ranks of soldiers and seamen, but the crowds parted in recognition, and nods of respect followed Roberts as he tiredly tramped up the gangplank.

Arterbury hailed him over the noise. "Good to see you on your feet, Captain Roberts!" he called out. "Your ship was full of dead men this morning. We hadn't the heart to wake you, sir, not when we heard you sailed through a storm over water to get to Commander Pickens' fleet." He grinned broadly. "You're the talk of the wharf, sir. Every merchant marine in Constantinople would sail with you."

Gesturing to the masses of soldiers, Roberts said, "The *Morning Star* is to go to the fleet?"

"Aye, sir, heavily loaded and with the blessing of Lord Creagan. She'll be ready tonight if your ship can take to air again. We'd be pleased to sail with her."

"What of your bilge? Captain Fosselweight said she was drawing water," Roberts questioned, stifling a yawn.

"Dry now, sir. Her pumps are back in operation." Arterbury waved at the crowded masses on the marine ship. "She's been swarmed with workers since dawn, sir, ever since you delivered Commander Pickens' letter. She's to go to the fleet, and she's been stocked with everything she needs."

Crowds parted and Fosselweight stepped forward. He was disheveled and tight with stress, but he greeted Roberts warmly. "You came back with laurel leaves, Captain Roberts," Fosselweight beamed, shaking his hand. "Is all well aboard your ship?"

"A bit of storm damage. She'll survive," Roberts said but Fosselweight looked worried.

"My orders are to depart as quickly as I can," he said. "When can your ship can take to the air again?"

"She should be able to fly by dawn," Roberts pronounced, hoping it was true. There hadn't been time to fully check the *Horizon* for damages, and Halloway's emergency patch job was only temporary. The airship could be stuck at port for days while the crew repaired her.

His worry proved unwarranted, and in the morning both ships were ready to leave Constantinople. The *Morning Star* was crammed full of supplies and provisions and the *Horizon* herself took on ten tons of cargo. The weight would dramatically increase her fuel consumption but the fleet needed all the supplies it could get.

Much to Roberts' chagrin, Miss Pickens and Jules appeared at the *Horizon's* gangplank and marched on board. Roberts greeted the pair with a restrained sigh and bowed stiffly. "Miss Pickens. Mister Pickens," he stated flatly.

She laughed delicately. "I do hope you have not forgotten our agreement, Captain Roberts."

"I don't go back on my word, Miss Pickens," Roberts responded. "But I'd advise you to stay in Constantinople. Your grandfather's fleet has seen hard action and the ships are full of starving, dying men. It's no place for a woman and I doubt that your grandfather would want you to take the risk."

"How sweet of you to worry." She brushed lightly past him. "But I am not as weak as you think. You needn't fret." Easily, almost gaily, Miss Pickens crossed the deck of the *Horizon* and breezed into Roberts' cabin as if she owned the airship. In passing, Jules nodded respectfully at Roberts and quietly entered the ship, carrying her two suitcases with him.

Roberts felt worry tighten in his gut. Despite Miss Pickens' assurances, he was unconvinced that Commander Pickens would welcome the appearance of his granddaughter in such hazardous conditions. The commander likely would not look favorably on the man responsible for bringing his granddaughter out of Constantinople and into a war zone. Roberts was halfway tempted to give Miss Pickens her money back and order her off the airship, but she had threatened blackmail, and he did not want to risk it. Instead, he turned his back on the closed cabin door and resolutely pulled his attention to his airship.

It was cooler in the air, but clear, and the *Horizon* quickly settled into her flight path, this time with a firm destination. A brisk tailwind lessened the work of her engines, and she could have easily pushed to forty knots. However, the *Morning Star* below could not hope to match paces with the airship. The *Horizon* settled into a sedate twelve knots, leading the *Morning Star* forward directly to the fleet.

Roberts estimated that two days would be enough to reconnect with Commander Pickens' fleet, bringing both supplies and the two reporters. He was musing on this during the afternoon of their first day out as he stood topdeck, keeping a sharp eye on his crew. Miss Pickens was also topside, swaddled in a heavy shawl, her glossy brown hair blowing loose from its upsweep and her eyes shining. She turned her enchanting smile Roberts' way and his masculine instincts temporarily overcame his better judgment.

"When will we reach my grandfather's fleet, Captain?" she questioned.

"Likely two days," Roberts responded. The scent of her perfume drifted towards him, further stirring up the unruly emotions in his gut.

Her expression turned canny. "I would be glad for a chance to see that fine Vandenberg gun in full display." Roberts' eyes narrowed, his internal alarms clanging. It would only take a well-placed word or two to Commander Pickens to throw suspicion on the *Horizon*. Roberts suspected Miss Pickens would not hesitate to place an accusation of theft against him if it suited her purposes.

She smiled, running a slender, well-shaped hand along the balustrade as Roberts stood icily at her side. Several spring-taut moments limped past as neither reporter nor captain said anything. Then a smile, genuine and touched with warmth, rose to Miss Pickens' lips.

"My grandfather will be exceedingly grateful for your efforts, Captain Roberts," she spoke kindly. "Captain Fosselweight is a fine sailor, but his men would have searched for weeks to locate the fleet. If conditions are as dire as you have reported, every hour means lost lives."

A soft hand touched his gently, and Roberts' senses jumped with shock and pleasure as smooth skin rested for a moment against the back of his hand. For one brief span of time, there was nothing coy or calculating about Miss Pickens, only feminine grace and warm acceptance.

Then it was over and her smile turned wily once again. "It will make a fine story," she stated. "A daring rescue at sea. One valiant airship battling a storm to locate a damaged fleet. Death averted at the last moment." She laughed, a pleased murmur that was twisted with a strange hardness. "The headlines will sell."

Roberts tightened his jaw. Looking her over, he wondered how much he could trust her. He had a deep-seated conviction that the answer was very little indeed. As if sensing his inner thoughts, the lovely reporter turned to him. Roberts unwittingly felt his deeper, baser instincts rising for control as Miss Pickens' charm bent itself his direction.

"Come, Captain Roberts," she cooed, her voice low and husky. "Let us have no quarrels between us." Her hand moved to place itself on his forearm, and Roberts felt the heat of her skin radiating through his sleeve. "I would have you think of me as a friend," she said with gentle kindness, yet an unmistakable tenor of enticement in her voice.

Roberts stiffened under her touch, gritting his teeth to bite back his rising desire. "Ma'am, I have an airship to run," he replied stonily. "I will take you to your grandfather's fleet as promised, but from that point on, I will consider my obligations to you fulfilled. You've caused me a heap of trouble, as you well know, Ma'am. I aim to have no more troubles added than I've already got."

With that, Roberts' tall frame bent slightly in a chilly bow before he turned on his heel and strode away, leaving the reporter behind.

Chapter Nine

Two days passed with clear skies, no signs of an enemy, and nary a storm on the sky, but morale on the airship was low and tensions high. Some of it was due to sheer tedium: although the *Morning Star* cut steadily through the waters, she could not begin to compete with the *Horizon's* pace. The journey was agonizingly slow for everyone on the airship. The crew's anxiousness to reach the fleet again, and the knowledge that they were racing against the clock only added to the general frustration on board.

The presence of the two reporters did not help matters, but Roberts observed that Jules was steadily earning some measure of respect from the crew. The big man took orders meekly and his considerable strength was a great asset to the *Horizon*. However, it was becoming increasingly more obvious that Jules was a bit of a simpleton, possessing little of his sister's canny intelligence. As the days passed, Roberts became more convinced that Jules' contribution to journalism was minimal at best. Likely, Jules was there simply to protect his sister so that she could travel freely.

Towards late afternoon on the third day, Miss Pickens loosed a cry of delight. "Captain! Captain, I've found them! I've found them!" She had been searching the waters with a telescope for hours, and her efforts seemed to have paid off.

Encouraged by the news, Roberts trained his spyglass on a distant speck that she pointed out to him, adjusting the lens carefully to capture as much detail as possible. There was precious little to see, even with the magnification of the telescope, but he could see a fleet of four ships ahead.

"I'd recognize the *Dante* anywhere, even at that great distance," Miss Pickens remarked, moving to stand at Roberts' side, the telescope not leaving her eyes. Roberts eyed the distance and calculated how long it would take to make contact. The *Horizon* could reach the fleet quickly on her own, but *Morning Star* would greatly hinder the *Horizon's* pace.

Miss Pickens' voice broke into his thoughts. "Now that we have found the fleet, we must make haste, Captain Roberts," she stated briskly.

Roberts shook his head. "We're backup for the *Morning Star*, Miss Pickens," he replied. "We stay in eyesight of her." At her impatient expression, Roberts amended his statement. "I'll have a click sent to the *Morning Star*. We'll see what Captain Fosselweight has to say."

A clicker message soon flashed across the distance between the two vessels, informing the *Morning Star* that the *Horizon* had possibly sighted the fleet. The seas around the merchant marine ship were clear and if she stayed her course, she would encounter no opposition. Fosselweight signaled back that the *Morning Star* would sail alone, and the *Horizon* was soon pushing forward, eager to reconnect with the fleet.

As their speed increased, the winds began beating across the deck. Miss Pickens stayed her position, one hand planted on her hat to keep it from escaping. However, the driving winds tore at her skirts and pushed her slender frame around, worrying Roberts about her safety.

"Ma'am, you should go inside the cabin," he called through the wind. "We're moving up to forty knots, and it will be rough going topside."

Miss Pickens frowned prettily as a lash of wind whipped a curly lock against her face, but she did not object as Roberts helped her to the cabin. Her long skirts swirled around her impishly and it was something of an effort to get all of her clothing inside the door. The airship bucked a bit, and Miss Pickens leaned heavily on Roberts' arm while attempting to corral her skirts and enter the cabin.

Roberts, distracted and a tad peeved about it, secured his passenger and shut the cabin door firmly before bellowing for his crew. Bloomberg was at the wheel, steadily guiding the airship forward under Oboe's tutelage. She seemed delighted to run free once again, and her crew shared her eagerness and excitement. Roberts felt the blood thrumming in his veins as his airship enthusiastically ate up the miles under her keel, the fleet ahead growing larger by the minute.

They were roughly ten miles from the fleet when Oboe's deep voice cut easily through the roar of engines and beating wind. "Captain! Enemy action ahead!"

Roberts hurried to Oboe's side, his spyglass training on the skies ahead. As the lens focused, his gaze fell upon two airships in the distance wheeling across the sky. The fleet of four lay directly under their hulls. Across the dark waves, two marine battleships were honing in on the crippled fleet.

Dammit, Roberts thought, straining his eyes through the spyglass. It was a bold move for two marine ships to attack four, but the enemy had the advantage of airships. Even the best anti-aircraft cannon were poor defense against an airship, and a bold flyer could seriously damage a marine ship. Even something as simple as flying overhead and dropping cannonballs overboard could sink a marine vessel. Commander Pickens' fleet, already damaged, would be harried both horizontally and vertically by the Russian attackers. The fleet had no airships to take the battle skyward.

Turning, Roberts exploded with orders. "BEAT TO QUARTERS, NOW! BARKING JACK, TO THE WHEEL! GUNNERY CREW, MAN YOUR POST! ENGINE ROOM, WE GO TO FORTY KNOTS. *NOW*!' Frantic movement erupted all over the *Horizon* as men hurried to their posts, breaths tense and blood pounding in veins. The airship roared forward, her boiler already pushing her to greater speeds.

Barking Jack grabbed the wheel from Bloomberg, freeing up Oboe who intoned over the shouts of the crew, "We attack, Captain?"

"I'm not leaving the fleet to fend off two airships when they've got a water attack to deal with," Roberts pronounced tersely. He lifted the spyglass, scrutinizing the enemy airships. Despite his words, he was not keen about taking on two airships at once. The *Horizon* was lightly equipped for battle, even with her Vandenberg. However, Russian airship technology was poor at best, and the two attacking airships were small and ungainly in comparison to the *Horizon*'s acrobatic grace. With her speed and agility, she could fend them off while the marine ships battled below for supremacy.

Oboe said nothing, but a keen light glinted in the corner of his eyes and his lips lifted slightly to show dazzling white teeth. Nothing more was said between him and Roberts. They plunged back in the mess of frantically moving bodies, pushing among the crew to keep order and prepare the airship for a scuffle in the air.

At a command from Roberts, a clicker message flashed across the aether, warning the *Morning Star* of the impending battle. At this distance, he doubted the message would reach the merchant marine, but after a few minutes, a reply winked back. It was somewhat garbled but clear enough to signal that Fosselweight was aware that the fleet was being attacked and that the *Horizon* was rushing forward to assist. A second message followed the first, but even Bloomberg could not begin to decipher it.

The miles raced under the *Horizon* as she surged ahead at forty knots, every spar and cog creaking with strain. Cannonfire boomed as the two Russian marine ships reached the unfortunate fleet and began raining a volley of grapeshot and cannonballs across the waves. From the air, the two Russian airships poured forth shot from their cannon, filling the air with gunpowder and smoke.

But the *Horizon* was nearly on top of them, roaring through the air as her gunnery crew loaded the Vandenberg and the other men held their hearts in their teeth, steeling themselves for battle. In the very thick of activity, pushing and shouting, Roberts nearly crashed into Miss Pickens who had exited the cabin and was stumbling across the deck.

"MA'AM, IT'LL BE A FIGHT! GET BACK INSIDE THE CABIN!" Roberts bellowed. As Miss Pickens turned to obey, a particularly vigorous blast of wind shot across the deck of the *Horizon* and smashed into her, shoving her right into Roberts' arms. For one millisecond, his world was suddenly void of imminent peril and very much full of warm softness and the heady perfume of roses as in a brief, electric moment, their eyes and bodies met. But it was only a moment in time, and the screaming of the battle soon wrested Roberts' attention away from sensuous distractions.

Another strong gust of wind roared across the deck as Roberts seized Miss Pickens' arm and towed her back to the cabin. She was lightweight and apt to blow away, and he put another arm across her shoulder, trying to shield her from the wind. Reaching his cabin door, he flung it back and pushed the reporter inside. Shutting the door behind him, Roberts left Miss Pickens in arguable safety while the crew fought to keep the *Horizon* on course.

No sooner had Roberts slammed the cabin door then Barking Jack yelled out, "Captain! They're engaging us!" Roberts hurried to the helm where the lanky pilot was struggling with the wheel, keeping the airship moving forward under her breakneck pace. The other two airships had abandoned their marine targets and were now swinging their noses towards the *Horizon*, cannon muzzles pointed her way.

"Steady on!" Roberts barked over the roaring winds and cannonfire as he fought his way to Barking Jack's side. "You know your orders!" Barking Jack nodded coolly, but his mouth was a thin, sharp line as he braced for the maneuver ahead, one the *Horizon*'s crew had practiced in case of an assault. It was tricky and dangerous, but it was the best way to maximize use of the *Horizon*'s one gun as well as take full advantage of her strength and agility.

"Aye, Captain!" Barking Jack called back. "I'll stick her arse in their faces," he announced with no small trace of humor. Roberts grinned dryly, but the two enemy airships were closing in, or, more accurately, the *Horizon* was bringing the fight to the Russians. Roberts judged that the two airships were not even breaking twenty knots. The *Horizon* roared forward at just under thirty-five knots, close enough for him to see mounting panic and fear on the other airship.

"STEADY! WAIT FOR IT!" Roberts bellowed as his men braced for an abrupt change of direction. Below deck, the gunnery crew hunched over the Vandenberg, cartridge loaded and primed to deliver a swift bucketful of oblivion. The *Horizon* was on a direct course of impact with the two Russian airships, her speed gauge clocking thirty-five knots. The Russian airships bustled with panicked activity as their crews swiftly realized that they were outclassed.

Under the *Horizon*'s hull, cannonfire roared as Commander Pickens' fleet, now freed from aerial attack, turned its attention to the two Russian marine ships. Battered but determined, and freshly encouraged by the sudden lack of airship fire, the fleet poured the full force of their cannon against the two Russian marine ships.

"NOW!" Roberts' roar cut through the turmoil of battle. At his command, the *Horizon* wheeled sharply to port, her nose jerking to the left as her tail spun outwards in a smooth arc, bringing the Vandenberg level with the two Russian airships. There was a juddering shimmy that threatened to flip the ship over. Barking Jack clung to the wheel, calling upon every last vestige of skill to keep the *Horizon* in the air and bring her around to face away from the enemy. The airship shuddered under his control, fighting for balance in the salty air.

She held true, staying her treacherous course in the sky. As the *Horizon*'s aft swung around to face the enemy directly, Roberts' bellow shook the airship's timbers. "FIRE!" he commanded. With instant obedience, the cartridge ignited and violently expelled bullets at one of the Russian airships.

Gunshot filled the air, mixing with great waves of steam as the Vandenberg's shot ripped through the airship's canopy, tearing the canvas and gouging the airbags inside. It wasn't a direct hit, but many of the bullets hit canvas, and their force took a significant bite out of the envelope. The Russian airship shuddered as panic broke out on board, men racing for the envelope in a frantic bid to repair the damage. Within a few moments, the airship began to sink towards the waves. Her pilot and engineers fought to keep her from touching the water, but she continued to drop downward.

Grapeshot rang out and the *Horizon* shook as the shrapnel grazed her keel. Barking Jack wheeled sharply to port, but he could not steer her clear of the grapeshot's wide scatter. A stream of projectiles roared across the topdeck. Pain tore through Roberts as a piece of shot sliced into his arm, ripping fabric and flesh and leaving a bleeding trail which stained his sleeve with red.

Adrenaline pushed away the pain when Roberts saw Bloomberg fall to the deck in a writhing twist of agony. Fighting his way to the pilot's side, Roberts lifted Bloomberg to see blood pouring down his face. Shrapnel had torn right under his left eye, leaving a jagged wound behind. Bloomberg was choking down a scream of pain as he tried to sit up.

"HARDING!" Roberts bellowed, and the surgeon stumbled forward to attend the stricken pilot. Roberts left Bloomberg in Harding's care and focused intently on the battle. The injured Russian airship was no longer a threat, and the other airship was struggling to train her cannon on the *Horizon*. Barking Jack was making the ship dance across the sky, nimbly avoiding the next volley of grapeshot which missed entirely. A thin trail of blood trickled down Barking Jack's face, but he held his position, the *Horizon* obedient to his will as Roberts mustered his troops for a fresh assault. The gunnery crew feverishly loaded the Vandenberg with a fresh cartridge, the minutes racing past.

Roberts ordered the *Horizon* forward, racing her towards the other Russian airship. Cannonfire blasted from her, and a cannonball skimmed along the *Horizon*'s gondola, scoring a light groove in the wood. "STEADY!" Roberts commanded. "STAY ON TARGET!" His men obeyed and at his command, the *Horizon* wheeled sharply to starboard, her Vandenberg aimed directly at the cluster of valves feeding steam into the overworked canopy of the Russian airship.

One hundred and fifty-two rounds of shot tore through the air in a deafening wave of sound. Instantly, the airship was enveloped in steam as bullets ripped through the pipeline system, peppering the metal with holes. Suddenly weakened, one of the pipelines burst under the pressure, geysers of boiling hot steam roaring out of the breech and enveloping the airship in clouds of agony. Men fled the rupture, but some were not so lucky; the screams of the dying filled the air.

"TAKE HER TO A THOUSAND FEET AND HOLD!" Roberts commanded. The *Horizon* wheeled sharply, her bowsprit edging towards the heavens as Barking Jack steered her out of the chaos and into open skies. None pursued her. The *Horizon*'s last victim was slowly plummeting towards the waves and none could save her from the mortal wounds she had incurred at the Vandenberg's hands. The first airship was struggling but still aloft, her belly just a few hundred feet above the sea and her crew laboring mightily to keep her afloat. Neither airship presented a threat. With a barked order, Roberts turned the *Horizon* towards the fleet and the battle raging on the waterline.

The two Russian marine ships were heavily armed, their cannon pouring out rounds of fire against Commander Pickens' fleet. They were swift vessels and intent on their target. However, they were outnumbered, suddenly bereft of their aerial backup, and now fighting a hard battle. As the *Horizon* turned towards the six marine ships, Russian anti-aircraft cannon began swinging skyward, training their sights on the oncoming airship.

Gunfire exploded through the air, missing the *Horizon* by several hundred yards. Roberts ordered his airship up well out of gunfire range. A fully armed marine warship was an enemy far beyond the *Horizon*'s abilities, and she could only hover in the sky and watch Commander Pickens' fleet engage the Russians. Volleys roared below as two of the fleet ships poured cannonfire on the Russian marine ships, wood cracking and bullets splintering the air.

Long minutes passed as the *Horizon* hung suspended in the sky and watched the battle. The Russian ships were fully rigged ships of the line, their broadside guns raining out massive volleys of cannonfire into the ironclad frigates who returned the shots with fury. Gunpowder filled the air, but Commander Pickens' ships bore down on the enemy and drove them back. The *Dante* loosed a ferocious volley and there was a great, groaning crack of wood as the mizzenmast on one of the Russian ships trembled violently. It hung suspended for a moment, then broke under its own weight in a tangle of sails and rigging.

With that, the remaining Russian ship took to its rudder, leaving its damaged companion behind and fleeing for safety. From the air, the crew of the *Horizon* watched as the Russian ship turned sharply, slipping between two of the British fleet ships attempting to block its passage. Strong winds filled its sails and bore it swiftly out into the open sea.

Commander Pickens' fleet did not pursue. Instead, they turned their attention to the damaged Russian marine ship that was unable to flee. Russian seamen lined the decks, bristling as if preparing for a battle to the last man. As the British vessels grew closer, a white flag of surrender fluttered from its bowsprit as resignation trumped bravado and the Russian captain laid down his arms to accept defeat.

Cheers roared along the decks of the British marine ships and from the *Horizon* as hundreds of tongues rose in triumph and elation. In the midst of his wildly celebrating crew, Roberts strode over to his cabin. The door opened as he approached it and Miss Pickens stood in the door frame, her dark eyes huge with tension and her hair falling in glorious tumbles past her shoulders. She was magnificently stunning, and Roberts' breath caught in his throat.

Smiling broadly, Roberts said, "Come with me. There's something you need to see."

Chapter Ten

When the *Horizon*'s lift basket hit the *Dante*'s topdeck and discharged Roberts, Miss Pickens, and Jules, they were greeted by a crowd of eager sailors. There was a certain flurry when the sailors realized a woman was on board, a second flurry when her lovely face swung their direction, and a third when her identification was made. It was obvious that both Miss Pickens and Jules were not unknown to the crew of the *Dante*, and a buzz of excitement ran through the ship.

Through the massed ranks, Commander Pickens strode forward to greet the newcomers. Roberts tactfully maneuvered around Miss Pickens to exit the lift basket, hoping to reach the commander first. Miss Pickens was far more agile than he expected. She artfully slipped under his arm and rushed forward, running through the ranks of crew members, her eyes alight. "Grandfather! Grandfather, we're here!" she announced over the babble of voices.

Commander Pickens was even more bedraggled than before. Gunpowder from his pistol dotted his face and blood trickled down his brow from a ragged cut. He froze in astonishment at his granddaughter's approach, saying nothing as she girlishly threw herself into his arms and prattled out a tumble of information. He did not return her greetings, and his hard eyes flashed in Roberts' direction, demanding an answer.

Miss Pickens' enthusiasm could not be contained and after a few moments of broken questions, the commander clasped his granddaughter to him with an expression of great joy. Jules, however, remained woodenly in the foreground, and Commander Pickens did not send a glance in his direction. Briefly, Roberts wondered about this, but his attention was quickly diverted. The commander turned towards him with a dark look, storm clouds gathering on his brow.

"So this is the man who brought my granddaughter out in the middle of the Black Sea during a battle," Commander Pickens thundered as he took a step towards Roberts.

Roberts gritted his teeth as anger roared up in him. The two men eyed each other narrowly, then Commander Pickens' face broke out in a wide smile. "Well, Captain Roberts, you're not the first man to fall victim to my headstrong granddaughter's smile and charms," he proclaimed heartily. "She's far too willful and stubborn for her own good. What am I to do with her?"

Miss Pickens dropped her eyes and looked suitably demure, but she was positively radiant with the glow of having her own way. Hastily, Roberts switched topics. "The *Morning Star* is not far off, Commander, and she's fair to bursting with supplies," he reported. "We left her side to assist with the battle, but now that the enemy is defeated, with your permission, sir, we'll return to her and bring her to you."

Commander Pickens nodded sharply. "We need her here soon as you can, Captain. We lost the *Falcon* two days ago, and the *Dauntless* is taking on water faster than we can pump it out. I need everything on the *Morning Star* and more."

He turned to Miss Pickens with a stern smile. "But this naughty young lady will be staying on the *Dante* where I can keep an eye on her." Miss Pickens beamed as her grandfather gave her a hard look that did not disguise his adoration.

Amidst all the stress and distraction of the current events, Roberts again noticed that Jules was merely incidental to the proceedings. It was obvious the man was not warmly welcomed on board the *Dante*: Commander Pickens barely acknowledged his grandson. There was a long story unspoken, Roberts could sense this, but he had neither the time nor inclination to suss it out.

A brief flurry of activity hastily commenced while Roberts reentered the lift basket to return to the *Horizon*. The airship was soon wheeling across the sky to reunite with the *Morning Star*. The *Horizon*'s crew was still scrambling to put her back to rights after her battle; she was nursing some wounds, nothing serious, but she would need some tending once they put down in Constantinople.

Within two hours, the *Morning Star* was at the fleet and discharging her cargo onto the *Dante*. Overhead, the *Horizon* lifted and carried, distributing heavier and more unwieldy supplies to the other three ships. Despite their hunger, disease, and recent battle, the sailors moved with impressive briskness, swiftly unloading supplies and distributing them as directed. As crate after crate of food, medical supplies, and other vital equipment made its way around the fleet, renewed courage and optimism rose in the battle-hardened, weary sailors.

With many hands eager to help, the *Morning Star* and *Horizon* were unloaded within eight hours and the supplies were distributed among the fleet ships. It was a heroic feat considering that everything either needed to be rowed from the *Morning Star* on longboats or lifted and lowered by the *Horizon*. The logistics were staggering but the need was enormous and the arrival of succor spurred the sailors on to greater activity.

Commander Pickens was not stingy with thanks. At the close of the herculean efforts, he presented both Roberts and Fosselweight with letters of commendation. The documents were inscribed with a large, florid signature and sealed with the commander's own crest. "Show these letters to any ship of the British navy and you're guaranteed merchant work with my express recommendation testifying to your excellence in service," the commander promised. "Both of your ships have well earned them."

The letters were followed by an invitation to a formal dinner on board the *Dante,* or at least as formal as a battle-ravaged warship in the middle of the ocean could manage. Roberts received the invitation with marginal interest. He was exhausted and in no particular mood to celebrate, but refusing would have been the gravest of insults. With some irritation, he dug out his one formal set of clothing and managed a shave and a quick sponge bath. There were four stitches in his arm, and pain nagged at him as he gingerly dressed around the wound. Wearily, he set off for the *Dante,* hoping the evening would be over soon.

The *Horizon* orbited the sky, waiting for her captain to return while her crew had their own feast. Commander Pickens had sent a choice dinner from his own table and a selection of wines to thank the men for their efforts. They deserved it. Bloomberg had just barely escaped with both eyes intact, Big Tom was nursing a new collection of steamburns, and Harding had a lot of shrapnel to pick out of the crew.

Dragging with fatigue and distinctly aware of the shabbiness of his attire, Roberts entered the commander's dining room. The officers present were equally haggard and clearly making the best of what meager sanitary opportunities were available at sea, and they welcomed him warmly.

Fosselweight, however, was dressed in an immaculate captain's uniform, his splendid mustache riding his lips like a ribbon of honor, his sparse hair carefully combed, and every fiber in his being resounding with alertness. Watching him carefully, Roberts surmised that much of Fosselweight's appearance and attention was centered on Miss Pickens, as well as on her grandfather whom the diminutive captain clearly wanted very much to impress.

Arterbury was at his captain's side and Roberts noted this with a frown. Oboe had not been included in the invitation and as first mate of the *Horizon,* excluding him was a serious breach in protocol. Looking around him, Roberts saw that every attendee at the dinner was white. The gentlemen seating themselves around the room would likely balk at dining with an African, despite Oboe's position and invaluable service to the cause. Briefly, Roberts thought about leaving the room in silent protest, but he held his position, grimly determined to get the evening done with as soon as possible.

His sour mood lifted considerably as Miss Pickens gracefully entered the room, stunning in an evening gown of deep green, the color repeating in the glints of emeralds shining around her neck and ears. There was a great rising of men as she sailed into the room and a great deal of gallant commotion as the men fell over each other to ensure that she was seated comfortably. Roberts struggled to remain impassive, but her presence was doing serious damage to his composure. Amidst the aroma of beef and potatoes, he could smell the perfume wafting from her skin.

Most curiously, Jules did not make an appearance at dinner. Roberts noted the absence and idly toyed with contemplation as the meal progressed. He had barely exchanged a dozen words with Jules in their weeks of travel and could make heads nor tails about any motives, ambitions, or original thoughts the man cherished. When he spoke, Jules had a pronounced stutter, which likely explained his rectitude. By all evidence, he appeared content to lurk in the shadows of his vivacious, forthright sister. None of that provided any insight into the obviously strained relationship between Jules and Commander Pickens.

Dinner followed the conventions of formality, but there was a strained rush hiding under courtesy. Commander Pickens was clearly trying to show his appreciation but was obviously distracted by dying sailors, broken spars, disease outbreaks, and other catastrophes clamoring for his attention. When port and brandy had been poured out and cigars began circulating, Miss Pickens made her farewells for the evening, to many gallantries displayed by the assembled officers. Fosselweight seemed poised to follow her out, but etiquette kept him at the table. With the conclusion of the meal, most of the diners were visibly anxious to return to their duties. Brandy glasses emptied and soon chairs were being pushed back as the men made their farewells.

With Commander Pickens' parting words of thanks and a fine cigar to take along for company, Roberts left the cabin for a brief stroll topdeck on the *Dante*, enjoying a few minutes of comparative solitude. The steady thumping of engines sounded overhead as the *Horizon* rotated in a holding pattern, patiently awaiting her captain, but Roberts wasn't quite ready to return. Leaning against the railing, he breathed deeply of the sea air mixed with the cigar. *Havana*, he thought, luxuriating in the smoke as the cigar's heady fragrance blended pleasantly with the tangy sea air. Waiting back on board the *Horizon* was an entire box of the cigars from Commander Pickens. Roberts had sent up the box to the *Horizon* with strict instructions about its safe-keeping. Rank had its privileges, and he wasn't about to let any of his men get their hands on his cigars.

Rich smoke drifted in the air as Roberts contemplated the vast expanse of night sky spreading before him. It was growing late and duty nagged at him, but he was not quite ready to return to his airship. His feet were cramping a bit, so he pushed away from the railing and began strolling along the main deck which was mostly deserted. Most of the crew were elsewhere: the ill and injured below deck and the able-bodied at dinner or attending their duties. As Roberts ambled forward, enjoying the cigar and the blessed solitude, familiar voices caught his ear.

"Oh, Captain, he didn't!" Miss Pickens' delicate giggle rose in the salty air. The night was dark but an oil lamp faintly illuminated the pair as they strolled across the deck. Miss Pickens' hand was resting on Fosselweight's arm and the man himself was practically strutting with pride as he regaled the reporter with some droll tale.

Roberts withdrew a few steps and watched the two under the cover of shadows as the cigar suddenly turned to ash in his mouth, sharp and acrid. Neither one noticed him, although they passed less than two dozen feet away, and he watched them covertly, his mouth a thin line. Pearly curls of cigar smoke wafted up to dance around the sailcloth flapping in the breeze until Roberts finally tossed the half-smoked cigar overboard. With a snort, he tramped off to signal the *Horizon* and return to his airship.

Chapter Eleven

"It's the humidity, Captain," a feminine voice caught Roberts' attention as he leaned against the *Horizon*'s balustrade and observed Constantinople ahead, barely visible through a veil of fog.

Turning, he saw Miss Pickens coming his way, yellow silk enveloping her slender frame and a delicate white lace shawl around her shoulders. "Constantinople is quite humid, and summers can be unbearable," she stated. "That is why the fog is so thick."

Lightly, she stepped to the rail while Roberts watched her guardedly. Whether her own choice or at the direction of her grandfather, Miss Pickens not stayed with the fleet when the *Horizon* and *Morning Star* turned back to Constantinople. Without asking, she had blandly entered the *Horizon* on the lift basket, Jules following her loyally, and breezed back into Roberts' cabin where many of her possessions still remained. Considering the growing familiarity between her and Fosselweight, Roberts was surprised she hadn't decided to sail with the *Morning Star*. Instead, she airily reentered the *Horizon* and took over Roberts' cabin while he said nothing, resignedly tolerating her presence on his airship once again.

Miss Pickens stood topdeck with Roberts, one slender hand to her forehead as she gazed into the distance. He wondered precisely what went on in that head of hers. For all her smiles and flirtatious looks, there was a keen, intelligent mind lurking just behind those enchanting eyes and coy smile.

"Constantinople will be aflutter with activity, Captain Roberts," Miss Pickens commented, her pretty brow wrinkling as she squinted in the distance. With some bitterness, she continued, "There will be thousands of young boys unaware that they will soon be packed off to Crimea to starve to death or die of Russian bullets."

Roberts said nothing, but he privately agreed with her. From what he had been able to gleam, Crimea was little short of bedlam. The war had been marked from the start by disorganization, chaos, and confusion, and the growing conflict did nothing to help ease these problems. England had entered the war haphazardly, and continual squabbling among the Allied factions greatly hindered their efforts to claim victory.

A tapping sound drew his attention. Miss Pickens was clicking her nails irritably along the railing as she gazed in the distance. Her mouth tightened which brought hardness to her delicate features. "There is scarcely *anything* available to the soldiers at the front. No food, no guns, no tents, no doctors, *nothing*. Thousands of them are poured into that wasteland and left scavenging for food where they can find it."

The words blasted from Miss Pickens' rosy lips with a force that surprised Roberts. He turned to face her, but she was lost in thought, eyes fastened on Constantinople ahead. "St. Arnaud would be well advised to listen to Lord Raglan, but I do not hold much hope that he will," she complained.

Miss Pickens was not alone in her opinions. British papers were beginning to issue stern articles decrying the French commander-in-chief and his inept handling of the war. If Miss Pickens' tight mouth was any indication, the French were due for a thorough journalistic thrashing when she returned to the *London Guardian*. Anti-French sentiment, always a popular topic in British publications, was being raised to a fever pitch, with more to come as the Allied troops marched through Europe in pursuit of Russian enemies.

"You seem well-informed on what should be done, Miss Pickens," Roberts commented dryly. Miss Pickens shot him a furious look.

"I am a journalist, Captain Roberts," she spoke with hard fervor. "I had my own reasons for wishing to board the *Dante*, one of them being that a dinner table full of military officers will speak quite freely once a few rounds of wine have been poured. I was able to glean quite a bit of useful information during this time. Particularly since," she gave him a sidelong smile laced with allure, "it is astonishing how unguarded a man's tongue will be when he is attempting to impress a woman."

Silence fell between the two for several long moments before Roberts spoke. "The Allies will win, Miss Pickens," he said evenly, but the words rang hollow on his tongue.

A harrumph was her response. "You seemed well-informed on what will happen, Captain Roberts," Miss Pickens replied caustically, throwing his words back in his face.

Roberts frowned deeply. "I'm not a military man, nor a political one, Miss Pickens," he responded icily. "But wars are won and lost over supplies and, by God, I'll not see us lose to the Russians because our soldiers had neither bullets nor boots. Not while I'm master of the *Horizon*."

"Yes, Captain," Miss Pickens replied with some softness. "And you will play that role well, I have no doubt. But," she paused as her voice grew thoughtful, "It would be far better if this entire farce was stopped in its tracks."

"Those are pretty thoughts, Miss Pickens," Roberts responded wearily. "But words will not stop a war."

"Mmm," Miss Pickens commented thoughtfully. "The *Horizon*, no doubt, will play her part. She will perform gallantly as she did for my grandfather's fleet, helping stave off death. As for myself..." she trailed her hand against the railing again as Roberts turned to her. There was a hard, calculating look on her face, and he could see the cogs working behind her brown eyes. He watched her suspiciously for several long moments while she gazed into the distance, lost in thought.

Then the cunning smile returned to Miss Pickens' face as Roberts' instincts twanged in alarm. "Well, we shall just have to see, shall we?" her voice oozed forth, replete with honey, as her smile turned silken once again. And with that, she flitted off with a twitch of her long skirts, leaving a whisper of perfume in the air and Roberts' senses rattled.

He shook his head a few times, trying to clear out her perfume from his nose, and forced his attention back on the *Horizon* and Constantinople ahead. As the airship moved forward through the thick, heavy fog, the city reared up in masses of white stone, arched domes and spiraling towers reaching towards the heavens. Through the sea air, Roberts could almost smell the odor of spices and perfumes rising up from the city. The droning of engines filled the air with noise as marine vessels clogged the waves and airships crowded the skies with sound and shape.

As the *Morning Star* worked her way through the Bosporus and fetched up at the crowded wharf, Roberts noted several Smothers marine ships at port: sleek, impressive-looking vessels, all bearing the Smothers crest in highly visible places. When the *Horizon* jostled her way into an air berth, she found herself rubbing shoulders with more than one Smothers airship. He pointedly ignored them. The *Horizon* had a perfect right to be in Constantinople and there were enough troops stationed on the wharf to put a lid on any harassment Smothers airships decided to dole out to the *Horizon*.

When the airship touched down at port, Miss Pickens and Jules exited Roberts' cabin, Jules loaded down with all his sister's baggage and Miss Pickens brisk and obviously eager to depart on her own errands. Roberts saw them off the *Horizon* with feelings of both relief and disappointment, and it did not help matters at all when Miss Pickens took his hands between her two soft ones and looked him full in the face.

"Captain Roberts, I cannot thank you enough for what you have done to assist me and my brother." Her eyes were warm and admiring, rousing all sorts of powerful emotions in Roberts, and the touch of her skin against his threatened to completely destroy his composure.

And then, with that, she was gone, her heels clicking against the gangplank as her skirts swept the ground. Jules trudged wearily after her, juggling her copious baggage. Roberts stood bewildered and vaguely angry, shaking his head a little and trying to restrain his unruly emotions. Turning sharply, he spotted Barking Jack, Farrington, and Carter smirking at him, and his frustration found a handy outlet.

"Get back to your duties!" Roberts barked harshly at the three men. "I don't pay you to sit around on your arses." Barking Jack made no attempt to mask his wide grin, and Carter snorted loudly as he sprinted away with Farrington at his side, Roberts snapping orders behind their backs, well aware that all three of them were laughing at him.

The crew was just putting final touches on a full shutdown of the *Horizon* when Roberts heard footsteps approach him and turned to see Halloway making his way forward. Abruptly, Halloway announced, "The patch job I put on Steamline F is holding, but it put too much damned stress on the other lines. I need to rebuild it."

Roberts scanned him. "How long will that take?" He didn't mean it as a challenge, but Halloway took it as such and anger flashed on his face.

"Do you want another burst steam valve, *Captain*, or do you want a fully functioning airship that can go forty knots on command?" he demanded sarcastically.

Roberts fixed him with a hard look and held it until Halloway's anger deflated a bit. "I can probably get it done in two days," he said in a sullen attempt at pacification. Roberts said nothing for several moments while Halloway fidgeted under his penetrating stare.

"Do what repairs you need, but the sooner the better," Roberts stated evenly. Halloway opened his mouth, thought the better of it, then turned away without a word, his feet stomping pointedly on the wooden deck. Roberts watched him go, frowning tightly. He knew Halloway was growing increasingly bored and frustrated. Although the airship demanded constant attention, there was simply not enough on board for Halloway to exhaust the limits of his energies and talents, nor was he keen on being crammed inside a small space with twelve other people. So far, Halloway had stuck by the *Horizon*, but Roberts had a quiet suspicion that the arrangement was nowhere near permanent.

Troubled, he saw to his airship and set his men to work repairing the damage from their skirmish a few days ago. They should have been preparing the *Horizon* for Crimea, but the *Morning Star* had floundered on their journey back to Constantinople, taking in far too much water and making heavy work of the flat seas. Fosselweight had pulled her into port and was determined to keep her there until she was fit to tackle the Black Seas again.

This left the *Horizon* at loose ends in Constantinople, and Roberts was restless and vaguely irritated. The next morning found him too impatient to stay on board the ship. Finally, he collected Oboe and set out into the city on no particular errand except to get away from the *Horizon* a spell. A few hours of walking found them seated on rickety stools outside a dark, smoky inn with two copper cezves of strong Turkish coffee in front of them. Oboe mostly ignored the beverage, but Roberts almost groaned with pleasure as he sipped the sweet, ferociously strong coffee spiced lightly with cardamom. Even though the cup was still half-full, he could already feel energy from the beverage racing in his veins. Turning to Oboe, he commented with feeling, "Give a man a drink like this and he could swim the Bosporus and back."

"That would be inadvisable Captain," Oboe stated calmly, his eyes fixed on the morning's copy of the *Constantinople Gazette* and his face betraying none of his struggle to translate letters into meaning. Observing Oboe over the rim of his cup, Roberts wondered afresh why his first mate didn't read with more ease. Oboe was fluent in three languages and possessed a spoken English vocabulary that would put a professor to shame, but it was a deep struggle for him to wrestle meaning out of a page of text.

Oboe carefully turned a page of the newspaper as Robert eyed it. A prior customer had discarded it on the table, and Roberts had pointedly ignored the paper when he sat down. However, Oboe had picked it up and idly perused it, subtle changes in his demeanor indicating he was not precisely pleased with what he found written down. Finally, Roberts reached out and plucked the newspaper from Oboe's fingers, not eager to know what he would find but determined to get the bad news out of the way as quickly as possible.

The *Constantinople Gazette* were full of bloodshed, sea battles, and the general collateral damage caused when nation decided to rise up against nation, but the headline *HMS FALCON SINKS!* immediately captured Roberts' attention. The article was accompanied by a large picture of the *Falcon* leaving Constantinople. She had been the youngest ship of the fleet, and the loss of her had been a deep blow to the navy.

Commander Horace Pickens, speaking from the deck of his flagship the HMS Dante, regretfully announced the sinking of the newly commissioned HMS Falcon.

"*We encountered five Russian marine ships and two airships on September 6th,*" stated Commander Pickens. "*The Falcon is the most agile ship of my fleet and she and her crew performed magnificently, sinking two of the enemy marine ships before the remaining three fled in retreat with their airships following. However, my fleet was heavily damaged by the attacking Russians and the Falcon was unable to be saved.*"

The next few sentences stated the number of men killed in action and then offered some platitudes about how their lives had not been in vain. Roberts skipped over this section, the following paragraph already clamoring for his attention.

"*The situation would have been significantly worse were it not for the courageous and gallant efforts of Captain Gavin Roberts of the airship Horizon,*" stated Commander Pickens. "*My fleet had been almost two months without seeing a merchant ship and we had been unable to inform Headquarters of our position. Food supplies were low, the Intrepid was on quarantine from an outbreak of measles, and my five remaining ships had sustained damages from enemy action. The airship Horizon braved a severe storm to locate us on the Black Sea and return with the merchant marine Morning Star, commanded by Captain Archibald Fosselweight.*"

Roberts digested the first two paragraphs. It wasn't as bad as he expected. There was no mention of record-setting time speeds or anything that would bring people's minds back to the unfortunate Smothers fiasco of a few months past. He continued down the page.

"*The Morning Star bravely sailed through enemy waters with only the Horizon as an ally and brought food and medical supplies to the fleet. Thanks to the skilled leadership of Captain Roberts and Captain Fosselweight, dozens of lives were saved.*"

Personally, Roberts never wanted to see his name in print again, but he suspected Fosselweight was exceedingly proud that he and his ship had been lauded publically. Fosselweight likely cherished the article, even more so because it had come from Miss Pickens. Snorting, Roberts kept reading.

"*While we often hail the sailors and soldiers who fight in wars, let us not forget that no war can be won without the dedicated, brave souls behind the lines who have the dangerous job of bringing the fighters what they need to be victorious.*"

There was more of that ilk, and Roberts scanned the rest of the text, alert for anything that captured his ire, but as a whole the article wasn't bad. A small ripple of pride straightened his shoulders, but common sense overrode it. The *Horizon* needed to keep a low profile, and Roberts didn't need to aggravate Smothers any further. The *Horizon*'s name plastered across the front page was not helping matters at all.

Irritated with the whole situation, Roberts tossed the newspaper aside and picked up the coffee cup. But the delightful, jolting beverage was suddenly harsh on his tongue. He sipped it a few times before setting the cup back down and digging into his pocket for a coin. Dropping it on the table, he rose to his feet. "Best get back to the ship."

The two men worked their way through the crowded, noisy streets of the city, the clamor of dozens of tongues rising in the air and mixing with the smell of garbage, spices, tobacco, and massed humanity all pressed together. Street children ran heedlessly through the crowds, pushing past British and French soldiers resplendent in their military uniforms, while a group of Dervishes whirled and danced in the crowded streets, their white clothing ballooning outwards and spinning around them in perfect cones of fabric.

The airship wharf was stuffed to groaning with vessels. Each berth was occupied, and several airships droned overhead, waiting impatiently for a landing spot. The crew of the *Horizon* was busy about the airship, setting her to rights after her air battle, and she was mending nicely. As Roberts and Oboe stepped on board the *Horizon*, the sound of metal against metal clanged below decks as Halloway's voice rose and fell in waves of sharp demands.

William stiffed in alertness as his senior officers reentered the airship. Saluting, he reported, "Captain, a man was looking for you, a Mister Grey Wulfe." He pointed down the wharf. "His airship is the *Horus*."

"Well then," Roberts said. "We'd best go see what he wants. William, you're with me."

The young steward flushed slightly in pride and his shoulders pulled up. "Oboe, you have command. Come, lad."

With that, Roberts turned on his heel, with William scrambling to keep up, skinny chest bursting with excitement and pride.

The two walked along the choked, noisy wharf. Engines roared as airships docked, downed engines, or began waking to life in preparation for flight. Steam hissed and airbags inflated and deflated, sun-bleached canvas snapping in the brisk wind. Men yelled in a panoply of tongues as dozens of nationalities raged across the wharf, fussing with the airships and moving cargo around. It was a commercial wharf and the airships present were a motley collection of vessels, wildly differing in size and shape.

Somewhere in the middle of the chaos was a collection of assorted planks shaped together into the rough approximation of a hull, hasty patch jobs evident here and there where cannonfire had blasted through the boards. The envelope was soot-stained and cobbled together from several pieces of canvas, and the relay network of valves and chute vents was a tangled pile of pipes and wiring. The entire combination looked as if it would have trouble staying in one piece right where it sat, much less keep its integrity in the air. The airship was tiny in comparison to the other vessels surrounding it. *Horus* was painted on the hull's port side in fading letters.

"There he is, Captain," William looked off to his left and gestured respectfully. Roberts turned to see a large man who headed toward them purposefully.

"Captain Gavin Roberts!" a thunderous voice boomed across the deck towards them. "Welcome aboard, sir! First Mate Grey Wulfe at your service!" A wild mop of bushy black hair and a tangled black beard enveloped most of the man's face, but what skin showed was ruddy and weather-beaten. Two light blue eyes twinkled merrily between the beard and thick eyebrows. Wulfe was not particularly tall but more than made up for it in width. His shoulders were enormous and rode the crescent of his barrel chest and wide torso. Thick legs carried the man forward with surprising speed and lightness, and Roberts found his hand quickly engulfed in a work-toughed paw the size of a barrel lid. He would have called the man fat but not to his face out of fear of being eaten in one hearty gulp. Wulfe, however, was more mass than fat, and the entire impression was of a solid, thick body, dense as a cannonball and strong as an elephant.

"Pleasure to make your acquaintance, sir!" Wulfe boomed out heartily. "The *Horus* here is a runner ship, sir, much like your fine *Horizon*." He grinned deeply. "This is a man's war and no mistaking. Guns and bullets are what's going to win it for us." Still crushing Roberts' hand between his thick fingers, Wulfe jerked the thumb of his free hand towards the derelict airship sagging on the berth. "My ship is full up with Moretti rifles for the front. Seen one of these in action before?"

Roberts managed to slip his hand out of Wulfe's grasp and shake his head no, but the broad First Mate was already stomping towards the *Horus*, beckoning Roberts and William to follow him. They did so, and Roberts was pleased to see that topside was neat and organized. The aether flyer looked close to falling apart, but she appeared to be a tight ship and her First Mate confident and skilled.

Wulfe bent over a heavily locked chest and fumbled with the locks. "Care to try a crack, Captain Roberts?" he questioned as he lifted a length of glossy wood and shining metal up into the air. Roberts took the weapon from Wulfe and scrutinized it intently. It was heavier than a standard rifle, the extra weight explained by the presence of two slim chambers resting on each side of the barrel and a network of fine tubing running from the barrels into the breech.

"Chemical propellants," Wulfe boomed proudly, directing Roberts' attention over to the deck and out into the open sea as he pointed out the weapon's various features. "Each of these two tubes contain a chemical. A squeeze of the pump here," he prodded a thin lever, "sends both chemicals down into the chamber and, mixed together, they propel the bullet forward. No gunpowder, no mess, no smoke. Quieter too, than a standard rifle, all the better for a battlefield. Here..." He reached out and guided Roberts through the process. "The magazine here holds thirty rounds of shot. It's gravity fed, so kick the nose up to drop a bullet in the chamber."

Roberts followed instructions and heard a chink of metal signaling the bullet dropping into place. "Now the pump," Wulfe directed. Roberts tugged at the lever and caught a liquid sound of the chemicals oozing into the chamber. "Alright, find yourself a target, sir," Wulfe ordered. Roberts scanned the open sea and saw an abandoned barrel floating in the waves about a hundred yards away. He sighted on it, held his position for a second, and pulled the trigger.

Bits of wood scattered into the air, rather surprising Roberts. The accuracy of the rifle was far better than he expected. "Fine shot, Captain!" Wulfe roared and slapped Roberts on the back. "That's rifling action you're seeing. Grooves inside the barrel put a pretty spin on the ball, giving it better accuracy. The old smoothbore muskets are a thing of the past. Can't win a war with them anymore, no sir, you can't."

Roberts jerked the muzzle up again, dropping a bullet into the chamber, and pulled the pump, aiming at a piece of barrel. Bits of wood exploded as the bullet found its mark. He repeated the action several times, marveling at how easy the weapon was to use: no ramming a cartridge down the barrel or long minutes of reloading. After several shots, he lowered the weapon to his side and noticed that William was examining the rifle with wholehearted longing. "Ever shot a gun before, lad?" he questioned.

"No, sir," William responded, eyes fixed on the weapon.

"No time to waste, then," Wulfe boomed heartily. "A boy needs to know his way around a gun." Carefully, Wulfe led William through the proper handling of the weapon. William pointed the muzzle out towards the ocean as Wulfe admonished, "Remember, boy, pull the trigger, and you're responsible for the bullet until it hits the ground. Don't ever forget that, lad, not when you have a gun in your hands."

William nodded and, with some hesitation, squeezed the trigger, aiming at a seagull that was bobbing peacefully in the waters. The recoil almost knocked William off his feet, but he had taken a firm stance, and Roberts had a hand on his back in support. The bullet landed several dozen feet away from the target, which gave an indignant squawk and took to its wings.

Wulfe loosened a great belly laugh. "Not bad, son, not bad at all! Practice is what makes a marksman. You can't expect to hit your target on your first shot."

Looking sheepish, William set his shoulders and tried again. Several shots later, he clipped the edge of a barrel fragment. Looking pleased with himself, he handed the rifle back to Roberts who sighted down the barrel. Without moving his eyes from the waves in front of him, Roberts said, "But you haven't said what I can do for you, Mister Wulfe. I doubt you called me on board the *Horus* just to show off your new toys."

Wulfe's grin parted the dense beard taking up much of his face. "Depends on if you're a man for risk, sir, and if the *Horizon* is willing to dodge some cannonfire. It pays out well for the run, but it won't be a pleasure cruise, that's for sure."

Roberts answered slowly, measuring his words. "I don't knowingly put my airship into danger. But the *Horizon* is fast and agile and my men are brave. What do you have in mind?"

"Orders came that all British soldiers are to be outfitted with these rifles, and we can't get them moved fast enough," Wulfe said, now serious. "Thing is, the *Horus* is currently flying alone. She followed the merchant marine *Cornucopia* to Constantinople but the ship fouled up in the Bosporus and damned near sank. She's currently crippled at port with no way of getting these Moretti up to the front. It's a blasted mess in Constantinople, and there's precious few merchant ships in the city that have room for extra cargo and are willing to risk Crimea. Until the *Cornucopia* can get herself fixed up or I can find more airships or marine ships willing to fly with the *Horus*, there's thousands of rifles stuck in Constantinople."

"The *Horizon*'s been sailing with the merchant marine *Morning Star*," Roberts responded. "She's down in Constantinople taking in water, and I don't know how long she will be in port." He paused, thinking. "I don't speak for Captain Fosselweight, but the *Morning Star* will be bringing supplies to Crimea when she can sail again. Captain Fosselweight might be inclined towards transporting some Moretti up to the port."

"Our boys at the front need these weapons now, Captain Roberts," Wulfe said solemnly. "The big nobs at the top say that there's going to be a big battle any day now and they want as many guns at the front line as possible." For a moment, mirth prevailed. "Nothing like doing a weapons drop in the middle of a battle to put a man on his mettle," Wulfe pronounced with obvious relish, then returned to seriousness.

"It'll be faster if the *Horus* and *Horizon* fly direct from Constantinople to Crimea without a marine ship slowing us down. The *Horus* is a little bird and about ten tons is what I risk on her, but she'll fly fast and agile with that. Between our two ships, I figure we can get several thousand rifles and a goodly amount of ammo up to the front, and quickly."

Wulfe wiped a massive paw across his face. "If I can find a marine ship to carry the rest, I'd be dammed glad of her help. But the *Horus* is flying up there, marine ship or none, and I'd be thankful for the *Horizon* flying at her side. We can get these Moretti and bullets up to the front lines, and my Molly won't have my head for letting her down."

"Molly?" Roberts repeated. Wulfe grinned broadly.

"My woman," the man responded. "Head matron of the nurses keeping our boys alive up there. She's waiting on me to get these rifles to the front lines, said she's tired of sewing up bodies and that I bloody well better help our soldiers win this damned war. Her words exactly."

"Well then," Roberts replied. "I say we not let your woman down. My ship is down in port for a good two days for some repair work, but she'll be up soon and I'll sail her with the *Horus*." Wulfe frowned slightly at the mention of a delay, but he said nothing and Roberts added, "I've a good notion Captain Fosselweight will agree to having the *Morning Star* carry some of your cargo when she is able."

A thought floated up. "I've heard no mention of the captain of the *Horus*," Roberts inquired.

"Ah," Wulfe's grin slacked. "In your ear, Captain Roberts, I'm sad to report that Captain Cork is, well, he was never what you'd call a stable man. Too much drinking and whoring tends to wear a man down. But it's been his mind, see? Addled a bit to begin with, and then we saw action about two months ago that gave the *Horus* a right good shaking. He got hit about the head pretty hard. I'd sooner see him off the ship and somewhere quiet, but the *Horus* is his and he won't let go of her." Wulfe shrugged. "I keep her going best I can, sir, and hope that the captain regains some sense one day. Molly thinks she can set him right, but she's got tentsful of dying soldiers to attend to and can't spare the time."

Roberts nodded, well remembering his days of trying to keep an airship together with an incompetent captain doing his best to tear it apart. It did somewhat temper the appeal of Wulfe's offer, especially since the *Horus* looked like it was about five seconds from disintegrating into a pile of splinters. However, there was a confidence without boastfulness that exuded from Wulfe, and Roberts instinctively felt positive about accepting the job.

He offered his hand. "Well, First Mate Grey Wulfe, I think we have an agreement."

Wulfe's smile reached his ears as his fingers crushed Roberts' in a vice grip. "Glad to hear it, Captain Roberts!" he thundered heartily, then dropped his voice conspiratorially. "Between the two of us, I think that a few spare Moretti might be finding their way to the *Horizon* because, take it from me, sir, you want all the artillery you can muster."

Chapter Twelve

A slight understatement, Roberts thought grimly as the *Horizon* flew high and tight, all eyes anxious as the crew examined their surroundings in search of the next attack. Cannonfire boomed underfoot in the dying light of the day, fiery sun streaking across the sky and long shadows casting eerie, distorted pictures on the blood-soaked ground. The screams of the dying and living alike broke through the smoke-clogged air as men fought and died several hundred feet below the *Horizon's* hull. A few war airships roared across the evening sky, trailing plumes of smoke and battling furiously, both with each other and with the massed troops below.

The *Horizon's* hull was peppered with grapeshot and a long tear in her envelope flapped in the wind where a cannonball had streaked past, tearing the canvas and just missing the airbags underneath. The *Horus* had suffered worse, adding two sizable holes to the collection of old scars on her hull and a slow leak in one of her airbags that her catwalk man was struggling to patch. But speed was on their side: the *Horus* was clocking in just under twenty-three knots, and Roberts knew that she would fly faster once she had dumped her bellyful of rifles and ammunition.

At that moment in time, Roberts wasn't confident that speed would be enough to get both airships out of the battle in one piece. For the dozenth time in as many minutes, he seriously reconsidered his agreement to send the *Horizon* near the front lines. Now, fighting to keep his men alive and the *Horizon* intact, he hoped that upholding his agreement wouldn't get everyone on board killed.

Ahead of the *Horizon* whined a small, nervous-looking military airship that served as an escort for the two merchant ships and appeared to be the sum total of British air forces over Crimea. In the distance, two French airships dueled vigorously with a pair of Russian vessels, keeping the enemy occupied as the *Horizon* and *Horus* roared forwards.

Roberts knew that Russia lagged far behind England in airship technology, and he was surprised to find enemies in the skies. Upon inspection, it was obvious the sluggish, ungainly airships were relying on out-of-date technology and were not much of a threat. Yet his marginal relief evaporated when three Russian airships broke out the dark clouds and began trudging forward to intercept the *Horizon*. Even loaded to her envelope, the *Horizon* could have easily outflown any Russian airship, but when the three oncoming vessels loosened a volley of cannonfire, Roberts knew it was time for the *Horizon* to prove just how nimble she really was.

One Russian vessel, slightly faster than the other two, pushed ahead of its companions, its cannon pointing directly at the *Horus*. The smaller aether flyer wasn't nearly as fast at the *Horizon* but she practically hopscotched across the air, presenting no steady target for the Russian airship. Several hundred feet away, the enemy vessel lurched, trying to get the *Horus* in its sights and failing.

"Duck and pull up!" Roberts roared to his crew. "Make them think we are retreating, and get us up to fifteen hundred feet!" He hoped Wulfe would see through the feint, but he didn't have time to wait.

The military escort ship shuddered into position and spat a cannonball at the oncoming Russian airship as the *Horizon* veered sharply and pulled up, nose to the sky. Her engines churned in effort, the boiler spitting out clouds of steam, and sent the airship racing up and away in a classic pattern of retreat. The Russian airship loosed a cannonball that veered past the *Horus* and missed by several dozen yards. One shot wasted, the enemy fumbled into position for another try, intent on the small aether flyer.

Most unfortunately for the Russian airship, it had abandoned the *Horizon* in favor of the *Horus*. This allowed Roberts' airship to swing around and attack. The Vandenberg rang out in the torrent of noise, hitting the enemy's envelope dead center. Steam poured out of the torn airbags like blood escaping from an artery and the Russian airship shuddered in the air, floundering helplessly.

With one Russian airship down, her two comrades were noticeably irate about the sudden turn of events and were making for the *Horizon* as fast as their bumbling clumsiness would allow. A roaring of engines and the *Horus* was just a few dozen feet from the *Horizon*. Wulfe waved a gigantic arm in salute. "My thanks, Captain!" he bellowed through the war-torn air. "I knew you wouldn't let us down!"

"There's still more of them, Wulfe!" Roberts called back. "Don't start the celebrations just yet!"

With a quick fishtail in the air, the *Horus* sailed forward to line herself up next to the *Horizon*. They squared up to meet the next attack, both of the *Horus'* small bore cannon alert and ready for action. She shot two cannonballs in quick succession, one that blasted through a Russian hull and threw men and broken bits of wood into the air and one that just clipped the enemy. But the *Horizon* was not idle; on deck, Roberts, Sparrowman, Bloomberg, and Oboe carefully aimed the muzzles of four rifles, two to each Russian airship, and let loose a volley of bullets.

Three Russian soldiers fell amidst the hysterical riot of splintering wood and escaping steam. Two cannonballs blasted from the Russians in response, hitting nothing but dust. Darting his eyes around, Roberts saw their military escort airship straggle far behind the *Horizon* and the *Horus*. The airship was laboring as if hit, although it had no visible damage. With two Russian airships in the skies and the scream of battle several hundred feet below their gondolas, the *Horizon* and *Horus* had only each other for backup.

Side by side, the two merchant airships raced forward to intercept the Russians flying their way. Roberts bellowed at Wulfe across the few dozen feet separating the two airships and the *Horizon* and *Horus* moved forward as one, directly in line to intercept the Russian airships. Bullets flew out of the *Horizon* and *Horus* and were returned by the Russians, but the merchant airships were far too fast and fleet and the Russian airships had trouble locking in on their target. By the time the two enemy airships swung their cannon into position, it was too late.

With balletic grace, the *Horizon* wheeled sharply, kicking her tail out and shooting her Vandenberg in a sharp volley that roared along the Russian airship's deck, pulverizing as it went. Without missing a beat, the *Horizon* pulled up sharply, leaving the way clear for the *Horus* to loose two cannonballs, one of which blasted through the main steam valve network of the Russian airship, sending boiling hot steam pouring from the broken pipes.

The Russian airship writhed in the sky, clearly too damaged to be of any further threat and sinking fast. In response, the remaining airship wheeled and turned towards safer skies, outnumbered and retreating as fast as she could. The *Horizon* and *Horus* made no move to follow, and Wulfe called over to Roberts, "Ahoy, *Horizon*! Skies are clear, we've just got to drop our load. Try to stay alive until we've finished the job!"

"We'll do our best, you daft bastard!" Roberts called back, adrenaline and the roaring heat of battle in his veins. The *Horizon* was battered but unbowed, still eager to race forward. Injuries among her crew were minimal. Harding was picking splinters of wood out of Oboe's leg and Carter was keeping one hand clamped to his arm where a trickle of blood stained his shirt, but for the most part the crew on board both airships were relatively unscathed.

The sounds of battle grew louder, and Roberts scanned the ground worriedly. Below, the river Alma snaked its way through a valley skirted by round hills that sloped to mounds. The Allied troops were spread out along several miles just north of the river while battalions of Russians clustered south of the river. Tens of thousands of troops swarmed the hills below, men dying by the minute, and the air was filled with shouts and gunfire.

For the moment, the two airships were safe, out of reach from Russian ground troops and with no other Russian airships attacking them. Seconds raced past as Roberts scoured the air for the next attack while the com device squawked with information from the catwalk and engine room. They still had a dangerous drop to perform in the middle of a battle, and there was still ample opportunity for spectacular damage.

"There, Captain Roberts!" Wulfe boomed enthusiastically. "Landing procedures like we arranged! Low and quick and let's get the hell out of here!" They were now flying over allied space, but a Russian airship could come sailing into the picture at any minute. The *Horizon* and *Horus* had to drop their loads quickly and flee for safer skies.

At the wheel, Barking Jack turned the *Horizon*'s nose around to pull her into a sharp spiral, rotating her around the radius of the drop zone and nosing her down to the ground. The maneuvers were intricate and dangerous. Barking Jack had the excruciating challenge of lowering the *Horizon* to within five or so feet of the ground and stabilizing her while the ground troops unloaded her. It was a situation perfect for disaster, and everyone on board was wracked with stress.

Both airships moved in a spiral, lowering to the ground as Roberts and Wulfe bellowed out commands and their men scrambled to obey them. "ONE HUNDRED FEET!" Roberts commanded to Barking Jack who was hunched over the wheel, his face grim and taut with effort. Below decks, the engine room yelled information through the com device.

The *Horizon* continued to spiral downward, shimmying as Barking Jack delicately nosed her closer to the ground. They were dropping right behind the lines, entirely too close to flying volleys of lead and cannonfire for Roberts' comfort. Under the *Horizon*'s belly, infantrymen swarmed in anticipation, desperate for what supplies the airships had brought. Roberts hoped that the men below had some experience unloading a moving airship. Getting the cargo up to the front lines had been difficult and dangerous enough. Getting it out of the airship and onto the ground undamaged was going to be even more challenging.

"TWENTY FEET AND TEN KNOTS!" Barking Jack shouted as Roberts snapped out commands to his struggling crew. The *Horizon* was fighting to slow her speed down, lagging far behind the *Horus*, who had quickly fallen into position and was now opening her bay door to the masses of soldiers below. She hovered steadily at five feet above the ground while soldiers eagerly bore away her cargo.

The *Horizon*, however, was having a much more difficult time performing the maneuver. After a few minutes of struggle, she dropped to eight feet, but she was moving forward at just under eleven knots, much too fast for the infantrymen on the ground to keep pace and take the cargo from her belly. Barking Jack was using all his skill to hold the *Horizon* still, but she still juddered and fishtailed in the air.

Oaths and barked orders filled the *Horizon* as she creaked and thumped in the air, vibrating with the strain. Soldiers pressed up around her, arms reaching out for what she carried. The situation was growing dire, and Roberts finally gave up. The *Horizon* was bigger than the *Horus* and the maneuver was too tricky for a battlefield. They'd have to use the lift basket to lower items.

Gears creaked in the heat of battle as the lift basket lowered to the ground. Roberts stood inside it and examined the ranks of soldiers waiting on the muddy battlefield, desperation in their eyes. The lift basket hit the mud with a squelching sound. Roberts vaulted over the side and began recruiting volunteers.

"You, you, you, and you, with me!" Roberts commanded, ordering four soldiers into the lift basket and signaling to be pulled aloft. The basket inched its way upwards to the open bay doors, where Carter and Long Tom caught it and hauled it forward, disgorging its passengers. "Load the basket! Now!" Roberts commanded. The soldiers obeyed instantly as Roberts directed their movements and sweated over his airship.

Long minutes passed. Every spare crew member of the *Horizon* and Roberts' enforced volunteers hastily loaded cargo onto the lift basket and lowered it to the ground. Below, it was promptly emptied by the milling soldiers, then brought back to the bay doors for a refill. The *Horizon* bounced and juddered alarmingly as the weight of extra bodies and the movement of cargo knocked her off balance. Barking Jack swore tersely as he struggled to keep the airship level while bullets and cannonfire roared around them and the screams of battle raged in the thick air. The *Horus*, who had quickly dumped her load, rotated in the sky, providing cover for the *Horizon* and waiting for her partner airship to finish the job.

Each moment inched by, Roberts fighting with every ounce of strength to keep his ship in the air and get the job over with quickly. At long last, the cargo bay was empty.

"Fine job, *Horizon!*" Wulfe roared across the space of the two airships. "A drop like this is tricky and you..."

"GREY WULFE!" a voice thundered through the oppressive clamor of battle. "WHERE IN GOD'S GREEN EARTH HAVE YOU BEEN, YOU FOOL MAN?"

Roberts turned to see a stalwart presence on the battlefield, hands planted on hips and feet braced, two blazing eyes glaring up at the *Horus* with a look that would melt gold. It was a Valkyrie, a vision straight from Norse tales, broad-shouldered and arrestingly bosomed. He guessed that this was Molly, the object of Wulfe's affection. Even viewed from several dozen yards away, the woman was formidably imposing and commanding. Roberts' respect for Wulfe's fortitude crept up several notches.

"CAN'T STAY, MY LOVE!" Wulfe boomed out cheerfully. "THERE'S A DAMNED WAR TO BE WON. BUT, WOMAN, DON'T YOU BE MISTAKEN. GREY WULFE WILL BE RETURNING FOR YOU!"

The woman's face was hard enough to cut glass, and Roberts fleetingly wondered if she was going to march forward, seize the *Horus* in her two massive hands, and shake it until Wulfe fell out. Instead, she cupped her hands to her mouth. "YOU'D BETTER RETURN TO ME, GREY WULFE!" she bellowed back as the two airships wheeled sharply and disappeared into the skies.

Shaking his head firmly, Roberts turned to face his crew. "Man your positions!" he roared. "We're heading back!" The *Horizon* churned in excitement and began climbing into the smoke-dark sky, engines roaring and steam curling in white waves behind her.

Chapter Thirteen

As night fell on Crimea, darkness was like a shroud hiding the carnage of battle that littered the hills. The *Horizon* and *Horus*, their cargo bays now empty, limped back to the British camp where a ramshackle airship wharf awaited them. Once the airships were berthed and attended to, the exhausted crews fell into their hammocks with groans of relief. The noise of the camp rocked both airships to sleep as in the distance, battle roared thick in the air.

Morning rose drizzly and gray with thick clouds piling on the skyline. Roberts limped his way across the *Horizon*'s rain-slick topdeck to greet the day. Yawning, he grimly surveyed the ragged lines of tents and massed throngs of filthy soldiers slogging wearily through knee-deep mud. Everywhere were the screams and moans of the dying. Hundreds of men lay wracked with injuries and illness. Harried medical workers moved among the casualties, but there were far too few doctors and nurses for the sheer number of patients.

Wulfe's Molly was audible as a deafening bellow that cut effortlessly through the noise of the camp. Roberts observed her for a few minutes from a distance as she harangued a frazzled-looking officer. Footsteps drew his attention to the *Horus* where Wulfe was just stepping down the rickety gangplank. He saluted Roberts with a wink, ever cheerful despite their circumstances.

Roberts quipped dryly, "There's an officer that needs rescuing from your woman."

Wulfe smiled unabashedly. "Aye, they've tried to push my Molly out of camp before, officers not liking to take orders from a woman, but she'll not be driven out by an army. She keeps the soldiers alive, and the men will stand by her thick and thin, and hang what the officers say!" He was already stomping towards the ladder, clearly intent on reuniting with his beloved. Roberts stopped him with a gesture.

"The *Horizon*'s a bit dinged, but sound, and I aim to take her back to the *Morning Star* as soon as she can get up in the air," he stated. "The *Morning Star* is sailing on her own, and I've no intentions for her to complete the voyage by herself."

When the *Horizon* and *Horus* had departed Constantinople three days ago, they had left behind the *Morning Star*. The merchant marine was nearing completion of her repair work and preparing to take to the seas again. Roberts hadn't liked leaving Fosselweight to sail on his own, but Wulfe was intent on reaching the front lines as soon as possible. In the end, the *Horizon* and *Horus* had set out with as many Moretti rifles as they could carry, leaving the *Morning Star* to follow them up to Crimea whenever she was seaworthy again.

Wulfe sucked at his teeth as he responded slowly, "The *Horus* took a bit of a beating but with a little work she can be back in the air."

Roberts shook his head. "She's a damn fast flyer, but the *Horizon* can get to the *Morning Star* quicker on her own," he countered. "Best you patch your ship up and get her back into fighting shape. We'll need her when the *Morning Star* arrives."

Wulfe frowned. "The Black Sea's a tricky patch for one airship, Captain Roberts," he said.

"She'll manage," Roberts stated firmly, but Wulfe's attention was elsewhere. He whipped out a salute as a man staggered forward into the bleak light and stood on the *Horus'* topdeck blinking in confusion. He was nearly bald and what hair was left had streaks of dark gray. A filthy captain's jacket hung off one arm, and his eyes were blank and vacant. He looked around for one moment, then shuffled back to his cabin.

Roberts watched with a frown, then turned to Wulfe, who shrugged helplessly. "Captain Cork," he pronounced simply. Roberts nodded but Wulfe was already transitioning smoothly back to the prior topic. They shook hands and parted ways, Wulfe to seek out Molly and Roberts to rouse his crew and get the *Horizon* back in the air.

Noon was well on its way before the *Horizon* took to the skies again, her canopy sewn up, her dents hammered out, and other problems remedied. The flight ahead was complicated and perilous. Fosselweight had stated his intent to leave Constantinople two days after the *Horizon* and had given Roberts details about his intended sailing path. Locating the marine ship on the Black Sea would not be an easy task, and

Roberts had no way of knowing if the *Morning Star* was sailing by now or if she was still stuck at port. The *Horizon* had just under seventy-two flight hours left in coal. If she couldn't locate the *Morning Star* quickly, she would have to hightail it back to Constantinople to refuel.

As the *Horizon* lifted into the thick air, Roberts watched the skies carefully. It was September 20th and the second half of the month was shaping up to be cold, humid, and foggy. On board the airship, tensions were high as the crew prepared themselves for a perilous solo flight across the Black Sea, watching their coal stores carefully and alert for enemies in the skies. Much to everyone's relief, the *Horizon* seemed unbowed by her recent skirmish. With no cargo to hold aloft, she flew easily through the air.

They found the *Morning Star* a few hours before dawn the next day, just as Roberts was close to abandoning the search and heading to Constantinople. The mounting tension on board the airship fell considerably as the *Horizon* dropped to a hover over the *Morning Star*. Although the airship had enough fuel to make it back to Crimea, Roberts ordered the crew to take on more from the *Morning Star*. There was no need to cut into the airship's fuel reserves, especially not over open water.

The *Morning Star* was sailing well and apparently had encountered no hazards, but when Roberts slid to the crowded topdeck, Fosselweight greeted him with a worried frown. They shook hands with the brief grip of two men glad to see each other but with too many worries on their minds to spare much room for niceties.

"The Black Sea treat you well, Captain Fosselweight?" Roberts inquired. "No damned Russians to bother you?"

"She sailed fair and true, Captain Roberts, and Poseidon was on our side," Fosselweight responded. "But..." his heavy expression deepened, creasing his forehead into lines as Roberts watched him worriedly. Finally, the smaller captain sighed. "You'd best see what is in my cargo hold."

Roberts followed Fosselweight across topdeck. Sailors scrambled out of the way of the officers, tossing up salutes. Below decks, the belly of the merchant marine was packed to the gills with neatly stacked cargo. Roberts trudged along behind Fosselweight, examining the cargo and wondering what had troubled the other captain. He stopped when his eyes fell upon several rows of mechanical automatons neatly lined up as if on parade.

"What the blazes?" Roberts growled as he stepped forward to examine the automatons in the dim light of the cargo hold. There were fifty of them by his quick count, each as high as a man's waist and twice his width: squat cylinders of metal, each with two mounted guns. Each automaton was supported on three tread-mounted triangles and seemed capable of independent movement. Roberts bent down to examine one carefully. From the looks of it, the automatons were the very latest of technological wonders, but they were patently inappropriate for the mud-choked fields of Crimea.

"Captain Roberts, I presume?" a bright voice rose out of the shadows and a man appeared. He was of medium height and build, unremarkable but for his forthright demeanor. "James Bothwell. Weapons inspector. I believe I have you to thank for the swift delivery of some of my Moretti guns."

He thrust out a hand at Roberts, who took it briefly, but then dropped Bothwell's fingers. Examining him for several moments, Roberts pointed at the automatons. "You're the man responsible for these?" he questioned darkly.

Bothwell cleared his throat. "Why yes," he fumbled the words. "Military contract, sir. I was one of three government-appointed officials who were part of the development of these weapons, and I'm to see them delivered to the front lines personally." He tried for a smile. "These are top-grade 1855 Orwille battle mechs, straight from the military labs after four years of development."

Roberts glared at him icily, but Bothwell seemed to have regained his momentum. Rubbing his hands, he continued with rising enthusiasm, "Each battle mecha is capable of auto or solo operation. In auto-operation, they can move independently in a direct line forward at a rate of eighty feet a minute and deliver one hundred rounds a minute under optimal conditions. In solo operation, one can deliver sustained fire or pinpoint fire for better target precision and optimal ammunition usage and..."

"Under what conditions?" Roberts demanded flatly. "Because if it's not in the middle of waist-high mud with cold rain coming down and hundreds of dead bodies clogging up the ground, these things aren't going to do any damned good."

"You will find, *Captain Roberts*," Bothwell spoke with some heat, "that each Orwille has been calibrated for high performance within a variety of war theatres and field conditions..."

Roberts laughed hollowly. "Mister Bothwell, there's thousands of soldiers in Crimea with no shoes, food, or guns. There's little space in Calamita Bay for what ships can make it up the Black Sea, and there's miles of impassible mud between the bay and the campsite. There's no place in Crimea for these things. They're a waste of cargo space."

That last comment was directed at Fosselweight, and the marine captain stiffened but said nothing. There would be a conversation between the two captains later, but for now, Roberts' attention was on Bothwell. He rumbled, "I'll take your guns to the front lines, Mister Bothwell, but the *Horizon* is not transporting these." He jerked his head derisively towards the Orwilles. "My ship has no room for useless cargo." With that, he left the bay, his boots echoing against the wood.

"Captain Roberts," Fosselweight said quietly behind Roberts' back as the smaller captain struggled to match paces.

"I wouldn't tell a captain what to do on his own ship, Captain Fosselweight, but those damned weapons are more useful as ballast in your ship than they will be on the battlefields of Crimea," Roberts replied tersely. "There's nothing up there but miles of mud and no roads."

"I'm contractually obligated to transport them," Fosselweight responded evenly. A sailor nearly collided with him before scrambling away at the last minute and throwing a hasty salute into the air. Roberts stopped, and the two captains exchanged a hard look before Fosselweight continued.

"Fortunately," he smiled marginally, "My contract only extends to delivering the supplies to port. I will sign them over to the quartermaster. If they disintegrate in port for lack of transport to camp, I have no control over that."

Roberts snorted, still not mollified. Fosselweight maintained his level stare and spoke firmly, "My hold has a thousand Moretti rifles, as well as a hundred thousand rounds of ammunition. I trust you will see them delivered?"

Roberts nodded tersely, his anger starting to dissipate in light of Fosselweight's even words, but tension still hung thick between the two captains. Fosselweight saw Roberts off the *Morning Star* with somewhat chilly courtesy, and Roberts returned to the *Horizon* still peeved. Fosselweight had the right to do with his own ship as he pleased, but a merchant marine and a merchant airship had different operational concerns. The Orwilles would have been exceedingly difficult for the *Horizon* to transport if Roberts had allowed them on board. They would do nothing more than litter Calamita Bay and clog up useful ground space.

Back on board the *Horizon*, coal was still moving up from the marine ship into the airship's hoppers. It was a slow and tedious process that still required the intent focus of everyone on board. Roberts called for a halt when the *Horizon* had enough coal for five flight days. That was plenty to see both ships back to Crimea, and there was no sense in the airship taking on more weight than she needed.

No longer hungry, the *Horizon* settled into her accustomed cruising speed for accompanying the *Morning Star*. Barring bad weather or enemy attack, they would reach Crimea in three days or less. The merchant marine cut easily through the dark waters, and both ships had a strong tailwind pushing them forward. Skies were gray with a garnish of thick clouds sagging wetly in the air. but with the steady tailwind and lack of potential danger, the ships made swift progress forward.

The next morning, Roberts moodily greeted the day when he exited his cabin. A line of low-hanging clouds filled the western skies, and moisture clung to every surface while a clammy cold seeped into his bones. Blearily, Roberts took inspection of his airship. She was flying well, leading the way while the *Morning Star* sailed below. The scent of breakfast porridge and coffee was in the humid air, and Roberts sniffed it, knowing that it would take more than one cup of coffee to wake him fully to life.

Oboe stepped forward to give his report after his shift on night command. As he spoke, his movements were uncharacteristically lethargic and his deep voice was slightly raspy. Upon close inspection, his eyes were watery-looking and there was a sluggishness in his movements that betrayed signs of a building illness.

Roberts stopped him mid-report and demanded, "Are you ill?" Oboe shook his head, but his lungs argued otherwise, and a sudden bout of coughing shook him.

"Go see Harding and get your head down," Roberts ordered. "I don't want to see you topside again until you've put some sleep under your belt."

Nodding, Oboe obeyed, and Roberts watched worriedly as his first mate stumbled his way below decks. Sickness on an airship could spread rapidly, and the cold, wet air was doing no one on board any good. Roberts alerted Harding to keep a careful watch on the crew and he observed his men carefully as the day passed.

The following morning, Oboe wasn't the only one feeling under the weather. William was the next to start coughing, followed by Big Tom. By the time the *Horizon* limped into Crimea's port a day later, four crew members besides Oboe were ill. Roberts himself was doggedly fighting off deep exhaustion and a heavy tightness in his chest by the time the *Horizon* came in for a landing in Calamita. It was nearly midnight, and a wet coldness was creeping up from the damp ground, adding further misery to the *Horizon*'s sick crew.

Calamita Bay was a chaotic mess of soldiers, haphazard stacks of equipment, lines of ragged tents, and disorder everywhere the eye could see. Campfires flickered in the dark wetness, and the ramshackle airship wharf was barely visible under the *Horizon*'s gondola as she cautiously landed on the rain-slick wooden beams. Roberts had expected a decent marine port in the bay, but he found only a rickety skeleton of a wharf that was already taken up by other ships. Nearby were two narrow berths for airships, and the *Horizon* landed gingerly on one. Looking over the bay, Roberts knew that getting cargo off the *Morning Star* and moving it to the British camp was going to be a strenuous and time-consuming task.

The *Horus* was down cold on the other berth, her crew below decks. Roberts was infinitely glad to see the aether flyer, yet he barely had the strength to see to his own airship. Exhausted and battling against the unshakable onset of illness, it was all Roberts could do to shut the *Horizon* down for the night and let his men rest. Wulfe and any further cargo transport would have to wait until morning.

Far too late in the morning of the next day, Roberts dragged himself upright. Calamita Bay looked no more inviting than it had the prior day, and the patter of rain continued. Big Tom, Long Tom, Sparrowman, and William were still coughing extravagantly, and Farrington had also started sniffling as well. Leaving his crew to their misery, Roberts hacked his bleary way to the *Horus*.

Wulfe greeted him warmly. "Safe journey, then, Captain Roberts? All well on board your ship?" he questioned.

Roberts tried unsuccessfully to suppress a cough, knowing that he looked ready for burying. "We've had some illness on board," he admitted.

A worried frown twisted Wulfe's mouth as he examined Roberts critically. "Can you fly?"

"We'll fly," Roberts responded, knowing the next several days would be hellish.

His pessimism wasn't disappointed. The ensuing week passed in a wretched blur of work, exhaustion, and dampness as the crew struggled to move supplies to camp while battling illness. Shorthanded and managed by miserable, coughing men, the *Horizon* trudged back and forth from Calamita Bay to the British camp while the *Horus* hovered anxiously around her, leading the way and lending assistance where she could.

Harding was busy with his patients and mitigated the illness as best he could, but only Carter, Jenkins, Halloway, and Harding escaped completely unscathed. The rest of the crew struggled with fevers, coughs, and weakness, but they fought to keep up with their workload and manage the airship. Though brutal, the illness quickly burnt itself out. By the time five days had passed, almost everyone was on the mend.

Oboe, however, was no better after a week of complete rest and isolation. Roberts had moved Oboe into the captain's cabin where the First Mate could cough in peace. Oboe did little but sleep, watched carefully by Harding, but rest brought no healing. His tall frame shook with chills and his coughs were audible outside the closed cabin door.

"I don't like the sound of his lungs," Harding stated quietly to Roberts. Oboe was sleeping fitfully while Harding measured his pulse. "This cold, wet climate is perfect for incubating pneumonia, and I suspect that he has it. If it is pneumonia, he will be a long time recovering from it."

"We'll be returning to Constantinople in a few days," Roberts intoned. "It will be warmer there."

Oboe stirred, but only to cough weakly, each ragged sound tearing sharply at Roberts. Oboe did not take kindly to cold weather, and Robert had long suspected that Oboe suffered far more in frigid temperatures than he evidenced. Four years ago, Oboe had suffered a bout of pneumonia that had nearly killed him, and his recovery had been lengthy.

Frowning worriedly, Roberts turned his eyes to Harding. "He's young and strong, Gavin. He'll live," Harding spoke reassuringly. Roberts said nothing, but a consuming worry ate at him. He left Oboe in Harding's care and stepped softly out of the cabin.

Outside was rainless but clammy. The air was still heavy with moisture and a clammy cold that seeped into the bones. Farrington and Carter were manhandling a crate across topdeck, and Farrington's lungs heaved audibly in the damp air. Under Roberts' feet, the *Horizon's* engines churned. She was lightly tethered to the berth while her crew and several soldiers filled her with cargo for one last trip to camp before shutting down for the night.

As Roberts supervised the loading, his attention was caught by the sound of gunfire rippling in the air. Turning, he followed the sound with his spyglass and saw approximately two dozen Orwille mechas being put through a field test. Yesterday's rainfall had increased the mud, and the automatons were making heavy work of crossing the field. At least half of them were buried past their axles in mud. Several were making vigorous efforts to move forward on their triangle-shaped wheels, but the mud was a foot thick and the automatons were effectively rooted to the ground.

Shaking his head, Roberts turned back to his airship. Bothwell would be livid, but Roberts highly doubted there would be any further demands for the *Horizon* to take the Orwilles up to the British camp. Perhaps if the war dragged into the summer and the ground hardened, there would be some use for the weapons, if they hadn't rust away in the wharf's ramshackle storehouses by then.

Sparrowman passed Roberts, sniffing and rubbing at his watery eyes, his footsteps heavy with fatigue and lingering illness. Sound echoed up from below deck as Jenkins yelled something over the noise of the engines. The *Horizon* was filled up with bullets, guns, and bandages and waiting for departure. When she lifted at last with the much-needed items, she left the useless Orwille mechs to flounder in the mud. while she joined the *Horus* in the dying light of the sun for one final transport before nightfall.

Chapter Fourteen

"Look, will you stop being a bloody idiot, Gavin?" Halloway barked loudly. "You work this daft bird into the ground and in six months you won't have an airship."

The boiler room was deserted except for Roberts and Halloway. The rest of the crew was keeping well away from the tense argument. Halloway's expression was distorted by layers of coal dust and other grime, but it was clear he was long past caring about Roberts' opinions or demands.

"If you plan on doing any more of those running drops, you're just going to overstress the engines. If she breaks down in Crimea, she'll stay here unless you can find a marine ship big enough to pack her up and bring her back to Constantinople."

Halloway slammed a toolbox lid and continued. "There's bloody nothing in that damned hellhole except mud and a lot of enemies. Stress her, drain out her boiler, then dump her into a warzone with Russians shooting at her, and she won't last and longer than your men will. You want to keep her going, you'll give me a week to get her into the right shape."

The *Horizon* was on her way back to Constantinople in the company of the *Morning Star*. Although both ships needed urgently to restock with cargo and return as soon as possible, Halloway was right. An airship required constant maintenance and repair, especially when performing heavy work in a high-stress environment. Roberts could push her and she would struggle to please him as long as she could. But the long months in Crimea would take their toll, and she'd eventually crack under the strain.

Her crew would fare no better. The spate of illness had burned through the men, but it left fatigue and lingering coughs in its wake. Even worse, pneumonia had fallen on Oboe, who hadn't stirred from Roberts' cabin in a week, Harding watching over him carefully. The entire crew needed a session of recovery in Constantinople's warmer climate or they would have no energy for Crimea.

They would need their strength. British military operations were currently being transferred from Calamita Bay to Balaklava Bay, a thin snake of water much too small for more than a few marine ships to navigate easily. There was no port or airship wharf in Balaklava, and the road leading out of the bay was a muddy rut that crested up over a pass cutting through the plateau. Roberts had seen this all on a quick reconnaissance mission the *Horizon* and *Horus* had flown before leaving Crimea. It was obvious at a glance that it would be nearly impossible to ground transport supplies from Balaklava to the British camp. If supplies were to be moved from Balaklava, it would be on airships.

Roberts sifted through all this while Halloway stomped around the boiler room, making a terrific racket and stonily ignoring him. He hated the thought of cooling his heels in Constantinople for a week while money and work opportunities slipped past him, but Roberts could feel his airship's strain and fatigue reverberating through her timbers. With all she had done for him, she needed some careful attention before he brought her up to Crimea again.

Finally Roberts spoke. "A week, then?" he questioned heavily, knowing the answer.

Halloway snorted. "Two weeks would be better, but since you're so damned impatient, I'll take a week."

Roberts didn't rise to the barb. "Do what you need to do," he said evenly. "It will be a long winter in Crimea. I need her at fighting strength."

A snort signaled Halloway's thoughts on the matter, but he said nothing more. He vigorously set to work, keeping his back firmly turned and making it clear that Roberts could hang himself for all Halloway cared. Roberts took the hint and left the boiler room, thinking things over.

Halloway's bad mood echoed throughout the airship. The crew was grim and consumed with thoughts about what lay ahead. Half the men was still recovering from their recent illness, and few of the men were at their full strength. The *Horizon* trudged listlessly through the cold air, her engines churning heavily as if exhausted and overstressed. At her side, the *Horus* flew wearily, Wulfe also consumed with getting his airship back to Constantinople where she could recuperate from her recent battle.

Tempers improved considerably when the two airships made it back down the Black Sea and landed in Constantinople. Their flight was relatively easy, and sunshine awaited them in Constantinople. The weather was almost warm, and this lifted the spirits of both airships' crews and helped remove the chill of Crimea from their bones.

Halloway quickly set to work , making a gigantic mess and yelling constantly at the long-suffering Jenkins and Sparrowman. While tensions between Halloway and Jenkins remained sharp, Sparrowman was developing a skill for managing Halloway. His words had a tempering effect on Halloway's personality, and he could quietly steer Halloway away from his bouts of irrationality. Arguments between Jenkins and Halloway had lessened the last few weeks with Sparrowman running interference between the two.

Roberts made mention of this to Sparrowman on their second day at port. The assistant engineer smiled lightly at the praise, but his face darkened as Roberts continued, "There's few men who can stand Halloway for more than a few hours without wanting to throw him overboard."

Sparrowman paused for several moments before responding. "I've been thrown off an airship before, sir," he pronounced quietly. "I wouldn't do it to another man."

"What?" Roberts demanded sharply, incredulousness filling his voice.

There was no answer for a moment. Sparrowman examined Roberts with a flat, unreadable expression. "I was a cabin boy on the airship *Bucephalus*. I was eleven," Sparrowman stated quietly. He set his jaw as if holding back his words, but with some reluctance continued.

"The captain had a taste for young boys," he continued with controlled anger, his voice even although each word was heavy as a stone. "When I fought him off, he dragged me out of his cabin and in full view of the crew, threw me overboard. We were three hundred feet in the air."

Roberts was appalled. It was true that occasionally a reckless airman or officer suddenly found himself taking an involuntary swan dive off the back of an airship. Life on board an airship was brutal, and a captain sometimes had to make the decision to drop a dangerous crew member overboard to preserve the safety of everyone else. However, to blatantly murder a young boy in full view of witnesses was despicable.

Sparrowman shrugged one thin shoulder. "I woke up in a puddle of mud with the wind knocked out of me. I walked to the nearest town." A ghost of a smile crossed his lips. "Later, I heard word that the captain of the *Bucephalus* was thrown overboard by his men. Apparently he had tried his tricks on his new cabin boy and stabbed the lad when he resisted. The crew decided they'd had enough."

Roberts gestured at Sparrowman's twisted leg. "Is that what did it for your leg?"

"This? No," Sparrowman smiled thinly but with more humor. "That was eight years later on the *White Squall*. I was one of her engineers. We were overtaken by three German raiders. A cannonball punched through the engine room and took me out with it. I fell out and managed to land topdeck on one of the German airships. As luck would have it, they needed an engineer and let me live. I was with them for six months until the ship was taken by our air force and I was released."

He tapped a fist against his bad leg. "I broke my leg in the fall and they didn't have a doctor on board to set it. It never did heal properly."

"Some men might have taken all that as a hint to stay the hell away from airships," Roberts quipped lightly.

Sparrowman smiled. "Well, sir, the good Lord has seen fit to spare my life twice. I reckon the skies are where I need to be since they can't seem to kill me."

"Good. Keep it that way," Roberts laughed and slapped Sparrowman on the shoulder. "Someone's got to keep Halloway and Jenkins from tearing the ship apart."

Sparrowman smiled, ducked his head in respect, and limped back to the engine room. where a gigantic mess of assorted metal parts and two irate engineers awaited him.

As Roberts stood topdeck, warm salt air rushed over him. He breathed it in deeply, thankful again for the change from Crimea's wet coldness. If the first two days at port were any indication, they were in for a week of sunshine and warm weather in Constantinople. The rest of the crew was hard at work in the full, warm sunlight and obviously enjoying the fine weather. The airship herself was luxuriating under the attention of her crew and clearly pleased at the chance to rest.

"Captain," Big Tom called out as he rolled across the deck, several yards of canvas in his hands. "Number fourteen, sir. Look at this bit of stitching here." Roberts took the airbag and examined it carefully. Airbags were sewn together with heavily waxed cording that was under constant stress from the pressure of steam and the decaying influence of moisture. Catwalk men had to constantly monitor the airbags and the canopy for signs of wear and tear, and the canopy's interior needed a full inspection every few months.

"Rotten almost through," Big Tom stabbed at the stitching triumphantly. "It was a blowout waiting to happen, sir. The fabric is rotting too. The whole airbag needs replacing."

Roberts nodded and handed the airbag back. "Well done," he said in approval. "Any other airbags you have the slightest worry about, replace them as well." Airbag canvas was prohibitively expensive; the cloth had to undergo a long treatment process to make it sturdy and durable. However, the canopy was the last place a captain could be afford to be stingy. There was frozen weather ahead, and that would put enormous strain on the canopy and the airbags.

As Big Tom left, Roberts smiled to himself and patted the railing affectionately. "You cost me a pretty penny, my lady," he said to his airship.

"Women do that, Captain," Barking Jack said in passing. Roberts laughed, feeling a welcome lightness brought on by the sun and warmth. He was further encouraged by the sight of his crew joking and ribbing each other as they went about their tasks. The promise of work and money ahead only further bolstered his mood. It was a near perfect day, and Roberts savored it, mentally storing up some of its warmth and carefree spirit to sustain him in the upcoming months.

The warm weather came as a great benefit to Oboe too. He began to rally during their second day at port. By the third day, he was shakily on his feet and making noises about returning to work, but Roberts laid down the heavy law. "You keep your arse planted on that chair," he commanded, pointing at a chair that had been set out in full sunlight. "You can sit there and yell at as many people as you like, but if you move, I'm demoting you to cabin boy."

Oboe smiled tiredly. He was thinner after his long illness and his ebony skin was dull, his steps hesitant and fumbling when his stride had once been strong and graceful. Without protest, he huddled under a blanket in the sunshine and kept an eye on the crew while William plied him with soup and tea. This process was repeated for several days as Oboe slowly recovered his strength.

In the midst of all the fuss and clamor, Roberts was both relieved and oddly disappointed that Miss Pickens did not make an appearance. He half-expected her to breezily appear at the gangplank, expecting a ride up to Crimea with some ill-conceived notion about reporting on the war from the field. Days passed, and there was no sign of either reporter. Roberts took this as evidence that the pair had returned to London where they belonged. He was thankful that Miss Pickens was no longer around to plague his existence. Still, deep down, there was a strange undercurrent of emotion that brought her to Roberts' mind with a nagging persistence, despite his best efforts to drown out the intrusion.

The weather continued with relentless sunshine and warmth as the days at port passed. By the end of the week, the *Horizon* had been thoroughly inspected and she gleamed with fresh paint and carefully scrubbed wood. Halloway, Jenkins, and Sparrowman were making excellent progress below decks and Halloway seemed marginally pleased with their efforts. Harding was busy puttering around in a tiny room that had been newly partitioned off as a sick bay, and the rest of the crew was rapidly finishing up the long list of tasks.

On the afternoon of their eighth day at port, Farrington and Carter left to go hunting with two airmen from the *Horus*. They returned with a young deer, still fat from the summer, and the combined crews of both airships roasted it on the beach that night. It was a full moon, a million stars winking in the sky while waves slapped softly against the white sand. Laughter floated up in the air and beer flowed freely. Through some small miracle, Sparrowman had coaxed Halloway from the boiler room to join the crew for a few hours of gorging and enthusiastic alcohol consumption. Surprisingly, Halloway took part of the festivities with little fuss.

By the time the men parted ways to their respective airships, there was little left but deer bones and two empty kegs of beer. A refreshed and elated crew stumbled back onto the *Horizon* in various states of inebriation and with high hopes for the future and Crimea ahead.

***   ***   ***   ***

Dawn was barely breaking over the waves when Roberts shook his crew loose from their alcohol-induced slumbers to get the *Horizon* ready for travel. Farrington and Carter were clearly worse for the wear, and Jenkins had a face like a pickled egg, but a cheerful morning sun saw them all on their feet with good humor.

A bit sluggish himself, and with a moderate-sized headache throbbing at his temples, Roberts was stomping about getting in everyone's way when a feminine voice floating over the babble stopped him in his tracks. Stifling both a groan and the sudden elation which stirred to life in the pit of his stomach, he turned to see Miss Pickens standing at the gangplank, arm-in-arm with Fosselweight.

"Hello, Captain!" Miss Pickens waved cheerfully at Roberts. She was all flutters and demure smiles, which put his suspicions on high alert. He had a looming premonition as to the reason for her arrival. Fosselweight was puffed up, proud as a turkey and likely unaware that Miss Pickens' flashing eyes meant serious business.

Observing the two, Roberts felt his gut twist. He strangled it, then irritably stepped forward to greet them. Nodding at Fosselweight, he said, "Good day to you, Captain Fosselweight." Turning to the reporter, he said in a voice of weary patience, "Miss Pickens, may I be so bold as to inquire about the purpose of your lovely presence on my airship?"

"Why, Captain Roberts, from whence did this formality come?" Miss Pickens said in a husky purr that played hell with Roberts' composure. "You see, our rather curmudgeonly acquaintance can present himself with courtesy when he chooses to," she cooed, leaning too close to Fosselweight for Roberts' approval.

Fosselweight patted Miss Pickens on the hand in a proprietary manner. "Quite so, Miss Pickens. But no courtesy, no matter how gallantly expressed, can do you the honor that you are worthy of receiving."

Miss Pickens laughed coyly. "Oh, Captain Fosselweight, you are truly too kind." With feminine grace, she released Fosselweight's arm and stepped forward boldly to claim Roberts'. He shifted in alarm as Miss Pickens was suddenly at his side, her soft body leaning against him as her head tipped up to stare at his face. Heat coursed strongly in Roberts' veins as Miss Pickens' voice nuzzled him with sensuous grace. "Our Captain Roberts, I believe, is a man of action, not pretty words."

Fosselweight's face darkened in jealousy while Roberts found himself in an interesting battle between desire and wariness. It was obvious that Miss Pickens delighted in playing the two men against each other, more likely for amusement than anything else, but the last thing Roberts needed was a squabble over a woman whom all of his better judgment ordered him to avoid.

Clearing his throat, he quickly changed the subject. Addressed the reporter, he bluntly questioned, "I imagine that you aim to find your way to Crimea, Miss Pickens?"

A delicate trill of a laugh rose in the air. "Captain Roberts, forthcoming as always, I see." She patted her white glove against her full lips. "In short, yes."

"Not on my ship," Roberts stated bluntly. "Crimea and the Black Sea are war zones, Miss Pickens. There is nothing for you there but mud and flying bullets and..."

"Oh, stop fussing," Miss Pickens said lightly, patting Roberts' arm in a way that sent thrills running up his spine. "Captain Fosselweight has been filling my ears with such warnings for three days. Now really, the two of you are being quite silly. Don't you know that we are on the cusp of history? There is not a more exciting place on this earth for a reporter to be than Crimea!"

Her eyes were wide with excitement, radiant femininity emanating from her skin. Roberts decided that he needed to reclaim his arm and leave Miss Pickens' presence before he did something foolish and possibly irremediable. Gently, but purposefully, he removed his arm from her grasp and said darkly, "It's too dangerous in Crimea."

Miss Pickens, however, batted the concern away and stepped between the two bristling captains. "Stop worrying, Captain Roberts," she said lightly. "The both of you. I'll be fine. My dear brother will be with me, and he would hold off an army to keep me safe. Besides," she gave Roberts' arm another pat. "Captain Fosselweight and I have an agreement, don't we, Captain?" She gave him a knowing smile and Fosselweight beamed a look of the obviously besotted.

"That is correct, my dear Miss Pickens, we do." He turned to Roberts. "Captain Roberts, Miss Pickens assures me that this trip is merely a chance to allow her brother to gain a lay of the land, shall we say, and report on what he finds. I have no intention of seeing a fine lady like Miss Pickens be exposed to the hardships and dangers of a military camp. However," he colored slightly, "I see no harm in allowing her to travel with the *Morning Star* to Crimea." Fosselweight puffed up a little more. "She will be well protected, Captain Roberts. No harm will ever come to Miss Pickens on board the *Morning Star*, that I can promise you."

Fosselweight had swallowed an obvious lie, and Miss Pickens was clearly in no hurry to disillusion him. She added brightly, "Jules and I will travel with the *Morning Star* to Crimea where he will gather the information we need. The *Constantinople Times* is desperate for fresh news, and Jules can provide this." She smiled innocently. "I will, of course, stay behind on the *Morning Star* while my brother is in the field. I won't risk myself needlessly."

Ah, Roberts thought with dawning comprehension. Miss Pickens and her brother had made good use of their time in Constantinople. They had filled the *Constantinople Gazette* with articles, many of them referencing to the *Morning Star* and her captain. Fosselweight obviously relished the media attention, and the glamour of seeing his name and ship in print was clearly overcoming his common sense. Miss Pickens likely knew that Roberts would deny her passage on the *Horizon* and had turned her sights on an easier target. Fosselweight was falling over himself to comply.

Sighing, Roberts grudgingly conceded to the inevitable. "Well, I can't stop you, Miss Pickens, but God knows I wish I could." Turning to Fosselweight, he said in a low growl, "I'm surprised at you, Captain Fosselweight, for allowing this."

"Captain Roberts, I will dictate what happens on my own ship," Fosselweight responded coldly as he gathered himself up sharply. "And if you will excuse me, Miss Pickens and I have other affairs to conclude."

With a chilly goodbye, the lovely reporter and the indignant captain left the *Horizon* while Roberts watched them angrily. There was a definite lilt to Miss Pickens' step that he recognized as the strut of a woman who had just bested two grown men. For a moment, Roberts wasn't sure if he wanted to throttle her or kiss her; both options were appealing.

Instead, he thundered toward his crew, sourly barking out orders. As he roared and stomped, Roberts had a sneaking suspicion that the little *menage-a-trois* had been observed by the whole airship. There were more than a few smirks visible, and the crew cheerfully submitted to his irritable commands no matter how forcefully he voiced them.

Irritated that he had been made a fool of by Miss Pickens and not happy about his current strained relationship with Fosselweight, Roberts got his ship back into the air, her prow pointed towards Crimea. At least there, his enemies were more straightforward and Roberts was allowed to shoot at them if he liked. Such a thought lessened the sourness of his mood as the *Horizon* settled down for another journey across the Black Sea.

Chapter Fifteen

Balaklava Bay was a mess. The harbor was more ships than water, with several dozen marine vessels effectively choking off the narrow, twisted bay. The *Morning Star* had scarcely any room to navigate forward and drop off her goods. Everything she was carrying would need to be rowed to shore on longboats or lifted by the *Horizon*, thanks to the complete absence of a dock. Along the shore, a number of ramshackle huts clung sullenly to the thick mud, which was churned deeply by the feet of hundreds of soldiers. Equipment, ammunition, and food lay everywhere, and teams of men tried to force carts through the mud with little effect.

The *Horizon* hovered in the air while her crew observed their new operating theater with extreme dismay. Calamita Bay had been bad enough, but Balaklava was a cesspool of confusion, disorder, and deprivation. Casting back in his mind, Roberts could not recall flying into a port that was this ill-equipped to handle an airship. Surveying it, he had serious doubts that the *Horizon* could perform adequately, considering what little she had to work with in Balaklava.

At Roberts' side, Carter stood fuming, shaking his head. "If Lord Raglan hadn't pissed around with the French over Sevastopol, we could have won this war by Christmas," he muttered loudly. "A siege was a damned fool idea."

Roberts said nothing, but he quietly agreed with Carter. According to rumor, Lord Raglan was currently bemired in a disagreement with the French commander-in-chief over Sevastopol. What could have been a swift and decisive victory was now sinking into a protracted siege, with winter fast approaching. Allied leaders hoped for a victory in Sevastopol before winter came, but Roberts strongly suspected that the war would stretch on for several months, if not years.

Carter crossed his arms and scowled, an expression mirrored by much of the crew. In the flight back to Crimea, morale had fallen, and their arrival at Balaklava Bay had not improved matters. The *Horizon* had flown alone after leaving the *Horus* in Constantinople to escort the damaged *Cornucopia* home. Upon arrival in Crimea, it appeared that the *Horizon* was the only British merchant airship present. They had spotted a military airship in Balaklava but where it made berth and refueled, Roberts was damned if he knew. For the *Horizon*, the lack of an airship wharf was an enormous concern. While the *Morning Star* could put down anchor and float in the waves, an airship eventually had to find someplace to land. There was a rough landing platform at the British camp, but nothing yet in Balaklava. Without a proper airship wharf, loading and unloading the *Horizon* would be enormously complex and a tremendous strain on the ship and her crew.

Carter apparently was thinking along the same lines, for he snapped out, "We could burn up our entire coal stores just moving cargo from the *Morning Star* to shore." He pointed angrily at the muddy fields. "And where the hell are we supposed to put everything? On the ground to rot?"

Roberts turned his worried gaze to the *Morning Star*. The merchant marine carried a generous supply of anthracite, but the *Horizon* couldn't afford to waste coal aimlessly hovering in the sky. Roberts had to quickly determine if Crimea held any coal deposits. If not, anthracite would have to be shipped up, at prohibitive costs.

With those thoughts chewing at him, Roberts ordered the *Horizon* down to a hover so that he and Carter could slide overboard. When their feet hit the ground, mud engulfed them halfway up to their knees. With a squelching pop, both men pulled their feet free of the mud and began slogging across the crowded ground in search of information.

It was slow and hard going. Mud sucked at their feet, and disorganized towers of equipment halted their passage. Soldiers, some in ragged uniforms and some simply in rags, milled around anxiously awaiting orders. Many of them were scarcely in their teens, and far too many clearly regretted their decision to enlist. A few glanced quizzically at Roberts and Carter but seemed too intent on their own private miseries to question two civilians in their midst.

Near a small huddle of rickety tents, Roberts and Carter found a cluster of harried officers in deep conversation. Roberts pushed forward, Carter at his heels. "Gentlemen, I'm Captain

Roberts of the merchant airship *Horizon*," he announced. "My ship has Class Five certification for military transport." His words had a remarkable effect, and looks of irritation vanished as Roberts' words took effect.

"A transport airship, thank God," an officer breathed out. "Captain, you're a sight welcome. All we have in the air are two military vessels, and we can't move supplies inland for love or money." He ran a distracted hand through his thinning hair. "I've got carts stuck from here to camp. My men have tried moving supplies but it's damned pointless with all this mud."

"My airship came ready to work," Roberts spoke firmly. "She flew with the merchant marine *Morning Star* who's in harbor, loaded to her stacks." He paused significantly. "Unloading her will be a job since you've no wharf here."

"I have plenty of men who can unload her," the officer responded. "I also have equipment and supplies here in Balaklava that need moving to camp." He smiled thinly. "We are in dire need of airship transport. As soon as you can get your ship in the air won't be fast enough."

Roberts nodded carefully. "And just what sort of enemy action am I flying my ship into, sir?" he questioned evenly.

The man shook himself, righting his shoulders. "Captain Grim," he stated. "I've the pleasure of commanding this fine harbor here. I can tell you, Captain Roberts, that you won't encounter much in the sky but yourself."

"The last sighting of an enemy airship was three days ago, five miles to the east of Balaklava," another officer added. "We have two military airships on constant patrol. They will be on the lookout for anything that wishes harm to your ship."

"With only two military airships, I can't offer them to you as escorts," Grim warned Roberts. "Still, it's barely five miles from here to camp. The main action is happening in Sevastopol. There's little to bother you in this part of Crimea as long as you keep your ship high enough in the air to avoid ground fire."

"Captain Grim, my ship is fast, and she'll dodge anything you throw at her," Roberts announced. "But she needs a place to land. There were two berths at Calamita Bay and damned poor ones at that. I bring my airship to Balaklava, and she's got nowhere to set down and load up. I can load her in air, but it's tricky and dangerous and will waste time she could use bringing supplies to camp."

Roberts paused significantly. "My airship is contracted with the *Morning Star*. I'll fulfill my contract and bring her cargo to camp. But," he paused again. "I will tell you this, Captain Grim." He fixed the man with a steely glare. "The next time I bring my airship to Balaklava, if there's not a wharf and a berth waiting for her, then she's turning back to Constantinople and not returning. That, I hold up as a promise."

Grim nodded wearily. "That is not an unreasonable promise, Captain Roberts." He smiled tiredly. "I will labor to ensure that you do not have to make good on it."

"My ship will need coal," Roberts continued. "Anthracite if we can get it."

"Sadly, our resources indicate that local coal supplies are scanty at best," another officer answered rather pompously. "Most of the merchant marine ships bring their own coal stores from Constantinople."

Carter stiffened in indignation. "Well, *sir*, marine ships don't run the risk of dropping out of the sky when they run out of fuel," he answered acerbically.

Roberts silenced his bosun with a hard look, then turned back to the officers. "Sirs, I've got brave men and a fast airship. She'll take on any Russian airship you care to name, and she's strong enough to transport what you need. But..." he let the words linger in the air as he looked at the faces of the officers. "She can't fly on an empty belly and she hasn't time to waste tracking down fuel. She can load in air but that triples her loading time. Every hour she wastes getting fueled and loaded up means less supplies getting to camp."

The officers made no motion to protest or counter Roberts' words. He looked them over again and pronounced heavily, "You get me what my ship needs, and I can promise you that she'll keep your men from starving."

Silence fell for a second, then Grim shifted his weight restlessly. "I'll do what I can, Captain Roberts," he announced wearily. "But you must understand that half my men don't have a decent pair of boots to claim as their own, food stores are rotting as we speak, and we are setting in for what promises to be a long and hard siege, not to mention that winter will soon fall."

"You want..." Roberts cut in, but the captain held up his hand for silence. "I can only work within the limits of my abilities and means, Captain Roberts," he stated quietly.

Roberts glared at him, but the captain continued, "If you will permit me, Captain, I will leave you in the hands of Staff Sergeant Prachett. He is the quartermaster in Balaklava and will assist you further."

Grim nodded at a rough, badly-shaved man standing a little apart from the others. Unlike the officers, this man had remained silent and unmoving, quietly observing the situation without betraying any of his inner thoughts. He looked like a sensible man, and Roberts let himself be escorted back to the *Horizon* by Prachett, an irate Carter trailing behind them.

Nothing was said for a few minutes as the three men slipped their way through the mud, fighting valiantly to keep their balance. Roberts had a suspicion that Prachett was sizing him up before speaking, and he remained silent until the staff sergeant spoke first.

"What's her fuel consumption per flight hour, Captain Roberts?" Prachett demanded, his voice gravely and clipped.

"Fully loaded and in these flight conditions, she'll take around a hundred pounds an hour, maybe a bit less," Roberts responded. "My ship flies on anthracite. If I have to put bituminous in her, she'll eat up a lot more."

He paused, waiting while Prachett chewed this over. "There's some mine works here in Crimea," the staff sergeant offered carefully. "I'll have a talk with the locals. There's not much work available here, and the local men take what jobs they can." He smiled marginally. "Your bird's a picky eater."

"It wasn't my choice," Roberts stated flatly. "But my ship demands anthracite and I'll find it for her."

Another thoughtful silence followed, then Prachett pointed at the shoreline where the remains of a marine ship lie.

She had been stripped, her skeletal ribs forlorn in the bleak sunlight. "The *Augustine* limped into port some three weeks ago, riddled with holes and good for nothing but scrap. There's good timber in her, enough to build a place for your little bird to rest her head."

"What about the other airships?" Carter interrupted angrily. "The military has contracts with other transport flyers, don't they?"

"Lad, we don't have the funds to feed half our soldiers, let alone fill the sky with transport airships," Prachett stated calmly. "Even if we did, most captains won't fly this far." He nodded at Roberts approvingly, then continued, "Best thing for us would be for a long-flight airship to make her way to Crimea, but even if she could get here, we'd have no place to land her. It's easier moving supplies hundreds of miles up the Black Sea than from Balaklava to camp."

"I'll hold to my terms with Captain Grim," Roberts warned. "If there's not a decent wharf waiting for my airship when she next flies up, I'm turning her back to Constantinople."

"I heard you the first time, Captain Roberts," Prachett said quietly but without rancor. "You keep your ship flying. I'll handle the rest."

His confident words mollified Roberts, who still had deep misgivings about the overwhelming logistics facing them. Thinking hard, he glanced across the bay and saw a longboat rowing quickly across the dark waters. Fosselweight was in command, and by his terse gestures to his sailors, he too was wholly displeased by what he found in Balaklava Bay.

When the longboat reached the shore, Fosselweight stepped ashore and Roberts introduced him to Prachett. Making little effort to suppress a sigh, Fosselweight questioned wearily, "Am I to understand that we are to unload my ship with longboats?" He looked pointedly at the noticeable absence of a wharf and the visible abundance of obstacles.

Prachett lit a badly formed rollup with unhurried movements. "I've plenty of soldiers with nothing to do but wait for orders. There's enough hands to get your ship unloaded, Captain Fosselweight." To Roberts, he said, "Captain Roberts, there's supplies rotting in the mud here in the bay. You know your work best, but if you'd be willing to transport the old goods up to camp before starting on the fresh supplies, you can name your transport price."

Roberts nodded, weighing the situation carefully. The old supplies clogging up the bay were soaked and rotting. Just prying them loose from the mud would be a challenge, much less loading them into the *Horizon* while she was airborne. He was surrounded by weeks of work but not nearly enough fuel to see it done. He would keep enough in reserve to bring the *Horizon* back to Constantinople, but the rest she would swallow up quickly.

Moodily pondering these thoughts, Roberts parted ways with Prachett and Fosselweight and signaled to the *Horizon*. As her engines roared closer, a yelp of surprise caught his attention. Turning, he saw Carter lose his balance and fall face-first into a deep puddle of watery mud. Brown droplets cascaded through the air and splashed Roberts.

Carter lay motionless in the thick brown slurry for a moment before pushing up on his forearms. His tanned features were completely unrecognizable under a thick coating of mud, and he was soaked from head to toe. Still prone in the slippery mud, Carter was silent for one moment before offering comment on his predicament.

"You know, Captain, I've heard Barbados is a fine place this time of year," he offered with a demented sort of cheerfulness. "Sunshine, rum, women, a bit of honest piracy." Scrabbling for purchase, Carter tried to rise to his feet. "Running rum pays a fine amount, so I've heard."

Roberts laughed. "Get your arse out of the mud, airman," he commanded with gruff joviality. "We've got work to do."

      ***   ***   ***   ***

And work they certainly had to do. Six days of grinding toil passed, and the *Horizon* spent very little of it stationary, catching only small rests on the decrepit airship wharf at the British camp. Otherwise, she trudged steadily back and forth from Balaklava to the camp, her belly loaded with food, ammunition, medical supplies, and clothing while her engines churned steadily.

Her crew ate and slept when they could, each man straining himself to the utmost. Wracked with fatigue and overworked himself, Roberts exhorted his men while monitoring them all for signs that he had pushed too hard. Both Harding and Roberts kept a worrying eye on Oboe who was not fully recovered and needed a month of convalescence somewhere warm. The first mate, however, would submit to rest with reluctance, duty pushing him forward.

The rest of the men kept grimly at their work, finding the strength somewhere to continue despite the demands of each day. Each time the *Horizon* flew into the British camp and gingerly set her keel on the rickety airship berth, there was a crowd waiting for her. Haggard, starving faces of soldiers lit up when the *Horizon* sailed in carrying food, bullets, bandages, tents, clothing, and other desperately needed items, and this was a tangible steadying point to the crew. It put fresh determination in them and kept the crew resolute, determine to play their part in the war.

In the midst of endless work, Roberts had little time to spare for anything but his airship and crew. He had almost forgotten about Miss Pickens and that she and her brother had sailed up on the *Morning Star*. It was a bit of a shock when a longboat rowed to shore on their third day in Crimea, and Miss Pickens gingerly stepped off it. She was helped off the boat by Jules and a solicitous Fosselweight who fussed about her, fretting over the mud and glaring at soldiers who dared glance her way, amazed at finding a woman in a war zone.

Wisely, Miss Pickens had dressed for rough conditions. Her customary elegant clothing had been replaced by a dress and coat of sensible, hard-wearing fabric, her long skirts trailing in the mud. Yet her plain garments did not disguise her beauty, nor her firm determination, and her eyes were serious as they swept the bay and turned in Roberts' direction.

Chivalry and longing compelled him forward, and Roberts squished through the mud to take Miss Pickens' arm in his, steadying her against the slippery earth under their feet.

"Captain Roberts," she said with warmth, her tones musical and low to his ears as her brown eyes searched his face carefully.

"How are you?" Concern touched her voice. "You look like you haven't slept in weeks."

"There's been little time for sleep, Miss Pickens," Roberts replied. Despite his fatigue, the thrill of having a lovely woman on his arm, especially one looking at him with such grave concern, rekindled his energy. For a moment, he felt a genuine wave of gladness at being in Miss Pickens' presence. This brief slice of time was quickly ruined by Fosselweight bustling up to possessively reclaim the reporter's arm.

Yet Miss Pickens continued with her thoughtful expression. "Our Captain Roberts looks quite worn out." She gave Fosselweight a look of mild sternness. "I do hope you have not been exhausting him, Archie."

Archie, Roberts repeated the word in his head, noting the familiarity with a low growl of jealousy. Fosselweight bristled momentarily but responded with graciousness. "I am afraid that, due to the *Horizon* being the only transport airship currently operating in Crimea, I am forced to overextend the good will of Captain Roberts and the strength of his men."

He gave a bow in Roberts' direction, a gesture that was lost on Miss Pickens, who was examining her surroundings with a calculating eye. When she swung her gaze back to the two men, there was hardness in her expression. "To have only one transport airship in the skies is an inexcusable laxity on part of our military," Miss Pickens responded with some heat.

Roberts shrugged his shoulders. "This is a bad patch of air for any airship to fly, Miss Pickens," he responded. "There's no coal, few places to land, visibility is poor six days out of seven, winter's setting in, and we're in a war zone."

A long, slender finger stabbed the air angrily. "Captain Roberts, I do not need to remind you that there are cartons of moldering food and supplies sinking in the mud as we speak. Only a few miles away is a camp where thousands of men are starving and dying of disease."

Miss Pickens swept her hand out, gesturing in the distance. "From this position, I count at least a dozen abandoned wagons buried past their axles in mud. It is patently clear to even the most casual observer that land transport throughout Crimea is an impossible feat, and it will remain so until the summer sun dries up the worst of this mud."

Light flashed darkly in her eyes. "It appears, sirs, that we have a government that has conscripted nearly forty thousand men and shipped them to this barren wasteland with little thought whatsoever to their provisioning. The casualty reports I have been able to gather have been inexplicably high, and winter will greatly increase the number of deaths."

Fosselweight grew quiet under the reporter's terse words, his indignation turning to solemn sadness. Reaching for Miss Pickens' arm, he said quietly, "Come, my dear Miss Pickens. We detain Captain Roberts, and you have stood in the mud far longer than is good for your health. I insist that you return to the *Morning Star*."

She did not protest, but her brows were hard as she stepped reluctantly away from shore, still examining the bay. With a few parting words, the pair left Roberts' side to return to the *Morning Star*. Roberts watched her go with longing clanging around in his innards. He tried to fight it, knowing Miss Pickens was trouble embodied, but he hadn't the strength to mount a successful resistance. It was all he could do to sigh wearily and slog back to his airship.

In the days to come, Roberts took pains to avoid Miss Pickens, and with nonstop work waiting for the *Horizon*, that was not a difficult task. After seven days in Crimea passed, he and Fosselweight had a serious conversation about the future. They were both slumped exhausted in Fosselweight's elegant state room and, despite the formality of the room, the two men inhabiting it were anything but. Roberts' clothes were heavy with mud and his chin was rough with hastily sheared stubble. Fosselweight's jacket was off and his cuffs flapped listlessly around his wrists.

"This is foolish," Fosselweight stated emphatically. "The *Horizon* cannot do everything. Your men are exhausted, Gavin. *You* are exhausted. You are pushing your ship and your men to the limits."

Wearily, Roberts noted the use of his Christian name, a first for Fosselweight. "What would you have me do, Archibald?" he questioned tiredly, running a hand through his greasy hair. A strand of it wrapped around his fingers and, examining it, he discovered it was grey from root to tip.

Roberts could not argue with Fosselweight; his airship was holding up bravely, but the strain was weighing heavily on her. All her cargo had to be brought up in the lift basket or hauled on board. This created enormous strain and a host of balancing issues that ate up hours of time and valuable energy. The *Horizon* couldn't continue much longer in these conditions, and neither could her crew.

"We must return to Constantinople," Fosselweight stated firmly. "We will partner with other marine ships and find more airships to assist the *Horizon*. Before we return to Crimea, we fill my ship with as much anthracite as she can carry. The military is searching for anthracite in Crimea, and I've a good notion that they will find it before long."

"More airships won't do any damned good without a wharf," Roberts shrugged. Staff Sergeant Prachett had remained true to his word, and construction had begun on an airship wharf, using wood cannibalized from the doomed *Augustine*. Roberts had serious doubts that the wharf would be finished before winter hit. Adding more airships in Crimea was pointless without enough places for them to land.

Fosselweight huffed. "If the *Horizon* were to remove herself from Crimea for a few weeks, it will take scarcely any time at all for the military to conclude that your airship's assistance is invaluable to the success of this war and the survival of our soldiers. I've a good notion that your entirely reasonable demands for a secure landing wharf and a local coal source would be then carried out with alacrity."

Fosselweight's logic was sound and his proposal reasonable. Roberts conceded and the two captains agreed to depart for Constantinople the next day. Leaving the *Morning Star*, Roberts sought out Prachett to inform him of their plans. He then broke the word to his crew, who cheered at the news. Not one of them seemed eager to tarry in Crimea.

The next day at dawn, the two ships left Balaklava. It was a poor day to travel: the waves were choppy and the sky was shot through with sullen grey, shrouding the air and reducing visibility. Low visibility could be fatal in a war zone, and Roberts' men kept a scowling watch on the air surrounding them, alert for the slightest sign than an enemy airship was lurking in the fog.

"I've seen better flying days, Captain," Barking Jack commented to Roberts with unaccustomed soberness. The pilot's face was haggard, exhaustion breaking through his normal lighthearted spirits.

Standing next to his pilot, Roberts caught the sound of grinding metal riding in the noise of the *Horizon's* engines. He shifted his attention to Barking Jack's construct arm. The limb moved with a strange jerkiness, then froze at the elbow.

"Dammit," Barking Jack growled and banged his arm against the wheel. A cog or two whirled sharply as the scent of burning oil filled the air.

Roberts took the wheel. "Report to Halloway," he commanded. "He'll fix it." Long hours on pilot duty, exposed to the corroding influences of rain and wind, wreaked plenty of damage on Barking Jack's construct limbs, and they frequently needed Halloway's attention.

Barking Jack obeyed, and Roberts tiredly steered his airship forward into the grey skies. She was moving well, but there was the slightest hint of vibration in her movements that suggested all was not quite perfectly tuned below deck. He suspected it was the Number Two engine.

"Is it too much to ask for everything on board to work properly for more than a day?" Roberts said conversationally into the air. As he voiced this statement, the *Horizon's* engines growled deeply and the airship shuddered in the sky. A yowl of frustration, most likely from Halloway, sounded below decks as feet pounded their way towards the engine room.

Feeling uncannily as if his airship had just laughed at him, Roberts wearily patted the wheel. "Come, pretty lady," he coaxed her tiredly. "Just get us to Constantinople in one piece."

Chapter Sixteen

"You damned fool, Captain Roberts," the rough, burly airship captain spat out, following the words with a wad of chewing tobacco that fell to the filthy decks of the wharf.

Roberts didn't budge. "There's good money to be made in Crimea," he proclaimed stoutly.

"And chance to get ship blown out of sky," the other airship captain retorted in broken, yet purposeful English, his swarthy complexion giving away his Spanish heritage. "I no fly my ship there." He stabbed a finger across the Black Sea. "I hear word from others. No coal, see? No wharf." He made a dismissive gesture, then pointed at the *Horizon*. "One gun, one ship." He rolled his eyes derisively. "Only *loco* man fly that."

Roberts sighed internally. They had touched down in Constantinople before dawn, and he had spent the morning trying to convince a few more airships to join their endeavors in Crimea. So far his efforts had been wholly fruitless. Airmen were risk-takers by nature and lived on the thin edge, but few were willing to risk the sheer insanity of operating in Crimea. Until the Army installed better infrastructure in Crimea, few airship captains would turn their prows that direction.

The Spanish captain gave Roberts another derisive look, then his expression shifted and a wolfish look crossed his face. "Look there," he said, jerking his chin to the right. His voice became a growl, deep and primal. "Like her in your bed, no?" he grinned salaciously.

Roberts shifted his eyes and saw Miss Pickens standing on the wharf with Jules at her side. His fists tightened as the other captain commented, "I pay good gold for her..."

Roberts' fist crashed into the captain's jaw with juddering force, knocking him backwards. Shaking his hand out, Roberts eyed the other man, poised to deliver another round of retribution.

"Stay the hell away from her," he snarled fiercely. With that, he stalked away, his hand still coursing with pain. The man's jaw had been particularly hard, but Roberts' fury pushed away much of the pain as he thundered down the wharf toward Miss Pickens.

By the time he had reached her side, Roberts had regained his control. His forced calmness was unsettled as Miss Pickens smiled at him, warmth in the curve of her lips. "Captain Roberts," she stated in a low purr. "An uneventful journey, I trust?"

"Fair enough," Roberts responded, determined to keep his jittering emotions in check. "Had you fair sailings with the *Morning Star*?"

Her smile increased. "Quite well, thank you," Miss Pickens said cheerfully. "Captain Fosselweight is a most affable host." At her side, Jules looked faintly green and his nod of respect at Roberts was brief.

"Ah, Captain Roberts, excellent, excellent," Fosselweight said as he appeared suddenly, bustling and rather distracted. "Back in jolly Constantinople again," he stated, his eyes not leaving Miss Pickens' face.

"Yes," she responded with a smile. "There is much work awaiting Jules and I at the *Constantinople Times*." She patted Fosselweight's hand, seeing his crestfallen look. "But do not worry, my good sirs. We will see each other soon."

Roberts saw it in a flash, the thin edge of unswerving determination and cunning in her soft smile. Fosselweight was oblivious, but warning clanged in Roberts.

She's plotting something, he thought to himself. *And Fosselweight is walking right into it, damned fool that he is.* Such thoughts did not leave him as the reporter and her silent brother bid farewell to both captains and disappeared into the tangled web of the city.

***   ***   ***   ***

It was October 25th when the *Horizon* turned back to Crimea again, this time in the company of the airship *Icarus* while the *Morning Star* and the merchant marine *Spirituous* churned through the waters below. Fosselweight had struck up an agreement with the captain of the *Spirituous* and Roberts had been successful in convincing the *Icarus* to fly with the *Horizon*.

The marine ships were heavily laden with supplies, and the *Horizon* carried a large store of anthracite. The *Spirituous* was full of bituminous for both itself and the *Icarus*. Roberts had warned the two captains that they would find little coal in Crimea, and they had planned accordingly. Roberts was expecting to find no anthracite waiting for his airship when she arrived at Balaklava. All he could do was let the *Morning Star* carry enough coal for the *Horizon* to complete the job.

As much as he was glad to have another merchant airship join him, it wasn't long before Roberts wished he was flying with the *Horus* again. Upon first meeting, Captain Firmin of the *Icarus* hadn't much impressed Roberts. He was younger than Roberts by several years and rather lackadaisical, interested mainly in what profit he could expect and unconcerned about the dangers ahead. Now that he had seen the *Icarus* fly, Roberts suspected that the airship would be more of a hindrance than anything else.

Thinking this over, Roberts approached the helm where Bloomberg stood on duty. Quietly, he cautioned the pilot, "Best keep an eye on the *Icarus*. I'm not liking how she's flying."

Bloomberg nodded. "Myself neither, Captain. I don't pride myself for being a master pilot and won't for a long time, but they've got a young fool at the wheel."

"Just keep her steady," Roberts said evenly. "Let's get to Balaklava in one piece."

"If they have a place for us, Captain," Bloomberg muttered unhappily.

"I made an agreement with Staff Sergeant Prachett," Roberts stated with a frown. "If the military wants a transport airship in Crimea, they'll make a place for us to land. If not, there's plenty of work elsewhere."

Bloomberg said nothing, but the question of what awaited them in Crimea weighed heavily on the crew during their flight. When the ships rounded the tip of Kamiesch Bay three days later, Roberts took the *Horizon* ahead to scout out conditions in Balaklava. He was pleased to discover a nearly finished airship wharf jutting up from the mud with two finished berths waiting. Men wrestled wooden beams into place and pounded nails energetically. However, the visual appearance of the wharf and the haste at which it was being constructed made Roberts question its structural integrity.

He and Oboe examined the new wharf from the safety of the *Horizon* while she circled overhead, waiting for the *Icarus* to fly into Balaklava. Arms crossed and chin sunk into his chest, Roberts commented, "Think it will hold us?"

"One would hope so, Captain," Oboe responded slowly, eyes steady and measuring.

The *Icarus*, however, answered the question for them by zipping forward and landing on a berth with haste. It didn't collapse under her weight, and Roberts finally called for the *Horizon* to land. Bloomberg gingerly set her down and to everyone's relief, the wooden structure didn't wobble or creak. With the airship secured, Roberts left the crew to tend her while he stepped into camp for information.

Just off the new wharf, Roberts was met by Prachett, who acknowledged him with a nod. "Glad to have you back, Captain Roberts." The staff sergeant measured him carefully and Roberts returned his gaze evenly, then turned his attention to the new airship wharf.

Prachett let the silence fall for a moment before announcing, "I've just had news from the local miners. They think they've hit a vein of anthracite. It's buried deep and a bugger to shift, but they seem confident they can get your ship the coal she needs."

Roberts was relieved, but he did not let his elation show. "You know my terms, Staff Sergeant."

"Your bird has a place to lay her head," Prachett responded calmly. "Not the prettiest, but it will hold your ship. No more loading in the air." With measured words, he said, "We have need of your ship as long as you will keep her here."

"So far, I haven't seen reason to lift her out of Balaklava," Roberts responded. Prachett took the words without a frown and, as Roberts watched, the staff sergeant turned towards the *Icarus*.

After several minutes of observation, Prachett said slowly, "We're badly in need of airships in Crimea, but if that dicey little tub can last the winter without a crash, I'll be hanged, hanged twice if she can handle a running drop like your ship."

"She flies like a drunken sow," Roberts stated tersely. "I've seen little I've liked of her captain and I'll be keeping two eyes on her when she's anywhere near my ship." He gave Prachett a meaningful look. "But she's all I could convince to fly up here. If she can do her work and keep away from my airship, I've use for her."

"If the *Icarus* can move supplies from bay to camp, then your ship would be more useful in the fields," Prachett said. "We've hundreds of soldiers starving in camps around Crimea. Ground transport of supplies is damned hard." He paused. "It would be a risk for your ship, but we need her to fly if you're willing. I can get you an airship escort when one can be spared, but I can't guarantee it for every trip."

Roberts cast his eyes up to the low-hanging clouds, thinking of what hazards could lurk in the skies. A soldier slogged past him, limping painfully on a rude crutch. It was the soldier's face, young and lined with pain and desperation, that steeled Roberts' resolve.

Heavily, he turned back to Prachett. "Where do you most need me to fly?"

Chapter Seventeen

Faces, gaunt and filthy, looked up in eager anticipation as the *Horizon* dipped down from the clouds toward the bedraggled camp below. Shouts rose in the air as a crowd of soldiers hurried forward, many hobbling from their wounds and some making do with just one leg. A ragged line of sagging tents was all the shelter provided, not enough to house the camp's soldiers. There was a line of prone bodies lying directly on the ground, either injured or waiting interment in a small graveyard visible to the south.

The camp below the *Horizon's* hull was small and perched on the very edge of the British-defended territory near the town of Kamara. From what Roberts had heard, the nearby Worononzoff Road had been impassible for over two weeks, leaving the soldiers at the mercy of the elements and subsiding on whatever food they could forage or steal. As a result, the growing crowd under the *Horizon's* hull was turning into a mob of crazed soldiers eager to get their hands on whatever she was carrying. Running drops were never easy under the best of circumstances, and this situation was particularly tricky. It was nearing dusk, fitful light from the setting sun casting distorted shadows across the mud while a light spatter of rain fell to earth. The soldiers below were only getting in the way and making it even harder to see the ground.

Roberts bellowed heavily, "Prepare for the drop! Steady, boys, we've got an eager crowd below. I don't want the ship mobbed." The *Horizon* had flown into isolated camps full of starving men before, and the desperate welcome she received usually meant that the soldiers would be nothing but hazard. Discipline was patchy at best in many of these camps, and starvation could easily turn a man feral.

Stepping up to the helm, Roberts ordered steadily, "Easy, Mister Jack. I don't want to take on any passengers." Aside from the risk of crushing soldiers under the *Horizon's* gondola or slamming the airship into the ground, the crew also had to watch for any desperate soldier keen for a lift out of camp. The crew had fended off several potential stowaways on earlier flights and were alert for more.

"I won't see her pulled down, Captain," Barking Jack ground out sharply, his one flesh hand gripping the wheel tightly and his back rigid. Roberts knew that the pilot hated performing running drops, but Bloomberg was not skilled enough to attempt the maneuver. Roberts wasn't even sure if he would trust Oboe or himself to perform a proper running drop. For now, the onus was on Barking Jack.

"Fifty feet, Captain!" Carter sang out as Roberts kept his eyes fastened on the scene below which was turning ugly. The massed crowd was growing in strength and size and making no attempt to clear a spot for the approaching *Horizon*.

"Captain," Oboe's voice sounded at Roberts' side. "I do not like the looks of what is below."

"Neither do I," Roberts replied grimly.

"Thirty feet and falling, Captain!" Carter announced.

After a second of thought, Roberts ordered, "Drop her to ten feet and hold, Mister Jack!" The pilot gave a stiff nod, his attention wholly focused on the intricate drop procedure.

After a few tense minutes, the airship lowered to ten feet and held steady, moving forward at eight knots. With the *Horizon* so close, the men on the ground were growing increasingly agitated. The able-bodied ones followed the *Horizon*'s path, getting underfoot and missing her propellers by mere feet. Officers were trying to restore order, but military discipline was tenuous. Roberts feared a riot once the *Horizon* got within grabbing distance.

He let out a long, tense breath as he ran through his options. A running drop was tricky enough as it was, and it required a cooperative ground crew below or at least people with enough sense to get out of the way. All it would take was some determined soul, and the mass of men clustered below could grow violent.

Frowning, Roberts gave the command. "Drop us down, Mister Jack! All hands, prepare for the drop! Mister Oboe!" he added, "The helm is yours. I will personally supervise the unloading."

The first mate nodded, and Roberts hurried down the ladder. He didn't like leaving topside at a moment like this, but below decks was more critical. Big Tom, Long Tom, Carter, and Farrington were in the cargo bay and opened the bay doors at Roberts' command. The doors swung open to reveal faces craning upwards desperately. Even with the airship ten feet above ground, men were still clustered directly under her as if poised to bear her away on their shoulders.

Officers bellowed for order, but Roberts could smell the tension in the air, the crowd a blade's edge from exploding into a mob. Soldiers crowded around the airship, the taller ones reaching up to bang their hands against her sides as she lowered down to eight feet. At Roberts' order, Long Tom and Carter pushed the first crate forward into the waiting arms of the soldiers below. A group of men directly underneath it caught it up and bore it away quickly, others stepping in to take their place.

Another crate was handed down and accepted, and a moiety of relief fell over Roberts. A riot was kept thinly at bay by officers threatening a lead earplug to any soldier who decided to grab what he could get. As the minutes sped by, this tenuous control frayed and the situation grew out of control. The crowd was pressing in too hard, too hungry, too wild, overwhelming the officers as they shouted for order.

One soldier, bolder and more desperate than the others, climbed up the back of another soldier and grabbed the cargo door frame, struggling to pull himself into the *Horizon*. Roberts stepped heavily on the unwanted fingers and bellowed, "MISTER JACK! TAKE US BACK UP TO FIFTY FEET AND HOLD!" Through the noise and chaos of the milling soldiers below, he wasn't sure if the pilot could hear the barked orders. Within a second or two, Barking Jack's voice piped out of the com device.

"Aye, Captain!" the pilot called back, but Roberts could hear the aggravation in his voice. The *Horizon* had just properly settled in at six feet. Pulling her back up in the air was a strenuous demand on her engines and her pilot. Roberts was aware of this but if he didn't get his little bird back into the sky soon, she was liable to be pulled to the ground and ripped apart by the starving soldiers.

Soldiers below cried out in dismay and anger as the *Horizon* began climbing upwards. Roberts, eyes on the crowd, saw a few rifles being aimed in their direction, but other minds, wiser and more steady, saw to it that no bullets were loosed. In several lightning-fast steps, he was topdeck. Eyes swung in his direction, seeking leadership and direction.

"Captain!" Barking Jack bellowed, the question hanging in the air. Roberts gripped his hands into fists, his mind spinning furiously.

There was really only one option available, other than heading back to Balaklava. The soldiers desperately needed the *Horizon*'s cargo. However, military discipline in the camp was threatening to break out into a free-for-all, and the airship and crew were in peril if they lowered close to the ground again. Bracing himself, Roberts gave his orders.

"Mister Jack! Dead ahead two hundred yards and drop to eight feet. Every man that can be spared, to the cargo bay. Once we drop to eight feet, shove as much as you can out the door. We'll lift when they get too close, then repeat until we've shoved everything out the door."

His orders were received with a palpable lack of enthusiasm, but the men were quick to obey. Barking Jack did not move from his hunched position over the wheel as he prepared to carry out his captain's commands. One running drop was tricky enough, and Roberts had just ordered Barking Jack to porpoise the *Horizon* through the air in a quick succession of waves, low and slow enough to get the cargo out but quick enough to stay one step ahead of the crowd.

It took four near landings before everything in the cargo bay had been shoved hastily out the door. The unloading crew didn't bother with finesse. Although some of the crates broke when they hit the ground, much of what they contained was food and clothing which stood a good chance of surviving the brief drop. Once the first load was dropped, the eager soldiers fell upon it and most of them ignored the *Horizon* as she performed the other three drops.

The moment they shoved the last crate overboard, Long Tom and Carter pulled the bay doors shut and Barking Jack jerked the *Horizon's* nose up to the sky. As she climbed upwards, moving quickly away from the disorganized scrum of bodies, Roberts caught a glimpse of several soldiers starting a fight over a crate. Shouts ripped through the air, mixing with the engines, but suddenly the crisp staccato of a revolver cut through the tension.

In the rush to get the *Horizon* up in elevation, Roberts only saw a brief flash of the event, saw an officer lower his pistol to his side, saw the crowd widen dramatically, forming a ring around a pool of blood and a limp body. A flour sack was ripped open, white powder scattered on the muddy earth, red blood like rose petals on snow. The fallen man was clutching a tin of something, likely potted meat worth a shilling at best. It had cost him his life.

You poor damned fool, Roberts thought as the *Horizon* lifted him away from the grim scene and into clean, empty skies once again.

Chapter Eighteen

"*No*," Roberts growled, the picture of a man unmoved.

Captain Grim stiffened, but his voice was almost pleading as he spoke. "They *must* be transported to camp, Captain Roberts. I have explicit orders..."

"I said no, Captain Grim," Roberts repeated with increased volume. He stared icily at the proposed cargo. There had to be sixty of the damned things, all stamping about inside a rickety pen. "I've no way to secure them and I'll not have them running around my airship shitting at will and throwing everything off balance."

Grim inhaled sharply. "I am authorized to offer you triple your standard transport fee," he stated, watching Roberts closely. "The cavalry is particularly desirous of their delivery. These are highly trained animals and their value is immense. In a difficult operation like this, I would trust only the *Horizon* to see them delivered safely."

Horses, Roberts thought with irate disbelief. A lifetime city boy, he knew little of the equine species save that it was fragile, noisy, and inclined to panic at the slightest provocation. The thought of even one of these damned things inside the *Horizon* made his head ache. The plum transport fee was tempting, but the wear and tear incurred to the airship due to the cargo could easily eat up all the profits. Rarely were airships pressed into service to transport livestock, for airship captains were disinclined to take on heavy cargo that moved of its own accord. Roberts had never lifted with animals on board, and he didn't intend to start now.

A Class Three marine ship carrying seventy-three cavalry horses from Gibraltar had arrived just that day in Crimea. Nine of the animals had died during the journey, and the rest were out of condition and restless after weeks of standing in their stalls. They pawed the muddy ground, snorting impatiently and flicking their tails. Roberts looked them over and tried to think of less desirable cargo to transport.

Carter and Farrington were at Roberts' side, surveying the proposed cargo with expressions of dismay. Carter whistled loudly and he scratched his head in thought. He turned to Farrington and said without much conviction, "Well, if we reckon ten each load..."

"Either we take the time to build stalls for them all or we tie them in place during transport," Farrington countered sharply. "They'll probably panic the second we take off..."

Oh God, Roberts groaned to himself, already picturing what might happen if he transported the horses. It would be far too easy for a horse to break its leg, fall over, or crash around in the cargo bay and knock the airship off balance.

Grim, however, was insistent. "I can make no promises, Captain Roberts," he stated quietly, "But I can tell you that the Earl of Lucan has been eagerly awaiting the delivery of these horses for months. An airship captain who can see them safely delivered to the Earl can be reasonably assured that his efforts will go neither unnoticed nor unrewarded."

He pointed to a massive dark stallion who was pawing the ground imperially. "That one there is especially for the Earl himself. The horse has a bloodline far superior to many noblemen. He's worth a king's ransom."

Eyeing the stallion, Roberts assessed it critically. He was no horseman but he could see that the animal was a magnificent beast of peerless lineage, exceedingly valuable and obviously full of its own importance, from its regal head to the proud swishing of its tail. On board an airship, though, there were a multitude of ways a prized warhorse could accidentally meet with a crippling injury. Roberts did not even want to entertain how dearly it would cost him should the *Horizon* deliver the stallion to Lucan in less than pristine condition. Once cargo was on board his airship, it was Roberts' full responsibility. The stallion pawing at the ground was a heavy responsibility indeed.

Trying to suppress a sigh of impatience, Roberts demanded of Grim, "Captain, the ground's firmer than I've seen it for weeks. You've got mud in Balaklava, but it wouldn't be impossible to move the horses inland. They've got four legs apiece. They can walk to camp."

Grim shook his head firmly. "Orders from the Earl himself. He wants them delivered by air." He gave Roberts a calculating look. "Your airship has been rapidly building a reputation for herself, Captain Roberts, and it has not been lost on my superiors. They know you are a man of your word who makes results happen."

Roberts' bark of a laugh was bitter in the cold air. "There's men starving as we speak and your superiors want to take up valuable time having my ship and crew fly a bunch of damned horses to camp."

"In blunt terms, yes, Captain," Grim responded. "The Earl was quite insistent on this point." He shrugged. "I have my orders, Captain Roberts."

Knowing that he would seriously regret this decision, Roberts sighed and turned to Carter and Farrington. Both men were deep in a hushed conversation about the logistics of transporting the horses. His lowered shoulders signaled defeat to Grim, who nodded in relief. "Alright, Captain," Roberts stated gruffly. "If the Earl wants to pay a pretty penny for the *Horizon* to transport horseflesh, I'll see them delivered. It's a damned fool's errand, but I'll see it done."

"Be sure that you do, Captain Roberts," Grim responded coldly, and it was on chilly terms that the two parted ways. Roberts returned to the *Horizon* with Carter and Farrington trailing behind him, still bickering about the best way to refit the airship as a livestock carrier.

Back on the airship, Farrington and Carter's debate was augmented by the addition of Oboe, Long Tom, and Barking Jack. Roberts moderated the discussion, carefully weighing his men's input, and the argument spilled over into the rest of the airship. Amidst the squabble, it was William who offered the most intelligent action plan. The young steward was standing quietly in the cargo bay amidst the rousing debate as various crewmembers tossed out various ideas. Roberts was doling out some swift mediation, his own mind chewing restlessly over the problem, when suddenly William's voice rose in the air.

"Sir, why not use slings?" William offered with some determination, pointing at the ceiling. Roberts had barely caught William's words, but the young lad was growing in insistence as his voice grew louder in the babble. "Horses, they can break their legs easily, sir, I know that. Even flying smooth, the *Horizon* could throw them to the floor."

Talk was dying down as the crewmembers began turning their attention towards William. "If we just tie their heads, it won't keep them from falling. But a sling under their bellies will hold them up so even if they lose their balance, they won't fall."

Thoughtful silence fell over the crew as they considered William's proposal. "It's not a terrible idea," Carter finally ventured. "It could work."

"Except for the fact that we would be suspending several thousand pounds of weight from the ceiling," Long Tom pronounced flatly.

"Not if the slings are loose enough so the horses can stand up on their own legs," Farrington countered. "I see where the boy's going. It's just a brace, see? Something to hold them up if they're a bit uneasy on their legs."

"We've got rope and canvas aplenty," Big Tom's quiet voice offered.

William lifted his chin. "We have hammocks."

The crew stirred at the idea, but Barking Jack broke loose in a rich laugh. "Give the lad a cigar, we've got a regular strategist on board!" he crowed and he slapped William on the back. "We'll praise him when we get these damned horses to camp safely, then curse him later when all our hammocks smell like horse shit."

"Where the hell is Halloway?" Carter snapped. "If this tomfool idea is going to work, we need his input." Now with a measurable plan, the knot of men disbanded itself as minds began turning their way towards prepping the airship for her first job as a horse transport carrier.

The next morning in the pale light of an early sun, the *Horizon* lifted for camp to the sound of whining engines and whinnying horses. There were six of them in the hold, Roberts having decided that for this first run, a minimum cargo load was best. Somewhat to his displeasure, one of the six horses was Lord Raglan's fine stallion. Captain Grim had insisted on it, all but marching the animal into the cargo hold himself.

Roberts had conceded with reluctance, preferring to make a few practice runs before committing the *Horizon* to transporting something so expensive and volatile. He lost the argument, and the stallion was currently ensconced in the belly of the airship along with five other warhorses.

The horses were accompanied by a thin, colorless groom and a small, frail-looking assistant who handled the horses with quiet skill. Five of the animals were obedient enough, walking calmly up the *Horizon's* wooden gangplank and into the straw-strewn cargo hold, where they were strapped into hammocks suspended from the ceiling which would cradle their weight if they fell during transport.

Lucan's stallion, however, had been an entirely different matter. Roberts watched with suspicion and alarm as the glossy black beast thundered up the gangplank, hooves whipping in the air, head high, and mane flowing in the wind. The groom, unmoved by the display of energy, calmly and determinedly moved the stallion forward and elbowed it into position. Enormous snorts and bellows of indignation roared from the stallion. The groom and his assistant fought to avoid its flying hooves while strapping the horse into its harness. To Roberts' surprise, Big Tom stepped forward to help. Under his deft hands, the energetic horse gradually stilled its stamping and begun settling down for the journey.

With the stallion calmed to a dull roar, all hands prepared to lift. Barking Jack was at the wheel looking calm but serious, knowing the delicate operations ahead. Topdeck, Roberts scanned the skies with a deep frown. Morning had broken over a series of low-hanging clouds, dropping visibility and heightening danger. Anything could be hiding in the cloud cover. The *Horizon* had not spotted an enemy for well over two weeks, but Roberts would not let his guard drop. In a war zone, he did not have that luxury.

To his pilot, Roberts cautioned quietly, "We've fragile cargo on board and poor skies ahead. Keep both eyes open and keep her steady."

"Not to worry, Captain," Barking Jack replied calmly as he patted the wheel affectionately. "She's a hell of a lady, sir.

She'll carry us well." True to his word, the pilot lifted the *Horizon* from her berth with exquisite grace and guided her upwards. As the airship began her ascent to cruising height, the crew busied themselves about her, tending to her needs, and shouts rose up in the cold air.

Five of the horses were quiet below decks and made no fuss. Lord Lucan's stallion, however, was indignant about its current predicament and intent on voicing its disdain. Great horse bellows filled the hull, sounding over the groaning cries of the engines and the shouts from the crew. Striding about his airship, Roberts wondered how one animal could make such a tremendous racket. From the sound of it, the stallion was keen on destroying anything it could get its hooves on. It was a short flight from Balaklava to the British camp, one the *Horizon* could easily make in a half hour or less, but every second seemed like an eternity with the trumpeting equine kicking up a storm in the cargo bay.

The *Horizon* had just settled into a comfortable cruising speed of twenty knots when a shout of alarm grabbed Roberts' attention. "Captain!" Barking Jack bellowed sharply. "Enemy vessel off portside, sir!" He pointed at the dark shape of an airship that had dropped unannounced out of the cloud cover and was roaring its way towards the *Horizon*, its prow a half-mile away and rapidly approaching.

God dammit, Roberts growled, sizing up the enemy in a hurried second. Russia was slow to capitalize on the latest of airship technology, and the few Russian airships the *Horizon* had encountered in Crimea had been relatively easy to evade. This one, however, was sleek and powerful, intent on the *Horizon* and zooming in for the kill.

"ENEMY SIGHTED!" Roberts' roar filled the *Horizon*. "GUNNERY CREW, MAN YOUR POSITIONS! ENGINE ROOM, FULL POWER!"

The crew immediately fell into evasive measures. The *Horizon* veered sharply, anticipating the fight ahead. If her crew could get her to the British camp, she could take shelter behind the cover of antiaircraft weapons, but the camp was over a mile away, and the Russian airship was closing in fast.

Nimbly, swiftly, it drew closer to the *Horizon*, blocking her path and driving her away from the British camp. It was a bold, reckless move. There were three British military airships in Crimea, and they patrolled close to camp. Any one of them could appear at once and rush to the *Horizon*'s assistance. The Russian airship flew alone and was smaller than the *Horizon*, yet it persisted in its attack. For one moment, Roberts felt admiration for the sheer bravado of its captain and crew.

Oboe was at Roberts' side in an instant, eyeing the Russian airship. "I suspect that our efforts in supplying the war have not gone unnoticed by the enemy," he said as the two hurried to the helm.

Roberts grunted shortly, but he knew Oboe was right. The *Horizon* was becoming a regular feature in the skies above Crimea. An observant enemy could realize that she was moving supplies and deduce that blowing her to smithereens would greatly hinder the Allied troops. That information could be enough to warrant sending Russia's best military airship into enemy airspace to take down the *Horizon*.

Not on my command, Roberts thought grimly. There was nothing else in the sky except the Russian airship, and he doubted a British military airship or the *Icarus* would come swooping in to assist the *Horizon* in her moment of need. Yet for all the enemy's speed and menacing cannon, the *Horizon* was faster, stronger, and fleeter. If her strength held and her crew's courage did not waver, she could survive the attack and escape the enemy.

Meanwhile, below decks, unholy hell broke loose as the horses protested mightily at the sudden instability under their hooves and vied to make their complaints known. Roberts fully intended to get his airship and all on board to the camp undamaged, the horses included. The Russian airship intended the opposite. It was practically on their tail, driving them over the rugged, vast terrain of Crimea. With the *Horizon* in peril, her whinnying cargo received scant attention.

In the midst of shouts from his crew and the screaming of horses and engines, Roberts tensed for the sound of cannonfire. He was astonished when a sudden volley of projectiles launched themselves at the *Horizon* unannounced. Shrapnel thudded into the *Horizon*'s gondola, ripping canvas and splintering wood. Searing pain ripped through Roberts as a sliver of wood embedded itself in his shoulder. He clamped down on the pain, willing himself forward as panic and confusion broke out on the *Horizon*. The shot had only grazed her, but there had been no gunfire, no puffs of white smoke, no cannonfire. Whatever firing mechanism the Russian airship had, the *Horizon* needed to get away from it, and fast.

"BARKING JACK! GET US UP INTO CLOUD COVER AND AWAY FROM THE ENEMY!" Roberts commanded with ringing clarity. "ENGINE ROOM! FORTY KNOTS NOW! WE HAVE A SHIP TO OUTRUN! GUNNERY CREW! ON YOUR MARK AND FIRE!"

The engineers were adroit in their work and the *Horizon* surged forward. Her engines screamed as the airship banked sharply and pulled up into the clouds, to the frantic trumpets of her equine cargo and the harsh bellows of the crew. Below decks, Long Tom swiftly marshaled his gunnery crew. They manhandled the Vandenberg into position, aiming directly at the Russian airship pursuing the *Horizon* with deadly intent. When the Vandenberg had been hastily loaded, Long Tom's warning cry filled the *Horizon*, and the crew braced for impact, waiting for the first volley.

Shot roared as one hundred and fifty two bullets rocketed across the sky and slammed into the Russian airship. She shuddered, reeling in the sky but clearly unbowed and undissuaded. The shot had scored her hull, but not enough to seriously damage her, and Roberts' men were already frantically loading another cartridge into the Vandenberg.

The Russian airship banked easily, following the *Horizon* upwards in a smooth dance that made Roberts' jaw clench. The enemy ship was swift and strong and her weaponry was baffling. What had been the catalyst, what power source had sent the bullets across the sky, Roberts did not know. By his best estimates, the Russian airship's guns had a range of about eight hundred yards: the *Horizon* had been almost out of range. The Russian projectiles had been erratic, filling the air with scattershot, and such shrapnel was deadly even at far range.

The *Horizon* roared forward, and the Russian airship struggled to keep up with her as she surged past thirty knots. Below decks, Long Tom held command and the Vandenberg exploded again, to the rousing tune of horses whinnying in alarm. The shot roared along the topdeck of the Russian vessel, felling men as it went and sending great clouds of splintered wood in the air. The *Horizon*'s gunnery crew was feverishly reloading the gun when a gigantic explosion filled the air with noise and sound.

The *Horizon* shuddered in the air, her crew yelling in alarm as great bellows of green and red smoke engulfed the Russian airship. Fighting his way to starboard, Roberts watched as the Russian airship bucked and flailed in the sky. Colored clouds of smoke filled the airship, her envelope already deflating and her shredded gondola falling to pieces. Below decks, Carter gave a great whoop of exaltation and Barking Jack let loose a manic cackle of triumph. Roberts stayed immobile, coolly watching as the Russian airship disintegrated into pieces, airmen tumbling from the sky with cries of panic as chunks of jagged wood, tattered shreds of canvas, and broken cargo fell to the earth.

Quickly turning his attention back to his own airship, Roberts wrestled order from the ensuing excitement. Within a few minutes, he received preliminary damage reports. The *Horizon* had not escaped unscathed: there were a few tears in her canopy and some dents in Engine One. The gondola was scored with holes, and Steamline B was dented. Blood leaking down his shirt, Roberts resisted Harding's ministrations, intent on getting his airship to the safety of the British camp.

When he thundered into the cargo hold, Roberts was relieved to discover six panicky but alive horses, all on their feet and uninjured. The groom and stable boy moved among the horses, clucking gently and attempting to sooth the animals, who would have none of it. William's idea had worked, and each horse was still trussed up in a hammock, undamaged yet determined to get back on solid ground.

Long Tom thundered across the floorboards with Carter and Farrington at his heels. Presenting himself to Roberts, he stated flatly, "That explosion wasn't our doing. Our shots couldn't have caused that. They must have been carrying some chemicals or combustibles that our shots ignited."

"On a warship?" Roberts demanded, grimacing as the wound in his shoulder blazed with increased intensity. "What would they have been carrying?" His words were nearly drowned out by Lucan's stallion who was still bellowing and kicking at anything in its range. The groom hung determinedly from its halter and spoke to it in firm tones.

"Hate to disagree with you, sir, but Long Tom has a point," Farrington commented respectfully. "That was a mighty big explosion, sir, and with those colors in the smoke, that wasn't gunpowder."

"It was chemical," Long Tom stated firmly. The other men considered the statement for a moment before Carter offered further elaboration.

"On a few of the trips we've made to camp, I've caught word from some soldiers that they've had a bit of problem with those Moretti rifles," the bosun stated carefully. "Damage in battle or other problems caused some of them to explode."

Roberts huffed, pain and tension making his words tight. "So your theory is that an exploding rifle sent an entire airship down in flames?" he demanded tersely.

Carter stiffened but responded evenly, "Could have been more than one, sir."

"Or the Russians have found a way to use chemical propellants in their cannon instead of gunpowder," Long Tom said darkly.

Soberly, the men considered this possibility. Farrington shook his head, then offered a short laugh. "If that holds true, then we've little to worry about. Let the damned bear-eaters blow themselves out of the sky like this last one did."

"The cannon on that Russian airship had a range of eight hundred yards if it was an inch," Long Tom stated darkly. "You saw her fly. Light as a bird and just as swift. She's not the typical Russian derelict we've seen in the skies."

"And just what is it you are saying, Mister Tom?" Roberts demanded sharply.

The airman crossed his arms. "I'm saying, *sir*," he enunciated the honorific with vitriol, "that we've been thinking, like the rest of Europe, that Russia can barely get an airship in the sky, much less one that can put up much of a fight. But that was a Russian airship we just had up our arses, and we're damned lucky she blew herself to bits before she did one over us."

Long Tom paused, then continued with sharper words. "I'm saying that we'd best consider the possibility that Russia just might be pumping out better airships now, and we'd best be mindful that we're over a war zone with just one gun. This doesn't look like a war that's going to be won soon, and these skies may start becoming a lot more crowded."

The *Horizon* shimmied a bit under their feet, and the men's attention turned back to her. Without much time to spare, Roberts intoned to Long Tom, "Point taken." The airman's sour expression did not lessen when Roberts delivered a swift volley of commands and the *Horizon* began moving back on course to the British camp.

Long Tom's words still echoed uncomfortably in Roberts' ears as he turned his attention back to his airship. She had veered several miles off course, but with Barking Jack at the wheel and Halloway and Jenkins shouting at each other in the boiler room, she was soon on approach to the camp headquarters with an empty berth awaiting her.

Chapter Nineteen

In the British camp, a sizeable crowd hovered anxiously at the wharf, just close enough to be a nuisance. As the *Horizon* settled down to rest, soldiers hurried forward to offer assistance. They were held in check by a cluster of officers directing traffic. Roberts guessed that someone had seen the *Horizon*'s battle in the sky and the crowd was anxious to know what harm had befallen her. The wharf's other berth was occupied by a military airship that had been preparing to lift, possibly to come to the *Horizon*'s aid. Her envelope was full and taut, and her engines were pumping rhythmically, but there was a decided movement among the crew that spoke of a sudden crisis averted.

Meanwhile, below decks, the stallion had decided it was getting the hell off the *Horizon* even if it had to kick a hole in the hull. Deafening blasts of angry horse bellows filled the airship as Roberts called for a full shutdown and the *Horizon*'s engines tapered off. He wouldn't lift her from the camp until a full inspection told him what damage the attacking Russian airship had done.

"Captain Roberts!" a harried voice called out. Roberts, still bleeding, turned to see a fatigued, bedraggled officer standing on the wharf. The man's face was familiar, but at that moment in time, Roberts could not recall the officer's name. He had more pressing concerns on his mind.

"We heard of your battle!" the officer rushed out, his eyes flicking over the oozing tracks of blood advancing across Roberts' jacket. "You are injured," he stated the obvious. "Did your airship sustain damages? Are all your men alive?"

Roberts ignored the questions. "Sir, I've got six panicking war horses in my hull and one of them is ready to kick to hell anything that gets near it. That would be Lord Lucan's horse. They're delicate cargo and damned noisy, and I'd be obliged if you'd get them off my airship."

The mention of Lord Lucan had a galvanizing effect. The officer nodded hastily and stammered orders to several subordinates. They obediently filed into the *Horizon* under Roberts' watchful eye to help unload the horses. Dramatically,

Lord Lucan's horse burst from the *Horizon*'s loading bay and reared impressively on the wharf, its glossy coat shining in the sunlight. The other five horses received less attention, but it was obvious that the collective horseflesh being moved out of the *Horizon* was exceedingly priceless. However, Roberts knew that plenty of the soldiers would have happily eaten the horses if given the opportunity.

Shouts, orders, and general noise filled the air as the horses were lead down the gangplank, soldiers moving out of the way. Roberts was relieved that one of his problems was finally solved. However, it wasn't long before a fresh quandary presented itself.

"Captain Roberts! Sir!" a young officer hailed Roberts imperiously from the back of a skinny, bedraggled horse. In contrast, the officer was crisply dressed and obviously proud of his sharp appearance. A white glove beckoned Roberts. "You are to see Lord Merriweather at once."

Cold indignation rose in Roberts, and he slowly turned to face the officer, his dark eyes boring holes in the young man. The officer wilted slightly under Roberts' gaze, but he was saved by Harding's cool, sardonic voice.

"Young man, surely it has not escaped your notice that Captain Roberts is in need of medical care. You can tell Lord Merriweather that after I have ascertained my captain will not fall victim to blood poisoning, I might persuade him to meet with your lord. Now, if you will excuse us," Harding propelled Roberts back onto the *Horizon* with a firm hand, "I have some bleeding wounds to treat."

Roberts turned his back on the young officer and allowed Harding to bustle him into the sick bay with brusque efficiency. "Sit down, you fool," Harding snapped out. "Twelve men escape with nary a scratch, and you decide to tempt fate with a wooden stake near a major artery."

"I didn't plan it that way," Roberts rapped back, but Harding was already digging in his worn medical bag and carefully laying out his tools.

Harding sniffed. "Well, I suppose it could have been worse," he commented.

"The ship's flyable. The crew's unharmed," Roberts retorted as he began peeling off his bloody jacket and shirt, exposing the wound underneath to Harding's ministrations.

Harding huffed, but he said nothing more, his eyes intent on his work. In a short time, Roberts was back on his feet, with a neat line of stitches sending throbs of pain coursing down his torso. A spare shirt and jacket soon replaced his torn clothing, which he left in a blood-splattered heap on the floor of the sick bay.

The cavalry officer was still waiting for him below the wharf's edge and he was holding the reins of another horse. Seeing Roberts, he stiffened to attention and gestured with the reins. "I took the liberty of procuring a horse for you, Captain Roberts. Lord Merriweather's tent is a fair distance from the wharf and the grounds are quite muddy."

And what makes you think I know how to ride the damned thing? Roberts thought, eying the beast with disdain. He had had quite enough of horses for now, and his proposed mount looked starved and barely capable of supporting its own weight. However, the alternative was slogging through thick mud, and Roberts was tired enough to grudgingly appreciate the offer of a lift. The horse didn't look like it would put up much of a fuss, but Roberts was only notionally acquainted with horses. He could just about trust himself to get up in the saddle facing in the right direction, and wasn't sure what to do beyond that.

Trying not to show his unfamiliarity with the process, Roberts moved to the horse's right flank and geared himself up for mounting. He had seen the maneuver performed dozens of times and it couldn't be that hard. It was a few undignified hops and much grunting before his buttocks touched leather, the horse shifting uneasily underneath him. The cavalry officer watched quizzically, but he said nothing until Roberts was marginally situated in the saddle.

"Follow me, Captain Roberts." Roberts' mount obediently trotted forward while he gingerly held the reins and tried to look competent. The horse fought to keep its footing in the mud, and its staggering pace jerked him about in the saddle. The two horses slipped their way across the camp, passing row upon row of ragged tents and hardened, despairing faces. The camp was swollen with soldiers, with more pouring in by the week to replace those felled by disease and starvation as the war dragged on.

As he gripped the pommel of the saddle, doubt nagged at Roberts. With so much starvation and deprivation facing him, the *Horizon's* desperately needed skills shouldn't have been funneled into transporting a herd of pampered horses. He had not overlooked the hopeful, hungry faces of the soldiers waiting on the dock for the *Horizon* to arrive, nor their looks of disappointment when her cargo was unloaded.

"Here, Captain," the officer gestured towards what was clearly an officer's tent, larger and better appointed than most of the camp's shelters. There were boards laid as a floor, elevating the tent's occupants above the mud that clung to Roberts' boots as he entered.

Humph. A damned boy, he scoffed as his gaze fell on the officer behind the small desk. The lad was barely twenty, pink-cheeked and smooth-skinned, even a trifle plump. He did not look up as Roberts thumped across the floorboards. "Sit down, Captain Roberts," the officer stated with a pompous crispness. "I will attend you in a moment."

For a brief, happy moment, Roberts toyed with slamming the officer's head down on the desk and seeing if he could crack through to the floor. Deciding that assaulting a lord would be of no benefit to his career, he settled for dropping pointedly in the visitor's chair so hard it creaked under his weight. Lord Merriweather ignored Roberts, intent on his paperwork, finishing only after several minutes of pen scratching. Roberts fumed internally but made it a point not to show his anger. He had a feeling his reactions were being measured, and he settled for a chilly calmness.

Finally the officer handed over the paperwork to an orderly, then turned his attention to Roberts. "Now, Captain Roberts," he intoned, his voice rising slightly high. Coughing a bit, he continued in a deeper tone, "Am I to understand that your airship was recently attacked by a Russian vessel?"

"Yes, and she's on the wharf peppered with holes," Roberts retorted impatiently. "I'd like to get back to her so she can get back to work. I've supplies to move."

"You will attend to me, if you please, Captain," Lord Merriweather stated imperiously, folding his smooth hands together. "Now, I understand from those who witnessed the attack from afar that the Russian airship that attacked you was far superior to what we have encountered in Crimea to date."

"She was loaded with long-range cannon, and she chased after my airship like a hawk," Roberts intoned. "She wasn't English, nor Spanish, nor German. I didn't get much of a look at her, seeing that she blew herself up a few minutes after engaging my ship, but I've no doubt she was Russian."

"Our reports have continually asserted that Russian airships are far inferior..." Merriweather began.

"Well, an inferior vessel can't damned near outrun my ship," Roberts interrupted. "She had cannon on board that went off without powder and near the *Horizon*. She damned well might have taken my ship if she hadn't had an explosion on board that dropped her. One of my men believes she had chemical propellants for her cannon that backfired and blew her up. If she's any indication, then the Russians have been investing time and money in their airship technology. There'll be more where she came from."

"One airship is hardly a basis for such a conclusion, Captain Roberts," Lord Merriweather stated with cold condescendence, drawing up his mouth arrogantly.

Roberts' dark laugh filled the tent. "Lad, you can say that with both feet on the ground, but in the sky, you don't overlook a warning when it presents itself."

"You will call me 'Lord Merriweather' Captain Roberts," the officer stated coldly.

Abruptly, Roberts stood to his feet. "*My lord*," he growled out with heavy mockery. "I'd be obliged if you and I could finish our little chat. I've work to do."

Lord Merriweather glared back, but his pompous bravado was swiftly evaporating in the face of Roberts' terminal lack of giving a damn.

They were interrupted by a tactful cough from a nervous-looking orderly. At Lord Merriweather's curt beckon, the orderly hurried forward to whisper in the officer's ear. Merriweather's plump face tightened with anger but by the time the orderly had saluted his way out of the tent, the young lord had regained some of his composure.

"Well, Captain Roberts," he stated, the picture of a man just controlling his temper, "It appears that Lord Lucan was quite pleased at the delivery of his horse."

"Good," Roberts turned his back on Merriweather. "I'd best get the others to him."

As Roberts flipped back the tent flap, Merriweather said indignantly, "I did not dismiss you, Captain Roberts!"

"No, my lord," Roberts retorted. "You did not." With that, he pushed through the tent to find light rain waiting for him outside. Inhaling sharply, he made his squishy way back to the *Horizon*, thick mud clinging to his feet and sullying his trousers to the knee. It was hard going, and Roberts was forced to admit that horses had their uses. At times like this, it was better than walking.

The *Horizon* was absent of an audience; she had no cargo save for the horses, and the hungry soldiers had abandoned her. Inside the airship, there was an impatient buzz of activity as the crew assessed her damages. Oboe greeted Roberts when he arrived and reported, "Mister Halloway is at work patching Steamline B. We were lucky, sir. It could have easily ruptured. Mister Jenkins reports less damage in Engine One than we suspected."

As Roberts stepped into the cargo hold, Oboe commented dryly, "Not all the damage incurred during flight was a result of our battle."

Roberts sighed as he saw generous ploppings of manure and damp patches of urine in the hold. Following Nature's protocol to jettison all unnecessary baggage in the event of an emergency, the horses had liberally smeared the *Horizon* with filth. Stepping around piles of horse droppings, Roberts examined several dents in the hull where frantic hooves had lashed out.

Oboe stood in place, arms crossed over his chest, and watched his captain look over the hold. Finally, he voiced the question Roberts had been chewing over the past hour. "Are we to transport the rest of the horses?"

Roberts didn't answer right away. He knew Oboe well enough to hear the unspoken words, could sense his quiet disapproval of the demanding, time-consuming job. There were fifty-eight cavalry horses in Balaklava waiting to be transported, and the *Horizon* could be days moving them all to camp. It was the last day of October, and the *Horizon* had to make as much use of each day as possible before winter hit and flying became exceedingly difficult and hazardous.

Oboe shifted his feet and absentmindedly began rubbing his right thumb and forefinger together. It was a subtle sign, but Roberts knew it well: his First Mate was growing angry. His voice even but tinged with firmness, Oboe said, "The horses are fragile, difficult to transport, and do nothing to relieve the suffering in camp. Is it truly worth our energy and time to transport them?"

Roberts grunted, bending down to examine a hoof-shaped imprint in the wall. "The payout is damned good, and I received word that Lord Lucan was glad his horse was delivered." He straightened up, then turned his attention to another dent scored into the wood. "The *Horizon* is building a fine name for herself in Crimea and making good money. I aim to keep it that way."

Oboe stiffened and his eyes darkened. Roberts rarely dispensed an order that Oboe did not instantly obey, but there was a deep well of determination in the First Mate. Roberts knew that they were rapidly heading into a strong argument just when he most needed Oboe's assistance and support.

A dark silence followed. It was a long moment before Oboe responded, with some heat, "There are thousands of hungry soldiers at the camp. I saw their faces when our cargo was unloaded and they realized that the *Horizon* had brought nothing to eat." Oboe's speech was absent its accustomed formalities, a clear sign that he was calling out Roberts for his actions and demanding a response.

A twinge in Roberts' back ran down his spine as he straightened up. Deep down, he knew Oboe was right: the *Horizon* had better things to do with her time than shuttling a herd of nervous horses to camp. Still, the money and prestige were too alluring. Roberts' bargain with Smothers never left his thoughts: even in the heart of barren Crimea, his debt nagged at his every step. Although the war steadily increased his savings, the deadline for his debt's repayment was growing closer every day.

Oboe's eyes were cold and heavy with disapproval. Glaring back, Roberts spoke sharply, "I'd be pleased never to see another horse on the *Horizon* again, but we came here to make money, and it's money we'll make."

Oboe said nothing as Roberts continued, "We'll get the job done as soon as we can, then get back to moving supplies. There was enough brought up from Constantinople to give us weeks of transport work."

Although the *Icarus* was operating in Crimea, she was lazy and slow. She had made little headway on moving supplies to camp. There would be plenty left for the *Horizon* to transport after she was done moving the horses.

Silence fell over the two men for a long moment. Finally, Oboe spoke. "I advise against this."

"Your objection is noted," Roberts retorted sharply. "Meanwhile, we've horses to move. Get repairs made and the crew in order. We're lifting off as soon as we can."

Oboe did not move for one long moment, then with fluid grace he departed the cargo bay without a word, leaving Roberts to swear under his breath. The last thing he needed was a squabble with his first mate. When he later ascended topdeck, there was a decided chilliness in the air that had nothing to do with the cold weather. The rest of the crew picked up on it quickly and it was an unhappy airship that lifted from camp and trudged toward Balaklava Bay.

The tension between captain and first mate continued in the upcoming days, and Roberts quickly realized that he should have taken Oboe's advice. Moving the horses proved to be a logistics nightmare. It ate up three days of backbreaking work and left the cargo bay of the *Horizon* reeking of horses and riddled with damage. When they had finally dropped off the last of the pernicious beasts and landed back at Balaklava, the crew wearily turned their attention to assessing what damage the horses had done to the airship. The answer was extensive.

"Hold that end," Long Tom snapped at Barking Jack, who was helping him repair a crack in the hull, courtesy of a well-placed horse kick. William, Carter, and Bloomberg were hard at work scrubbing the floorboards, but the odor of manure and urine was still strong in the air. The entire ship reeked of horses; Big Tom complained that the smell had permeated the airbags and the canopy.

"All the food we transport is going to taste like horseshit," Carter grumbled.

"Government grub usually does. Military men won't know the difference," Barking Jack quipped. This garnered a few laughs, but the mood below decks was irritable. No one had rejoiced to see the horses on board, and Roberts was distinctly aware that no one but him had supported the idea.

Abruptly, Halloway marched directly into the cargo bay with a ball of something furry in his hands. "Look at this," he snapped, dropping it on the floor in front of Roberts. "Do you know how much horsehair I just pulled out of the engine fans?" he complained.

The rest of the crew eyed the ball of hair as Halloway pulled himself up to deliver an indignant chastising. Roberts was already cherishing deep misgivings about their last job, and he silenced Halloway with a glare. Halloway spun on his heel and marched back into the engine room, barking over his shoulder, "Next time, shave the damned things first!"

In the midst of the fuss, Oboe went about his duties as normal. There had been no silent admonition, no smugness, no justified indignation, and that only made Roberts more irritable. The chilliness between the two refused to thaw, but pride prevented either man from addressing the issue directly.

Later that evening, Roberts moodily calculated sums in his tiny cabin, his brow furrowed over the equations. The *Horizon* had been paid well for her efforts, but the plump sum had to be set against damages which had mounted up quickly. It would take a few days to put the airship back together, and she didn't have the time to spare. Balaklava was still full of cargo from the *Morning Star* and *Spirituous*, and thousands of soldiers were desperately awaiting it.

As Roberts bullied the numbers together, a light tapping caught his attention. "Enter," he grunted, knowing by the sound that Oboe was knocking. The first mate entered and Roberts gestured at a chair. "Sit down," he sighed gruffly.

With quiet grace Oboe settled his tall frame into the chair and waited. Roberts pinched the bridge of his nose, feeling a headache throbbing at his skull. "Look, you were right," he stated bluntly, closing his eyes for a moment. "The job paid well but it caused a hell of a lot of expensive damage to the ship, and we'll be down for a few days for repair."

Roberts opened his eyes and looked at Oboe directly. "I made a poor decision. It was mine to make, but I should have taken your thoughts into better consideration."

Oboe nodded, accepting Roberts' words quietly as the frozen tension between the two men began to thaw. The dreaded horse transport was over, for better or worse, and the captain and first mate were back on speaking terms. Conflict resolved, it was time to get back to business.

"I believe two days will be sufficient to repair the damage, Captain," assessed Oboe.

"If I can keep Halloway from tearing Engine One apart," Roberts commented dryly. "And if the patch job on Steamline B holds. We'll probably have to replace it completely."

The two men buried themselves in repair work issues for several minutes before Oboe rose to take his leave. At the door, he paused, one hand on the doorframe. "Captain," he said quietly.

"Hmm?" Roberts grunted, his eyes going back to the sums in front of him.

Oboe set his mouth thoughtfully. "Despite the damage and inconvenience of the horse transport," he said slowly, "I do not believe we should be hasty at fixing a price on a commendation from such a man as Lord Lucan."

Roberts' eyes lifted up to Oboe, who continued thoughtfully, "It would be...advantageous for the *Horizon* to garner as much support as she can from those of high ranks. This may prove to be worth more than mere money."

"What, so I can have more horses on my ship?" Roberts quipped tiredly. Oboe smiled wearily, trying to cover up a yawn. "Go get some sleep," Roberts commanded with rough kindness. "You look half dead on your feet."

"One could say the same of you as well, Captain," Oboe responded and shut the door, leaving Roberts to stare belligerently at rows of numbers before giving up for the night. Chilled, bleary of mind, and vaguely aware that his boots would likely smell of horses for the rest of their natural life, Roberts rose to his feet for a final round of his ship before bed. Another day of cold, mud, and work awaited him.

Chapter Twenty

To the crew's relief, a full day at port in Balaklava was enough to repair the damage that the horses had kicked into the *Horizon*. The crew did their work well, and the airship was ready to lift the next morning. The smell of horses, however, still permeated the *Horizon*. Scrub as they might, the odor lingered for days as a reminder of the ill-advised transport.

The *Horizon* quickly fell back into her accustomed pattern of loading and unloading, bringing supplies from Balaklava to the British camp. She shared airspace with the *Icarus*, but the other airship performed poorly in the field, and cooperation between the two vessels steadily eroded. From hearsay, Roberts understood that Captain Firmin had demanded to transport some of the cavalry horses and was deeply peeved when the *Horizon* had been given the job. After that, Firmin kept his airship to himself, avoiding the *Horizon* and refusing Roberts' offer to coordinate flights between the two vessels. Flying solo was risky, especially after the *Horizon's* encounter with the Russian airship, but Firmin was deaf to Roberts' warning and flew his airship on his own schedule.

Although she performed far less work than the *Horizon*, the *Icarus* gobbled through coal with reckless abandon and was constantly down for refueling. That, and the influx of steamships in and out of Balaklava put a serious strain on what coal supplies the military could find. Local miners were digging as fast as they could, finding both anthracite and bituminous, but unearthing the coal and getting it to Balaklava was a complex process. The *Morning Star* had long departed for Constantinople and would return with anthracite for the *Horizon*. Roberts, however, was worried that his airship would not have enough fuel to last until Fosselweight returned.

As November commenced, rain continued to fall and the ground below never had a chance to harden. Poor visibility and fog were chronic, further increasing the dangers of flight. Roberts had to ground the *Horizon* regularly for bad weather, much as he knew that every hour down was wasted time and money. However, flying in bad weather was sheer folly. He would not risk his men or his ship.

A few days after the complicated horse transport, Roberts stood topdeck a few hours before sunset, examining the weather and wondering if they could safely complete another run or two before nightfall. A trickle of rain was dripping down on the bay and visibility was dropping by the hour. He had kept a worried eye on the weather all day and had just about decided to ground the *Horizon* for the night when Staff Sergeant Prachett appeared on deck. Something in his bearing indicated that he had serious business to discuss. Roberts motioned the Prachett on board with some reluctance; an airship captain occasionally had to reason with an irate customer who didn't understand that flying through a thick fog or driving rain was all but guaranteed suicide.

Prachett hailed Roberts with steady quietness and examined him for a moment as if gathering his thoughts. Finally he spoke. "Bit of good news for you, Captain Roberts."

"I'd be glad for a bit of it, or more if you've got it to spare," Roberts said, trying for a stab at humor.

Prachett did not smile, but there was a slight lifting of his eyes that indicated humor. "I've just had word from the local miners. They found a new vein of anthracite closer to the surface and easier to get to."

"That's mighty good news, Staff Sergeant. I've need of whatever they can get me," Roberts stated with relief.

Prachett began rocking on his heels, humming a strange tune to himself. Roberts, picking up the not-so subtle signs, waited for Prachett to speak again, letting his eyes travel out over the muddy, sticky expanse that was Balaklava.

"I'm damned grateful for any airship that will risk Crimea," Prachett spoke thoughtfully, "but there's word on the ground that the *Icarus* doesn't intend to stick around long." He waved a hand over to where the *Icarus* sat belligerently. She hadn't moved all day, and Captain Firmin had complained to Roberts in passing of engine problems.

Prachett looked as if he had more to say but they were interrupted by a harried soldier hurrying towards the gangplank and calling out to him. With a nod, the staff sergeant left Roberts to contemplate the weather and ponder his next options. The spatter of rain had all but dried up. Visibility remained low, but Roberts had an innate airman's sense that tomorrow would see an outbreak of sunshine.

We could damned well use it, he thought with a grunt as he turned his attention back to his airship.

***   ***   ***   ***

The next day did indeed break uncannily sunny and dry, and decidedly warmer than it had been for days. The warmth and sunshine put great heart in Roberts' men. It was with relatively buoyant spirits that they got the *Horizon* heated up for her first flight of the day. However, no man on board had forgotten the swift Russian airship that had accosted them a few days past, and the recent attack was still a main topic of conversation and concern.

The attack was clearly weighing on Long Tom's mind. He sought out Roberts that morning. "Captain, we need some firing practice," he stated. "We've not practiced for a while."

Roberts nodded. They were heavily pressed for time as it was, but he knew Long Tom was right. "We can clear out some time tomorrow morning," he replied. "I'll talk with Prachett so the military knows why we're firing."

"We need to practice with a full load," Long Tom said. "We've always fired her empty, but it's another game with cargo on board." In the past week, Roberts had taken to loading the *Horizon* with up to twenty-five tons of cargo. Colder weather had increased her lift power, her flights around Crimea were short, and she didn't need to carry much fuel, so there was all the more room for cargo. Long Tom was correct in his assessment: defense and offense were an entirely different game when the airship was fully loaded.

"Tomorrow morning, then," Roberts pronounced. "We'll load her full and run her gun out. I'll advise Staff Sergeant Prachett so we can get air clearance for practice."

The next morning, the *Horizon* rose steadily in the air, just over twenty-two tons of cargo in her belly. Her sights were set on the coast, where she could run out her gun without interrupting anything on the ground. Trailing behind her was a military airship, an escort vessel in case the *Horizon*'s rhythmic firing drew attention from Russian airships. The escort ship kept itself well out of the *Horizon*'s way as Roberts' crew devoted their attention to blowing up target balloons.

Below decks, Long Tom, Carter, and Farrington worked carefully, struggling to compensate for the heavy weight of cargo dragging the airship down and slowing her response time. The cargo itself, although carefully loaded and secured, shifted under the repeated juddering of the Vandenberg's shots. Halloway's retractable chassis and carriage system was effective, but could not completely absorb the Vandenberg's tremendous recoil. In the cargo hold, Oboe, Bloomberg, and William managed the cargo, reshifting stacks and checking knots to keep everything in place.

A noisy but fruitful three hours passed before the *Horizon* burned through almost all of her cartridges. Roberts' ears were ringing, but he was pleased with their efforts: they had hit seven targets in a row dead-on and had managed a reload time of just under one minute. Carter, Farrington, and Oboe were already in a spirited conversation about new cargo securing ideas, and the mood on board was elated as the airship returned to Balaklava Bay.

The crew's spirits were further bolstered when they discovered a newly arrived merchant marine ship in the bay. A line of longboats paddled supplies to shore, and an airship circled overhead. Roberts was pleased to see the airship, hoping it would be of more assistance than the *Icarus*, which was currently down at the wharf, engines cold.

"About damned time," Farrington said cheerfully to Roberts, pointing at the merchant marine. "I wonder what she has for us, sir. We could well use the work."

Roberts nodded, wondering himself. Balaklava was starting to look decidedly bare, and the *Horizon* was running out of supplies to transport. Just four days ago, a warship had arrived bearing news that the *Cambridge*, the pride of Smothers; marine fleet, had sunk during a storm with nearly all hands lost. The ship had carried nine hundred tons of supplies for the British troops, including thousands of winter uniforms to help the soldiers withstand the upcoming months. With these vital supplies lying at the bottom of the sea, the already grim situation in Crimea would only worsen.

With these thoughts, Roberts directed his airship to land at the wharf, and moved through the routine patterns of securing her. The arrival of the merchant marine had filled the bay with noise, but he was dimly aware of a growing disturbance on shore. Something had captured the attention of the ground troops and the crowd was growing. Distracted with his airship, Roberts wondered what all the fuss was about, but it didn't seem important enough for immediate investigation. He kept to his work, minding his crew as they put the airship to rights and prepared her for another loading. It was some time before Roberts poked his head above decks in the direction of the growing noise.

Oh God, not again, he groaned as his eyes fell on a slender figure sashaying her way along the muddy shore, with a growing gaggle of soldiers crowded around her. Like a queen on parade, Miss Pickens sailed through the ranks of dazzled soldiers, spreading awe and astonishment by the second. Much to Roberts' dismay, she had locked in on the *Horizon* and was heading his direction purposefully. Jules trailed a step behind his sister, keeping an eye on the soldiers beside themselves at seeing a woman for the first time in months.

Without preamble or waiting for an official welcome on board, Miss Pickens marched adroitly up the *Horizon's* gangplank, her smiling yet intent eyes never leaving Roberts' dark expression. "Good day to you, Captain Roberts," Miss Pickens announced cheerfully, a coaxing smile upon her lips. "A pleasure to see you, as always."

Silence was his response until Roberts could trust himself to speak dispassionately. "Miss Pickens." He turned his eyes to the silent figure of Jules. "Mister Pickens."

Jules nodded, but Roberts' focus was wholly on the woman facing him. She was dressed for the elements in a thick skirt and warm coat that, while sturdy, were tailored to subtly enhance her curves. Her presence sent bolts of annoyance, anger, and longing shooting through his gut, much as he tried to suppress the emotions.

The crowd of women-starved soldiers gathered at the foot of the *Horizon*'s gangplank, pressing forward to examine the stunning newcomer. Roberts frowned at the audience. He guessed Miss Pickens' intentions, and he didn't need witnesses observing what promised to be a rousing argument.

"Miss Pickens, I doubt very much that this is a social call," he said with weary gruffness. "Whatever you two have to say to me, I'll hear it inside my cabin, if you please." Courtesy nagged him and he added in somewhat kinder tones, "It's cold topdeck. You'll be warmer inside."

"Such courtesy, Captain Roberts," Miss Pickens said in a low, husky voice that made Roberts' toes curl up inside his boots. Boldly, she took his arm, a gesture that filled him with pride and irritated desire. With a slight strut, Roberts escorted Miss Pickens into his cabin, Jules following, as the gathered soldiers watched enviously.

Roberts shut the cabin door, then gave Miss Pickens a penetrating look, watching as she drew up all her reservoirs of persuasion and will. Before she could speak, his deep tones filled the tiny cabin. "I see that you did not sail up here with Captain Fosselweight, Miss Pickens."

"Ah, no, we did not, Captain Roberts," Miss Pickens responded, seeming to fluster a bit under the mention of Fosselweight's name. She rallied quickly. "The *Morning Star* left Constantinople for Gibraltar two weeks ago."

"Which, I presume, would explain why you are here now, in Balaklava and on my ship," Roberts stated flatly. "You'd best not play coy with me, Miss Pickens. I've a good notion that you're aiming to find a ride into camp and well knew that Captain Fosselweight wouldn't bring you up to Crimea if he knew of your intentions."

Miss Pickens bristled under his words but her response was quick and even. "I have my own purposes and agendas, Captain Roberts, and I do not require the permission of Captain Fosselweight to fulfill them," she stated with some coldness. "Jules and I are here on business. I will have you know that the *Times* sent one of their own reporters to the front lines, a Mister William Russell. He has been with the troops for weeks."

Miss Pickens' lips tightened with controlled anger. "Mister Russell's dispatches and subsequent reporting on the war have greatly increased circulation of the *Times*, not only in London but abroad as well. As a result, the *London Guardian* and the *Constantinople Times,* as well as other publications owned by my father, have seen a drastic decline in readership."

Miss Pickens smoothed the front of her sensible yet attractive coat. "If my father's publications are to remain competitive, there is no alternative but to have our own journalists on the front lines as well. We need first-hand information, gathered fresh, from a journalistic perspective."

Roberts' humorless laugh filled the tiny cabin, but Miss Pickens' determined look did not waver.

"And you were your father's best choice for a war correspondent, Miss Pickens?" he stated with disbelief. "He cares so little for your well-being that he would send his only daughter, a beautiful woman, to a camp full of desperate, starving men?"

"As the only correspondents of both publications who are stationed in Constantinople, who else but us would be best fit for the task?" Miss Pickens answered briskly, but Roberts noted that she gently skated around the question and had not answered it directly.

"Let me rephrase that question, Miss Pickens," he said firmly. "It is on the orders of your father that you are bent on becoming a field reporter?"

Her lack of an instant response was answer enough for Roberts. "Not in such precise terms, Captain Roberts," she responded slowly, hand-picking her words diplomatically. "However, staffing at the *Constantinople Times* has been greatly reduced in the past six months, and those who are left do not have the necessary contacts and resources to be at their most successful in Constantinople. Jules and I are simply the most experienced and skilled."

"I'm not questioning your abilities, Miss Pickens," Roberts replied, struggling to keep his voice even. "I'm saying that it's a tomfool idea for you to be here. War is no place for a woman, especially a fine lady such as yourself."

As normal, Jules was standing quietly at his sister's side, but there was a hard cast to his eyes that Roberts did not think was directed at him. Unless he was mistaken, there had been conflict between brother and sister, and Jules had lost the debate. Abruptly, his clumsy voice broke into the conversation. "Not the battlefield." His hooded eyes flickered over his sister and stayed there. "Camp only. You promised."

Miss Pickens' brown eyes flashed with sudden fire, but Jules did not cease his steady gaze. A silent fight between the two raged for a few moments until Roberts' voice broke in on their struggle.

"This is madness," he rumbled. "You don't belong here, Miss Pickens." A touch more softly, he added, "There's little in camp but cholera, starvation, and misery. If I put you down in camp, you could be dead in three days. Crimea's full of dead bodies, Miss Pickens, and the gravesites are plenty crowded already. You don't need to be joining them."

She said nothing, her face hard but her eyes thoughtful as she considered his words. For one brief moment, Roberts thought he had actually won the fight, but a flash in her eyes quickly reminded him how wrong he was. "It is commendable of you to worry over me, but my safety and well-being are my concern," Miss Pickens replied firmly. "Jules and I have a commitment to this war."

Her slender, gloved hands clenched. "It is not bullets or cannon that will end this foolish war, Captain Roberts, but sound journalistic reporting. Mister Russell has…" she bit her lips sharply as if strangling an ill-chosen phrase, "…certain skills, I will concede that, but from what I have gathered, he is a rather…common fellow. He may be able to coax information out of foot soldiers, but unless I am very much mistaken, the upper levels of the military, those exactly suited to deliver important information, are beyond his reach."

She smiled coyly. "I, however, and Jules," she added with some hastiness, "with our positions and support, will be more effective at gathering useful information."

Roberts didn't doubt her for one moment. He knew that, turned loose at camp, Miss Pickens would soon have every officer fawning at her feet. It would be amusing to watch the chaos erupt if she touched down at camp, but Roberts had no intention of subjecting Miss Pickens to the horrors of war.

"We will, of course, compensate you for your time and efforts," she stated, but Roberts shook his head.

"Miss Pickens, I am not taking you to camp," he announced flatly. "As I said before, it's a damned fool idea. You've little notion what you would face there."

They glared at each other, but it wasn't long before Miss Pickens stiffened and drew up her chin tartly. "Well, then, if you have made up your mind, Captain." Roberts crossed his arms, resolute and determined. "Then we will go," she announced, turning on her heel. "Come, Jules."

The sudden lack of opposition took the wind neatly out of Roberts' sails. He had expected Miss Pickens to insist more forcefully. An odd pang of disappointment was beginning to stir in his belly when her next words grabbed him by the throat. "I see that there is another airship here in Balaklava," she stated cannily. "Perhaps her captain would not be adverse to allowing us a place on board."

"Oh, no you don't," Roberts rapped out, as he placed a heavy hand on the cabin door, preventing Miss Pickens from opening it. "The *Icarus* flies like a drunken seagull. I'll not have you on that airship, Miss Pickens."

Her smile was triumphant. "Well, Captain Roberts, if you will refuse us passage, we must find an alternative way into camp."

Roberts' fingers pressed against the door, nearly scoring grooves into the wood, while Miss Pickens watched him with an air of barely suppressed gloating. Roberts wrestled with his options, the inevitable looming in his face. Dark silence filled the room as the seconds ticked by. Finally, and with great reluctance, he lifted his hand from the door.

"We leave in one hour," Roberts stated through his clenched jaw.

Miss Pickens didn't even bother to hide a smile of triumph. "Why, Captain, how kind of you to offer," she said, her every word grinding like glass against Roberts' nerves.

You always do manage to get your own damned way, don't you? Roberts was positively aching to shout. Instead he jerked the door open with a rough, abrupt gesture. "I'd advise you pack wisely, Miss Pickens. It will be hard accommodations at camp, with little but cold, mud, and disease."

"We'll manage, Captain," Miss Pickens said lightly, but now that she had accomplished her mission, her attention had already turned from him. With a firm step, she strode through the cabin door that Roberts held open stiffly and marched across the deck of the *Horizon*, the crew watching as she passed.

Jules, however, stayed put, shifting his weight uneasily. Roberts stood, still holding the door open. He waited impatiently, but he could see that Jules was worriedly sifting through ideas in his mind. The big man was rarely anything but placid, but Roberts could see that Jules was becoming agitated. Inhaling sharply, Roberts addressed him. "Your sister's damned determined to go, and I doubt there's a force of nature that could stop her. I'd watch her with both eyes constantly. Do what you came to do, then get her out of there before she freezes or dies of dysentery."

Jules frowned darkly, and Roberts felt a stab of angry helplessness. It galled him to see Jules meekly following his sister's lead instead of standing up to her foolishness, but the big man clearly looked to his sister for leadership. Resisting a strong urge to kick him, Roberts watched as Jules sighed deeply, then exited the cabin, obediently trailing behind Miss Pickens as they left the *Horizon*.

With table-rattling force, Roberts slammed the door shut and indulged in a fit of cursing until he regained some control and could face his crew again. Belatedly, he realized that a woman was going to be inhabiting his cabin again. That notion brought with it no small amount of conflicted emotions, which did nothing to sweeten his temper. It was with a sharp tongue that the master of the *Horizon* eventually roared out of his cabin and begin shouting orders to get the airship back in the sky, this time with a highly volatile payload to deliver. With newly arrived supplies, she wouldn't make the trip empty and the crew scrambled to load her with fresh cargo.

In well under an hour, Roberts spotted Miss Pickens and Jules heading his way again. He sullenly watched them approach, grudgingly prepared to transport passengers once again and uncannily aware that he'd much rather take on a cargo load of war horses. The honest stink of horse manure and the crash of frantic hooves shattering wood now seemed curiously welcome in contrast to the beguiling scent of perfume and the mass chaos Miss Pickens unleashed every time she stepped on board the *Horizon*.

Back on deck, three suitcases at her feet, Miss Pickens turned to Roberts. Sunlight danced rainbows across her glossy hair and her full lips parted into a welcoming, radiant smile. Stepping forward lightly, perfume scenting the air, she flirtatiously took Roberts' arm. Her husky voice threatened to completely destroy what composure he had left.

"Well, Captain Roberts," Miss Pickens breathed out, low and almost dangerously intimate. "Shall we fly?"

Chapter Twenty-One

The *Horizon* settled into a berth at camp, her engines churning rhythmically. She would lift soon after unloading, and her crew kept her envelope full and her engines running. Casting an eye over the British camp, Roberts could see nothing but mud and weary, resigned faces everywhere he looked. Heads perked up hopefully at the sight of the airship, and men surged forward, no doubt eager to avail themselves of what the *Horizon* was carrying.

One element of the airship's cargo was an exceedingly attractive female, and Roberts guessed she would be as eagerly welcomed as the beans, cots, and bandages filling up the cargo hold. He wondered if Miss Pickens realized that her and Jules' presence in the camp meant two more mouths to feed. Their positions as guests could easily result in soldiers going hungry while the reporters dined on the best the camp could offer. Roberts doubted any officer would care if a couple privates had to starve in order that the new visitor, a vision of loveliness and charm, could eat.

Miss Pickens observed the camp carefully, her eyes flittering from the mud to the gaunt-looking soldiers to the rows of inadequate tents. Further down the line was a cluster of primitive medical facilities surrounded by an ocean of prone bodies. Some men were lucky enough to be sleeping on stretchers but most were lying directly on the ground, whether dead or simply very still, Roberts didn't know.

There was a hard, calculating set to Miss Pickens' jaw, and Roberts hoped that she had the fortitude for what was ahead of her. Glancing at her, he rumbled, "There's still time to change your mind, Miss Pickens."

"Certainly not, Captain," she responded briskly. "Who else will tell England what is happening to our boys here?"

"It'll be rough and dangerous," Roberts warned, but his words were unheeded. Miss Pickens had already shifted her attention to the men working their way towards the *Horizon*, officers and soldiers alike. A triumphant smile rose to her lips. With one hand lightly on Roberts' arm, Miss Pickens tripped elegantly down the gangplank to the edge of the wharf and fluttered her gloved fingers at the crowd below. "Hello, gentlemen!" she said in a voice that was light and warm, but carried a steely undertone that hinted at her resolve.

A ripple of astonishment shook the crowd. Dozens of eyes stared up in astonishment at the sight of a living, breathing, attractive young woman in their midst. The murmur grew in size and volume, as men began pushing forward to get a better view, eyes frank and hungry-looking. Miss Pickens continued to beam and flutter as several officers hurried up to greet the newcomers, their bodies practically vibrating with soldierly bearing. Roberts reflected that at least Miss Pickens' presence would be a morale-booster to the homesick, fatigued fighters. There was nothing like the sight of a lovely woman to put a strut in a man's steps.

"Ma'am! Welcome to Headquarters!" an eager but just slightly confused voice echoed over the burgeoning sounds of surprise and excitement welling up from the still-growing crowd of men. Word was spreading like gunfire, and more men were walking or hobbling forward to see if the news were true.

"I'm Major Bryson, Ma'am, Cedric Bryson." A hat was briskly snatched off a head and a long, lean frame bowed. "At your service, Ma'am, and you too, Captain Roberts."

Miss Pickens quickly stepped forward and seized the major's hand in a firm grip, eliciting consternation from the officer. By etiquette and custom, women didn't shake hands, much less initiate a shake. After a few fumbled moments, the major covered up his awkwardness by pressing Miss Pickens' hand to his lips while bowing over it.

"So courteous, Major Bryson," Miss Pickens cooed, and Roberts recognized the purr waking to life in her tones. However, in an instant, the purr was gone. "But we need not stand on courtesy, sir, not when thousands of your men are dying or dead from disease and hunger," she said firmly.

Major Bryson paused for a moment, consternation rising deeper in his face. "Ma'am?" he said, packing a paragraph of questions into one word.

"Of course," Miss Pickens answered quickly. "Forgive me. I am Miss Pickens, granddaughter of Commander Horace

Pickens." The major froze at the name, and the murmurs from the crowd grew louder. "This is my brother Jules," Miss Pickens continued, gesturing at her brother. "We are both reporters for the *Constantinople Gazette*, a subsidiary of the *London Guardian*."

"Reporters?" Bryson repeated dumbfounded. "But...but, Ma'am, I'm...I'm sorry, but a war camp is simply not a place for a woman. It's rough living, ma'am, and winter's coming. Not a place a fine lady like you should have to suffer. Besides," he said, as if just now remembering. "We have a reporter here, Ma'am, a Mister William Russell with the *Times*. He's been with us for almost a month now."

Roberts had to give Miss Pickens credit for she held her emotions well in check. Only a bare glimmer of anger flashed before her beguiling smile returned. "Ah, but Major, I had explicit orders from my father to come to the camp and report on what I see." She pulled a dutiful, innocent face. "My father owns the *London Guardian*, and my brother and I are intrinsic parts of its operations." Her innocent look grew more cherubic. "I am simply being an obedient daughter, Major Bryson."

It was a bald-faced lie and Roberts knew it, but he kept his tongue. Bryson ran his hand distractedly through his hair, caught between two social demands. Far be it for any man to hinder a woman carrying out her father's orders, especially one with a high-ranking grandfather. However, the order put her in a place of discomfort and danger, which was any gentleman's bounden duty to prevent.

Thoroughly frustrated with the situation, Roberts turned to go. With any luck, a few days of hard living in camp would make Miss Pickens change her mind. The *Horizon* could pick her up once she had received her fill of cold, rain, and misery. Turning to the reporter, Roberts said dryly, "Miss Pickens, I am sure your father would be pleased to see the both of you carrying out his instructions to the letter. I..."

"Just what is going on here, Major?" a thunderous, deep-toned voice boomed. Heads turned and bodies parted to make way for Molly, who was moving through the crowd like a pike through a fish pond. Roberts had only seen the woman at a distance, and up close she was no less formidable. She was a handsome woman, in a broad-shouldered, sturdy sort of way, but the determined set of her chin would send all but the most courageous of men running.

"And who's this pretty little thing?" Molly rumbled out, hands on hips and eyes drilling into Miss Pickens'. Roberts watched in amusement as the reporter shrank under her penetrating stare. It seemed that the wily, artful Miss Pickens had met her match at last. Here was one foe she could not coax and charm into submission.

Miss Pickens made a stalwart effort to stand up to the oncoming attacker. Pulling herself upright, she said proudly, "Miss Victoria Pickens, granddaughter of Commander Horace Pickens, and reporter for the *London Gazette*."

"Another reporter? Excellent," Molly said with an evil little smile. "Nothing like first-hand experience to make a news story real, that's what I've always said." The smile grew sharper. "You can start by reporting on the number of dead and diseased men we have in camp, thanks to the pitiful amount of supplies our army has been sending us."

Seizing Miss Pickens' arm, Molly turned abruptly and began carting the reporter with her. "I'll be glad to show you the tents full of dying men, and that's just the ones lucky enough to be inside a tent, pitiful shelter as they are. Most of my patients are lying out in the mud. You can do your reporting just as well while helping pack the maggoty wounds of dying soldiers as you can just standing there, my girl, once we get you some proper clothes..."

Looking aghast, Miss Pickens was hauled off towards the medical tents, Jules hurrying after them. Roberts was suddenly seized with an overwhelming urge to scoop up Miss Pickens in his arms and carry her back onto the *Horizon*, away from all this danger. A less saintly part of his nature wanted to laugh at the sight of her getting more than she'd bargained for. He restrained both impulses. Most likely a day or two with Molly would send the reporter fleeing for the safety of the *Horizon*, and she would be done with this foolish nonsense.

Major Bryson sheepishly turned towards Roberts. "We're hardly fit to entertain ladies in camp, much less the granddaughter of Commander Pickens," he said worriedly.

Roberts shrugged. "I've little influence over Miss Pickens, Major. What I know of the lady is that she's of her own mind, and there's little reasoning with her. Best let her have her own way. A few days of cold and mud at camp should bring her to her senses again."

But the major was already turning away, a thousand demands calling for his attention, and Roberts had his airship to unload. The *Horizon* disgorged her cargo easily and was soon lifting in the air back to Balaklava. Roberts' spirits were sour. His thoughts constantly shifted back to the image of Miss Pickens disappearing into the diseased carnage and filthy mud of the British camp.

***   ***   ***   ***

Roberts welcomed the work of the next few days as a bulwark against distraction over Miss Pickens' ordeal. The new merchant marine ship, the *Mary Girl*, had come to Balaklava fully loaded, and her companion airship, the *Pelican,* was capable and steady. As if galvanized by the extra competition, Captain Firmin of the *Icarus* displayed a marginal amount of cooperation and his airship soon joined the *Horizon* and *Pelican*. In tolerable union, the three airships lifted and landed in endless loops across the sky from Balaklava to the British camp.

November was half-over and the war continued to build. It was this precise topic that led to a huddle of airship officers on the wharf one damp, cold day. Late afternoon was galloping towards evening and there was a tang in the air that promised oncoming snow. Roberts and Oboe stood with Captain Brunswain of the airship *Pelican* and his first officer. Staff Sergeant Prachett was also among the men, and his granite face was even harder than normal. On the wharf, the *Horizon* and *Pelican* were being loaded by soldiers while the *Icarus* circled overhead in jerky circles waiting for a landing spot. Seeing the group of airship officers, Captain Firmin and his first mate lowered to the wharf in a lift basket and stepped forward to join the conversation.

The men parted to let Captain Firmin join them. He returned the courtesy by interrupting the discussion. "There will be nothing but starvation left in camp once the *Mary Girl*'s cargo is transported and consumed," he spoke indolently. Languidly waving a hand at the *Mary Girl*, he pronounced, "There will be no more ships coming to Crimea this winter."

"Word is, the *Omnia Vincam* will travel to Constantinople with supplies," Captain Brunswain said uncertainly, but Firmin snorted dismissively.

"Sir Smothers lost the *Cambridge*. He will not risk the *Omnia Vincam*." Firmin coolly straightened his cuffs and set his chin. "Gentlemen, when the *Mary Girl* leaves, my airship will travel with her. I advise you to do the same. In the coming months, there will be little work, bad weather, and a hard winter. I have no wish to further risk my airship."

With that, Firmin all but sauntered out of their midst, his first mate hurrying to catch up as he signaled for the *Icarus* to pull them aloft. The airship reclaimed her captain and first mate, then resumed circling in the sky, waiting for a berth to open so she could land in Balaklava.

The other men were silent in Firmin's wake until Prachett's dry voice cut through the brittle air. "Well, if you gentlemen have had time to properly grieve Captain Firmin's imminent departure," he quipped, "I'd be obliged if you'd advise me of your intentions."

Brunswain worried his bottom lip intently while Roberts weighed his options. He had made fine money in Crimea but at the expense of his crew. All the men were exhausted, overstressed, and overworked. Farrington was visibly struggling with the long absence from his family, and all the men were missing London. The older crew members had originally signed up on the *Lucky Lady* with the understanding that she was a short-flight vessel. Her rebirth as the *Horizon* and her abrupt departure from London had caused tremendous changes in the lives of her crew, and the ramifications were building daily. This was to say nothing of the hardships of Crimea, which would multiply a dozen times over when the full wrath of winter poured forth.

A gust of wind tugged at the men's clothing as Prachett waited quietly for a response. Brunswain shifted his expression to his first mate, silently seeking his input, but the young man's thin face was tight with worry. Heavily, Brunswain shuffled his feet and stated, "My ship will fly, but I don't need you telling me, Staff Sergeant, that flying conditions will be poor at best, suicide at worst." He shuffled his feet again, thinking hard, while Roberts kept quiet, uneasy in his mind and not willing to commit to anything.

"I don't need an answer now, but I need one soon," Prachett stated. "With winter coming, I need to know if I can count on your assistance or if the Army has to figure out other ways of getting supplies to forty thousand soldiers. Both your airships are mighty welcome in Balaklava for the winter, but there's little predicting what you will find in the next several months. You could have weeks where you can't fly for weather and nothing to transport on days you can fly. I can promise you good transport fees on the cargo you transport, but I can't promise that there will be much of it for you."

Roberts and Brunswain digested the news solemnly while Prachett observed them keenly, then nodded in farewell. "I've leave you to think it over," he said, taking his leave and walking away from the men, his footsteps echoing on the bare wooden planks.

Brunswain blew out tiredly as he rocked a little on his feet, both hands clasped behind his back. "It's a hard gamble," he said solemnly. "A good payout, but money's little use if your airship gets shot out from under your feet."

Roberts grunted in agreement, his own gaze turning toward his airship where she rested on her accustomed berth. Worriedly, his eyes followed her lines, examining her furls and angles with solicitous care, seeking out any evidence of damage or weariness. She seemed solid and courageous to his eyes. Although he hated to risk the *Horizon* in the unknown hardship that winter in Crimea would bring, his little bird seemed strong enough to shoulder the challenges ahead. Still, Roberts was deeply uneasy in his mind if he wanted to risk it, despite the potential gains.

Movement on board drew his attention. Roberts watched as Oboe and Harding stepped across the topdeck, deep in conversation. His mouth tightened as he observed the pair, thinking hard about what he was asking of his men: Oboe to suffer through long months of cold, Harding to do a young man's work of caring for the crew while helping manage the airship, Farrington to yearn for his family and the child he had yet to meet. Heavily, Roberts mentally ran through his crew roster, considering each man carefully.

Brunswain grunted. "There's good pay here, but the army didn't give near enough thought to provisioning their soldiers through the winter." He waved a hand over the bay, encompassing it in a gesture. "If it continues like this, every soldier in this wasteland will be dead come Christmas."

A muscle danced in Roberts' jaw. "Without airships to transport cargo, they'll be just as dead." He didn't intend this as a challenge, but Brunswain took it as one.

"You can risk your men's necks and your ship if you like, Roberts," Brunswain pronounced coldly. "But I won't see my airship shot out of the skies or my men die of cholera. You're a damned fool to stay." With that, he left, his heavy boots thundering significantly on the wharf and his first mate at his heels, leaving Roberts alone.

It seemed as if the *Horizon* was the only airship considering staying on in Crimea for the winter. Moodily, Roberts retraced his footsteps back to his ship, holding his coat closer as the temperature continued to drop with the oncoming evening. The airship was about ready to lift with her full load, and once she landed in the British camp, she would stay there for the night. There were only two berths in Balaklava, and one of the three airships had to stay in camp each evening. It was the *Horizon*'s turn that night. She'd shut down at the camp's wharf so her crew could get some sleep.

The last transport of the evening was uneventful. The crew landed the *Horizon* in camp and unloaded her quickly. As they shut her down for the night, warm smells wafted up from the galley; William was hard at work on dinner. Roberts saw his airship secured and shut down, then moved across the deck towards his cabin, needing some time alone to process his thoughts. Preoccupied, he didn't notice Oboe heading his way.

Oboe paused, sensing that his captain didn't want to be disturbed, and let Roberts pass. Roberts went into his cabin where he could mull over his plans for the upcoming months.

Roberts was still deep in thought when Carter's quiet knock summoned him to dinner. Below decks, the crew was crowded around the plain board set out for meals. Still preoccupied, Roberts paid little heed to his surroundings, but when a bowl slid in front of him, he was astonished to find that it contained beef stew. Shooting a look at William, Roberts demanded, "Where did you get beef?" Such meat was a luxury in Crimea. Although Roberts fed his men well, they had little access to beef.

William flushed, but Carter came to his rescue. "An old ox dropped dead at port earlier this morning," the bosun stated cheerfully. "A couple of soldiers stopped by with one of the legs as a present. It was as tough as teak and didn't have much meat on it, but a good stewing will soften up anything."

Roberts gave him a hard look, but Carter wore an innocent expression. There was a general tenor among the men that said they didn't want their captain digging too closely into the mystery of the appearing beef. Roberts was hungry and distracted and let the matter go, his attention focused on more important matters. Soon after spoons began to rise and fall in a rhythmic thumping of cheap pot metal against wooden bowls, Long Tom broached the matter.

"Captain, are we staying in Crimea for the winter?" Long Tom questioned abruptly. Conversation around the table had been muted, the delicious stew garnering everyone's attention, and Long Tom's words fell with sharp clarity.

Eyes lifted to Roberts, who paused in the act of lifting a loaded spoon to his mouth. He glanced coolly across the table at Long Tom who returned his gaze. A significant hush fell over the other crew members as they waited, the question clearly one that had been chewing at them all. Roberts set the spoon back down in the bowl. "I've words for you all, but after dinner," he said firmly.

The men returned quietly to the stew, but the initial cheer of a good meal rapidly diminished. Conversation was subdued as William passed a tray of bread he had baked that day. Roberts toyed idly with a slice, noting its steady improvement from the first time William had attempted to bake bread. Barking Jack had joked that the resulting loaves were a fine substitute for anthracite. The slice Roberts now held was a bit doughy but entirely passable and certainly better than what most of the soldiers were eating.

When the men had eaten their fill, heads turned to their captain in uneasy anticipation. Roberts had been turning over words in his head and, without preamble, he began.

"As of now, the *Horizon*'s the only merchant airship in Crimea. The *Icarus* and *Pelican* are leaving with the *Mary Girl*. With a hard winter coming, it's a safe guess that we'll be on our own till spring."

Barking Jack and Carter nodded thoughtfully, their brows knit with worry. Bloomberg simply looked exhausted, while Oboe and Big Tom wore their normal illegible expressions. The rest of the crew looked solemn and leaned forward to more clearly hear Roberts' words.

He continued. "As the only merchant airship in Crimea, that will give us plenty of transport opportunities, but only as long as the military keeps sending in supplies. As winter comes, it will be harder to get marine ships across the Black Sea. We could be here all winter and see damned little work or we could make a fortune this winter. We've no way of telling which outcome we'll get."

"You all know the risks we face staying here," Roberts stated. "We've seen plenty of bad flying days, and more will come this winter. It wouldn't take much to see us grounded at port with no way of getting back to Constantinople. There are enemies in the skies and on the ground. We're operating daily in a war zone, and you all know that."

"If we stay, we won't see London for a time, most likely late spring or even summer," Roberts added. "Some of you have families that you've been away from for going on five months now. Those of you that were with the *Lucky Lady* didn't sign up on a long-range airship, and you got a hell of a lot more than you bargained for with the *Horizon*."

"However," Roberts paused firmly. "You all know that your efforts on board the ship have saved lives. I don't need to remind you that these fields are full of dying men. If half of them can make it out of Crimea alive, I'll be surprised. If we leave and no other airships take the *Horizon's* place this winter, the death count will be a lot higher. If we risk it, we at least risk it for a good cause."

He paused again, letting his words settle on the men before continuing. "I aim to keep the *Horizon* in Crimea," he announced, watching closely as his crew reacted with quiet nods, sighs, and looks of weary fortitude. "She's needed here. But," Roberts let his words grow deeper. "I'll not risk any man here against his will. We'll be returning to Constantinople with the *Mary Girl* to restock and make what repairs we need. Any of you wish to leave the ship, he'll have his pay in full, with a bonus and no hard feelings."

"Those that want to stay," Roberts continued, "you'll all receive a wage raise of ten pounds more a month for as long as we are in Crimea. Even if we don't transport anything else, that pay bonus is for any man who sticks it out in Crimea for as long as we're here."

His announcement caused a considerable stir among the men, and Roberts felt a sinking somewhere in the region of his wallet at the thought of what the winter could possibly bring: high wages for a crew that had no work. He had already raised their wages once the *Horizon* had started earning money, and the new wage increase had nearly doubled the men's pay. However, he stared down the worry, knowing that his decision had been the right one. Considering what he was asking his men to do, they deserved it.

"It's not my intent to make any man here misjudge his better instincts for the sake of money," Roberts announced. "If you were thinking of leaving before I offered you a pay raise, then you'd most likely be best trying your luck elsewhere. However," he moved his eyes down the table, looking each man full in the face, "If you're committed to staying, then I intend to make it worth your while. I'd not ask any man here to break his back for nothing.

"Make no mistake," Roberts concluded. "I need every man here. I would hate to lose one of you. I've a good ship and fine crew, and I'm damned proud of both. But the decision to stay or go is yours alone. I only ask that you make a decision and abide by it." With that, he stood to his feet, signaling that the moment of rousing speech was over. "We leave for Constantinople in two days," he announced, then left the table, intent on seeking the one crew member who wasn't present for the meal.

Halloway, as per normal operating standards, was holed up in the engine room, taking advantage of the stilled engines to perform some maintenance. Either that, or he was tearing apart the engine room out of sheer boredom. He was half visible under Engine Two, his thin legs sticking out as he banged irritably at something and muttered a fluid stream of barely audible words. Roberts observed from the doorway before calling out, "Halloway."

"What?" the engineer called back irritably.

"Get your arse out from under there," Roberts ordered amicably. "I've got some questions for you."

A muffled snort echoed from Halloway. "Can it wait, *Captain*? I'm busy."

Roberts crossed the room and squatted down to better get his words across. "We're leaving for Constantinople in two days," he announced.

Halloway snorted derisively again. "Had enough risking her over a war zone?"

"We need a few days of repair and downtime," Roberts frowned, warning in his voice.

"If you'd stop running her into the ground, there wouldn't be so much for me to fix," Halloway complained.

Abruptly, Roberts seized Halloway's bony ankle and pulled, dragging him forward until his grease-smeared face was visible. Halloway looked indignant, but Roberts cut him off. "I'm not talking to your feet," he said evenly. "What I have to say concerns you as much as the rest of the crew."

Roberts stood up, with Halloway following suit, bristling and ready for a fight. He was all but drawing his fists into balls before Roberts' calm voice stopped him. "James, you are the one who has suffered the worst on board my ship," he said with honest sincerity. "You're the only man on board who didn't want to be here in the first place. You've stuck it out with a loyalty you didn't need to offer, and there's not a day I'm not grateful for it."

Halloway huffed but his belligerent expression softened as Roberts continued. "I'll repeat what I said to you before and what I just told the rest of the men: you've a right to leave when you want, and I'll not be stopping you. But the *Horizon* is staying the winter in Crimea. She's got thousands of soldiers to feed. It will be a hard winter. Whether it means work or long days of twiddling our thumbs, I don't know. I need you at my side but only if you want to be there."

Halloway inhaled stiffly; Roberts saw his frustration. He knew Halloway was mad to get off the *Horizon* and back to his own interests, but he said nothing. He merely picked up his tools and wriggled back under the engine. Roberts thought about forcing an answer but decided to bide his time. He knew Halloway was deep in thought, trying to figure out his next course of action.

As was Roberts himself. Fatigue was screaming in his veins and his wire-taut nerves groaned under the burden of long months of back-breaking work and the incessant press of constant worry. Doubt and uncertainty followed at his heels, chewing at him, as he left Halloway and moved through his airship, mentally gearing up for the risky trip back across the Black Sea to Constantinople.

Chapter Twenty-Two

Constantinople was a city at war. Massive screw-powered marine ships cut through the narrow Bosporus while fully-rigged sailing ships proudly displayed their cannon and unfurled their sails in the bright sun. Several war airships droned overhead, their high-powered engines filling the air with noise as they circled like beasts of prey. The streets of the city were packed with soldiers, and ranks of uniforms moved in orderly lines, rolling imperially past citizens.

The *Horizon's* journey to Constantinople had been smoother than Roberts anticipated. In a surprising show of cooperation, Captain Firmin had offered to fly his ship with the *Horizon* rather than joining the *Mary Girl*. Roberts suspected Firmin was intent on returning to Constantinople quickly but did not want to risk flying alone. Without a marine ship to slow them down, the two airships kept steady at twenty-five knots across the Black Sea. Winds were cold and brisk, but halfway through the trip they picked up a steady tailwind that blew them forward. Enemies lurked in the skies, but aside from a few scares, the two airships traveled unmolested.

In Constantinople, the *Horizon* found a berth with some difficulty and landed gratefully. When the airship was secure and shut down, Roberts granted the crew a day of ground leave. The men departed the *Horizon* with hasty enthusiasm, heartily sick of being penned up on board together and eager for some recreation. Constantinople had long been picked clean by hordes of hungry soldiers, and there were only paltry delights to be found in its streets and taverns. However, most of the crew departed the airship with prompt haste, eager to spend their wages.

Left to his own devices, Roberts was plagued with a restless energy that belied his exhaustion. There was much to do but he had no crew to accomplish it. He didn't begrudge the men their ground leave, but the airship needed careful preparation for Crimea's upcoming winter. Thoughts of Miss Pickens nagged at him. She had been in camp for ten days and he had scarcely seen her during that time and had no word if she was well or ill.

Halloway was hard at work below decks and didn't want Roberts' help. Frustrated, Roberts finally left the airship and headed for the nearest market, although he knew all their wares would be prohibitively expensive. The *Horizon's* food stores were growing leaner by the day, and she needed to bring plenty of supplies up to Crimea for the winter. Roberts was pondering whether or not they should restock at another port when he entered the main street of the marketplace and paused, his brows drawing into a dark line.

Rows of raggedy tents lined the street, and many of the vendors were obviously running on a thin margin with little to offer hopeful customers. However, dotted here and there were several thriving shops well-stocked with both food and customers. Roberts observed carefully, watching as dark-skinned men, veiled and graceful women, and handfuls of soldiers ducked in and out of the tents, bearing away items. A soldier hurried past Roberts with several tins of Ramornie brand tinned meat cradled in his arms. Roberts knew the brand well, having transported tons of it to the British camp in the past several weeks.

Suspicious, he stepped into the tent the soldier had hastily exited. Its flaps were drawn far back, welcoming potential customers in to peruse its generous food wares. In just a glance, Roberts knew that everything inside had been originally intended for the frontlines. He wasn't surprised; most wars contained certain soldiers and officers out to make a fat profit selling military supplies. Constantinople was hungry, and its people were eager for whatever they could find.

"Good sir, we have food here," stated the proprietor, a tall, handsomely-proportioned man with gracefully enunciated English. "Please see." Roberts ignored him, intent on assessing the items for sale. The prices grabbed his attention.

"Six lira?" he repeated in disbelief, holding up a small can of tinned meat to the vendor, who nodded serenely. The man's handsome face was pleasant but a trifle smug, the pleased look of a seller who knows his customers have few other options and would pay whatever price he felt like demanding. Still, six lira was a staggeringly inflated price.

Roberts put the tin back down and exited the tent despite the vendor's efforts to entice him back. More browsing showed him that the better stocked tents all held military goods. He had no interest in paying high prices for stolen supplies. The *Horizon* would have to restock at another port. Roberts briefly considered reporting the stolen goods to Headquarters, but he knew it would do little good.

Finished with the market, he made his way back to the *Horizon*. As he walked, he noted that Constantinople was beginning to resemble London: a nonsensical mishmash of modern and medieval. Ancient buildings sagged against each other, crumbling tilework bleached slowly in the sun, and animals filled the air with noise. Three steam-powered automobiles rolled importantly down a narrow street, carrying a cluster of pompous military officers who ignored the thick crowds pressing in around their vehicles. Soldiers marched in ranks, many of them carrying Moretti rifles, their uniforms crisp and impressive. Roberts thought briefly of Grey Wulfe, wondering how the *Horus* and crew were fairing and if he would see them soon. He would give much for Wulfe's courage by his side in the months to come.

A metallic noise caught Roberts' attention, and he turned to see several Orwille mechas rolling down the street escorted by a squad of soldiers. Unlike in Crimea, the mechas seemed to function well in the city. Passing citizens drew back from them in fear, and Roberts recalled hearing about riots in Constantinople that had been brought to a swift halt. He guessed that the battle mechas had played a part in this role.

Shaking his head a little over the rank foolishness of war, Roberts returned to the wharf where his airship waited. However, his restlessness could not be stilled and he found himself pacing the marine docks, not exactly certain what he was looking for and not finding it. Later in the afternoon, his mood brightened slightly when he spotted two merchant marine ships sailing into port. Three airships looped around the marine ships, fussily escorting them.

Roberts watched the spectacle carefully. He had an idea that the ships were bound for Crimea, which was entirely welcome. One of the airships reminded him of the *Horus*: a bundle of mismatching wood and canvas held together by rope and optimism, while the other two were bigger, sleeker-looking machines. Roberts ran his eyes over their well-trimmed hulls, mentally gauging their agility and strength. They were strong-looking airships and deftly handled, but his ears were tuned to the sound of their engines. German-made was his guess: powerful and dependable, but fuel-hungry.

Deciding he wanted a better look, Roberts strolled along the wharf, watching as the marine ships slid into port and the airships found berths on the wharf. Waiting while their engines stilled and their crews finished settling the ships down, Roberts observed the newcomers intently. His presence was noted, it seemed for after awhile, an airman abruptly stepped off his ship and strode towards Roberts purposefully. Roberts gave him a measuring look, instantly recognizing the cut and bearing of a captain, but there was something in the man's demeanor that made Roberts' fists clench.

The oncoming captain did not waste words. "Ye have been looking at me ships a goodly time, sir," the man snapped out. He planted his feet wide, his hands on his hips while he spat out "sir" derisively. "What was it ye wants with the master of the *Specter*?"

Roberts deliberately moved forward, standing squarely and looking down a few inches at the other man. "Captain Roberts of the airship *Horizon*," he rumbled darkly. "As for what I wanted, I'll start with your name."

The man spat loudly on the deck, an inch from Roberts' boots. "Captain Ronald Dunlap." He tapped himself on the chest, then pointed to the other two airships. "Mine as well, the *Black Nell* and the *Dark Squall*."

"You aim to take your airships to Crimea, Captain Dunlap?" Roberts questioned.

"Aye, and I see naught why it is any business of yers," Dunlap barked out.

Roberts' blood rose, but he spoke calmly. "My ship's been flying in Crimea for over three months. I know the skies and the land. It's a tricky patch for any airship."

Dunlap interrupted him with a hard laugh. "If ye be trying to drive me ships away, Roberts, ye be wasting breath. I know who ye is. There's talk aplenty of the *Horizon* and I know that ye has made good coin in this war." He stuck his chest out aggressively.

Darkness was settling over Roberts' brow. "There's need for your airships and mine in Crimea," he continued in the same even tone. "There is little that can be moved overland. When the supply ships arrive, they need every airship available to transport goods."

"I've no need of any other airship captain at me side," Dunlap growled. "I've three good ships of me own. I'll be taking over transport in Crimea." He and Roberts were nose-to-nose, and neither man had any intent of backing down.

They glared angrily at each other before Roberts spoke. "Take your ships to Crimea, if it please you, but the *Horizon* is returning there tomorrow. She's got her own contract and work waiting for her, and she'll be in Crimea. There's rough skies ahead, and I'd be grateful to know you're watching my back and the *Horizon* yours. But," he raked Dunlap with his eyes, "you seem hell-bent on going your own way."

"I'm not losing transport fees to the likes of ye, Roberts," Dunlap pronounced. "My ships are more than enough for Crimea, and there not be room enough there for ye and myself."

Roberts' shoulders stiffened. "I came to Crimea to make profit, not enemies," he growled. "But if you're dead-set on being competition, your three ships are no match for mine. She's fast as the wind, and I've a better crew that you'll find in the air. I've made a name for myself and my ship in Crimea and by God I will not lose it to a man like you."

Dunlap laughed unpleasantly. "Ye talk big, Roberts, but ye have one ship to your name." He spat again. "And I've little time to waste on ye."

With a final hard look he turned, but not before throwing back at Roberts, "I'd be keeping my ship in Constantinople if I were ye, Captain Roberts. There will be little for ye if ye return to Crimea."

Roberts glared hard at the back of Dunlap's head. "I'll see you in Balaklava," he intoned purposefully. Dunlap's parting laugh grated on Roberts' nerves as he turned deliberately and stalked his way back to the *Horizon*.

Oboe was the only one visible topdeck, having returned from ground leave early. Limbs stilled and face upturned to the sunlight, he sat quietly on a bench, still as a stone and taking his ease. He did not open his eyes as Roberts rolled up the gangplank onto the airship and crossed over to him. Silently, Roberts leaned against the railing and gazed out over the wharf. His eyes kept turning towards Dunlap's airships as he chewed over their brief but tension-filled interview.

A slight sound and Oboe rose to his feet. He moved to the railing to stand at his captain's side. Roberts dropped his weight onto his forearms, leaning heavily against the railing while Oboe stood tall, arms crossed over his chest. He waited patiently until Roberts felt like unburdening himself.

Finally he did. "We can be expecting some competition when we reach Crimea again."

Oboe was silent for a moment before responding, "I saw two merchant marine ships coming into port with three airships as escorts."

"A captain by the name of Dunlap commands all three airships," Roberts stated darkly. "I offered a partnership, but he seems angling to take over all airship transport in Crimea."

"An ambitious goal," Oboe stated with mild humor.

Roberts shook his head. "He's got a trio of good airships, but I've a notion two of them are German-made. They'll spend most of their time looking for coal. The smallest one seems likely to fall apart in a strong wind. Still..."

He let the sentence hang in the air until Oboe picked it up. "The *Horizon* has made a fine reputation for herself in Crimea," Oboe reminded Roberts with quiet assurance. "She can name her own fee and has gained the respect of many of those in power."

Moodily, Roberts sunk a little lower into his shoulders, worry tensing along his spine. "Dunlap strikes me as a man who doesn't let much stand in his way."

A thoughtful hum emanated from Oboe. "You anticipate opposition?" he questioned.

His back cramping, Roberts stood erect, his jaw tightening. "I wouldn't put it past him," he responded. Hardness gleamed in his eye. "Though he's in for a fight if he thinks he can run my ship out of Crimea."

"I doubt that will be necessary, Captain," Oboe responded. "The *Horizon* can speak for herself."

"As can her crew," Roberts asserted firmly. He shifted his weight back and forth, feeling the aching in his feet, but his internal energy pushed past the sensation. Turning his head to face Oboe, he commanded, "We lift at dawn tomorrow."

Oboe's face stirred slightly. "Captain, we return to Crimea alone?" he questioned respectfully, but with the faintest twist of concern.

"No," Roberts stated curtly. "We'll accompany two merchant marine ships, ones fresh to Constantinople with little knowledge of the seas ahead and only too glad to have an experienced airship as a guide."

Oboe grinned. "As you wish, Captain."

***　　　　***　　　　***　　　　***

Morning sunlight gleamed off the shoreline as the *Horizon*'s engines roared enthusiastically, sending the airship forward as clicker code flashed across the water. Bloomberg was hunched over the clicker, his stubby fingers rapidly tapping out a message to the two marine ships moored in the blue waters: the *Delhi* and the *Adolphone.*

The *Specter, Black Nell,* and *Dark Squall* were down cold at the airship wharf; Roberts had made certain of that before lifting. The *Horizon* made quickly for the two merchant marines in a way that might very well have attracted the attention, not to mention the firepower, of Dunlap had his airships been aloft when the *Horizon* approached. A few other airships dotted the sky, but the *Horizon* was the fastest and her flight to the marine ships was direct.

Sooner than Roberts expected, an answering click flashed back, signaling that the *Horizon* was cleared to approach, which she was doing anyway, with or without permission. Normally Roberts wouldn't have dropped his airship so unexpectedly and quickly on another ship. Doing so could meet with a volley of warning shots, but both marine ships were moored at bay, their crews occupied and their cannon ports closed. Roberts was taking a risk, but he was gambling that the marine ships wouldn't feel sufficiently threatened, not with so many war ships close by and a military airship patrolling a half-mile away.

The crew of the *Horizon* was in fine form. Roberts had warned them that competition was on the increase in Crimea, and the men were keen to make it very well known that the *Horizon* was the best in her class. Barking Jack was at his best, sending the *Horizon* racing forward, then dropping her into a startlingly quick and showy hover directly over the *Delhi*. He held her rock-steady in the air while Roberts and Oboe slid below on quick drop lines.

The *Delhi*'s topdeck crew was a bit scattered from the *Horizon*'s abrupt approach. Roberts took full advantage of the confusion to single out the captain and bear down heavily upon him. Sailors scrambled to get out of Roberts' way as he strode forward, Oboe a step behind him.

The captain of the *Delhi* was a giant bear of a man with shoulders mighty enough to erect monuments upon. He was imposing from his mane of yellow-white hair to his highly polished boots. "You and your airship have made a mighty big show for yourselves," he boomed ominously, his hard eyes fixed on Roberts.

"My ship needs little showmanship," Roberts responded confidently and loudly. "She speaks fine for herself as do my men." He squared evenly with the other captain, summing him up in a glance. The two men were almost exactly even in height. The other captain had a good twenty years on Roberts, but he was hard as teak. There wasn't a shred of weakness in his frame, and his steely eyes bored through Roberts, testing him openly.

Before he could lose the initiative, Roberts made his introductions. "Captain Gavin Roberts of the airship *Horizon*. My ship's a Class Five military transport vessel in Crimea."

"I see your airship, Captain Roberts," the other captain looked sharply at the *Horizon* hovering over the *Delhi*. "I also see I've three fine airships that have followed me from London all these weeks."

"True," Roberts conceded. "But you don't have an airship that has been flying in Crimea these past four months. One that knows the land and the seas well enough to keep your marine ships from being blown out of the water and your cargo safe. Balaklava has no port, sir, just a narrow bay and a pile of timbers that calls itself an airship wharf. You won't find a half-decent road and mud's three feet thick on the ground. That's if you're lucky enough to make it to Balaklava Bay. The Black Sea is full of Russian ships, and I've seen more than one good Russian airship in the skies over Crimea."

The older captain's face was a cracked riverbed of deeply rutted lines, his expression unreadable. Roberts was aware of Oboe a few feet behind him and the none-too-friendly stares being directed their way. There was a subtle shifting in the air that hinted the situation could sour rapidly, but Roberts was not cowed. With easy yet purposeful strength, he pronounced confidently, "One experienced airship at your side will do you damned more good than three airships who don't know Crimea's skies and land."

"I paid for three airships and they've served me well," growled the other captain. "I'm not a man to break contract when I've not strong reason to do so."

"I wouldn't ask a man to go back on his word," responded Roberts. "My airship is returning to Crimea tomorrow morning. If you care to have your ships sail with the *Horizon*, she knows these skies. Times like these, a captain can do with as many eyes watching as he can find."

Not a twitch registered in the other captain's granite face, but Roberts had a distinct feeling that his words were being carefully considered. He continued, "Both your marine ships look heavily loaded. Three airships could shift your cargo, but four would help ensure that you get your cargo where it needs to go before the war's out. I've seen plenty of shipments rotting in port at Balaklava for lack of airships to transport it. But," he paused before the other captain had a chance to protest, "first, sail your ship with mine for a time. Let her show you what she can do."

By now, the two captains had gathered an audience. Sailors hovered nearby, going about their duties while carefully eavesdropping. Roberts ignored them, his gaze cool, intent on the other captain who was thinking hard.

Finally the man spoke. "Don't believe I gave you my name." At once, the granite expression softened marginally. "Captain James Oldham. The *Delhi* and *Adolphone* are mine."

Roberts nodded as Oldham continued, "You've got guts, Captain Roberts, I will give you that. But I'll see the cut of your jib first before I'll make up my mind about you."

With that, he thrust out a hand that engulfed Roberts' in sheer agony, his fingers grinding together like gears. Roberts fought to return Oldham's grip before all the bones in his hand disintegrated from the relentless pressure. After several seconds of torturous squeezing, Oldham released Roberts, who resisted the urge to massage his hand back to life. He turned to Oboe and signaled for the *Horizon* to pull the two aloft.

The airship reclaimed her captain and first mate and the crew stared at them as they reentered the ship. Roberts smiled broadly and encouragingly. The crew turned the *Horizon* back to the airship wharf in a jubilant mood. To Roberts' great satisfaction, there was a berth open right next to the *Specter*, whose topdeck was occupied by a visibly furious Captain Dunlap. He gave Roberts a dark look packed full of malice as the *Horizon* touched down on the empty berth. Roberts returned the expression with a salute, then jauntily stepped away from the railing.

Oboe watched the exchange quietly, and as Roberts stepped his way, the first mate commented dryly, "It would appear, Captain, that you are developing a remarkable talent for accumulating enemies."

Roberts snorted. "My ship's been run out of London. I'll be damned if I'll let her be run out of Crimea."

Slowly, Oboe's head nodded. "As will I, Captain."

Chapter Twenty-Three

It was with supreme satisfaction on the following day that Roberts directed the *Horizon* to lead the fleet of air and marine ships through the Bosporus as they departed Constantinople. The *Horizon* flew boldly through the clean air, the five other vessels trailing behind her. Roberts watched Dunlap's airships carefully, knowing the other captain was furious about the *Horizon*'s addition to the fleet. Surprisingly, Dunlap kept his airships trim and in good formation, and they manifested no sign of aggression.

The crowded skies and waters of the Bosporus left little room for any arguments between the *Horizon* and Dunlap's airships. Dozens of vessels wiggled their way forward, near collisions threatening and tempers flaring. Clicker code flashed in the air as airship captains signaled position reports and bickered over flight paths, while a few vessels blatantly ignored regulations, putting themselves and other airships at danger. In the waters below, marine ships scrimmaged irritably, battling over right of way and favorable streams while the narrow waters of the Bosporus pressed from both sides.

Out in the open skies and waters of the Black Sea, the fleet of six settled into a more comfortable sailing pattern: the *Horizon* in point position front while the *Specter*, *Black Nell* and *Dark Squall* fanned out in a wide arc, all the better to see any possible danger approaching. Despite his initial conflict with Dunlap, Roberts had to admit that the man was a skilled captain and his three airships were a credit to his name. For the time being, professionalism took precedent over competition. The four airships flew together smoothly, passing along information about headings, speed changes, and potential enemies in the sky or water.

If Roberts' first encounter with Dunlap had not nearly come to blows, he would have been glad to fly with him. However, Roberts knew that Dunlap's threat had not been idle and that his temporary cooperation was likely due to Oldham's eye watching them carefully. The minute the fleet hit Balaklava Bay, Roberts fully expected that Dunlap would disavow all further collaboration with the *Horizon*.

Pacing the decks of his airship, Roberts observed his men at work and passed on quiet words of praise or correction as deserved. He was pleased to note that they were moving with extra briskness, eager to show the *Horizon* at her full strength and ability. As he passed through the airship, Roberts encountered Big Tom, who had unearthed himself from the envelope and was standing topdeck, carefully observing the other three airships with a telescope.

Roberts paused by Big Tom's side and waited, knowing that something had captured his attention. Big Tom, like Halloway, spent almost all his waking hours at his post and was intently focused on his work. For him to be taking keen notice of the other airships in the fleet meant that something was nagging at him.

Several moments passed before Big Tom dropped the telescope from his right eye and frowned through his generous beard. "I flew on the *Dreadnought* three years past, sir," Big Tom commented, nodding at the *Specter*. "She had a Heimdall envelope like that one."

Roberts took in the information thoughtfully. German-made envelopes were rare on airships, most captains preferring one from a well-known English canopy factory such as Dunningham. Plenty an airship made do with a handmade envelope stitched together with whatever spare canvas was available. An artfully engineered envelope meant all the difference between a vessel that sailed fast and true and one that was sluggish and unresponsive. When she had passed into Roberts' hands, the *Horizon* had come with a nearly new Dunningham envelope that had served her well.

Big Tom sucked his teeth. "A Heimdall is light, sir, and that's a strong point. You'll shave a quarter in weight off your envelope." He passed the telescope to Roberts and gestured at the *Specter*. "See the tucking along the portside duler line? That will cut your drag down. A Heimdall's for speed, sir, tight and tucked to keep her flying clean.

"But you lose maneuverability and strength and you need more hands to maintain it," Big Tom added thoughtfully. "We had three men on the *Dreadnaught*'s catwalks at all times."

Roberts grunted, but he was pleased by the information. Any edge he could gain on Dunlap was helpful. "How do you think she'll fly in Crimea?"

The catwalk man hummed a little in his throat. "Difficult to say, Captain, but I'd not use a Heimdall in a hard winter." He pointed a stubby finger toward the *Black Nell*. "That one there is losing too much steam, sir. She's overworking her boiler to keep her airbags full. Too much strain. The other," his finger moved towards the *Dark Squall*. "A good ship," he conceded grudgingly. "Not much to look at, but she's tight and full in the envelope."

It occurred to Roberts that this was the longest speech Big Tom had ever given in his presence. The words had been expressed almost grudgingly, as if stockpiled for use only in dire occasions. Having said his piece, he fell silent. With a nod, Roberts let Big Tom clamber back into the envelope while he pondered what the man had uttered.

The thoughts stayed with Roberts through the journey back to Crimea, five days of uneventful travel. The winds blew cold and bracing and the seas below were choppy, but the *Delhi* and *Adolphone* filled their sails with wind and cut easily through the frigid waters. The *Specter*, *Black Nell* and *Dark Squall* left trails of black smoke as they flew steadily through the air. Observing the smoke output from Dunlap's airships, Roberts guessed they were burning through their fuel stores and would be eager for fresh coal the moment they hit Crimea. They could squabble over the scanty supply of bitimous while the *Horizon* filled her hoppers with anthracite courtesy of the local mines.

The fleet reached Balaklava on November 22nd, and Roberts would have paid dearly to see the look on Dunlap's face as the airships entered the air over the harbor and began easing towards the wharf. The weather had grown bitingly cold, and stiff winds were gusting in and out of the harbor, setting the *Specter* and *Black Nell* vibrating in the air. Even Barking Jack was visibly struggling to keep the *Horizon* flying true. The ramshackle airship wharf was empty, but in the stiff winds it looked even less sturdy than normal. Although a third berth had recently been constructed on the wharf, there were now four airships over Balaklava. Dunlap's airships circled the wharf uncertainly as their crews wondered if it was strong enough to hold them and who would land first.

Seven warships were anchored in the bay, and the *Adolphone* and *Delhi* eased into the narrow harbor, edging past the warships and moving to shore. Dunlap's airships droned overhead, fighting the winds while his men surveyed their new operating theater. On board the *Horizon*, Roberts bided his time, keeping the *Horizon* steady in the air while his crew worked with practiced ease. When he calculated that frustration had taken a firm enough hold on board the other vessels, Roberts called for Bloomberg to hail the *Delhi*.

The *Horizon*'s clicker code was answered promptly, and soon Roberts was sliding on board the *Delhi* with cool ease. Oldham stood stalwart, mighty boots planted wide and face like the sheer side of a cliff. As Roberts moved in his direction with a confident gait, Oldham eyed him stormily, then boomed deeply, "I've sailed into worse ports before, Captain Roberts."

"I've no doubt," Roberts replied calmly, at ease and unruffled. "You're a man that will finish the job before him. Question is," he smiled thinly, "how long do you wish to take to finish it?"

Oldham's beard twitched as Roberts returned his steely gaze with equal strength. "The *Horizon* can unload your ship right here in the bay, and you needn't drop a longboat to do so. She can hoist all your cargo ashore without touching down."

"True? And risk your airship tangling my sails to bits?" Oldham thundered.

Coolly, Roberts lifted his chin towards the *Horizon*. "Captain Oldham, I'd be obliged if you'd notice my airship is the only one rock-steady in the skies." The *Horizon* was hovering with barely a tremor while the *Black Nell* and *Dark Squall* cut jerky circles around the bay and the *Specter* vibrated in place. It took calm weather and exquisite piloting for an airship to lift cargo from a sail-rigged marine ship without a catastrophe. The *Horizon* could handle the task, something Dunlap's airships could decidedly not do.

"My ship is ready to work," Roberts emphasized. "Captain Dunlap's ships likely need berthing and recoaling, and her crews need a lay of the land before they can load and lift." It was early afternoon, but Roberts doubted if Dunlap's ships would be ready to transport before evening fell. In contrast, the *Horizon* was still carrying almost half the anthracite she had brought from Constantinople. Her crew was ready to start work, still eager to show off their airship in the face of Dunlap's antagonism.

Oldham pondered Roberts' words while Roberts waited calmly, willing himself not to show the slightest sign of anxiety. Finally, and with another twitch of his beard, Oldham pronounced his edict. "I'll see you take on a load, Captain Roberts," he intoned ominously. "But if your ship, your ropes, or your men come an inch closer to my sails or masts than I care for, well," he grunted, "My cannon have blown airships out of the skies before can and will again."

"I'll not call you an unreasonable man, Captain Oldham," said Roberts. Oldham's lips parted in a marginal smile as Roberts took his leave, acutely aware of hard eyes drilling into his back. Confidently, easily, he crossed the topdeck and signaled for the *Horizon*.

The next two hours were packed solid with tension as the *Horizon* carefully lifted nine tons of cargo from the *Delhi* and settled it into her cargo bay. Barking Jack keep a running commentary of muttered swear words as he battled valiantly against the effects of strong wind, shifting cargo, and bodies moving about the airship. Muscles strained and groaned with effort, and spines ran wire-tight with stress. Shoulder-to-shoulder with his men, Roberts kept his cool, exhorting his crew as his own strength flowed into the demanding work.

Despite the multitude of ways something could go terribly wrong, operations on board the *Horizon* progressed smoothly. As the last basketful was hoisted off the *Delhi*, Roberts was rewarded with a grudging nod of approval from Captain Oldham. He took this small triumph away with him as the *Horizon* reclaimed her captain and began maneuvers to bring her load to camp.

Elsewhere in Balaklava Bay, operations did not fare as well. The *Dark Squall* and *Black Nell* had finally touched down at the wharf, and their boilers were steadily cooling, but stiff winds blew across their topdecks, snapping ropes and flapping canvas. In the bay, the *Adolphone's* crew was hard at work rowing the supplies to shore on a small fleet of longboats, but the waters were choppy and progress was slow. One longboat tipped over, its contents lost to the wave. A hasty rescue party came to the aid of the longboat's crew.

Meanwhile, the *Specter* continued to cut circles through the air. Dunlap kept her aloft, but she stayed out of the *Horizon's* way during the loading process and wasn't a bother. As the last basketful of cargo lifted from the *Delhi*, a clicker message flashed across the sky.

"Captain!" Bloomberg called out. "The *Specter* asks permission to accompany us to camp."

Roberts frowned, then responded, "Signal back that permission is granted."

Bloomberg flashed the message and the *Horizon* turned her nose towards camp. With every sign of courtesy, the *Specter* settled in place behind the *Horizon* at a respectful distance and followed her out of the bay. As the two airships moved out into open country, the *Specter* showed absolutely no sign of antagonism, nor any indication that Captain Dunlap intended to make good on his threat.

As Oboe and Roberts stood observing the *Specter*, Oboe inclined his head in her direction. "She is sailing well and true, Captain," he commented.

Roberts snorted. "Dunlap has a keen mind," he pronounced with a small measure of grudging admiration. "A man doesn't rise to his position by being a fool. He's biding his time." Narrowing his eyes, Roberts added, "He's good and angry now but he doesn't know the land and he knows this is not the time. No. He'll wait, he'll watch, then he'll strike when he's ready."

Oboe nodded thoughtfully, but there was a sharp gleam of cunning in his eye which was mirrored by Roberts. The two men said nothing more as the airships moved forward.

The approach of camp several minutes later drew their attention and the *Horizon* was soon touching down on her accustomed berth while the *Specter* hovered in the sky, waiting for the lead airship to land first.

The camp had continued to swell in the time the *Horizon* had been away. Hunger and desperation were etched into the faces of the soldiers who unloaded the *Horizon*, and disappointment reigned supreme when the *Specter* proved to be empty. Dunlap and his crew kept to their airship, doing nothing to hinder the *Horizon* as she dropped her load. With only nine tons in her, the *Horizon* was quickly unloaded and both airships soon lifted to return to Balaklava.

Back at the bay, the *Delhi* had managed to edge closer to shore, but there were still far too many warships blocking her way. Some of her cargo was moving ashore on longboats, and work continued slowly across the choppy waters. Roberts ignored them, intent on the *Delhi*. At his command, the *Horizon* sailed lightly through the gusty air and lowered him overboard on a quick drop line.

Confidently and with pride running through his veins, Roberts slid to the *Delhi*'s topdeck, to be greeted by a steely-eyed Oldham. The two captains met face-to-face, and Roberts smiled broadly in greeting, not bothering to disguise his look of triumph. Oldham's face was discouragement embodied in flesh but after a staring contest that Roberts refused to lose, the older captain's frozen expression thawed a trifle.

"Well, Captain Roberts," Oldham thundered impressively. "I will hand it to you. Your ship held true to her captain's word and she did her work well." He spoke the words with reluctance, as if unaccustomed to doling out anything resembling praise.

Taking the grudgingly-bestowed compliment, Roberts pressed the point forward. "You need the *Horizon*," he stated confidently. "You've seen the lay of the land and you've seen my airship fly." He nodded his head in the direction of the *Specter*. "Dunlap's a good captain, but you know as well as I do that his three ships aren't a match for the *Horizon*. Not here, not with these flying conditions. You need my ship."

Oldham shifted his eyes to his second-in-command, but before either man could speak, Roberts calmly fired his next volley. "And you'll be paying me forty-five pounds a ton." It was a steep price, though lower than what the *Horizon* could command in Crimea. Roberts suspected his demanded price was significantly less than Dunlap's fee.

Oldham startled, then loosened a great bear laugh of incredulousness. Borrowing Oboe's enigmatic smile, Roberts refused to budge and merely waited calmly while Oldham got the laugh out of his system.

"By gods, is there room in your trousers for those stones you're carrying, Captain Roberts?" Oldham demanded with clear admiration.

Grinning quietly, Roberts pointed out over the bay. "You'll be days rowing your cargo to the mud they call a shore," he emphasized. "None of Dunlap's airships can lift cargo from your ships, not with the wind and choppy waters. Not if you want to keep you sails intact and don't fancy lingering in Balaklava for weeks. Lifting cargo straight from a marine ship plays hell with my engines and my crew. That's wear and tear on my ship and a hazard risk. Lifting cargo eats up coal by the ton, and my ship runs on anthracite which is damned expensive. All this comes at a cost."

Pointing out over the hills, Roberts pronounced, "The fields are littered with camps of starving men that can't move half a mile for the mud. My ship's been flying around Crimea for weeks dropping off supplies at these camps. To reach them, I'm flying my airship over a hell of a lot of battleground with enemy airships in the skies to dodge. That's hazard pay. My ship is agile and strong enough that she can unload near the ground and doesn't need to put down at a wharf. But doing so overloads my engines and puts her at good risk for a crash."

"So you're asking me to pay nearly a third more than what I pay Captain Dunlap?" Oldham demanded, bearing down on Roberts.

"No, sir," Roberts responded calmly. "I'm telling you the *Horizon* and my men are worth a hell of a lot more but I'll settle for forty-five pounds a ton."

Dunlap's glare could have melted iron, but Roberts held it unwaveringly, refusing to put aside his thin smile, until the other captain's face cracked into a wide, knowing grin.

"You've got to be one of the biggest bastards I've ever had standing on my ship!" Oldham thundered heartily. His hand clapped down on Roberts' shoulder with crushing force. Triumphantly, Roberts savored the complement, but Oldham tempered his praise. "I expect damned good use out of my forty-five pounds a ton," he warned ominously.

"You won't be disappointed," Roberts promised. The urge to gloat was nearly overwhelming but he kept his ego tethered down. With a little more dithering, he and Oldham hammered out the terms of their contract. When the *Horizon* pulled Roberts off the *Delhi*, elation was still running high in his veins and he vaulted easily over the railing with a youthful exuberance. His feet thumped heavily on the topdeck.

Bloomberg and Carter watched hopefully as their captain jumped back into the airship, ready at the railing to help him aboard. They gazed at him in anticipation while Roberts stood grinning, letting the tension build dramatically for a few moments. Finally Carter, impatience breaking through his restraint, demanded, "Captain? Any word?"

Roberts' grin increased. "Best make yourselves comfortable in Crimea, lads, for we've work ahead of us."

"Old Dunlap will be pissed," Carter announced with glee while Bloomberg smiled broadly. Word quickly spread and the rest of the crew caught the news. Roberts waved his men off before elation turned to carelessness.

"We've cargo to move," he admonished, pushing the men back to their work. "Get her loaded."

Oboe, however, stayed at Roberts' side. "Well done, sir," he said, smiling his approval. Then his eyes shifted as his voice rose up in quiet warning. "Captain Oldham will tolerate no mistakes,"

Frowning, Roberts narrowed his eyes in determination. "I don't aim to make any."

Chapter Twenty-Four

There was little sleep to be found in the upcoming days as the *Horizon* raced feverishly in a locked battle with Dunlap's airships. As Roberts had predicted, all cooperation between the *Horizon* and the three other airships swiftly evaporated. In its place was an onslaught of antagonism that was no doubt aggravated by the rapidly spreading news of how much Oldham was paying Roberts for the *Horizon*'s expert skills.

The *Specter, Black Nell,* and *Dark Squall* aggressively asserted their position in Crimea, commandeering all three berths on Balaklava's wharf and refusing to allow the *Horizon* any professional courtesy in the sky. With three airships and forty-three men at his command, Dunlap had the advantage of numbers, and he drove his crews mercilessly. His men struggled to adapt to the increasingly colder weather and the limited infrastructure in Crimea, but Dunlap spared them no pity in his determination to best Roberts and the *Horizon*.

"Right bastard, isn't he, Captain?" Barking Jack commented wearily to Roberts, gesturing at the *Specter*. It was three days into the massive transport job, and the *Horizon* had spent very few of them grounded, just enough to let her crew catch some sleep or load up on coal and cargo. She needed coal now, but the *Specter* wouldn't clear from the wharf despite being fully loaded and ready to lift. The *Horizon* had just sailed into the bay, and Roberts swore the *Specter* had been lifting off as they approached. When the *Horizon* moved closer to the wharf, the *Specter* remained on her berth and refused to budge. Running low on coal, the *Horizon* circled over the wharf, waiting for a landing spot to open. Dunlap's airships, however, stayed put and did not lift.

"This is bullshit," Farrington snapped irritably at Roberts' side. "We've less than an hour of fuel before we hit our reserve. Dunlap better get his damn birds off the wharf."

"They'll move," Roberts stated. He'd so far held his temper where Dunlap was concerned, happy in the knowledge that the *Horizon* was performing far better than the other three airships. However, if Dunlap's actions imperiled the *Horizon*, Roberts would make him see the error of his ways in a hurry.

Barking Jack sighed heavily, wiping a hand over his taut, haggard face. While Bloomberg's piloting skills continued to increase, the stiff uptick in competition and the hazardous flying conditions meant that Barking Jack spent long hours at the wheel. The endless hours of high-stress work were etching deep lines of worry and stress into his face.

Shifting his concerned eyes from his exhausted pilot to the airship wharf, Roberts spotted purposeful movement heading towards the direction of the *Specter*. He was grimly pleased to see Staff Sergeant Prachett marching towards the *Specter* with several burly soldiers trailing behind him, rifles over their shoulders. A visibly tense conversation followed. From the *Horizon*, Roberts watched Dunlap grow agitated, waving his arms in a threatening manner. Prachett stood immobile and resolute, his bearing indicating he was not about to take any sort of bullshit from anyone.

The end result was Dunlap storming back on board the *Specter* while Prachett stood, arms folded and watching sternly. Through the air, the *Specter*'s engines began whining with urgency, indicating the airship was grudgingly preparing to lift into the air and make room for the *Horizon*.

"About damned time," Farrington grunted.

Roberts nodded at him, then called into the com device, "All ship, prepare for landing. Full shutdown and hold. We'll be at port awhile for fueling and water." His men obeyed, fatigue dragging down their movements. At the wheel, Barking Jack was operating on his last crumbs of energy. If a herd of naked women was running around on the wharf, Roberts suspected that Barking Jack would barely notice.

His suspicions were proved correct when the *Horizon* thumped down into her berth with a surprising jolt, shuddering the airship and knocking loose a few crates below decks. Barking Jack shook himself and began scrabbling at the wheel, trying to right the airship and clearly surprised at the hard landing.

"Captain! I...I'm sorry, sir...I...," he stammered.

A few quick glances and a general empathy with his airship gave Roberts a firm impression that the airship and crew had both taken a hard jarring, but no real damage had been done. Reaching Barking Jack's side, he admonished sharply, "Easy, man."

Barking Jack's face tightened into stoicism, mentally preparing himself for the tongue-lashing his carelessness earned him. Roberts glared at him. "You're walking drunk with fatigue. You're not taking the wheel again until you've got some sleep in you. That's an order."

Barking Jack nodded marginally, then obediently turned and stumbled his way down to the berthing area. Roberts roamed the airship, checking her carefully for damages and finding none, save a few broken crates. He castigated himself silently for the accident, knowing that he had pushed Barking Jack far too hard in recent days. Resolving to monitor his pilots more closely and step in to take the wheel more often, Roberts walked the rest of his airship in a grim frame of mind. Disaster was never more than a step away on an airship, and Crimea dealt severely with carelessness.

A week passed as the four airships prowled the skies, lifting and carrying cargo in endless circuits. As November came to a close, the temperature continued to plummet. The winds increased, and fog routinely appeared. As predicted by Big Tom, the *Specter* was fleet but unstable in the sky, and the battering winds of Crimea made for hard flying. The *Dark Squall* and *Black Nell* fared a little better, but harsh flying conditions, low coal stores, and winter weather dragged all the airships down. Dunlap struggled mightily to keep his three ships flying, but it was hard enough just to get them from Balaklava to camp.

The *Horizon* flew to camp but also ranged across Crimea to small campsites where starving, desperate soldiers waited for supplies, enemies, and orders. The endless succession of running drops created enormous strain on the *Horizon* and her crew, straining her engines and exhausting the men keeping her in the air. Roberts himself battled grimly through the days, his mind wracked with worry over both his airship and crew while he wrung out every last drop of energy and strength from his own flesh.

It was November 29th on a cold, clear day when the *Horizon* moved through the air with a half-load in her belly. Skies were clear and the sun was shining, increasing visibility and producing better flight conditions than they had seen for days. Less welcome was the sound of gunfire in the distance as battle raged on the ground. The *Horizon's* crew had long grown accustomed to the sounds of distant warfare, but Roberts did not allow them to slacken their vigilance. William and Carter were on deck watch, carefully surveying the ground and skies for any potential hazard.

The *Horizon* was soaring through the air at a steady thirty knots, winds still and skies clear, when William's voice rose up in alarm. "Captain! You should come see this, sir!"

Roberts was at his side in an instant, spyglass in hand. Through the lenses, the ground below unfolded in living color as specks of movement sharpened into clear detail. There was a battle in progress, and the hills swarmed with action: cavalry rushing forward under a battery of fire pouring in from three sides, Russian flags fluttering on the hills. Even at the distance, Roberts could see that the British cavalry was heavily outnumbered and racing into an imminent slaughter.

He lowered the spyglass and narrowed his eyes into a thoughtful squint. Seized with a sudden impulse to gain a better look, he turned to Bloomberg and gave an order. "Move us closer in," he commanded.

"Captain?" Bloomberg questioned with reasonable confusion. Roberts couldn't blame him. Actively getting closer to a battle was foolhardy, but there were no other airships present in the clear skies. If the *Horizon* kept eight hundred feet in the air and a half-mile from the conflict, she would be reasonably safe while Roberts assessed the situation. Precisely why he wanted to do so, he wasn't entirely sure, but an inner compulsion goaded him forward.

Turning back to his crew, Roberts snapped out a volley of commands which they obeyed reluctantly. As the airship moved closer, the sound of cannon fire filled the air and the action ahead swung into sharper focus. It was madness. Five units of British cavalry were charging forward under an unstoppable volley of bullets pouring in from both hills and from the direct front. The lightly-armed cavalry troops were heavily outnumbered and could do little against the onslaught of multiple artillery. But the chargers were bearing up magnificently, racing zealously across the field even as their comrades fell around them.

It was suicide to continue, madness to keep moving forward. But not a charger wavered from his path, all of them dead-set on the Russian battery in front of them, men dying every second as bullet after bullet ripped through their ranks. Bullets continued to pour in, men falling, horses screaming as their riders were shot off their backs, the cries of battle and the sounds of determined, fearless fighters continuing to rise up in the air.

Even to the uninformed, the heroic suicide charge below clearly served no purpose. What commander would knowingly send a small group of lightly-armed men to face these odds? What soldiers, when confronted with such heavy opposition, would attack wholeheartedly without regard for their own skins? But they were coming, and the endless volley of bullets did not slow the mad charge.

"Captain!" Bloomberg called out nervously over the tense air. "It isn't safe here, sir! We should leave!" Although the skies were empty, a Russian airship could appear suddenly. Even without the threat of an attacking ship, the *Horizon* was entirely too close to the field of battle.

William's look gave Roberts pause. "Can't we do something, sir?" he questioned, pointing at the battlefield.

"Captain!" Bloomberg repeated, this time angry. Tension and alertness tore through the crew as they attended the airship while keeping a sharp eye on the slaughter below. The *Horizon* was no warship. There was only one way she could help the fighting warriors below.

Turning, Roberts voiced his orders. "Hard to port and a straight path back to camp!" he barked out. He strode over to the com device. "Engine room, get her up to forty knots!"

"Aye, Captain!" Jenkins shouted back. "Is there a problem, sir?"

"We need air and speed," Roberts repeated. The British camp was just a few miles away, and time was precious. However, getting to the camp to spread the alert was a virtually pointless endeavor. The cavalry was being cut to pieces. It would be a miracle if any of them survived the charge. Reinforcements would not reach the warriors quickly enough to make a difference. The cavalry was doomed, and there wasn't a damned thing the *Horizon* could do about it.

That didn't mean that Roberts wasn't going to try. After ten minutes of high-speed flying, the *Horizon* touched down on the camp's wharf. Barely had she landed than Roberts vaulted off the railing, leaving Oboe behind to supervise the airship. To his relief, he was greeted by Major Bryson, who had spotted the *Horizon*'s approach.

Without preamble, Roberts growled out, "Major, you've got several units of cavalry a few miles from here. They're sandwiched between Fedioukine and Causeway and getting hammered from both sides and the front by a damned big number of Russians."

The officer paled under the mud and rough stubble on his face. "Oh, my God, the Light Brigade..." he gasped out as Roberts cut him off.

"You'll be damned lucky if a handful of them make it out alive," he said darkly.

Major Bryson gave Roberts a harried look, then gestured over his shoulder. "You'd best come with me, Captain Roberts. We'll report to Lord Raglan."

The two men threaded their way the mud clogging up the camp. Gaunt, haunted-looking faces peered at them as they passed, overwhelming misery dulling hundreds of eyes. But Roberts' thoughts were intent on the task ahead. He knew whom he was about to face: FitzRoy James Henry Somerset, the First Baron of Raglan and the general of the British troops in Crimea. Lord Raglan had personally commended the *Horizon* for delivering the cavalry horses, and the *Horizon* had earned a name for herself in Crimea. Roberts didn't want to wreck his first interaction with Lord Raglan, and his thoughts were heavy as he followed Bryson through the camp.

Bryson hurriedly pushed them both through several strata of the military pecking order until he and Roberts were standing in a crisply ordered tent, surrounded by a group of officers. Bryson stuttered through a hasty introduction of Roberts, who was silent and observed his surroundings with a critical eye. Lord Raglan was well past sixty, and while his craggy, stern face was lined with crevices, his curling hair was still thick around his temples. He had the look of a man who was conceding to age only with a fierce struggle.

He kept his sharp eyes fastened on Roberts while Bryson spoke, then interrupted abruptly. "What did you see, Captain Roberts?" he demanded sharply.

"My airship saw several units of lightly armed cavalry getting killed in the valley between Fedioukine and Causeway," Roberts reported bluntly. "They were heavily outnumbered by Russians on both sides and the front. It was a slaughter, sir," he finished simply.

Lord Raglan's brow was like a growing storm. "I gave Captain Nolan specific orders to..."

"Lord Raglan!" a harried voice cut through the air as a mud-bespattered officer arrived. "Sir, Captain Nolan! He's dead, sir, and the Light Brigade is falling as we speak!"

"What?" Raglan shot to his feet, knocking his chair over.

"The Light Brigade, sir, it went into the valley!" the officer continued hurriedly. "There are Russians on both Fedioukine and Causeway and..."

Raglan stormed around his desk toward the tent's entrance. He stopped midway, then pointed a finger at Roberts. "Captain Roberts, I'll thank you to keep your airship in my camp until I give you leave to depart. I may have need of you." The general didn't wait for a response as he thundered forward, officers hurrying behind him.

Roberts and Bryson exchanged a weary shrug, then left the tent as one. Already, the camp was roaring with activity as fresh reports from the battlefield began flooding in, quickening the noise and disorder. Commands were yelled and soldiers swirled in a maelstrom of movement. Bryson was quickly sucked into its force, leaving Roberts alone.

Glowering to himself, Roberts slogged his way back to the *Horizon*, chewing moodily over what had just transpired, when a feminine voice caught his attention.

"Captain Roberts!" He turned to see a woman heading his way, but it took him a second or two to place her as Miss Pickens. Gone was the elegant, dainty clothing and instead there was a plain, coarse skirt and man's greatcoat, both overlarge and heavily splattered with mud and gore. Her hair was caught up in a messy bun unraveling around her neck, and her face was drawn and haggard-looking.

Roberts hurried to her across the mud. "Miss Pickens, are you well? Are you injured?" he said heavily, eyes assessing her carefully. She was bedraggled and obviously fatigued but seemed reasonably intact.

Miss Pickens pressed a hand to her lips. "Captain, it's...it's simply terrible here," she said, almost in a sob.

"It's war," Roberts growled heavily. Before he could stop himself, he continued, "I just witnessed a group of cavalry being slaughtered a few miles away."

"The Light Brigade?" Miss Pickens said, her eyes widening. "I've heard bits of news but..." she shook her head tiredly, then seemed to pull energy from a hidden source. "Captain Roberts," she said firmly. "You must take me to that battlefield at once."

"What?" Roberts said incredulously. "That is out of the question, Miss Pickens."

"You must, Captain," Miss Pickens said with conviction.

"No," Roberts replied flatly. "There were at least fifty Russian artillery on those hills and more bullets than I care to think about." More gently, he added, "It was a slaughter, Miss Pickens. There won't be survivors."

Miss Pickens started to protest, but something crumpled in her face. Roberts caught her as she bent at the knees, and her small frame rested against his for one moment. She sighed deeply before she pulled herself to her feet again and lifted her chin with quavering determination.

Examining her carefully, Roberts stated the obvious. "You're exhausted."

Miss Pickens tried to stand taller. "No more so than you, I imagine." There was a paleness to her face that caught Roberts' attention, and he reached out to touch her forehead. Her skin was hot under his fingertips. She flinched slightly at his touch but there was no hiding her condition.

He frowned deeply. "You're ill." Miss Pickens shook her head in protest but Roberts' frown only increased. "You're getting back on the *Horizon*, Miss Pickens," he stated flatly. "This is not up for debate." Her shoulders stiffened but then drooped. With submission likely born of sheer exhaustion and illness, she meekly let him guide her toward the *Horizon*. Miss Pickens did not refuse Roberts' offer of his arm and as she clung to him, he could feel her strength draining away with every struggling step through the mud.

Miss Pickens' appearance filled the *Horizon* with surprise. Her exhausted, ill condition was apparent; the crew looked on in concern as she stumbled on board. Roberts directed her toward his cabin, collecting Harding as he went. He pushed them both inside: Harding to work his doctoring skills and Miss Pickens to rest, something he suspected she had lost acquaintance with in the prior weeks.

Most of the crew had gathered at a respectful distance, watching the proceedings. When Roberts turned back to them, William piped up, "Is Miss Pickens badly ill, sir?"

Roberts waved a hand in dismissal. "Overworked and overtired and running a fever. Harding will look after her." He spoke the words easily, but worry chewed at his stomach. The camp was thick with diseases and Miss Pickens could have picked up a number of them, not to mention that she'd grown thinner since their last encounter.

Worriedly, Roberts kept his airship grounded while Lord Raglan decided what he wanted to do with the *Horizon*. With nothing to do but wait at the airship for further orders, the crew dispersed into small knots to talk quietly and keep a sharp eye out for more news. Roberts kept the *Horizon*'s envelope full, ready to lift, and hoped they would be on their way soon. However, he had a feeling they would be stuck at camp for awhile.

Not too long after Miss Pickens had entered the *Horizon*, Jules appeared and stomped up the gangplank with a solid determination that discouraged any attempts to get in his way. He caught Roberts' eye, who merely gave a shrug in the direction of the cabin. Jules nodded curtly and thundered towards the cabin as if he suspected Roberts of dishonorable actions where his sister was concerned. Roberts let him pass. The cabin door slammed pointedly behind Jules.

Movement and noise increased in the camp and within an hour, the first wave of wounded cavalry started to arrive. Bloodied, half-dead men were slung across horses, blood dripping down the horses' flanks to pool onto the muddy ground. A wagon, overloaded with mud and groaning bodies, squished its way forward. Other soldiers arrived on foot, dragging the wounded or carrying them on stretchers. Medical personnel, already overworked, staggered forward to attend the newly-arrived Light Brigade survivors.

Roberts surveyed the chaotic turmoil and said to Oboe, "I'm surprised to see any survivors."

Oboe looked grim. "I do not believe that there will be any survivors past the end of the day, Captain," he intoned solemnly. Roberts had to agree. The camp's paltry medical facilities were overflowing as it was, and the fresh influx of wounded would only overtax their scanty resources.

Sighing, he turned his attention back to his airship. With newly arrived wounded, the camp was in dire need of the medical supplies waiting back at the bay for transport. He wondered impatiently how long the *Horizon* would be detained at camp at Lord Raglan's pleasure. To his infinite relief, an orderly soon brought commands from Lord Raglan that the *Horizon* was to take to the air again. Whether the general wanted the *Horizon* to get back to work or merely wished the camp clear of non-military personnel, Roberts didn't know. He was simply relieved to leave the carnage behind and return to Balaklava Bay.

When the *Horizon* cleared the hills and lowered into the bay, all three of Dunlap's airships were sitting on the wharf. Roberts' thin temper reached the snapping point as the *Horizon* moved to hover near the wharf. He could see that the *Black Nell* was loaded and nearly ready for takeoff but her engines were starting to taper off, a clear sign that she was staying put simply to spite Roberts.

God damn this, he growled and bellowed for a quick drop line. The *Horizon* dropped him off at the edge of the wharf, nearly depositing him in the chilly waters of the bay. He had to scramble for purchase on the rotting boards before his feet stabilized and sent him storming heavily down the wharf towards the *Black Nell*. She was supervised by one of Dunlap's first officers, a squat man who watched with cool insolence as Roberts approached.

Roberts wasted few words. Towering over the man, he thundered, "You've got five minutes to get your damned ship off the wharf. My ship's got a sick woman on board and she's bringing news of a slaughter that happened less than two hours ago in the Heights." Roberts stabbed a thick finger into the distance to emphasize his point. The other man flicked his eyes in the direction of Roberts' finger as uncertainty broke through his defiance.

"My ship saw the event first-hand and I'll be damned if the likes of you will prevent me from bringing word to the officers here," Roberts snarled. "Get moving. *Now.*"

The officer conceded, and with a few commands began moving the *Black Nell* off the wharf, allowing the *Horizon* to quickly slip into the berth. During the noise and bustle of landing, Roberts felt his senses tighten in warning. He turned to see the dark figure of Dunlap rolling towards him. Behind a scowling Dunlap was Staff Sergeant Prachett, and a few feet behind him were three soldiers.

Planting his feet firmly, Roberts waited for Dunlap to approach. The conflict between them had been building long enough. By the sharp cast of Dunlap's body, he was keen to even the score with fists, knives, or an all-ship brawl if necessary. His own anger burning in his gut, Roberts thundered toward his oncoming opponent. Both men halted in the middle and hands were already curling into fists, but Roberts pointedly ignored Dunlap for Prachett.

"Staff Sergeant Prachett, have you heard news of the Light Brigade?" he demanded, knowing that it was unlikely a messenger had reached the bay with word of the slaughter.

Dunlap reddened with anger at being ignored, but Prachett stepped forward meaningfully, all but shouldering the other airship captain aside. "What news?" he questioned calmly but urgently.

"Wiped out by Russians flanking on both sides of Causeway and Fedioukine just about two hours ago," Roberts announced with brutal finality. "A few survivors made it back to camp, but it was a bloodbath. We saw it from the air."

Prachett inhaled sharply for one long moment, then spoke in a level tone. "I'll pass on word to my superiors," he stated, then turned carefully. He moved back down the wharf with a stiff motion that indicated the enormous control he was exerting over himself.

With Prachett gone, Dunlap immediately swung back to Roberts with murder in his fists. Roberts stopped him with deep, hard words. "You ships are carrying medical supplies?" he demanded. He well knew that Dunlap's vessels were loaded up with the last of the medical supplies from Oldham's ships.

Dunlap barely nodded in grudging acknowledgment. "Then get your ships in the air and to camp," Roberts commanded. "They need every bandage you're carrying."

"Ye telling me what to do with me own ships, Roberts?" Dunlap threatened ominously, his fists clenching.

"Dammit, man, there's men dying in camp," Roberts replied with heat. "Whatever quarrel you have with me, I'll meet you fair and square when all this is over. But you and I have a job to do."

Dunlap's jaw clenched with pure rage as he met Roberts' glare. However, to his credit, Dunlap deliberately loosened his fists and stepped back a pace, not turning his furious eyes from Roberts. Through gritted teeth, he stated, "I'll get me ships in the air."

Roberts nodded curtly but Dunlap did not budge. "I'm not finished with ye yet, Roberts," he warned ominously. "This is not done between the two of us."

"You know where to find me, Dunlap," Roberts shot back, watching with angry satisfaction as Dunlap turned and strode away from the *Horizon*.

Turning to his own airship, Roberts saw several of his men hovering at the edge of the gangplank and watching him anxiously. He turned his hard gaze on them all. "We're getting a load out in double-time," he ordered sharply. "We've lives depending on it."

Chapter Twenty-Five

With haste, the *Horizon*'s crew loaded her with supplies and food, then sped back to camp. When they arrived, they found the wharf full of all three of Dunlap's airships. There wasn't room to perform a running drop, so Roberts called for the crew to unload using the lift basket. This was a tricky and time-consuming task that constantly unbalanced the airship and strained her engines, but piece by piece her cargo lowered to the ground.

In the middle of the unloading process, a tall, emaciated-looking figure pushed his way through the crowd of soldiers handling the cargo and waved frantically at the *Horizon*. His voice was deadened by the airship's engines, but he made gestures that signaled for permission to board. Roberts waved back an approval, and the man entered the empty lift basket to catch a ride up topdeck. Roberts helped him on board and the man awkwardly threw his legs over the railing, already talking hurriedly.

"Doctor Howard Reid, head surgeon, at your service," the man said by way of introduction as he rushed to the point. "Captain Roberts, I've got hundreds of patients needing transport to the military hospital in Scutari. Would you be willing to transport them?"

"The *Horizon* is hardly fit as a medical transport ship, Doctor Reid," Roberts answered slowly, briefly envisioning his airship's hull crammed with dying soldiers.

The surgeon shrugged helplessly. "I've heard your airship is fast, and that's a better guarantee of getting soldiers down to Scutari than the best equipped medical transport ship. We lost much of the Light Brigade and the survivors are badly wounded. I've also got thousands of other patients that badly need to get to Scutari. I've just been given permission to contract your airships for patient transport if you are willing to accept them." He gestured towards Dunlap's airships. "Captain Dunlap as well, if he will carry patients."

"Doctor Reid," Roberts said with some force. "The *Horizon* is the best transport airship in Crimea and the only one who can bring supplies at other camps. You've got camps full of starving, dying men with no food, medical supplies, or clothing. With winter coming fast, airships are the only thing that can move supplies in Crimea. The *Horizon* is fast, sir, but she can't do everything. If she transports patients down to Scutari, she's not here moving supplies."

Reid rubbed his face tiredly as Roberts turned the request over in his mind. Thoughtfully, he stated, "There are currently four transport airships in Crimea, and we've near cleaned out Balaklava of supplies. I don't know when we'll see fresh supply ships again. With no cargo to transport, my airship could move your wounded soldiers. But if a new supply ship arrives while we're away, that means cargo rotting at port and soldiers starving."

Reid pressed his fingers to his temples. "Captain Roberts, I am authorized to contract with you and Captain Dunlap, as well as Captain Oldham. Four airships and two marine ships could move several hundred wounded patients down to Scutari."

"Could the hospital take on that many patients at one go?" Roberts questioned practically.

"The poor souls would have a better chance in Scutari than here," Reid shrugged. "It would be a strain on the hospital, but most of my patients will die here if not moved. If you would be willing to transport them, lives may be saved."

Roberts wasn't convinced. Scutari was four hundred miles away across the Black Sea, far too long for the gravely injured or ill to survive the journey. Simply lifting patients from camp to Balaklava would be extremely delicate and difficult; he doubted many of the patients would make it to the bay alive. Fragile human cargo on the brink of death would make for a terribly difficult transport.

Reid looked at Roberts expectantly. Roberts shrugged his shoulders and said, "I'll talk with Captain Oldham and Captain Dunlap." With as much tact as he could, he bundled Reid off his airship and lowered the surgeon to the ground. There was still cargo in Balaklava to transport, and Roberts moodily pondered Reid's proposal while his crew finished unloading the *Horizon* and prepared to lift for Balaklava.

The *Horizon* moved back to Balaklava with her captain in a gloomy state of mind. The airship was running low on coal and needed more water for her boiler. She also urgently needed some down time to shut off her engines and let Halloway perform some maintenance. Roberts had been pushing her as of late, and she was beginning to suffer from it, her speed lessening and her responsiveness thickening with stress. Roberts knew that he couldn't afford to push her more. However, first, he had a grim meeting with Oldham to arrange.

Oldham listened to the proposed transport with flinty eyes. "I'm not running a hospital," he stated bluntly. "And you're a damned fool if you think I'm going to let a passel of sick soldiers on board my ships. I'm not going to watch my men die of pneumonia or dysentery."

"There's been enough deaths in Crimea," Roberts stated with weary conviction. He was nearly punch drunk with exhaustion and the world had a high, sharp tang to it that layered his senses with acute alertness. "Some of the soldiers could make it if transported."

Oldham's granite expression did not budge. "I've heard of this hospital," he spoke with derision. "Charnel house for soldiers, it is, entombing the living with the dead. They've a better chance in Crimea."

"They've no chance in Crimea," Roberts replied with some heat. "If you've been to the camp, Captain Oldham, and seen dying men stacked like firewood out in the cold, you might be of a different mind. In the hospital, at least, they've a chance at a bed and some food, and that alone can make the difference between life or death."

Roberts and Oldham stood eye-to-eye for several moments, neither man willing to concede a millimeter. Finally Oldham spoke. "There will be little money in it, Captain Roberts, mark my words."

A shrug of his weary shoulders was Roberts' answer. Oldham watched him narrowly, something unreadable in his face. "You're set on this, then?" he demanded.

In truth, Roberts was dreading the proposed transport with every fiber of his being, but somehow he knew he had little choice but to see it finished. "My airship has near cleaned your vessels of cargo and there's not much left in Balaklava to transport. We could be weeks at port without work. It's a rough transport job, not one I would choose willingly, but it's work and it will help save lives."

Oldham had not left off scrutinizing Roberts, his mouth hard and unyielding. Wearily, Roberts realized that the *Horizon* might be the only vessel willing to turn herself into a medical ship. He wondered how many soldiers she could carry at one go. Oldham's next words surprised him.

"My son is serving in the Baltic," Oldham stated gruffly. "He captains the warship *Ragnarok*." Oldham spoke the words with some quietness, but the fierce pride in his voice was unmistakable. Roberts kept silent, observing the struggle raging in Oldham's face as he weighed the needs of his crew versus the call to brotherly arms.

Finally, Oldham appeared to have made a decision. Fixing a fierce eye on Roberts, he demanded, "You and I will be paying a visit ashore, Captain Roberts, while I determine just what sort of fee I am risking the health of my men for."

"That's a question I want answered for myself," Roberts responded. He knew that whatever the army offered wouldn't offset the danger and cost of transporting several hundred wounded, ill soldiers across the Black Sea. Yet he also knew, deep in his soul, that he had little choice in the matter.

Oldham gestured up at the *Horizon*. "With your permission, Captain Roberts," he stated in a demand coached as a request, "your airship will take me and a few of my officers to camp. I've things to discuss with those idiots running this war before any of their soldiers set a foot on board my ships."

"I'd gladly take you to camp, Captain Oldham, but I've run my airship too long," Roberts said. "She needs coal and water before she can lift again."

Oldham glared but made no move to press the matter. Instead he switched topics. "If we are going to attempt this folly, we will need Dunlap's airships as well. If your ship is the only one lifting soldiers out of camp, the wounded and sick will be dead before we leave harbor." Glancing up at the *Dark*

Squall, which had just crested the hill into Balaklava, Oldham announced, "I'll have a word with him."

"We need Dunlap's ships. The *Horizon* can't do it all on her own," Roberts said with what grace he could muster. He would happily see Dunlap and his airships go hang, but if they were going to attempt this transport, every airship was needed. Dunlap would likely balk, but Oldham's pressure would force his compliance.

The whining of the *Horizon's* engines reminded Roberts that his airship was ready to shut down for a spell. That and his own hunger pointedly demanded his attention. Oldham had already shifted his focus back to yelling at his crew and, with parting words, Roberts left the *Delhi.* The *Horizon* pulled him homeward and made a beeline for the wharf, settling down into a berth with hasty speed.

Knowing his men and his airship were exhausted to the point of stupefaction, Roberts called for a full shutdown with no intention of making any demands on anyone until morning broke. Somehow his crew found enough energy to shut down the airship and eat something before stumbling toward their hammocks. Roberts, his mind dull with exhaustion, made for his cabin and remembered only at the last moment that there was a woman inside it. He backed away hastily while a small but vocal part of him insisted that he wasn't *that* tired. Crushing the thought, Roberts resolutely headed for the berthing area for a hammock and found a chorus of snores rising up in breathy syncopation. Brief seconds passed before he was dead to the world and oblivious to anything.

Morning rose with cold clamminess as the crew of the *Horizon* reluctantly woke and got the airship ready for the day. Without fuss or preamble, Jules stepped forward to help the crew, completing tasks and following orders calmly. Roberts was thankful for the extra pair of hands, enough so to call out, "Glad to see you back on the *Horizon.*" He thumped Jules firmly on the back. "I've more work than I have men to do it. You're damned welcome on board."

Jules smiled shyly at the compliment, but the pleased expression disappeared from his face as he glanced at the door of Roberts' cabin. He frowned in worry and he shifted restlessly in place.

"She'll be alright," Roberts assured him. "Harding is looking after her."

Jules did not seem convinced, but he turned his gaze away from the cabin door. Roberts tried to hide his own worry. He had seen nothing of Miss Pickens since yesterday, and Harding had given only brief reports about her condition.

The *Horizon* clamored for Roberts' attention, and he turned her way. Miss Pickens' condition worried him, but he had only so many thoughts to spare and most of them were occupied. He was deeply troubled about the proposed medical transport and consumed with moving the rest of the cargo.

In the midst of the noise and damp unpleasantness of the morning, Miss Pickens emerged shakily from Roberts' cabin and made her hesitant way across the deck. She looked frankly terrible: dark circles rimmed her eyes, her hair was lank and bedraggled, and her coarse clothing was splattered with mud and blood. She was thinner, and the luxuriant, blooming beauty Roberts had once known was fading. As he observed her approach, he felt a sharp prick of outrage rising in his gut. Although Miss Pickens could be wily and self-serving, she was a fine, high-class lady who deserved better than this.

Roberts stepped forward to greet her and, without thinking, growled out, "You look terrible, Miss Pickens." *Charming*, his internal monitor grumbled. *Fine choice of words, you daft idiot.* He had meant something more solicitous, but his brain had apparently decided on a more direct phrase.

Miss Pickens' already tight mouth thinned. "Courteous as always, Captain Roberts," she responded haughtily.

Roberts loosened a tight sigh. "I meant that you look exhausted and overworked, Miss Pickens. What in the... what have you been doing to yourself?"

"Trying to keep men from dying," Miss Pickens replied shortly. "Getting first-hand information. Writing. Staying alive."

Roberts scanned her for signs of injury or illness. She was thinner and weak from exhaustion, but the fever seemed to be moving out of her cheeks. With luck and some rest, she would hopefully recover without any lingering side effects.

"Well, you're not going back to camp," Roberts stated bluntly. Miss Pickens glared at him, but her steely eyes had little effect. "End of story, Miss Pickens," he pronounced.

She bit her full lips but rather than opposition, her words took a different tact. "I have a proposition for you, Captain Roberts," Miss Pickens responded softly but firmly.

"And just what is that?" Roberts answered suspiciously. Whatever she had in mind, he knew it would mean aggravation and inconvenience for everyone on board.

She pressed her lips together for a moment, then said firmly, "I am prepared to offer you a thousand pounds if you will fly Jules and I to London as fast as you can."

"That's a pretty penny to offer, Miss Pickens, and a fair distance to fly," Roberts replied carefully. He was surprised by the offer; it instantly set off all his suspicious alarms. He chose his response with particular care. "I'd sooner see you back to London as quickly as you can, for your own safety and health, but the *Horizon* is needed here in Crimea."

"Captain, you have seen how atrocious this entire war is," Miss Pickens pressed with some heat. "There are countless numbers of men dying from starvation, disease, and cold. If our government had been properly supplying our troops as they should have been, hundreds, if not thousands, of deaths could have been averted. And then there is the matter of the slaughter of the Light Brigade. This entire...*farce* is a complete disgrace."

Miss Pickens' eyes were blazing. "England, if not all of Europe, needs to know of this," she insisted firmly. "Our leadership has failed us and our soldiers are paying the price. I will *not* stand by and let the incompetence and neglect of those in command go unchecked." Her fists clenched at her side. "Jules and I can write articles that will expose all of this. This war must be stopped, or at least our soldiers must be better equipped. Articles in the *Constantinople Times* are not enough. Jules and I must get back to the *London Gazette*."

Roberts shook his head. "Miss Pickens, the *Horizon* is the fastest airship in Crimea and the only one that can fly supplies to other campsites. If she leaves Crimea, that leaves a lot of supplies not getting into the hands of those who need it."

"If she leaves Crimea to get Jules and I back to London, she will save lives," Miss Pickens insisted. "The faster we can relay information to the *London Guardian*, the better for every person involved in this war." She added quickly, "In the time I have flown on your airship, I have seen her ability. If I am not mistaken, she could reach London in less than two weeks. You could be to London and back before a month passes, even sooner if I am not mistaken."

"Constantinople is closer, Miss Pickens," Roberts said.

"I have dozens of articles to publish, Captain," Miss Pickens burst out impatiently. "I simply must get to the *London Guardian* and place them in Henry Whiteside's hands." Her shoe tapped impatiently on the deck, and Roberts noted that bits of dried mud flaked off it.

Despite the enormous number of logistical problems, Miss Pickens' proposition had some merit. A thousand pounds was a significant amount of money, even offset against the cost of getting the *Horizon* to London. If they stripped her down, she would fly fast and burn little coal. The *Horizon* needed supplies, equipment, and tools, all which could be had cheaply in London. The crew with families deserved to see them, and all on board had affairs to conclude. If they wanted to see London before the hard winter set in, this was the time to leave.

Roberts was just as keenly aware that leaving Crimea would put all further transports in Dunlap's hands, an opportunity the other captain had been bucking to accomplish. Conceding to Miss Pickens' offer could very well mean risking a dangerous journey across Europe while Dunlap grew rich off transport fees in Crimea. Conversely, it was any man's guess whether more transport ships were due in Balaklava: Roberts could refuse Miss Pickens' offer and stay in Crimea only to see weeks pass with no more work.

As if sensing Roberts' thoughts, Miss Pickens said quietly, "I do not believe you will see many more supply ships this winter, Captain." Her words were tinged with concern and worry. "I have labored to gather as much information as I can while in camp and from what many of the officers have said, there is little word about ships inbound, nor much hope that more will come. With increasingly more enemies in the Black Sea and winter approaching, this is a dangerous place for a merchant captain to sail or fly."

Miss Pickens paused while Roberts considered her words, wondering if she was speaking the full truth or simply trying to finagle her way into getting what she wanted. Not answering her immediately, Roberts gazed out over the harbor while Miss Pickens waited impatiently at his side, energy burning through her fatigue and traces of fever. When he spoke, he chose his words with care.

"Miss Pickens, the *Horizon* will be soon moving a score of injured and sick soldiers down to the military barracks in Scutari. With luck, Captain Oldham's ships and Captain Dunlap's airships will move patients as well. We'll bring several hundred souls down to Scutari. I'll make up my mind once we're done with that job."

"Captain, I must..." Miss Pickens protested, but Roberts interrupted her.

"The *Horizon* will be full of sick, dying men, Miss Pickens, and it will be sheer luck if none of my crew falls ill during the transport. It will be a dangerous spot for you on board, but it's dangerous everywhere you turn in Crimea, and I'm not bringing you back to camp," he pronounced flatly. "You and Jules can ride with us to Scutari. I'll make my decision after that."

He expected her to protest, but instead she set her eyes in a narrow line. "Excellent. That will make for a fine article," Miss Pickens announced sharply. "While our military airships scour the air of England searching for miscreants and our merchant ships deliver spices and silks from India, there is not one medical airship stationed in Crimea to attend the ill and wounded. Instead," she smiled very much as a sneer, "the stalwart *Horizon* and her brave crew, a merchant airship and one lightly armed, must deliver our injured troops to safety."

She was interrupted mid-harangue by Oboe. As the first mate approached, he loosed a loud cough that captured Roberts' attention. Damp and cold were continuing to play havoc with Oboe's lungs, and Roberts knew that his first mate was particularly susceptible to illness. Against that, Roberts was preparing to introduce hordes of sick soldiers onto the *Horizon*. The repercussions could very well prove fatal.

He stepped forward to intercept Oboe and frowned at him. "Are you alright?" he demanded.

"Captain, we should be able to lift in thirty minutes," Oboe skated over the question but Roberts was not distracted.

"You know we've been requested to serve as a medical transport airship," he stated bluntly, examining Oboe intently. "I'm well aware that doing so puts every man on board at risk for disease. More so, you," he pushed the point home firmly.

"We have work that awaits us," Oboe responded, a hint of firmness in his voice.

Roberts emphasized his scowl. "If you get sick again..."

"*Captain.*" The slightest growl of warning hovered in the air as Oboe stiffened slightly. Roberts glared back at his first mate in frustration. Oboe rarely put his foot down, but when he did it stayed down. From his stance and demeanor, he was clearly not in the mood to put up with any fussing. While Roberts wanted to press the point, now was not the time or place to start an argument.

He settled for snapping out, "Don't get sick on me or I'll take it out of your hide." Oboe took the words coolly and left his captain's side without another word.

To Roberts' dismay, Miss Pickens had observed the encounter, but she wisely said nothing as Roberts turned back to her. "We'll soon be filling the ship with sick and dying soldiers," he warned. "You'd best keep in the cabin and out of danger." As she turned her head, weak sunlight highlighted the sharp plane of her jawline and the hollowness in her cheeks. "You're not half recovered yourself," Roberts added firmly.

Miss Pickens' mouth thinned. "I am stronger than you think, Captain Roberts," she responded coolly. "You needn't concern yourself so greatly with my well-being."

"You don't seem much concerned with it yourself, Miss Pickens," Roberts retorted, noting the weary, almost haggard expression in her face, the cracks lining her fingertips, the thinness of her wrists.

"There are other concerns which are currently occupying my thoughts, Captain," was her tart answer. "A little deprivation on my part is hardly comparable to the sufferings of thousands in Crimea. You of all people should understand that." With that, Miss Pickens brushed the front of her skirts then turned with a flounce to Roberts' cabin, shutting the door behind her with an angry thump.

Muttering choice words about the female race, Roberts pushed away from the railing and plunged back into the bowels of his airship, its empty bay waiting to receive what was likely the airship's most perilous and fragile cargo to date.

Chapter Twenty-Six

Fetid air struck Roberts in the face, almost gagging him, as he stepped gingerly into the *Horizon*'s hold, taking great care where he placed his feet lest he inadvertently trod on a patient. Sixty-seven of them lay on the wooden floor, only a thin layer of blankets cushioning them from the airship's movements. The *Horizon* was holding steady at thirty-seven knots in a determined effort to get the soldiers to the hospital quickly, and every bump jarred the airship and its human occupants. Moans and cries of pain rose up whenever the *Horizon* hit an air pocket. The crew was doing their best to ensure a smooth ride, but the airship could not avoid every meteorological flutter.

Harding, his face sagging with strain and weariness, moved among the patients, dispensing what care and comfort he could offer. He was assisted by one army nurse, a young man whose medical training was patchy at best. Jules was also present, and he showed no hesitation about wiping away vomit and changing bandages as he gently ministered to the patients.

Roberts could not spare any of his men to assist with medical efforts below decks, not with the *Horizon*'s engines straining mightily to maintain thirty-seven knots for the duration of their journey. Halloway, Jenkins, and Sparrowman labored in the boiler room to coax every last ounce of speed out of the *Horizon*'s engines while the rest of the crew fussed over her carefully. The patients amounted to less than five tons of weight and with no additional cargo, the *Horizon* had little to load her down.

Roberts could not think of more dreadful cargo to transport than a hold full of weeping, dying soldiers. The twelve hour flight from Balaklava to Scutari was burned in his memory for many years after that. It visited him on the edge of dreams: the screams and moans of the wounded, the vomit and the stink of urine filling the hold, the bodies that sighed out their last breath and grew quiet. A few of the patients were grown men, but the vast majority were barely in their teens. Some of the lads were younger than William, a thought that haunted Roberts the few times he passed through the hold to examine the passengers.

He could not afford to spend much time in the cargo bay. His airship demanded all hands and eyes, especially because she flew alone over the Black Sea. It had been decided in Balaklava: the *Horizon* would take the most critical patients and fly solo to Scutari while the *Delhi* and *Adolphone* sailed on with the *Specter*, carrying the rest of the patients. Dunlap had conceded with extreme reluctance, and, Roberts suspected, heavy pressure from Oldham. The *Specter* had forty-five soldiers on board while the *Dark Nell* and *Black Squall* stayed in Crimea in case further cargo arrived. Even at her best, the *Specter* had no hope of matching the *Horizon*'s pace, and with his airship full of soldiers clinging to life, Roberts had made the decision to fly hell for leather to Scutari in hopes of saving as many as possible. If they encountered enemies, the *Horizon* would need to rely on her blazing speed and her Vandenberg to see her through safely.

Thankfully, the day was clear with low winds and good visibility. At eight hundred feet, the *Horizon* had a panoramic view of the Black Sea and could easily spot any potential attackers. She had left Balaklava at sunrise, and Roberts was determined to make the four hundred mile journey before dusk. Freshly stocked with coal and water, the *Horizon* was moving through the air with energetic determination. Roberts could feel through his boots that his airship was in a good mood and didn't seem inclined to give him any trouble.

The passengers, however, were a different story, although the main trouble they offered was dying. Seventy of the most critical soldiers had been loaded into the belly of the *Horizon* at Balaklava. Although they were only five hours into the journey to Scutari, three soldiers had already died. There was nothing to be done with the bodies but cover them and pray that no more of their companions followed suit. Many of the patients were hovering between life and death, and the stress of transport was aggravating their condition.

In all, nearly eight hundred patients had been lifted out of the British camp by the four airships and transported to Balaklava in preparation for the journey to Scutari. This had taken three days of grueling effort, and Roberts had lost count of how many patients had died during or shortly after the move. Many of the patients had been far too unstable to transport and had demonstrated so by dying quickly, a hard fact that had spurred Harding into more than one bitter argument with the army surgeons.

"They're pushing the dying on us rather than focusing on those who could be saved," Harding snapped tartly at Roberts in the midst of moving patients into the *Horizon*. Roberts had been unconsciously holding his breath, trying not to see the blood, the vomit, the faces of abject misery and suffering. "The damned fools," Harding continued. "They're leaving men in the camp that, with some care, could recover. We're transporting dead men, Gavin. I hope you realize this."

Harding's words echoed forcefully in Roberts' ears, particularly when the surgeon lifted his gaze from a motionless patient, then shook his head at Roberts. Yet Harding, for all his complaints, tended the soldiers with grim resolve and did not let himself rest during the flight to Scutari.

In the dim, stench-clogged light of the cargo bay, Roberts was surprised to find Miss Pickens sitting at the side of a horrifically wounded soldier while jotting in a notebook. For one moment, anger surged in him that she would exploit a dying soldier simply to garner more fodder for a newspaper article. As he drew closer, he realized that she was taking down a letter the patient was dictating.

She did not notice Roberts as he stood a few feet away, watching the scene. The wounded soldier was barely able to express his words through numb lips, but Miss Pickens smiled encouragingly and carefully took down his words with a gentleness that moved Roberts in ways he could not quite express. Emotion churned in his innards as he watched Miss Pickens finish writing, then gently help the soldier scrawl his signature on the letter. Her small hand carefully guided his trembling fingers.

By the soldier's face, the effort was exhausting. When is hand finally dropped the pencil, Miss Pickens closed her fingers over his for one moment. "I will see that your family receives your letter, Paul. I promise this."

A weak smile twitched faintly to life on the wounded soldier's face before his eyes closed. Roberts stiffened in alarm, then swiftly bent down to feel for a pulse on the patient's wrist. It was present but weak, fluttering under his finger like a fish gasping on the shore. Unexpectedly, Miss Pickens reached out and gently took the soldier's wrist from Roberts' grip, shaking her head slightly as she carefully placed the soldier's hand back on his chest. Her fingers brushing against Roberts' hand filled him with warmth and he stood to his feet, his heart pounding a drumbeat against his ribs.

Miss Pickens tightened her jaw and made to rise, hindered by her skirts and the fatigue which lingered after her ordeal in camp. Roberts helped her to her feet, trying to remain passive at the presence of her slender frame so near his and the touch of her palms against his own. A tear glimmered in her eye, and he suppressed an urge to brush it away. Instead, he turned tail and fled to the safety of gruffness.

"You should rest," he stated roughly, looking her over carefully and noting the patches of fresh vomit and blood on her clothes. "Harding doesn't need another patient."

Miss Pickens shook her head. "We will reach Scutari before night, yes?" she questioned.

"I'm not aiming on sailing over the Black Sea at night," was Roberts' answer.

"Then Jules and I can both watch over these poor souls until this journey is over," Miss Pickens replied with firmness. "Mister Harding has enough work on his hands. He needs as much assistance as he can muster."

Roberts was too tired to argue, and he wasn't about to start a fight in the middle of several dozen dying men. Fatigue, stress, and longing were all fighting for his attention, so he merely growled out, "Don't exhaust yourself." With that, he abruptly departed, leaving the moans of the dying behind him, along with one lovely woman who was doing uncanny things to both his mind and sense of self-preservation.

Roberts forced himself to focus back on his airship and crew. To his immense relief, the *Horizon* sailed through her journey without any sign of problems or hint of an enemy. It was just after nightfall that she touched down on a well-lit airship dock in Scutari. The military hospital was a beacon of illumination in the falling darkness, an extremely welcome sight to the crew and still-living patients on board.

There was a guard on the wharf, and Roberts swiftly dispatched him to the hospital. The *Horizon* had just settled down on a berth when a squadron of nurses arrived and began emptying her of human cargo. They were commanded by a small, dark-haired woman who briskly directed operations with the skill of a general dispatching troops. Harding, fussing and growling, swiftly found himself outgunned by the dark-haired woman. She bowled over his concerns, making it unmistakably clear that this was her turf and she was giving orders, despite what Harding had to say on the matter.

In the midst of unloading, the woman hailed Roberts with an imperious air and moved towards him with a brisk, yet jerky pace, her motions falling into an arrhythmic pattern. Light from the wharf fell on her face, illuminating her features, and as she moved closer, Roberts could see the seamless blending of metal and flesh, intricately sculpted brass plating flowing over what were clearly old burn marks. A half mask of sorts hid much of the scars on her face, and over her left eye was a network of lenses. The skin of her left hand was reddened, pitted scar tissue, over which a network of fine wires and tubing seemed to provide structural support for the hand and fingers. The hissing, rhythmical thump of gears at work and the odd lurch that characterized her step indicated a metal left leg hiding under her sensible skirt. Her jaw was set in a determined manner of one who walks with pain as a daily companion, yet will not bow to it as her master.

"You are the captain of this vessel?" the woman stated quickly as she gave him a sharp, measuring look.

"Captain Roberts of the airship *Horizon*," Roberts managed to get out before she offered her name.

"Florence Nightingale. Head nurse here at Scutari." A stiff nod of the head followed, and Roberts responded in kind.

The nurse swiveled her head in the direction of the *Horizon*. "How many poor souls did you bring?"

"We loaded seventy," Roberts responded carefully. "Not all of them survived the trip." Miss Nightingale nodded again, and Roberts guessed that the news did not surprise her.

"This is only a tiny handful of what Crimea has to offer, Captain Roberts," the nurse stated firmly.

"My airship took the most critical patients. Behind her are two marine ships and one airship carrying patients. All told, we left Balaklava with a little under eight hundred souls." Roberts felt a trifle off-guard in the presence of the indomitable nurse. He had no doubt that Molly and Miss Nightingale together would make a formidable force. If Miss Pickens took it in her head to join them, the three women could conceivably conquer the world.

"Eight hundred?" A very brief moment of apprehension crossed the nurse's face. She shoved it away and pulled her chin up in the air. "Well then, Captain, I suggest you get your airship off my wharf to make room for the other ships." With that, Roberts realized that he had been briskly dismissed. Feeling vaguely stunned, he hastily slunk away from the dark-haired woman and headed back to his airship to make sure all the patients were unloaded.

When the last of them had been carried out, Harding slumped to the filthy floor, not minding that he was sitting in blood and vomit. Roberts was exhausted himself, but he managed to help the surgeon above deck where the air was cold, yet mercifully clean.

"Seventeen," Harding muttered weakly. "Seventeen poor souls didn't make it."

Roberts accepted the news quietly. "That's fifty-three still alive."

"They were just boys," Harding sighed as the two men stumbled across the topdeck. With Nurse Nightingale's admonition in his ears, Roberts lifted the *Horizon* from the hospital wharf and secured permission to land at a nearby military wharf. Hastily, the crew shut the airship down for the night. Her cargo bay desperately needed scrubbing, but it was too late in the night to do anything but turn off her engines and find some sleep. One by one, the crew finished their tasks, then headed for their blankets and hammocks. Roberts held out until the end, making sure that the airship was secure for the night before he fell like an anvil in the berthing area, the snores of the crew lulling him to sleep.

***   ***   ***   ***

The sun was barely a glimmer in the sky when Roberts was on his feet and calling for his crew. He anticipated a long work session before the *Horizon* was ready to fly again. Her hull had to be thoroughly scoured to remove all traces of the patients, and the airship needed to be checked for potential problems. Halloway and Jenkins took advantage of the break to swarm the envelope and engine room. Unsurprisingly, several issues presented themselves for repair.

Roberts was negotiating irritably with Halloway and Jenkins when Miss Pickens made an appearance topdeck. Somehow, she had managed to track down a bath and she was fresh and lovely once again, if a bit thin. As she stepped forward, a current of wind blew the scent of her perfume towards Roberts. It worked a trill along his spine.

"Ah, Captain, I believe that we will be soon returning to London?" Miss Pickens stated innocently, but with a canny look on her face.

Roberts sighed audibly and stamped three paces forward to face her. "I didn't say that we have an agreement to return, Miss Pickens," he pointed out.

"I do recall that I offered you a thousand pounds, Captain Roberts," Miss Pickens replied smoothly. "Jules will sign any agreement you wish to write as a guarantee that we will keep our word. We can pay two hundred now and the other eight hundred when we reach London."

In spare moments during their journey to Scutari, Roberts had considered Miss Pickens' offer. They needed to return to London at some point, Roberts knew this. The airship was low on just about everything she needed, and the long months away from home were hurting the crew. Yet the proposed journey meant a trans-Europe crossing in early winter. It would be the longest distance the *Horizon* had flown on her own. Their path would take them over much of Europe with mountain ranges, unfamiliar skies, and unfriendly vessels roaming the air. The *Horizon* would need to be stripped light, then raced to London before she ran out of anthracite.

Then there was the matter of whether Miss Pickens and her brother could uphold their end of the bargain. A thousand pounds was no trifling sum, and Roberts questioned their ability to pay it. The pair obviously came from a wealthy family, and Jules' signature on a legal document would bind him to paying the transport fee. However, Miss Pickens had a talent for wriggling her way in and out of situations. Roberts suspected she would try to renege on their agreement.

Then again, any number of weeks could pass before more supplies appeared in Balaklava. When the *Horizon* had left Crimea the prior morning, Balaklava was empty of cargo. The *Dark Nell* and *Black Squall* had stayed behind, ready to work when the next transport marine ship appeared, but there was no word of one heading up the Black Sea. With December bringing harsh weather, Roberts did not want to keep the *Horizon* in Crimea waiting for a supply ship to turn up. It was too costly and hard on the airship. If she didn't have work, there was no point staying in Crimea.

Miss Pickens watched Roberts keenly, almost impatiently. He suspected that she had little inkling of how difficult it would be to fulfill her proposal. Finally, he said slowly, "It would be a long and difficult flight, Miss Pickens. I've things to consider before I have an answer for you."

She bristled coldly. "Captain Roberts, I must remind you of the urgency of the situation. Every hour that passes is one more hour that the world does not know of the utter atrocities committed in this war..."

"Miss Pickens," Roberts interrupted flatly. "If I accept your offer without thinking it through, my airship's liable to crash into a mountain or run out of fuel. That will not do you, nor anyone on this ship, any good. The *Horizon* has never flown that far on her own, and it will take careful planning for her to complete the journey safely."

"Surely you..." Miss Pickens started but was fielded again by Roberts.

"I'll have an answer for you," he said firmly. "But it's not a request I'll consider lightly." With that, he left her and sought out Oboe for his input.

Oboe listened to the prospective journey carefully as Roberts briefly laid out the situation. When he finished, Oboe said carefully, "It would be the longest flight a short-range airship had ever attempted, Captain."

"Think she can do it?" Roberts questioned.

Oboe was silent, his forehead furrowing slightly in thought. "I do." A sharp spasm of coughing sent him doubled over for a few moments before he straightened up again.

Clearing his throat, Oboe continued in a labored voice. "Speaking plainly, Captain, I will say that the ship is exhausted, as are the men. We have seen enough to know that this winter will be brutal. If your intent is to keep us in Crimea over winter, I do not think the ship will survive it unless we can restock and refit her with what she needs."

Practically, Oboe pointed out, "We pay five times over in Constantinople for half of what we need. Even with the thorough inspection and servicing we gave her in Constantinople two months past, it was not enough." Firmly, he continued. "She needs London. I would urge this journey."

"With the costs it will take to get to London and back, we won't make any profit," Roberts stated logically.

Oboe shrugged. "The odds are high that we will spend the next few weeks in Balaklava with nothing to transport."

Roberts nodded thoughtfully and looked out over the bay, weighing his options. Darkly, he spoke what had been troubling him most in regards to their journey back to London. "We won't find a warm welcome in England's airspace," he warned Oboe. "Smothers does not let go of his anger."

A snort, and Oboe said something caustic in his own tongue. Roberts suppressed a smile. Although his spoken vocabulary was normally impeccable, Oboe would occasionally loose a tirade in his native language that needed no translation. These rare outbreaks were a source of amusement for Roberts, mostly because it took a great deal before Oboe was sufficiently peeved to utter them.

"Smothers does not own the air," Oboe said. His verbal outbreak over, he was already falling back into his calm tones.

"I'll make sure to remind him of that when we reach London," Roberts grinned tiredly.

"We have yet to see one of his airships in Crimea," Oboe stated. "He will have little cause to entice conflict with a ship that carries the recommendation of Commander Pickens and Lord Raglan himself."

Looking across the topdeck, Roberts saw Miss Pickens standing at the railing. Her arms were crossed tightly over her chest as she looked intently at Scutari's barracks. He didn't realize Oboe had followed his gaze until the first mate spoke quietly, "She will be safer in London."

"If she has the sense to stay there," Roberts huffed, shaking his head.

"For her shortcomings, Miss Pickens is a young woman of extraordinary intelligence," Oboe said, albeit begrudgingly. None of the crew was pleased to have Miss Pickens back on the *Horizon*, and Roberts suspected Oboe still harbored a deep mistrust of her.

This suspicion was confirmed when Oboe edged his approbations with a warning. "I would proceed with caution," he advised. "That is no mean sum Miss Pickens is offering. I..." he paused and amended his words. "There is a possibility of a default, whether intentional or accidental."

"I'll have her brother sign for the amount," Roberts shrugged. "If he defaults, I'll set the law on him.

"And you have assurance he can deliver as promised?" Oboe questioned.

"I'll take it out of their grandfather's hide if I have to," Roberts replied curtly.

Oboe said nothing in response, and Roberts' eyes were drawn to the barracks housing the wounded of Scutari. The building structure was impressive, white walls and sharp towers hiding the masses of writhing human misery, stink, and fear inside.

Abruptly, Roberts pushed away from the railing. "Let's get out of this damned hellhole and back to civilization."

Chapter Twenty-Seven

Three days passed on Scutari's wharf while the *Horizon* was scoured and prepped for the journey. Harding spent his days and nights in the hospital, adding his efforts to assisting the ill and injured. Roberts had only set foot inside the hospital once, and once was enough to convince him that he would gladly choose falling off the *Horizon* at a thousand feet to being a patient at Scutari. The interior was overcrowded with moaning, vomiting, crying soldiers, most still in their teens. Filth and suffering were as epidemic as cholera and tuberculosis. Miss Nightingale, as it transpired, was newly arrived at Scutari and diligently working to turn a den of filth and disease into a well-ordered, clean facility.

"Nurse Nightingale has few friends among the doctors and superiors of this hospital," Harding commented to Roberts on their second day at Scutari. "However, I have yet to meet her equal," he continued with admiration. "A most resolute and intelligent young woman. Indeed, some of these poor souls we transported might just have a chance after all."

Roberts was glad to hear it, but he had little time to worry about the fate of the patients. The *Horizon* had done her work and brought her load to Scutari. Roberts' next concern was getting his airship to London. The upcoming journey was riddled with complications, particularly concerning their flight plan. Deciding the airship's course was a difficult endeavor that consumed much of Roberts' and Oboe's time over the three days they were in port.

"We'll stop in Naples and take on coal and water if we need it," Roberts grunted, stabbing at a map. It would be a much quicker flight to London if the *Horizon* could simply cut a straight path from Scutari to Rome, but Greece was still a volatile mess from their rebellion. Despite the blockade France and Britain had strong-armed on the ports of Greece, entirely too many Ottoman sympathies lay in the country. To avoid this, the *Horizon* would need to swing south, away from the conflict, before finding herself in allied air over Italy. This flight plan was safer, but required more time and miles than Roberts cared to give.

Oboe rubbed a thumb and finger together absentmindedly, and Roberts caught the gesture with a worried frown. Slowly, the first mate responded, "Such a flight would put us very close to Tirana, as well as several mountain ranges peaking at over fifteen hundred feet. We would avoid many problems were we to sail to Athens."

"We would add on about two hundred extra miles with that flight path," Roberts countered with a frown. "We've little time to spare and Greece is too volatile right now."

"As is Tirana, if not more so. Greece is less of a risk," replied Oboe. His words were measured but carefully enunciated. He rarely needed to raise his voice: generally a deepened note of meaning in his tones was enough to drive his point home. It had been a frustrating three hours in front of maps, and captain and first mate were gradually working themselves towards an argument.

With weighty insistence, Oboe continued, "Tirana is known to be a popular destination for Macedonian pirates. If the *Horizon* was keen on finding potential opponents in the sky, Tirana would be an ideal spot to begin her search."

For Oboe, this was biting sarcasm. Roberts took it with bad grace. "*Alright*," he growled. "We'll make for Athens."

Oboe didn't gloat, but some of the stiffness left his expression. Roberts knew that his first mate was right, but he did not want to add any more miles to their journey than strictly necessary. It would be a long flight as it was and heavily taxing on everyone aboard.

The flight from Scutari to Athens was roughly five hundred miles; flying well, the *Horizon* would complete that leg from sunup to sundown. From Athens, it was approximately six hundred miles to Rome, then a further six hundred miles to Paris. Paris to London was a matter of two hundred and fifty miles. So simple on paper, so inordinately difficult in practice.

Roberts suppressed a long sigh as he retraced their flight path on the maps. Much as he quietly dreaded the long journey ahead, he had driven his men and airship long enough. It was time to return home, even if it was only briefly before the *Horizon* turned her prow back to the war.

The *Horizon* lifted from Scutari on a cold, clear day, winds steady at ten knots. She cut south across the Sea of Marmara and skimmed the coastline of Turkey before flying across the Aegean Sea to Athens. As they flew, warmer air began to waft across the topdeck and the sunshine intensified despite it being mid-December. The crew luxuriated in the sunlight, pulling strength from its energizing rays. The promise of Athens ahead was a further boost to morale.

The *Horizon* moved steadily across the Aegean Sea, and three hours into her flight encountered two Greek vessels hovering in the skies dead ahead. At a command from Roberts, Bloomberg hailed the two airships, signaling the *Horizon's* position through clicker code, but neither vessel seemed inclined to move. Instead, they held their position in the sky, far apart enough to permit the *Horizon* to fly between them, but close enough to represent a threat. Roberts was not going to send his airship between two vessels lest she find herself in the middle of a crossfire, but neither ship yielded airspace.

Turning to Bloomberg, Roberts commanded, "Send the code again and this time, tell them to clear the path." Bloomberg's fingers flew, clicker code springing to life and racing across the air toward the Greek airships. Not a flicker of light signaled back, and Roberts frowned sharply. The absence of a response could have been a studied insult, the prelude to a threat, or simple carelessness; there was little way to tell at that distance. It was not uncommon to find airships without a clicker mechanism on board: clicker code standards had yet to be fully embraced by all nations that flew airships.

Still, the lack of response and the position of the ships generated deep suspicion in Roberts. With a sharp command, he ordered the gunnery crew to the Vandenberg while the rest of the men held their positions with watchfulness, eyes trained on the two Greek vessels.

"Rise to fifteen hundred feet!" Roberts commanded as the crew hurried to carry out his order. With smooth fluidity, the *Horizon* rose higher into the air, leaving the two Greek vessels a few hundred feet under her hull as she gracefully sailed over them. Roberts' eyes did not leave the Greek vessels;

the nonchalance with which they hovered in the air was studied, he was certain of it. He harbored a deep suspicion that their crews were carefully measuring up the *Horizon*, weighing the merits and risk of an attack.

They made no threat, and the *Horizon* soon left them in the dust, her fleetness carrying her swiftly away from the potential attackers. When she had sailed beyond reach of the two Greek airships, Roberts called for the gunnery crew to stand down. Normal operations were resumed, but tension rode in the crew as they hurried the airship towards Athens, eager to reach the safety of port.

As the airship approached Athens, the crew could see long beaches of glowing white sand, inviting aquamarine waters, and the sheen of hundreds of white buildings. Roberts heard the seductive call of port and longed to abandon himself to it: plop the *Horizon* down on the nearest berth and disembark for several days. He wearily resisted the urge, both out of duty and the sharp awareness that several ports they had passed were heavily locked down by Allied forces. Any traffic coming in and out of Greece had dozens of muzzles trained its direction, and gaining clearance to land was difficult.

Roberts received permission with some struggle, and he directed the *Horizon* to land at Athens for a night of rest. Miss Pickens had fussed about the stopover, but Roberts was adamant: Greece was a political hotbed, and the Ionian Sea was notorious for airship traffic. It was sheer folly to continue the next leg of their journey overnight. They slept hard and rose with the light of the new dawn for another day of flight.

The next morning dawned with a golden sun rising in a clear blue sky. As the *Horizon* worked her way across the country and towards the Ionian Sea, Roberts kept a keen eye on the airspace which was dotted with other vessels. Greek airships were substantially better than Russian vessels, but Greece was nowhere near leading the world in airship development and flight. Many of the ships he observed were piratical and shifty-looking, on the hunt for the nearest target. Roberts kept the *Horizon* at thirty-five knots and easily outstripped any potential danger in the skies.

As Roberts moved about the airship, he could see the exhausted determination in his men's faces. There was little joking or ribaldry, had not been for a long time. The horrors and numbing workload of the war had robbed much of the crew's cheer, especially during their last transport. Roberts was halfway convinced that the moans of dying patients had etched themselves permanently into the *Horizon*'s planks and echoed in the clanging of her engines.

Stepping below decks, he moved toward the engine room. The door was flung wide open, emitting voluminous plumes of steam and clangs of metal against metal. As he stepped into the room, Jenkins appeared in the middle of the steam, stomping from the room in a fit of temper. When he spotted Roberts, his face tightened with anger and he rolled his eyes in frustration.

Stepping closer to his captain, Jenkins spat out, "I haven't been able to get a word out of that damned idiot all day. I don't know what's eating him, Captain." By common assumption, Roberts guessed that Halloway was the topic of conversation. That was confirmed when he entered the engine room and saw no sign of Sparrowman.

It was the sight of Halloway rifling absentmindedly through a toolbox that grabbed Roberts' attention. The inventor was clearly not searching for anything specific, and he didn't look up as Roberts entered the room, though a stiffening of his frame indicated he knew someone was approaching.

"She running alright?" Roberts shouted over the engines, peering intently at Halloway. The inventor merely shrugged without bothering to look up.

Roberts stepped closer to Halloway, trying to force eye contact. "We've got nearly five hundred miles to Rome and we're coming up over the Ionian Sea. I need her running at full power and strength. She has a few hundred miles of open water to cover."

Halloway shrugged again, still not meeting Roberts' eyes, as he fiddled aimlessly with a file. "Look at me," Roberts demanded, forcing Halloway's eyes upwards. "Something on your mind?"

The inventor shrugged a third time, a listless gesture that barely clung to life. Halloway had become markedly less argumentative during his long months on board the *Horizon*, but he had sunken more into himself. He was prone to increasing bouts of dark moods that settled on the airship like tar. Examining his old friend, Roberts wondered if returning to London would be painful for him. Halloway had little for him in London except a ruined workshop filled with the burnt remains of his life's work.

Picking his words carefully, Roberts said, "We'll be in London a week, most likely more. That's time you've got to call your own if you like." The news made zero impression on Halloway, so Roberts tried a different tact. "It's also a week to do any repairs you've a mind to."

There wasn't a glimmer of interest on Halloway's face, but he managed to mutter out, "She's running fine."

For Halloway not to instantly seize a chance to enthusiastically tear the airship apart was severely out of character. Roberts' forehead creased heavily. He had seen Halloway in a black mood before, but not one nearly this deep. Roberts had to suppress an urge to shake the inventor back to his senses again. Before he could do anything, Carter called down the ladder, drawing Roberts' attention to the topdeck.

"Captain! We've got another airship in our sites, sir!"

Sighing, Roberts turned back to Halloway. "We'll talk about this later," he said, not quite certain himself if that was a threat or merely a statement of fact. Abandoning the engineer to whatever inwards struggles he was fighting, Roberts hurried topdeck to see what now hovered in the sky near his ship.

***   ***   ***   ***

Despite his grave doubts about the journey, Roberts had to admit that it was running surprisingly smooth. There were hazards in the skies, but the *Horizon* did not fire her Vandenberg once from Scutari to London. Her nearly empty hold allowed her to stay above thirty-three knots the entire journey, putting her comfortably beyond reach of any other airship. Her engines ran well, nothing vexed Big Tom in the canopy, and a hundred issues that could have cropped up did not manifest. Miss Pickens kept to herself in her cabin, no doubt still recovering from her long ordeal, while Jules made himself useful about the *Horizon*.

They stopped in Rome for water and a night of rest, Roberts anxious to determine if his airship was suffering any stress from their long, high-speed journey. Much to his relief, Rome's port had anthracite, and at better prices than he expected to pay. The *Horizon*'s coal hoppers were still more than half-full, but at the asked price, Roberts couldn't afford not to fill her with coal from Rome's mines.

The airship was still flying well, but she had a few hundred miles more of open sea to cross before she flew over French soil. Roberts knew he would not breathe easy until there was solid ground under the *Horizon*'s hull. They would fly over Corsica in crossing, but the leg from Rome to Marseille would be hazardous, and the strain of their trans-Europe flight was already showing heavily on the crew.

Skies were turbulent and cloudy when the *Horizon* left Rome for Corsica, and it was a jolting ride over the choppy grey waters. Grim and worried, Roberts ordered the *Horizon* to land in Corsica and refused to move her for six hours until the wind died down and the skies cleared. The weather improved towards mid-afternoon, clearing the way for a safer passage, but the journey from Corsica to Marseille was still hazardous. It was to everyone's great relief when the *Horizon* entered French airspace and put land under her hull.

"Good to be back in civilized airspace, Captain," Barking Jack called out to Roberts with tired cheer. Roberts nodded in agreement. France was rapidly threatening to overtake England in airship technology, and the skies of France were well-patrolled with military vessels. Overland travel presented its own hazards, such as mountain ranges, but as a whole their journey to Paris was much less tense and worrisome than the earlier parts of their flight.

With growing excitement and anticipation pushing away the strain of travel, the crew of the *Horizon* kept the airship flying true, London in the distance and growing closer by the hour.

Chapter Twenty-Eight

The skies over London were crisp and cold, bright sun pouring from the heavens and barely a wind in the air as the *Horizon* sailed toward the commercial air wharf at Kingston. Roberts had weighed the merits of quietly slipping into London to try to prevent detection, and he had briefly considered landing at Cheapsides again. Upon further thought, Roberts had decided that Smothers be damned, the *Horizon* had the right to fly where she pleased.

He had, however, paid care that she approached London from the southwest, avoiding the most highly trafficked flight lanes and keeping well away from Smothers' bustling air wharfs. Kingston's wharf provided plenty of security for the steep docking fees it charged. Though guards could be bribed, Roberts was confident his airship would pass the week in London unmolested.

His confidence was further boosted when a stout man in the uniform of a port master hurried to the *Horizon* to conduct the necessary business. "Riester, sir, Owen Riester. Port Master First Class," he introduced himself with a tip of his hat. "Welcome to Kingston wharf, Captain."

"Captain Roberts of the *Horizon*," Roberts responded, and there was a glint of recognition in the man's eye.

"Where have you flown in from, Captain Roberts?" Riester asked genially as he scribbled in a thick book.

"We were in Crimea a few months for some military supply transport," Roberts began. Riester's expansive face split with a grin.

"You come welcome, then, Captain, you and your ship!" Riester boomed, seizing Roberts' hand in a hearty grasp. "My boy shipped over to Crimea six months ago. Got a letter from him the other day, I did, and he talked of your airship by name. Said she was a fine flier and that they had been starving before your little bird showed up."

Riester's fingers tightened in enthusiasm as he bobbed Roberts' arm up and down. "My boy was born and bred on this wharf, and he can name any airship by sight and ear. He said yours was the finest he had seen in the sky, and she worked like a champion. Fine ship, sir! Honored to have you on my wharf! Lads!"

The last word was bellowed at a cluster of young dock hands, who sprang instantly to attention and hurried forward to the port master. "Set this fine airship here to rights," he ordered. To Roberts, he said, "Whatever your ship or crew needs, Captain, you just say the word. I'm beholden to you, and I thank you for my boy's sake."

Roberts said in a low tone, "I'd appreciate it if your workers could keep a close watch on my airship. There's those in town I don't want crossing her path."

Riester visibly squared his shoulders. "Not a worry, Captain Roberts, not a worry. My wharf is well-guarded. Nothing goes in or out of this wharf without my say." He waved an expansive hand at two burly guards patrolling the length of the wharf, alert for trespassing, thieving, or loitering. "I'll tell my lads to keep an extra close eye on your airship, Captain Roberts," promised Riester.

"Much thanks for the offer, Mister Riester," Roberts responded with relief, even more glad he had touched down at Kingston. Riester, however, wasn't paying attention: he looked over Roberts' shoulder and straightened up even more.

"Ma'am, welcome to Kingston," the port master called out. Roberts turned to see the heart-catching sight of Miss Pickens standing topdeck. She was back to her faultless attire, a dark wine-colored skirt and jacket fringed with lace and a confectionery of a hat perched on her head. Every curl was in place, and from her mincing steps and elegant clothing, no one would suspect that less than a fortnight ago, Miss Pickens had been splattered with mud, blood, and exhaustion. On the flight to London, Harding had spent much of his time coaxing various nostrums and food down Miss Pickens' throat. She had recovered well and regained her former glory.

"Mrs. Roberts, I presume?" Reister saluted her crisply. Longing flooded Roberts even as embarrassment boiled hot in his belly. He rapidly shifted his eyes to Miss Pickens, wondering what she would make of the question. His varied emotions fled under a sudden surge of disappointment as the beautiful reporter laughed delightfully, her white-gloved hand floating dismissively in the air.

"Oh no, dear sir, I am merely a passenger on this vessel," Miss Pickens fluted with a casual dismissal that grated like broken glass on Roberts' nerves. He was ignored as Reister hurried forward to help Miss Pickens disembark. Jules was standing a few feet behind her, loaded with her baggage and resigned to his role as mobile luggage carrier.

Despite the turmoil in his gut, Roberts' thoughts immediately shifted to the pending financial transaction the two reporters had yet to complete with him. For one moment, he suspected them of trying to skip out on the deal. But Miss Pickens smiled at him.

"I believe we have a bank to visit, Captain Roberts." Her words were light, but she was obviously in a hurry. "Jules and I have a great deal to accomplish, and we must quickly conclude our affairs with you."

It was with more emotional conflict that Roberts dragged his attention back to his airship. Knowing that his men would be agitating to jump ship the second she touched down in London, he had dispensed pay before landing, and every pocket was heavy. Most of the men were taking away months' worth of wages with them, not having had much recent opportunity to spend their money. There were money transfer businesses available, but they were notoriously corrupt and charged hefty fines. It was far safer for a traveling man to bring his wages home personally.

As he stepped back on board, Roberts could feel the sharp anticipation, especially from Farrington, whose mind was clearly elsewhere. Spotting his quartermaster fumbling with a barrel, Roberts roared, "Mister Farrington!"

Farrington jumped, then reluctantly turned to face his captain. "What are you still doing on the ship?" Roberts demanded. "You've a family waiting for you."

"But I...the ship...I still have work..." Farrington fumbled, disarmed by his captain's harsh words, coupled as they were with a smile. The *Horizon* still had an hour or two of work left before she was fully shut down.

"We can live without you," Roberts grunted. "Get your arse off my ship," he said with gruff geniality.

"Go on, you idiot," Carter called out encouragingly. "You're about useless. Go home."

The quartermaster did not need to be told a third time. With hasty thanks, Farrington grabbed his sparse belongings and sprinted off the *Horizon*, Roberts yelling after him, "Be back in a week!" The rest of the crew set to their work with renewed energy, determined to get every task done in double time so they too could be freed from their duties.

Miss Pickens was beginning to tap her foot impatiently as Roberts dispensed orders, but he ignored her. She would have to wait. She was visibly fuming when Roberts emerged from the *Horizon*, cradling a heavily locked chest. It contained much of the profit his airship had earned for him in the past several months. Keeping all his earnings on board the *Horizon* was foolish and risky. It was time for Roberts' money to earn some interest and wait for him in London.

For the journey to the bank, Roberts had his pair of Smith & Wesson revolvers with him, as well as Jules, whose massive presence was an automatic deterrent to any potential mugger. He left the *Horizon* in the hands of Oboe and Halloway as well as a stolid-faced guard patrolling the wharf.

Miss Pickens' luggage was stowed on board the cab with some difficulty. She settled in the front seat with the driver while Roberts and Jules squished themselves in the back. As Roberts' shoulders competed with Jules for space, he examined the streets, noting what changes had been wrought in the months he had been away from his home city. As always, London was a mulligatawny soup of contrasts: ancient buildings housing science laboratories, cows bellowing as steam-powered transporters bore them through the city, airships roaring over cathedrals. To his right, Roberts saw an elegant gentleman in natty attire strolling along, obviously highly pleased with his appearance, only to have a chamberpot appear in an open window and spatter its contents on him. Small children ran here and there, helping themselves to apples off grocery stands and gleefully evading irate adults.

The streets were packed with traffic, and the cab crawled forward. It was sunny, but the weather was cold and clammy, settling into the bones. The ride became increasingly more chilly as the minutes ticked past. It was a long stretch of time before the steam cab pulled to a halt in front of Rothschild Bank and the passengers could disembark to thaw out and conduct their business inside.

Miss Pickens in her lovely clothing was warmly welcomed and ushered into the bank with solicitous care from the head cashier. Roberts, travel-stained and roughly shod, was examined with snobbish disdain until he made clear that he was quite happy to take his money elsewhere. The opening of the chest he carried had a remarkable thawing effect on the cashier. Jules authorized a withdrawal of a thousand pounds signed over to Roberts, who left just under thirty-five hundred pounds in the care of Rothschild Bank. Relieved that his money was safe, Roberts departed the building in the company of Miss Pickens and Jules.

It was only then, on the threshold of the bank, that he realized that the time had come to part ways with the fair-skinned reporter. Miss Pickens, her debts cleared, was already tracking her thoughts another direction, deep in hushed conversation with her brother as the pair stepped forward into the sunlight. Fighting a jumble of emotions, Roberts helped Miss Pickens back into the steam cab. He was taken aback when she warmly clasped his hand.

"Thank you, Captain Roberts, for all that you have done. Jules and I owe you a great deal, far more than a thousand pounds can repay." Her eyes were soft and luminous, enchanting under her hat, and Roberts had to force himself to surrender her hand.

He wasn't entirely certain if he responded with words or merely made a strangling noise in the back of his throat. Miss Pickens spoke to the driver and the cab roared to life, whisking the two reporters away into the hurly-burly of the city and leaving Roberts in the streets. Among the various emotions welling up inside him, relief and disappointment were waging a close war for mastery. He suddenly very much wanted a drink, perhaps several, and then quite possibly the chance to punch someone. Instead, duty strangled emotion in a chokehold, and he resolutely hailed another steam cab to transport him back to the *Horizon*.

It was reaching late afternoon when Roberts' feet hit the wharf at Kingston. He was vaguely surprised to find Oboe waiting for him topside. "You still here?" Roberts demanded with a mock frown. "We've been in home port several hours, and you've yet to leave. Get your arse off my ship," he commanded with rough affection. "You're missing out on a lot of drinking and pretty women."

Oboe smiled, white teeth against dark skin. "I could say the same for you as well, Captain." He inclined his head below decks. "Mister Halloway is still in the engine room."

"He is?" Roberts frowned, not surprised. A banging noise was starting to echo up from the inner bowels of the *Horizon*. After admonishing Oboe a second time to go on ground leave, Roberts went below to investigate.

He found Halloway covered in grease and chips of metal and characteristically intent. Roberts was relieved to see that his old friend had regained some of his former enthusiasm. There was still a sober intent about Halloway, and he moved with a preoccupied air. Not looking up as Roberts entered the room, Halloway called out, "About time you got back. There's a lot of little things I've been putting off, but now that we're in London I've got access to a lot of parts I need. She needs some serious work."

"Do what you need to do," Roberts responded, wondering how much it would cost him. In the past four months, the *Horizon* had earned more than Roberts had just deposited at Rothschild, but the cost of maintaining and equipping an airship could easily match the amount of income she earned. Halloway's expertise had averted numerous costly problems, but even with the best care an airship could quickly become a financial drain. Before she returned to Crimea, the *Horizon* would need supplies, provisions, armament, winter clothing for her crew, and an onslaught of other items, all of which would make a significant dent in Roberts' earnings.

Pondering this, Roberts watched Halloway move across the room, purposeful but curiously lackluster. Neither man said anything for a few moments, until Halloway questioned, apropos of nothing, "You leaving the ship for the evening?"

"I hadn't quite decided," Roberts responded. There were guards carefully patrolling the wharf, but Roberts was still acutely aware that the *Horizon* was in enemy territory, even more so than in Crimea. She had every right to be in London, but Smothers' influence was far too widespread in the city for Roberts to comfortably leave his airship undefended.

"You should. You look like shite warmed over," Halloway stated bluntly in what, for him, was solicitous concern. Roberts knew that he had seen better days, and he was positively barking for a long bath, a good meal, and a decent bed somewhere away from the endless droning of engines. However, he felt uneasy leaving the *Horizon*.

As if reading Roberts' thoughts, Halloway sighed heavily. "I'm not leaving your precious airship, Gavin," he grumbled. "I'll keep an eye on her. There's guards on the wharf and for what they charged you to land here, they damned well better watch her carefully. She'll be fine."

Halloway seemed settled in for the night; by any indication he would be diligently wrestling with tools until the early hours of the morning, longer if his energy held out. He would be noisy enough to make it clear someone was on board, and a simple yell would bring guards running. Roberts toyed with this as he climbed back topdeck, telling himself that the *Horizon* would be fine without him for a night.

Footsteps thumped on wood as a pair of guards marched towards the *Horizon* with Riester leading them. The men halted at the gangplank, and Riester hailed Roberts, who stepped forward to inspect the newcomers. "If you was thinking of a night on the ground, Captain Roberts, I've these two lads here to watch over your airship if you'd like," Riester proffered generously. "She's a pretty little thing, and I'd not see a square of her canvas harmed. My lads will keep her safe." He gestured at the two guards who were well-endowed in the shoulder department and apparently carved out of bacon.

Not one to ignore a hint when the universe insisted on offering it, Roberts nodded at the port master. "I thank you, Mister Riester. My men are getting up to hell-knows-what in the city, except for an engineer below decks tearing my engines apart. He's damned handy with a wrench, but he's not exactly the type to scare off intruders." The two guards, however, appeared very well capable of scaring off just about anything. With a command from Riester, they marched forward to take watch over the *Horizon*.

With another word of thanks to Riester, Roberts left the *Horizon* in the guards' care. A few locks secured his cabin, and the watchmen would guard against any industrious souls with a crowbar. With that he left, disappearing into the smoky depths of London, thoughts of soap, food, clean clothes, and a solid ten hours of rest dominating his thoughts.

Chapter Twenty-Nine

The *Horizon* was still intact and unharmed when Roberts strolled onto Kingston's air wharf that next afternoon, clean from head to toe, well-fed, and rested. The two night guards had been replaced by a brawny fellow who saluted Roberts as he stepped on board the *Horizon*. A close inspection uncovered nothing that drew his attention. Halloway was propped up in a corner of the engine room in a sleeping position that virtually guaranteed a backache when he awoke. Roberts let sleeping engineers lie and patrolled the rest of the airship until he was satisfied nothing had harmed her while he was away.

Halloway woke not long after, or so Roberts surmised based on the sounds of noises emanating from the engine room. He repaired to his cabin and shut out the sounds of Halloway at work, counting the minutes before the inventor appeared and began making clamorous demands on Roberts' wallet. There was paperwork calling his name; he shuffled through it listlessly, at a loss for what to do with himself. There was a long list of things to be done, especially since London had more supplies and resources than the airship could possibly need. Without a crew, Roberts couldn't begin to start on this list. Instead, he was left twiddling his thumbs and wandering aimlessly around the *Horizon*.

Two days passed, leaving Roberts oddly at ends. He had little to do but stay out of Halloway's way and mentally plot out what tasks he would dump on his crew once they returned from ground leave. Halloway required little of him, save that Roberts occasionally shove food through the door. His offers of assistance were soundly rebuffed, and Roberts guessed Halloway wanted to be left alone. This left Roberts to his own amusements, a situation hindered by the fact that leisure was not a concept he easily embraced. He had his own errands to run, and his own personal affairs to tend, but this still left him with large blocks of time on his hands. By the third day, Roberts was going quietly crazy from lack of activity, coupled with a crushing preoccupation with how many work opportunities in Crimea might be slipping past him.

London was in full festive mode, preparing for Christmas, and the streets were full of holiday decorations. Thick snowflakes drifted from the sky and turned to slush the moment they touched down. Yet even the joviality of the season could not push away the concerns of war. Talk of the conflict filled the streets, and family members waited anxiously for word about loved ones overseas. Newspapers sold instantly, each edition full of news about the war. Although Christmas celebrations were well in hand, the season's cheer was tempered by the sobering realities of battle.

The third morning found Roberts in a dingy coffee house listlessly stirring a cup of brown sludge that called itself coffee but barely deserved the name. He had entered the establishment with low expectations, and reality had triumphed over faint optimism. The result was a muddy drink that Roberts grudgingly swilled down as his eyes trawled a stack of yesterday's newspapers bearing copious stains from previous messy drinkers. A name caught his attention, and his heart skipped in response.

Victoria. With forced nonchalance, Roberts smoothed out yesterday's *London Guardian*. A long article graced the front page, with the name of Miss Victoria Pickens printed clearly and boldly in the byline. Roberts managed to set aside his seething emotions enough to approach the article with a detached eye, resolutely keeping his focus on the information it contained and away from the twanging feelings it aroused. He had read enough of Miss Pickens' work to spot her writing style: graceful yet direct, crushingly accurate, and with the right touch of *pathos* to incite action and outrage.

A growl of warning emanated from Roberts' innards and his forehead wrinkled, his stomach tightening. To fortify himself, he reluctantly choked down a shot of lukewarm coffee and settled back for some critical reading. The *London Guardian* had printed a sunrise and sunset edition the prior day, no doubt to accommodate the content Miss Pickens and Jules had brought back from Crimea. Roberts had a copy of the sunrise edition in his hands, and he carefully scoured it for any trace of the *Horizon*'s name or his own, his better instincts warning him that fully trusting Miss Pickens was not a wise course of action. The sunrise edition was thick and heavy, Miss Pickens' name showing on many of the pages.

As was the *Horizon*, Roberts noted this coolly. Miss Pickens had skillfully woven horrific tales of the British camp into brutal condemnation for how poorly the British government had provided for its soldiers, then gracefully highlighted the *Horizon*'s critical work in the war. Roberts carefully measured these references to his airship, noting that Miss Pickens had restrained her hand where the *Horizon* was concerned. She had given praise and thanks to the airship and crew, but avoided potentially inflammatory information.

Roberts continued reading, a growing sense of pride welling up in him. He had a damned fine airship and an excellent crew, and there was something delightfully satisfying about seeing both praised in such a public format. Around him, the coffee shop slowly emptied of customers, and the elderly proprietor began to shakily bustle his way around the tables cleaning up the debris. Passing Roberts' table, the proprietor put down a fresh copy of the *London Guardian* and filled Roberts' cup before he had a chance to protest. Ignoring the coffee, Roberts picked up the new newspaper. It was that morning's edition, and the screaming front page was full of news about the Light Brigade's slaughter.

With piercing poignancy, Roberts absorbed the article, Miss Pickens' words hitting him afresh. He recalled that fateful day with sharp clarity. Yet, he was surprised at how much detail and information she had managed to dredge up about the battle. Miss Pickens had not witnessed the event, nor had she much time at camp to interview survivors of the slaughter. She had boarded the *Horizon* shortly after the Light Brigade's ill-fated charge, feverish and in need of several days of recovery. Where she had come by her information, Roberts did not know, but as he continued to read, clarity began unfolding.

Turning to an inside page, Roberts scanned through an article highlighting the plight of soldiers suffering over in Crimea. The heavy crease on his forehead etched itself further across his face as his eyes fell on a particular passage.

The belly of the airship *Horizon* became a vessel for the dying, speeding wounded and ill soldiers across the Black Sea to Scutari in a desperate race against time. On board, she carried Corporal Edwin Paget of the 13th Light Dragoons, one of the few souls who survived the catastrophic slaughter that felled over a hundred of his companions. Yet the wounds he bravely received in valiant battle were mortal indeed, and even the swiftness of the *Horizon* was not enough to save the young dragoon and many of his brother soldiers from death.

Intaking sharply, Roberts narrowed his eyes and continued to read down the page. He began to realize where exactly Miss Pickens had gained her valuable information: from the lips of dying cavalry men in the *Horizon*'s cargo bay. A little further down, another segment made his gut tighten.

Dear Mother, Father, Paul, and Judy,

When I left home last year, I promised you all I would return. I'm so sorry to fail you. I tried, God knows I tried. But the enemy was strong and I wasn't strong enough. I'm sorry.

With growing fury, Roberts scanned the lines, his memory violently jerking him back to a poignant moment of two weeks ago: Miss Pickens tenderly writing down the last words of a dying soldier, her hands gentle and her face filled with concern. Roberts had witnessed the scene. It had cracked some of the barriers he had firmly erected against the tempting, wily reporter. However, common sense roared back to life as he kept his eyes fixed on the page.

Miss Pickens had reproduced the dragoon's letter, its heartfelt words intended for a private audience now splayed across the newspaper for thousands to see. Roberts cherished almost no hope that Miss Pickens had sought the approval of Corporal Paget's family before printing the letter. Most likely his poor family had heard of their loved one's death through a newspaper article, their private grief aired in public.

With cold anger, Roberts finished reading the article, then flipped through the rest of the newspaper. The *Horizon* made another appearance in an article about the cavalry, making mention of the equine transport that had caused Roberts so much grief. A brief word of praise from Lord

Raglan, mentioning the *Horizon*'s efforts, stood out on the page. Roberts took the praise, but his enjoyment was soured by his fury over the way Miss Pickens' journalism had soundly reverted to muckraking.

Finally he stood to his feet, tossed a coin onto the table, and thundered out of the cafe. The street outside was crowded. Roberts' determination to walk off some of his anger was hampered by the pressure of the many bodies clogging up the road. As he rolled along, his eyes lit on a familiar figure. He shifted his head to see Bloomberg strolling down the street with a lady on his arm. The pilot was ramrod straight, chest puffed out with pride, and his attention wholly focused on his companion. The woman in question was a trifle plump and a shade plain, but her round face was pleasant. Even at this distance, Roberts could tell she was giggling delicately. Behind the pair stalked a no-nonsense figure covered in several yards of respectable black crepe.

Roberts momentarily forgot his anger and watched in surprised amusement as the trio walked by, taking in the Christmas festivities and enjoying the day. *Well, I'll be damned*, he thought as he uttered a brief laugh. Shaking his head, Roberts decided not to hail Bloomberg. The crewman was clearly happy with the company he had found and likely not interested in his captain getting in the way.

Still shaking his head in amusement, Roberts continued forward, not exactly sure of his destination. As a result, a goodly spell of walking led him to the Broken Spar. There was a high likelihood of running into some of Smothers' employees in this particular part of London, but Roberts decided he didn't give a damn. Besides, he needed something to wash away the taste of yesterday's warmed-over coffee.

Tom the landlord was clearing a table when Roberts strolled in, and he nodded curtly. "Still alive then, Roberts?" Tom grunted by way of greeting. "Heard you were trying to get your airship and men blown up in Crimea."

Roberts grinned, taking the one free hand Tom offered to shake, then made his way up to the bar. Tom followed behind, while managing to carry seven steins in one enormous hand. He filled an empty stein with one economic movement and slid it under Roberts' nose. "You don't look half-bad," Tom said, examining Roberts. "All well on your ship?"

"All's well," Roberts responded, trying the beer. It was better than he remembered. "There's good money to be made in Crimea. It's a hell of an airspace, and it takes a ship like the *Horizon* to get the job done. She earns her keep and more."

Tom sniffed. "Word is, she's the talk of the papers." He gestured towards a neglected newspaper lying on the edge of the bar. Reading was not an overwhelmingly popular pursuit among most airmen.

"A bit." Roberts played with the beer.

"Hmm," Tom sniffed again. He picked up a stained cloth and began wiping down the bar or, more accurately, spreading the dirt around more evenly. Roberts rested his elbows on the bar, simply enjoying the moment of silence, but also waiting quietly. Tom had the look of a man with something on his mind, and it wasn't long before he spoke.

"Some might say it was mighty brave of you to return to London, Roberts," stated the barkeep in an undertone.

"I fly my ship where I please," Roberts grunted with an edge of hardness.

Tom looked worried. "I'd keep my eye on her while in London. There's some here that have a long memory. There's talk," he said quietly. "You know how airmen talk, and your airship's made quite a name for herself."

Roberts frowned heavily. "Any man that wants to come against my airship or my crew has got a fight on his hands."

"I'd just keep an eye out, is what I'm saying," Tom spoke in a conciliatory tone. With quick movements, he topped off Roberts' beer. "You're a good man, Gavin. I'd hate to see anything happen to you or your ship."

Roberts took the beer as well as the solemn words, and he brooded over them both carefully. He was lost in thought when the tavern door opened and men entered.

"You started drinking without us, Captain!" a voice called out. Roberts turned to see Carter, Jenkins, and Harding enter, carrying boxes, cases, and valises.

"Careful with that!" Harding snapped out as Carter dropped a box on the table. The surgeon gently lowered a heavy medical case onto the floor and then winced, pressing his hands to his back. Jenkins set down his armload as Roberts stood to greet his crew.

"I'd always suspected my landlord was the devil incarnate, but it seems I have misjudged the old man, or at least his good lady," Harding commented as he straightened up gingerly. "Gavin, it appears that you have at least a few supporters in this city. Mrs. Cooper told me that she was proud to see men take on the Smothers empire and live to tell the tale. Apparently she has been keeping my supplies against the day I returned to London to claim them." He waved a hand at the boxes and cases. "We will need all this in Crimea."

Carter was already moving towards the bar, slapping a few shoulders in greeting and generally making noise. As if drawn by his magnetism, two more airmen entered the tavern and were quickly sucked into the wake of Carter's enthusiasm. Although it was barely noon, a party of sorts was quickly warming up. The bar began to fill and the beer started flowing in steins. Roberts was glad for the chance to let loose some steam. His anger over Miss Pickens' latest editorial offerings was still burning in his veins and Tom's quiet warning hovered in the air. Roberts joined his crew with forced enthusiasm and the party continued to gain momentum. It lasted well into the wee hours of the morning.

   ***   ***   ***   ***

The sound of noise in the street pulled Roberts from the depths of alcohol-induced slumber. He blearily opened a pair of eyelids that were nearly glued shut. His internal clock pointed at late morning, but the dull greyness outside the window showed no sign of the sun. Wincing, Roberts pulled himself from the chair where he had spent an uncomfortable night and rose gingerly to his feet, trying not to jar his aching head. Memory blearily uncovered his location: one of the dank rooms above the bar. He dully recognized it as the same room where Farrington, Carter, and Jenkins had recovered following the *Lucky Lady*'s boiler explosion several months ago.

Jenkins and Harding were snoring on the narrow bed, Jenkins hanging partially off of his side. Carter, inexplicably wearing his coat, hat, one boot, and no trousers, was out cold on the floor with only a thin blanket across his torso. Roberts stepped carefully over the sleeping bosun. He hazily recalled that Harding had called it quits early in the night and disappeared upstairs. The party hadn't wound down until well past midnight, and Roberts couldn't remember when he, Carter, and Jenkins, had staggered into the room. Yawning, he left his men sleeping and limped downstairs.

The bar was deserted, the front door locked and no sign of Tom. Roberts wandered around the tavern, wondering if he could stomach eating something, when a rap at the door caught his attention. He unlocked the door to discover William on the other side, his face taut and his jaw clenched to keep back the shivers. Roberts stepped back to let his young steward pass. With a nod to his captain in greeting, William stepped across the room to the fireplace where a few logs smoldered. Silently, he stirred the fire back to life. By the time Tom groaned his way out of his sleeping quarters, a brisk fire was beginning to fill the room with warmth.

William continued to say nothing, simply setting about the morning with quiet determination. Roberts watched him carefully but did not press the issue. The young lad had obviously sought out his fellow crew members for a purpose; he would speak up when he made up his mind to do so.

Footsteps sounded, and Carter, Jenkins, and Harding made their groggy appearance. Tom's wife soon arrived with a cauldron of steaming porridge. With the remains of last night's festivities still burbling uncomfortably in his stomach, Roberts had little appetite for breakfast, and, from the faces of his crew, neither did they. However, they made as much headway as they could on the porridge.

William remained silent as breakfast ended, and he mutely fell in line as Roberts mustered his troops to move Harding's medical supplies back to the *Horizon*. Roberts settled the bill with Tom, and the five men left the hospitality of the Broken Spar for the mud-slick streets. Outside, a mixture of rain and snow fell down in a drizzle that thinned the streets of traffic. Although it was a long walk to Kingston's wharf, there was little to bar their way.

They arrived at the wharf chilly and damp and glad to set down Harding's supplies, which had grown heavier by the mile. Investigating below decks, Roberts saw that Halloway was intently focused on his work. While Harding moved his supplies into the infirmary, Roberts, Carter, and William did a walkthrough of the *Horizon*. They had left the airship well-organized, and there was nothing out of place. Jenkins moved towards the engine room, only to be driven out of it by Halloway, who clearly didn't want any company.

With not much to do and the rainy snow still falling, the crew wandered around the airship. Carter soon broke out a cheap pack of playing cards, and the five men settled down for a round of poker, betting on chestnuts. They whiled away a few hours at cards, and William won an impressive pile of chestnuts before the game broke up in favor of roasting and eating the chestnuts. Outside, the drizzle began to taper off. As late afternoon approached, a few tentative rays of sun began poking through the thick cloud cover.

Harding soon headed off to the berthing area for a nap, while Carter and Jenkins left their airship to find other amusements. This left William and Roberts. The boy mooched aimlessly around the airship, fiddling with this and that until Roberts spoke up.

"You've still got four days of leave, lad," he said kindly. "Your time is your own while we're in London."

William shrugged, his eyes downcast, and he began digging at the floor thoughtfully. "You've something on your mind?" Roberts questioned, knowing the answer was yes.

The floorboard excavation continued for several moments before William flashed Roberts a brief look, then dropped his eyes again. "Granny died last month," he finally stated in almost a whisper.

"I'm sorry to hear that," Roberts responded. He waited a few moments, almost asking about William's aunt, but decided to hold his tongue and let the boy speak.

"She...she was old and sick but...she was my granny still," William said, almost defiantly, as if anger could overcome tears. He bit his lip harshly. "It's just Auntie Mae and me now." He stopped, his foot twisting harder on the floor, visibly struggling with some internal battle, before he finally burst out loud, "Captain, I couldn't stand being in that damned house any longer! I..." he stuck his chin out. "I told Auntie we were flying out this morning."

"Well, that's not the truth, boy, and you know it," Roberts stated plainly but without condemnation. William shot him an angry look, but Roberts returned it with sympathy. Having met Williams' grandmother and aunt only once, he had a strong notion that the aunt had collapsed the full force of her grief and helplessness on William the second he walked through the door. No wonder the boy had escaped the moment he could and fled to the masculine safety of the *Horizon*.

William wiped his nose. "She's my aunt. I love her," he said as if reassuring himself and Roberts.

"I'm not questioning that," Roberts stated. "But nothing says that you've got to spend all your ground leave with her. It would do you good to spend some time with lads your own age. You've friends still in London, yes?"

Another shrug followed. "The boys I ran with are street kids, sir," William stated honestly. "They're going nowhere. No jobs, no schooling, nothing." His words were a reminder of Roberts' own experience, coming home on his first ground leave to discover just how much he had changed in six months, vastly outgrowing the friends he left behind.

William looked at his captain half-hopefully, half-fearfully, and Roberts let himself smile. "You can stay on the airship if you've a mind to, lad," he said genially. "That's not to say I won't put you to work," he warned. He had little use for idle hands, and if William was determined to hang around, Roberts would find something for him to do.

Looking slightly cheered, William nodded. "Can I have some money, sir?" he requested hesitantly. "Two of the cook pots need some soldering and one of the carving knives has a cracked handle."

"We'll take them in for repair," Roberts said. "The market will be open now that the rain's stopped. We should also start pricing supplies out. It will be a long, cold winter in Crimea, and we need to stock up as best we can."

With lighter steps, William scrambled to fall in place beside Roberts as the two left the *Horizon* for a nearby market. He stuck to Roberts' side, and it occurred to Roberts that William was perhaps pleased to have his captain all to himself. The boy was good company, and the next couple days, the pair of them managed to accomplish quite a bit of work while Halloway continued his efforts below decks, ignoring everything but wires, gear, and tools.

The week passed and, as evening fell on the last day of ground leave, the *Horizon*'s crew began trickling back on board, well-rested and re-energized for the struggles ahead. Bloomberg was unexpectedly jovial and full of talk about his new young lady, a pleasant thing by the name of Ruth, with whom he had struck up a rather fast-paced courtship. The pilot prattled happily about Ruth to anyone who stood within ten feet of him, and he endured a great deal of good-natured tormenting by the other men. The rest of the crew was full of talk about wine, women, and song, trading insults and filling the airship with noise as they prepped her for the long and dangerous flight back to Crimea.

Only Farrington failed to make an appearance that evening. The sun was well in the sky the next morning before the quartermaster returned to the airship. He hurried quickly up the gangplank, only to run almost directly into the arms of his stern-faced captain.

"You're late," Roberts thundered, his arms crossed firmly over his chest.

"Sorry, Captain," Farrington responded sheepishly, but his glowing face was so infused with happiness that Roberts' sharp words failed entirely to penetrate.

Roberts barred Farrington's way, watching as the quartermaster dutifully mustered himself to absorb a curt dressing-down. Roberts glared at him one long minute, then demanded with a smile, "Boy or girl?"

Farrington's grin could have illuminated a building. "Two boys," he responded with beaming pride. "Twins, sir. They're doing fine and so is Mary."

Roberts thumped Farrington's shoulder soundly. "Congratulations!" News spread quickly, and the crew clustered around to pound on Farrington's back and exchange jokes until Roberts shooed them back to their work. They had much to do before the *Horizon* was ready to brave the dangers and deprivations of Crimea once again.

Two days of noisy activity followed. The airship was inspected from top to bottom, and Roberts' money climbed out of his pocket with disheartening speed. There was a dazzling array of things to buy, and Roberts was determined to take with them as much as they could think of needing. Halloway grudgingly allowed Jenkins and Sparrowman to reenter the boiler and engine room, and the last of the overhaul was swiftly completed, the *Horizon* tuned with exquisite care to handle what work she had coming her way.

Christmas Day came and went, but not without a fine dinner on board the *Horizon*. Roberts didn't stint, and the crew had enough to eat to make them all sick. William's cooking skills had greatly improved, but the traditional roast goose and plum pudding were far beyond his abilities. London's many food markets and taverns sold prepared meals, and Roberts could buy anything that his crew wanted to eat, which was both varied and copious.

Boxing Day dawned the next morning, and found the crew groggy and hung over from stuffing themselves. Roberts was easy on them, passing out extra wages as part of Boxing Day and turning a blind eye to slackness. The *Horizon* was just about ready to lift and in the spirit of the holidays, he didn't want to push his men. Yet, soldiers were waiting for them back in Crimea, and the airship had money to make. It was time they got back to work.

As Boxing Day drew toward evening, the crew finished up the long list of tasks Roberts had for them and moved about the airship looking for anything that needed attending. Roberts was preoccupied with thoughts of departure and did not notice that Halloway had made an appearance and was hesitantly trying to capture his attention. Roberts finally made the connection and looked over to where Halloway stood fidgeting uncomfortably. With a gesture, Roberts signaled Halloway to follow him into the cabin, which Halloway did with surprising muteness.

Roberts shut the door behind them, feeling in his bones that the following conversation would be difficult and serious. Halloway's behavior had been exceedingly withdrawn as of late, and Roberts suspected that Halloway had been putting off a confrontation until he had no choice but to address it. Trying to keep his voice light, Roberts sat down in his chair and offered, "Have a seat, Jacob."

Halloway looked at the proffered chair, and Roberts repeated himself. "Sit down," he said, trying to be cheerful and failing by several notches.

Halloway awkwardly lowered himself into the chair, and the two men looked at each other for a second. Roberts guessed what the conversation would entail, but Halloway seemed unable to find the right words. Shifting in his chair, Halloway opened his mouth a few times but nothing came out.

Finally, Roberts broke the silence. "I meant what I said, Jacob, to you as well as to the crew. I'll hold no man on the *Horizon* that doesn't want to be here."

Halloway's face twitched and he began drumming his fingers on the table, still reluctant to catch Roberts' eye. Roberts waited quietly, knowing that eventually Halloway would speak his mind.

"Jenkins may be an idiot, but he can keep the boiler and engines running about as well as I can," Halloway said abruptly. "He can get you forty knots and keep this daft bird of yours going. Sparrowman's not half bad either. "

Roberts nodded, sadness twanging in his stomach. He wasn't surprised Halloway was leaving, but it was still a blow to hear the words. "We'll damned well miss you on board," he said sincerely. "I know you didn't want to be, but you're one of my crew. There's not a day I'm not thankful for what you've done for my ship."

Halloway looked marginally pleased, but he shifted uncomfortably, clearly anxious for the conversation to be over. Roberts, though, was already thinking ahead. "London is not the place I would choose to set up a new shop," he warned Halloway. "Even if you leave the *Horizon*, you carry her reputation with her. Smothers will just as soon run you out of town as look at you."

"You fuss like an old woman," Halloway mumbled.

"Forget what Smothers did to your shop?" Roberts responded with more harshness than he intended.

"No I didn't," Halloway snapped. "And I'm not going to be run out of town by that old bastard."

Roberts shook his head. "Jacob, listen to sense for once," he said in exasperation. "Your name's welcome across Europe, There are hundreds of cities that would be proud to have you set up camp. You could trade off your reputation and name your price anywhere." His words fell on deaf ears, Roberts knew that. Time on board the *Horizon* had not instilled in Halloway a greater ability to comprehend reality. Halloway could command a fortune at his feet, but Roberts knew that he'd never move in that direction.

"Don't be daft. I've had enough of foreign countries, courtesy of the *Horizon*. I'm home now, and I intend to stay here." Halloway swallowed hard, and Roberts suspected his old friend was covering up emotion with hard words.

"Well, I can't stop you," Roberts sighed. "I do wish you'd come to your senses. You're always welcome back on board if London grows too hot for you."

Roberts barely heard the soft "Thanks" echo from Halloway before the inventor cleared his throat.

Silence descended, then Roberts added carefully, "You need some money? I'd be pleased to give you what I can spare." Halloway had received wages the same as the rest of the crew, but getting him back on his feet would take significant cash stores.

Halloway shook his head, dismissing something so elemental as money. "I've got a bit put aside," he said almost impatiently, as if was of no concern.

Roberts nodded. "Well, good then." He was suddenly at a loss of what to say, and Halloway didn't seem to have much else to offer. It wasn't long before Halloway stood to his feet, shifting his weight anxiously.

"I've got some things to tell Jenkins and Sparrowman before I go," Halloway muttered. He snorted. "Make sure they don't blow up the damn ship, will you?"

That got a small smile from Roberts. "If they do, I'm holding you responsible for not training them right." Halloway's lips lifted in a wry half smile and the two stood awkwardly for a few moments, not meeting each other's eyes. Finally, Halloway bobbed an awkward nod and ducked his way out of the cabin, leaving Roberts to run his fingers through his hair and process the information.

He wasn't entirely surprised at Halloway's departure. The inventor was clearly bored and sick of being stuck on board the *Horizon*. Yet still, it was a tremendous blow to lose him. Jenkins was a talented engineer and Sparrowman functioned well as an assistant, but the tricky boiler system Halloway had devised really needed two expert engineers. The *Horizon* needed Halloway, and Roberts realized that the months ahead were going to be even harder without the inventor's skills.

It wasn't long before Halloway had barked out last-minute instructions to Jenkins and Sparrowman and gathered up his few possessions. The crew took the news with soberness, and it was with genuine regret that they watched Halloway leave the *Horizon* for the last time. Never one for emotions, Halloway muttered an awkward goodbye to everyone before departing in haste.

Roberts walked Halloway off the gangplank and down the wharf, the thick silence hanging uncomfortably between them. At the end of the wharf, Halloway paused and inhaled sharply but said nothing. The silence grew palpable.

Finally Roberts said, "Jacob, you know I owe my ship to your skills. In return for all your help, I've brought you nothing but trouble. That's not a fair way to treat an old friend. You've put up with more than anyone else on board."

Halloway's thin cheeks colored slightly. "Save your speech, Gavin," he said huskily. "We both know that bastard Smothers had it in for me. Never liked the fact that the best of his engineers couldn't ever top me."

Somewhat to Roberts' surprise, Halloway stuck his hand out for Roberts' grasp. The reclusive inventor normally shunned all physical contact, and it was a gesture of magnanimous generosity to offer a handshake. Gripping it firmly, Roberts shook Halloway's hand in farewell. "Take care of yourself, Jacob. If London gets too hot for your tastes, there's always room on the *Horizon* for you."

"I'll remember that, Gavin," Halloway said with evident sincerity, then sniffed. "You keep that blasted bird of yours in the air until she can pay off Smothers for you. If she falls to pieces or Jenkins blasts a hole in her, I might be persuaded to patch her up again."

"Alright you, get your arse out of here," Roberts rumbled affectionately, as he slapped Halloway on the shoulder. Halloway snapped off a mocking salute and stepped forward, his lanky frame eating up the ground as he left the wharf and disappeared into the filthy maw of London.

The mood on the *Horizon* was solemn when Roberts reboarded. Halloway was not exactly a favorite of the crew, and there wasn't a man on board who hadn't dreamed of tossing him over the railing, Roberts included. Though intractable, Holloway was the brains behind the *Horizon*'s operation, and the loss of him echoed throughout the ship.

Quietness remained on board the *Horizon* as the men finished their preparations. Morale fell rapidly in the wake of Halloway's departure, as the men contemplated the next few months without his skills. It was a sober crew that turned in for the night, waiting for morning to see them out of London and back into the skies of war.

Chapter Thirty

It was a cold, dark, and damp morning when the crew of the *Horizon* reluctantly dragged themselves to their feet again. Wet snow fell at irregular intervals and melted as soon as it hit the ground, turning the air clammy. Roberts had fitted the crew with sturdy, warm clothing for the upcoming months in Crimea, but the new clothes were soon damp, and morale was equally soggy. Halloway's sudden departure and the crew's worry over their long flight ahead sapped spirits as they prepared the *Horizon* for flight. She, in turn, was sullen, her boiler sluggish and her engines whining irritably. Jenkins and Sparrowman coaxed and cajoled the airship, but she seemed determined to stay grounded.

Roberts roamed the decks, spitting out commands and trying not to be angry with Halloway, whose tardy resignation had been particularly ill-timed. If he had announced his intentions at their arrival in London, Roberts could have spent the week looking for a replacement. Good airship engineers were hard to find and expensive to hire, and London was the best place to search for one. However, Roberts was already pressed for time as it was; he'd have to lift his airship from London and try his hiring efforts elsewhere.

Eventually, and albeit a few hours later than planned, the *Horizon* grudgingly lifted from the wharf and began climbing up in the grey heavens. Bloomberg carefully directed the airship to the southwest, well away from Smothers' wharf and London's more crowded flight paths. There wasn't much else in the sky. The *Horizon* had airspace to claim as her own, but Roberts kept her at fifteen knots until the city was well behind them. The light snowfall meant low visibility, and with as much air traffic as London generated, there was no sense in risking an accident.

The airship grumbled her way out of the city but gradually warmed up and settled into her pace. Not too long after they lifted, the snowfall tapered off and sunlight feebly penetrated the clouds. Through the gray haze, Roberts spotted the shape of two airships following the *Horizon* at a distance. Frowning, he examined them through his spyglass, straining to capture any detail about the vessels. After a few moments of careful scrutiny, he could just make out Smothers' crest emblazoned on both airships.

Oboe, passing by, paused at his captain's side. Roberts wordlessly passed the spyglass to his first mate, who also examined the two airships. Oboe did not have long for reflection before Roberts gave orders.

"Gunnery crew, man your post!" Roberts commanded sharply. "We've two Smothers airships on our tail." Long Tom, Farrington, and Carter hurried below decks while the rest of the crew tensed for action. The *Horizon* was scarcely out of London, and Roberts doubted the two airships would attack, but he vividly remembered several months ago when the *Horizon* was harried in the sky not five miles from London.

Over the sound of tension and voices rising up in alarm, Oboe's voice demanded Roberts' attention. "We are to fire on them, Captain?" he questioned.

"If they keep their distance, no," Roberts retorted sharply. "But I'm not risking being logjammed between two Smothers airships again." He slammed the spyglass shut. "We'll outrun them. We'll only fire if we must."

Visibility was still poor, and Roberts didn't want to kick up the *Horizon*'s speed, not this close to London. Instead, he fastened his eyes on the two Smothers airships and watched sharply as they continued to fly behind the *Horizon*, staying far enough away to be polite but close enough to make their presence known. Roberts directed Bloomberg to fly southwest towards Southampton. With a potential conflict on their tail, he did not intend to send the *Horizon* out over the Channel where an intentional "accident" would be easier to hide, the waters covering up the evidence.

Yet no conflict presented itself, and the Smothers airships did nothing to threaten the *Horizon* or encroach upon her flying space. Below decks, the gunnery crew waited, tense and irritable with anticipation, as minutes ticked by with nothing happening. Roberts himself was fighting back anger as well as a primal desire to have a spat break out, just for the pleasure of unleashing the Vandenberg on two of Smothers airships. After nearly twenty minutes passed with no change in status, he'd had enough.

Bellowing into the com device, Roberts roared out, "Engine room, bring us to thirty-five knots! We're putting those damned airships behind us." Jenkins barked back something unintelligible that sounded like compliance, and increased noises sounded from the engine room. As the *Horizon* picked up speed, she bobbed and weaved a little, not liking the flying conditions. It was somewhat of a fight to get her up to thirty-five knots and keep her there, but Jenkins and Sparrowman struggled grimly and won in the end. After efforts and oaths from her crew, the *Horizon* reluctantly set her pace at thirty-five knots and held it grudgingly.

She surged forward, leaving the two Smothers airships behind. Somewhat to Roberts' surprise, they made no efforts to pursue and did not react to the *Horizon*'s increased speed. By the time Southampton was visible ahead, there was no sign of the Smothers airships. The *Horizon* rounded the city and flew out over the Channel with extreme care, her captain and crew watching carefully for any hint that she was being followed. Aside from light airship traffic in the sky, they were alone.

Reluctantly, Roberts called for the gunnery crew to return to their normal duties, but the lack of Smothers' airships did not relieve him. Rather, the entire encounter left him perplexed and angry, and his temper surged, much as he struggled to keep it at bay. The *Horizon* settled down as she flew out over the Channel but her crew, picking up on their captain's foul mood, was agitated and tense.

It was an unhappy airship that crossed the Channel and entered France's airspace, but things began to improve once they passed Le Havre en route to Paris. Some of the boost in morale was due to the scent of beef stew wafting from the gallery. The *Horizon*'s larders were well-stocked with fresh food, and William was making copious use of it, no doubt sensing that a good meal would go a long way toward reducing tension on board. Roberts' own mood refused to lift, even when William set a generous bowl of stew and a mound of fresh-baked bread in front of him.

He had been too careless in London. Roberts became more convinced of that with each passing hour. He had been lulled into a false security by their trouble-free entry and their unimpeded movements around the city. Roberts hadn't been foolish enough to assume that Smothers knew nothing about the *Horizon*'s arrival, but none of the crew had reported any suspicious activity or possible threats, and the airship had gone unmolested. From all appearances, it had seemed that Smothers had wholly ignored their presence in London.

The two Smothers airships that had followed the *Horizon* out of London had shaken Roberts into sharp alertness. Their appearance had been deliberate, calculated, and pointed, deadly threatening although no cannon were aimed. They were a warning, a sharp reminder that the *Horizon* had a powerful enemy who neither forgave nor forgot.

Such thoughts consumed Roberts as his airship flew through the clear skies over France, a full moon glowing like a pearl in the velvet night.

*** *** *** ***

Athens was a gorgeous stretch of graceful white buildings under an azure sky. Waters the color of an aquarium lapped delicately at the city's ancient stones and pristine beaches that stretched for miles. The golden sun turned the air nearly warm and filled the skies with light. Work-weary, the *Horizon*'s crew flew her into the embargo-locked port and began a long, maddening process of securing permission to land. Allied forces patrolled the sea port and airship wharfs, keeping a tight lid on the political situation. The *Horizon* flew with extreme care to avoid a potential skirmish.

An hour of communicating with ground command via clicker code and impatiently hovering in the sky finally secured the *Horizon* permission to land at a berth. A squad of well-armed soldiers waited for her. Without asking permission from her captain, the soldiers boarded the *Horizon* for an inspection. Roberts watched narrowly as soldiers stamped over his airship, freely probing into whatever caught their attention, but they conducted themselves with prompt professionalism and were soon gone.

When the soldiers departed, Roberts glanced along the length of the airship wharf. Much of it was taken over by an absolutely enormous long-range airship sitting in the one berth large enough to just barely accommodate its massive frame. It was surrounded by a horde of workers and several squads of soldiers. Roberts had spotted the ship from the air and knew what it was: an airship this gargantuan could only be the *Omnia Vincam*, the biggest long-flight airship in existence and the pride of Smothers' airship fleet.

Roberts examined the *Omnia Vincam* carefully. Although the airship could easily carry twenty times what the *Horizon* could transport, if not more, its incredible lift power came at the price of slower airspeed, enormous coal consumption, and landing difficulties. Few airship wharfs could accept a massive airship like the *Omnia Vincam*. Her captain had to plan her flight path meticulously to ensure that she had a place to land when she needed to come down to earth. Her immense boilers gobbled up hundreds of pounds of fuel every hour, and her coal hoppers were gigantic. Yet, properly managed, the airship could roam from Europe to the Indies to China and back, making the trip in weeks, while a marine ship would sail for months, if not years.

Roberts did not have much time for the *Omnia Vincam*, for Farrington quickly drew his attention to another vessel.

"The *Morning Star*, sir!" Farrington called out in jubilation, waving his spyglass. "I knew I spotted her from the air. She's in port, Captain!"

Roberts took the spyglass and followed Farrington's pointing finger. The marine port was overloaded with ships, both sail and screw-powered, and Roberts had to hunt before he spotted the *Morning Star*'s colors.

"I'll be damned," Roberts commented, more to himself than Farrington, as a broad grin rose on his face. Barking Jack and Carter hurried to the railing with Oboe, William, and Harding following behind. Word spread through the *Horizon*, and the news was received with enthusiasm. Most of the crew abandoned their tasks to examine the *Morning Star* and eagerly speculate about her possible course.

Carter leaned over the railing, hands on his brow. "Think Captain Fosselweight will sail with us again, sir?"

"Could be," Roberts said evenly. He did not want to raise his crew's hopes, nor his own. He'd give much to fly with Fosselweight again, but he didn't know where the ship was headed, nor what prior obligations Fosselweight had made. Meanwhile, the *Horizon* was still only half shut down, and soon Roberts was shooing his men back to their tasks. The *Morning Star* would have to wait.

Thankfully, the wait wasn't long. "Ahoy, *Horizon*!" called a voice from the gangplank, not long after the crew had finished shutting the airship down. Roberts looked over to see a tall man standing at attention, light glinting off a lensed contraption covering his left eye.

"Ahoy, Captain Roberts!" Arterbury called out across the dock. "Permission to come aboard?"

Roberts called back permission and Arterbury strode up the gangplank, then presented a salute and a wide grin. "We saw you in the skies, sir, and damned glad we were to clap eyes on you again. Captain Fosselweight sent me with his greetings. He would have come himself, but you can't take a shite in this port without permission, and he was too tied up to break away." His grin deepened. "When you are free, sir, Captain Fosselweight welcomes you on board the *Morning Star*. Your ship has been sore missed, and we've work for her if you've a mind to take it."

"I'd sail my ship with the *Morning Star* again," Roberts said with pleasure. "What's she carrying?"

Arterbury jerked his head to the right. "Captain Roberts, see that great fat bird taking up almost the whole damned air wharf? That's the..."

"*Omnia Vincam*," Roberts interrupted. "I know the ship."

Arterbury continued without missing a beat. "You heard of the merchant marine *Cambridge*," he questioned in a statement. "Well, Captain Roberts, word is, Smothers is running half-arsed right now. The loss of the *Cambridge* was a big blow to the old bastard. He sent the *Omnia Vincam* to Constantinople and her cargo's bound for the front lines."

"The *Morning Star* made contact with *Omnia Vincam* three days ago here in Athens. We saw her fly into port. She came alone to Athens, and she'll be stuck in Constantinople once she gets there, sir. There's no way Balaklava can handle a great big bird like her. She'll need lighter transport ships to move cargo from Constantinople to Balaklava."

Proudly, Arterbury stated, "Captain Fosselweight saw an opportunity and earned a contract for the *Morning Star*. We'll be moving supplies up to Balaklava." He gave the *Horizon* an approving nod. "We could do with your fine airship once we reach Crimea."

Roberts nodded back, but his attention was on the *Omnia Vincam*. "How's she fly?" Roberts questioned.

Arterbury's face stiffened. "Like a damned boulder with wings, sir. Beats me to hell how she stays aloft." He shrugged. "She pays well, sir, and we'll leave her in Constantinople and good riddance."

Roberts' mood was thoughtful after Arterbury saluted and took his leave. As glad as he was to see the *Morning Star* in port, Roberts knew that her partnership with the *Omnia Vincam* could easily disintegrate if the *Horizon* was brought into the equation. He didn't wish to bring any trouble or conflict of interest to Fosselweight.

Later at the *Morning Star*, Fosselweight heartily welcomed Roberts and Oboe on board. He graciously poured them both tumblers of port while Roberts examined him carefully. Fosselweight's hairline had receded a bit more, as if his mustache was sucking energy from his scalp's follicles. He was still energetic and brisk, and the *Morning Star* seemed as capable and well-handled as ever.

"Is your ship sailing well, Captain Fosselweight?" Oboe questioned, accepting the port.

"We've been delayed in port the last week," Fosselweight replied patiently. "The *Omnia Vincam* had some engine problems. Then there is the matter of the embargo. If you wish to move as much as a teaspoon from one ship to another, you would be aghast at the paperwork you must finish. However, we should be departing within a few days."

Brightening, Fosselweight set his glass down with a thump and questioned, "And what of the *Horizon*, Captain Roberts? How has your ship fared in the past few months? Are your men well?"

Roberts briefly summarized their recent efforts in Crimea while Fosselweight listened attentively. He was particularly captivated by Roberts' tale of the Light Brigade's slaughter and the *Horizon*'s journey to Scutari. Roberts was stingy with details about Miss Pickens; Fosselweight would be outraged if he knew the reporter had spent weeks in camp. However, when Roberts began describing their flight back to London, Fosselweight interrupted in excitement.

"An airship of her class and size making that long of a flight? Unaccompanied? In winter?" Fosselweight's eyes shone with admiration and astonishment. "Captain Roberts, you will continue to make history with that fine ship of yours, sir!"

Roberts took the praise with quiet pride. "It was damn hard on my ship and my men, but she carried us through." Turning back to the business at hand, he announced, "I aim to get her back to Crimea as soon as I can. With luck, she'll stay there the winter through. She's strong enough to take it, and I know she's needed."

Fosselweight toyed with his port before continuing, "As much as I am glad of the chance to sail with your ship again, Captain Roberts, I do not need to tell you that forging a partnership between the *Horizon* and the *Omnia Vincam*...would present unique challenges," he finished diplomatically.

"You mean Smothers would be damned if his cargo ends up on my ship," Roberts translated flatly.

Fosselweight took a nonchalant sip from his glass. "Once the *Omnia Vincam* reaches Constantinople, a good deal of her cargo will be loaded on my ship. From that, it is contractually my obligation. Captain Mountjoy will have no further say over any further partnerships I may forge with support vessels. I will have vital need of an airship in Crimea.

"However," Fosselweight paused delicately. "It may be in the interests of all parties if the *Horizon* were to travel independently to Constantinople."

"We'll meet you there," Roberts agreed, eager not to cause Fosselweight any potential trouble. The *Horizon* could tarry in Athens a few days, getting a last burst of sunshine before Crimea, then fly to Constantinople. Already it was growing clear that the *Horizon* needed another engineer, and Roberts could put in some time searching for one before their rendezvous with the *Morning Star.*

"Excellent." Fosselweight looked visibly pleased. He raised his glass. "To the *Horizon*. Here's to another partnership."

Chapter Thirty-One

The *Horizon* tarried four days in Athens, killing time and waiting to join the *Morning Star* in Constantinople. Roberts was impatient to get the *Horizon* back to work, but Athens invited leisure and enjoyment, two things they would not find in Crimea. Although the embargo gripped the city, the beaches and inexpensive wine made it no hardship to wait out the days there. With few tasks for his men, Roberts gave them plenty of ground leave and they took their fill of the city.

January 2nd came and went, and Roberts did not register his birthday until the day was halfway over. In celebration of the event, he collected Harding and Oboe and repaired to a small, bustling restaurant recommended by several other airmen. Inside, an olive-skinned maiden supplied their needs in terms of bread, wine, oil, and a number of exotic dishes where tentacles played a starring role.

Roberts ate with gusto, trying everything and consuming an entire bowl of olives on his own. Oboe was a more cautious eater and more than once quietly edged a dish towards Roberts that was too unusual for his tastes. Harding surveyed everything set before him with extreme suspicion, warily poking it with a knife as if expecting it to explode.

"What in heaven's name is this?" the surgeon demanded, holding up something long and slightly purple.

"Looks like octopus," Roberts answered.

Harding hastily set the offending tentacle back in the serving dish. Grinning, Roberts speared it and gulped it down, watching Harding blanch. "Good God, man, if you wish to live to see your thirty-fifth birthday, as your physician I highly recommend a diet free of things that are capable of strangling you," Harding commented dryly.

Watching the surgeon closely, Roberts speared another tentacle and slurped it down, while Oboe laughed quietly. Despite Harding's dismay over the kitchen's offerings, their small table was full of cheer, and Roberts was particularly buoyant. They eventually left the restaurant in high spirits and ambled pleasantly through the city, taking in the sights and enjoying the fine weather.

Strolling along the road, Roberts found himself humming in contentment, more jovial than he had been for days. Meeting with the *Morning Star* and the promise of work had lifted the spirits of everyone on the *Horizon*, and their mood improved by the day in Athens. Roberts would get his airship back to Crimea, she'd collect her fat transport fees, and in a few years, he would be a free man with an airship wholly his own and no debt owed to any man.

When the *Horizon* lifted from Athens for Constantinople, she had a new man on board, a wizened engineer of German stock by the name of Hans Abelman. He was one of the few remaining members of the first generation of airmen, old enough to remember when airships first began to dot the skies. Abelman's skin was a network of steam burn scars, old and new, and he was quick to fill anyone's ears with harrowing tales of crashes, boiler explosions, and engine failures, all told in an accent thick enough to hammer.

Roberts was cautiously optimistic about Abelman. The engineer had far more experience with German engines; the *Horizon*'s engines were English made and her boiler was Halloway's own creation. Abelman, however, quickly proved to be a skilled engineer, and he handled the *Horizon*'s innards with deftness. Although there were some minor hiccups, the combined forces of Jenkins, Abelman, and Sparrowman kept the *Horizon* flying. As the miles passed, Roberts grew more confident that Abelman would be an asset on board. Nothing would replace Halloway but with luck, the *Horizon* would not suffer too greatly from his loss.

They met the *Morning Star* in Constantinople, where the *Omnia Vincam* was being unloaded laboriously and with far too much fuss and bother, in Roberts' estimation. There was more waiting while the cargo made its way onto the *Morning Star* and the two ships prepared for their upcoming voyage. On January 9th, they left Constantinople for Crimea, both carrying cargo and grimly prepared for what was ahead.

The voyage across the Black Sea was long and perilous, enemy ships in the water and the skies. Cold increased with every mile, and visibility was hazy. Stiff winds beat determinedly against both ships and tried to push them off course. To Roberts' relief, the *Horizon* flew well and gave him very little fuss. He had enough troubles keeping a close eye on the weather and a sharp lookout for potential enemies. Roberts kept in constant communication with the *Morning Star* and routinely steered the merchant ship away from airships and marine vessels ahead that looked like potential attackers.

It was January 13th when the two ships sailed into Balaklava Bay, grateful to put the Black Sea behind them. The bay, however, was not inviting. It was rimmed with ice, and the *Morning Star* had to edge her way carefully inside, fighting ice and the waves that beat at the mouth of the bay. Inside, seven battleships clogged the waters and blocked the *Morning Star* from the shore. She dropped anchor while Roberts sent the *Horizon* forward to the empty airship wharf.

As she landed on a berth, Roberts examined the wharf carefully. He had an uncanny feeling that it had not been used for a few weeks. There was no sign of Dunlap or his airships, and Roberts pondered this as he secured the *Horizon*. She had five tons of cargo with her and was ready to lift to camp as soon as her captain made contact with ground command. He wouldn't lift again until he had properly assessed the current situation and what flight risks he could expect.

The *Horizon* did not go unnoticed. Before long a small cluster of officers hurried onto the wharf and hailed the airship. "Captain Roberts, sir, welcome back to Crimea!" an officer called out over the noise of the *Horizon*. Roberts stepped off the ship and greeted the men. He recognized them under the mud, ragged clothing, and overgrown beards but could not remember all of their names. However, the officers were clearly not interested in formalities.

"Do you have food on board, Captain Roberts?" another officer asked anxiously.

"My airship is carrying five tons of it. The *Morning Star* is anchored in bay and a hundred tons more."

The officer sagged in relief. "Thank God. We've seen only one supply ship since the *Horizon* left Balaklava and we've barely the airship power to transport it."

"Where's Captain Dunlap and his airships?" Roberts demanded sharply.

"The *Black Nell* was shot down three weeks ago by a Russian airship," stated another officer. "All hands lost." Roberts shook his head but the officer wasn't finished.

"The merchant ship *Gallant* arrived two weeks ago and she came without an airship. Captain Dunlap drove the *Specter* and the *Dark Squall* to transport the cargo, but they couldn't keep up under the strain. The *Dark Squall* burst two steam valves and nearly crashed, more than a week ago. She's been grounded in camp and can't lift off the wharf."

"The *Specter* and *Dark Squall* managed to transport about half of what the *Gallant* brought up," said a man Roberts recalled as Captain Ayers. "When the *Gallant* returned to Constantinople, the *Specter* went with her. Captain Dunlap wanted parts and supplies for the *Dark Squall*. He hopes he can patch her up enough that she can get back to Constantinople for repairs. We've been without air support since then."

"We've got supplies freezing on the ground and thousands of men starving," another officer stated with tired bitterness. "We can't move a damned thing overland."

"My airship is here," Roberts pronounced with firm determination. "She's ready to work and so are my men."

"Then get moving," the officer snapped. He was frozen into silence by a cold look from Roberts.

"My ship is not lifting until I have a full report of air activity and flying conditions," Roberts responded sharply. "The *Black Nell* was shot down. I'm not risking my ship until I damn well know what she'll be flying into." As he spoke, he was relieved to see Staff Sergeant Prachett approach the airship wharf. Coolly, Roberts stepped through the group of huddled officers and stamped across the wharf to deal with someone he knew he could trust.

Prachett greeted Roberts quietly. "Wasn't sure if you were coming back, Captain Roberts," he said evenly. "Your ship well? Your men?"

"All well," Roberts brushed the inquiries aside. "What happened with the *Black Nell*?"

"She flew alone to a winter camp close to the Russian line," Prachett responded. "Dunlap's ships can't do running drops, but they can throw supplies overboard or lower them on ropes. Captain Grim convinced Dunlap to send the *Black Nell* to one of the winter camps that was in dire need of supplies. I warned him against the transport, but he's gone reckless in Crimea. The *Black Nell* strayed too far north and met a Russian airship she couldn't dodge."

Prachett shrugged marginally. "There's no room in this land, or this war, for carelessness," he finished simply.

Roberts went quiet at the news, digesting it thoughtfully. Prachett examined him carefully. Finally the staff sergeant spoke. "With the *Horizon* gone, we made do with Dunlap's airships. He's now down to just the *Specter* and she's currently in Constantinople. Damn knows when or if she's coming back. With the worst of winter to come, I'd be glad to know if you intend to keep the *Horizon* here."

"If there's Russian airships in the skies, I'm not risking my airship running her out to camps across Crimea," Roberts stated flatly.

"Most of the men are in the main camp for winter," Prachett stated. "We've got smaller camps scattered around Crimea and they're pretty well starved out but..." he shrugged again. "You take your risk as you feel comfortable. We've lost two military airships in this war, and the one I have left is grounded five days out of six. She flies like a rock in this weather, and I can't promise that she will be any use to you as an escort vessel." He gave Roberts a hard look. "If you fly, Captain Roberts, you'll fly alone."

"What have you seen in the sky from here to camp?" Roberts demanded.

"Nothing but clouds," Prachett reported. "The airspace is clear. It's not well patrolled since we are down to one military airship, but it's one of the safer airspaces you'll find in Crimea. Weather will be your main concern. The damn fog sets in fast."

The news was not encouraging: fog was feared by all airmen. As if to further dampen Roberts' spirits, a few flakes of snow shook loose from the clouds and landed on his shoulders.

In a sober mood, he returned to the *Horizon* and grimly gave orders for her to lift. Afternoon was burning away, and he wanted to take a flight to camp to assess the situation and decide whether the *Horizon* should stay in Crimea.

With some difficulty, the *Horizon* lifted from the wharf and flew toward the British camp. The light flakes of snow did not thicken but the air was bitterly cold and visibility was marginal. Roberts kept his eyes on everything at once, noting how difficult flight conditions had become in the few weeks the *Horizon* had been away. Crimea had already been a difficult patch to fly, and January's weather made it even more perilous.

Their journey was uneventful, and the grey skies held nothing but air and the occasional bird. Nevertheless, Roberts was greatly relieved when the camp rose into sight and the *Horizon* moved in to land on the wharf. Part of it was occupied by the *Dark Squall* whose topdeck suddenly filled with activity at the *Horizon*'s approach. Roberts guessed that the crew hoped the *Specter* had returned. He caught a few disappointed looks as the *Horizon* landed, and the *Dark Squall*'s crew quickly filed below decks and disappeared.

The *Horizon* soon had plenty of company. Hundreds of soldiers hurried to the wharf, ready to strip her of anything edible she contained. Her cargo looked paltry in comparison to the number of soldiers pressing up against her, desperate and frozen, and she was speedily unloaded. After a hasty conference with several officers, Roberts quickly lifted his airship from the camp, determined to bring the *Morning Star*'s cargo to camp where it was so urgently needed.

His determination was severely tested over the next two days. Brutal cold fell over Crimea, filling the air with snow and hampering all efforts aboard the airship. The engineers worried over the ship's innards with solicitous care, well-knowing that a cold boiler could freeze and explode and that harsh cold played havoc with the engines. The rest of the crew grimly battled the elements and the demands of the airship, fighting exhaustion and risking frostbite.

On the *Horizon*'s third day back in Crimea, the *Specter* flew into Balaklava and landed solidly on the airship wharf.

Almost instantly, Dunlap was off his airship and stamping toward the *Horizon*, clearly furious at finding his rival back in Crimea. Roberts, frozen and exhausted, had quite enough on his plate and didn't feel like dealing with more bullshit from Dunlap. Watching the other captain roll in his direction, Roberts wondered if he shouldn't just punch Dunlap in the face and be done with it.

Dunlap had lost flesh in the few weeks the *Horizon* had been gone, and his face was harder and more worn. His intensity was in no way lessened as he roared down the wharf. "Ye have got stones to show your face back in Crimea, Roberts," Dunlap pronounced with a low growl of rage.

"I fly my ship where I please," Roberts stated evenly but with an edge of warning.

Dunlap's face was a rictus of fury, inches from full attack, and Roberts had half a mind to give Dunlap the fight he desperately wanted. He knew that brawling was pointless; it was obvious that Dunlap was smarting from his losses and striking out blindly.

"I'm sorry to hear of the *Black Nell* and her crew," Roberts said solemnly, meaning the words. "She was a good ship. That's a hard loss."

Dunlap's knuckles whitened but he stayed his hand, masterfully holding his grief from breaking through the angry hardness of his face. Roberts' condolences were ill-received.

"I need no tears from ye, Roberts," Dunlap pronounced harshly. "Just get your damned bird off the wharf and stay the hell out of the way. I've work to do."

"There's more work than both our ships can handle, visibility's piss-poor, and it's damned dangerous to be flying these skies," Roberts measured each word, but his tones were heavy. "I well know you've got a grudge against me, but dragging a grudge across Crimea could get all of us killed. If we watch each other's backs, we'll a better chance of getting our ships out of this alive." He was striving for reason, but it was transparent that Dunlap would have absolutely none of it.

"Watch your own back, Roberts," Dunlap snapped. He seemed poised to deliver another volley of insults but apparently thought the better of it. He stormed off angrily, leaving Roberts to fume alone. Dunlap would not see reason, so there was nothing Roberts could do but return to the *Horizon*. She would find no ally in the *Specter*.

Once back in Crimea, Dunlap quickly resumed his campaign of aerial antagonism toward the *Horizon* and her crew. Fosselweight initially refused to give Dunlap a contract, but Roberts' better judgment moved him to appeal the decision. Despite Dunlap and Roberts' dispute, cargo needed to be moved to camp. The *Specter* was better than nothing. Roberts grudgingly shared airspace with Dunlap, who did his best to annoy and inconvenience the *Horizon* at every step.

It quickly became obvious that the *Specter* was floundering heavily in the brutal winter. She took nearly twice as long as the *Horizon* to load and three or more times longer to fly from the bay to the camp. She was down on the wharf more than the *Horizon* and lifted far less, and her engines sounded strained and overstressed.

Dunlap had returned from Constantinople with parts for the *Dark Squall*, but her repair work progressed slowly and she had yet to lift from the camp's wharf. The wharf's third berth was now too dilapidated to land on, and the *Horizon* and the *Specter* squabbled over the one available berth in camp, further increasing the tension between them.

Both airships labored mightily, but neither could begin to meet the needs of the swollen camp and its numerous soldiers. Food supplies were consumed almost the second they hit camp, leaving many soldiers hungry and with nothing for the next day. Thousands of soldiers languished from disease, wounds, and exposure in campsites around Crimea, and the graveyards consumed and expanded daily.

In the midst of hardship and deprivation, Roberts was astonished to receive a dinner invitation from Lord Lucan. The offer was unexpected and deeply puzzling: high-ranking military officers carried impressive titles, not the sort of men to mingle willingly with a common-born airship captain.

Roberts examined the gilt-embossed invitation critically for several long minutes before opening it. His suspicions rose as he scanned the words enclosed inside. There were fulsome references to the *Horizon*'s service to Queen and country and praise for her captain, but Roberts' cynicism was not easily dissuaded: Lucan wanted something. There was no other reason why a decorated earl would extend a dinner invitation to a common merchant captain.

With a grim sense of prescience, two days later Roberts made his appearance on the earl's luxurious yacht, moored in Balaklava Bay. He knew the yacht well; it had been a damned nuisance clogging up the narrow bay and hindering merchant ships from reaching the port. To the earl, it was a welcome relief from the filthy realities of camp as well as a place to entertain select guests, all of whom, save Roberts, were decorated officers.

Roberts had prepared for the event as best as he could, digging out his one formal set of clothing and performing what ablutions he could in a small tin bath full of rapidly cooling water. With his brawny, work-toughened hands and rougher manners, Roberts was easily distinguished from the privileged gentlemen filling the room. Surprisingly, he was received by the officers with a measure of cordiality, a gesture he did not exactly reciprocate, especially when he saw the copious champagne dinner spread before the eleven guests, far more food than they could all eat.

As dinner progressed, Roberts could not help noticing how carelessly the officers dealt with the food on their plates, helping themselves to choice morsels and leaving generous amounts uneaten. Remembering the thousands of starving men just a few miles inland, Roberts was angered by the waste, knowing the leftovers would likely be tipped overboard rather than given to those who would gladly accept it. Yet, it had been a long time since he had eaten so well, and with only a small prick of guilt, he felt to it with a relish. The maze of cutlery and drinking vessels was annoyingly complex, but hazy remembrances of formal dinners with Captain Albert helped Roberts identify the fish knife and red wine goblet.

The gilt surroundings and paunchy, well-fed bellies crowding up the luxurious dining room were an insult to the sufferings in camp, but Roberts kept his feelings to himself. The *Horizon* had earned an admirable reputation and he did not want to sabotage that. Besides, as the wine flowed and tongues flapped loose, information spilled out that captured his attention. What wine was unable to uncover was likely to be let loose once the after-dinner brandy was poured.

Roberts kept a wary eye on his glass, still unable to shake the deep suspicion that his presence on board was no mere gesture of thankfulness. At the beginning of the meal, Lucan had actually stood and formally recognized Roberts in their midst, personally thanking the "gallant captain" and the crew of the *Horizon* for their efforts in the war. Roberts acknowledged the praise with graciousness, but his suspicions were not averted, and it was not merely the high-class surroundings that rendered him coolly aware and alert.

The conversation around the table, unsurprisingly, was centered on the war. Plenty of complaints and accusations floated in the air. Roberts said little, acknowledging the occasional pleasantry directed his way, but mainly keeping his ears open for useful information while he waited for the true nature of this little dinner to manifest itself. It came eventually, when the dessert plates were cleared and brandy and cigars were being handed out. Voices sharpened as the conversation turned to the touchy subject of the Light Brigade.

In the midst of the babble of voices, Roberts heard a sentence ring out clearly. "Damned pack of lies, that's what it is. Don't you agree, Captain Roberts?"

A sudden silence fell over the room as eyes swung Roberts' way. He turned to see Lord Lucan, his brandy glass held high, and the beginnings of a flush creeping across his balding dome. Like many of the officers present, Lucan showed clear evidence that age and gluttony were overthrowing the trim, disciplined waistline a military man should possess. His baggy, hangdog eyes and red-veined nose hinted at serious alcohol use, and his veneer of joviality covered an undertone of anger as his voice rose.

Tension twanged up in Roberts as his eyes narrowed. Casually he set down a particularly fine cigar and turned to the earl. "I beg your pardon, my Lord?" he said calmly. *So you're finally getting to the point of this sham,* he thought coolly. *Alright, old boy, show your hand.*

"I'm referring to this...garbage disguised as journalism," Lucan responded with forced cheerfulness. "Come, Captain Roberts, surely you have seen some recent publications. I believe you have the acquaintance of that," the earl made an attempt at a tight smile, "charming young lady reporter and her brother who recently graced us with their presence."

Not looking at the earl, Roberts lit the cigar and took a leisurely puff before answering. "Mister Pickens and Miss Pickens were passengers on my airship. That's all."

Lucan waved the comment away. "If I am not mistaken, Captain Roberts, you have some...clout with Miss Pickens."

"I've acquaintance with the lady, my lord, but I've no say in how she conducts her affairs," Roberts stated evenly. "She answers to her father and her grandfather Commander Horace Pickens." He put emphasis on the commander's name.

"And a dammed fool he is," a general interrupted drunkenly. "Letting his granddaughter roam about unchecked and unchaperoned save that idiot brother of hers." He hiccupped loudly. "There's no place for a woman in a military camp or a newspaper. If the commander had a grain of sense, he'd marry her off as soon as he could and be done with her. Utterly disgraceful, it is."

Lucan gestured, and servants began setting down newspapers in front of the diners. Several copies landed in front of Roberts. There were some editions of the *London Guardian* and the *Times* as well as a copy of the *Constantinople Gazette*. The dates were within a few weeks, and Miss Pickens' name was clearly evident on many of the pages. The Charge of the Light Brigade, as the newspapers dubbed it, was front-cover fodder in several editions.

Around Roberts, his fellow diners ruffled through the publications and commented loudly, anger rising in the air. As Roberts flicked through the papers, he understood the building indignation around the table. Miss Pickens had spared no punches, condemnation bordering on vitriol spilling out against the military leadership and the British government. William Russell's articles graced the *Times*, and he was no more gentle than Miss Pickens.

"Blast it to damnation!" a white-bearded, portly officer threw a paper down and reached for his glass with a shaky hand. "Reporters! They ought to be hanged, the plague-ridden lot of them. My officers have kept their mouths closed, but the common rank...bah! Give 'em a drink or a cigarette, and they'll spill anything." He sniffed loudly. "Disgusting, really. Cholera take them all if the Russians don't."

"Starvation to the lot of them," echoed another titled lord, and Roberts felt his fists tighten. Rank had its privilege, but it did not extend to fluently cursing the common man dying of starvation in a muddy camp. However, he kept his anger. Lord Lucan had still not fully played his hand, and Roberts waited for the events to unfold.

The Charge had been a fiasco, that Roberts knew. Preliminary reports stated that an unclear command passed from Lord Raglan to Lord Lucan had sent the saber-armed Light Brigade into what Miss Pickens had colorfully referred to as "The Valley of Death". In the valley, more than twenty Russian battalions had poured out their attack from three sides. Rumor was spreading that the suicide charge was not what Raglan had intended, and fingers were pointing. Captain Norlan, who had carried Raglan's original order to Lucan and died in the battle, was under suspicion and his death left many questions unanswered. Lord Cardigan, who had led the Light Brigade and survived the ordeal, was under censure as well. Lucan, however, was bearing most of the blame.

"I imagine our Miss Pickens will eventually return to Crimea?" Lucan interrupted Roberts' musings.

He gave Lucan a cool look. "My airship transported her and her brother to London around Christmas, my lord. I left her there and don't know of her plans."

"Humph, good riddance I say," a white-bearded officer harrumphed into his nearly empty glass.

"She'll be back," another officer stated darkly. "Man or woman, a reporter is a moth to a flame."

"I've written to her grandfather and asked him to intervene as he should," interjected a third. "It's damnably improper for her to be carrying on about. Commander Pickens should be ashamed of himself. I've known the old boy for decades, we served together. He'll listen to me."

Lucan thoughtfully swirled the brandy in his glass, ignoring the words around him. "Nuisance or not, Miss Pickens could be suitably harnessed to our purposes if she insists on continuing with her writing." His words fell like a stone on the table, crushing grumbles of malcontent. Faces started wrinkling in surprise, then calculation.

So that's what you want, Roberts thought, anticipating the next sentence. He wasn't disappointed. With some lightness that did not cover up his serious intent, Lucan said, "I am hoping you can use your influence with Miss Pickens, Captain Roberts, to help us cast this situation in a more truthful light."

Roberts said nothing. He did not need Lucan's words to tell him that the Lieutenant General was intent on cleaning his coat of arms. A hundred and eighteen men had fallen in the charge, and England had not taken the news kindly. The hunt was on to find the best candidate to blame, and since Lucan had relayed orders to Cardigan, he was first in the running as the one responsible.

Eyes turned expectantly Roberts' way as the diners shifted their chairs to better face him. He coolly ignored them, keeping his focus on the newspaper in his hand. Finally Lucan spoke. "Well, Captain Roberts?" he said impatiently.

A few seconds of silence followed, long enough for Lucan to shift angrily. Finally, Roberts answered slowly, "I'm not quite sure what you are asking of me, my lord."

Lucan visibly bristled, making a poor attempt to cover up the expression with a stiff smile. "Captain, I have it on good authority that the *Horizon* was near the battleground and that you, sir, saw the battle unfolding before your eyes."

"I don't see how that relates to Miss Pickens," Roberts answered evenly.

"Surely you saw that sending the Heavy Brigade into the valley would have been suicide!" Lucan snapped, the flush in his face deepening, as a servant mutely refilled his brandy glass. He took a stiff drink, knocking it back angrily while Roberts observed him carefully. Lucan was linked to Cardigan as a brother-in-law, and the animosity between the two was legendary. The supposedly muddled orders could have been a convenient way for Lucan to rid himself of an adversary. Even without the hatred between Lucan and Cardigan, Lucan had a point. Roberts had seen the battle unfold and could testify that sending in the Heavy Brigade would have only added to the death toll.

But Lucan wasn't finished. "Lord Raglan has continued to grant me scarcely a morsel of discretion in carrying out his orders. Throughout this campaign, he has hampered me at every step, demanding that his orders be carried out to the letter. And after all this, I am being blamed for not having used my discretion in ordering the charge!" Angrily, Lucan threw an edition of the *Times* across the table, where it landed unceremoniously in front of Roberts. "See how I am censored to be made a scapegoat for this damned slaughter!"

Roberts scanned the publication. It was dated December 10th and the front page was a dispatch from Lord Raglan himself. It only required a few seconds of reading before it became clear that Raglan blamed Lucan for bungling the Charge and the subsequent death toll.

Pushing the paper aside, Roberts puffed his cigar in thought. The situation was tricky, and he was wary of making a mistake that could jeopardize the *Horizon*'s continued employment in the war. Lucan was growing furious, and angry men seldom made good decisions.

"I want you to go to London and bring that reporter of yours back to me," Lucan commanded bluntly.

"For what purpose, may I ask, my lord?" Roberts responded evenly.

Lucan flushed even deeper, his balding head sweating under the influence of alcohol and agitated emotion. "If she insists on spilling ink across the page, she can do me the courtesy of allowing me to defend my reputation and my decisions to England and my superiors," he snapped. "I have been vilely painted and my name has been dragged through the mud. I simply will not allow this."

Remembering how Miss Pickens had besmirched his own name, Roberts considered warning Lucan that the reporter would likely do far more harm than good. But Lucan didn't seem as if he was in a mood to listen. Aloud, Roberts said, "You still have the reporter from the *Times*, don't you, my lord? Why not have him write a rebuttal for you?"

"Lord Raglan has forbidden all officers from speaking to him," Lucan replied irately. "The woman, Miss Pickens, is a different matter." He smiled without humor. "So far, Lord Raglan has given no order regarding her."

"That may change with these articles," Roberts commented dryly, lifting the newspaper in his hand.

Lucan waved the comment away angrily. "I will not allow my name to be sullied!" he exclaimed furiously, his voice rising. "Captain Roberts, you and your airship have been granted an extraordinary amount of freedom in your transport activities throughout Crimea, not to mention that you have generated astonishingly high transport fees. May I remind you that your generous contract can be rescinded at any moment."

It was a threat, but a hollow one. A few reasonably sober officers blanched, knowing what would happen if Roberts took offense and pulled the *Horizon* out of Crimea. The tension in the room increased dramatically but Roberts was unruffled. Lucan was descending into thoughtless bluster, and he was quickly losing support around the table.

Roberts let silence fall for a few moments before responding. "Let me repeat, my lord, I don't answer for Miss Pickens. I left her in London a few weeks ago. She might be trying to find her way back to Crimea now for all I know. I could waste weeks chasing about Europe looking for her. Or," he paused, "I could get food, bandages, and bullets to your men, my Lord." He turned his head, meeting the eyes of each man at the table. Many made brief eye contact only to look away uncomfortably.

Over the deafening silence, Roberts continued. "January is almost over, and the snows are falling steadily. Merchant marine ships will have an even harder time bringing supplies up to Crimea. Last I saw, Constantinople was cleaned out of food. With the *Dark Nell* shot down and *Black Squall* broken down, that leaves the *Horizon* and the *Specter* as the only transport airships in Crimea. Between the two, my ship's the superior airship. I'm sure, my lord, you will agree that her skills as best put to use helping you fine gentlemen win this war than chasing after some fool woman reporter."

An icy chill suddenly fell upon the room. Roberts ignored it and took a luxurious drag from his cigar. While the situation was tense, he knew the balance was tipped his direction. More than one officer was examining his glass thoughtfully, and a few glanced at Lucan with measured expressions. Although the officers might publically side with Lucan, they valued food and medical supplies over the reputation of their cavalry commander. It could very well be their own bellies that went unfilled if the *Horizon* was dismissed from her transport duties.

Roberts took a few more puffs on his cigar, then spoke. "I'm a merchant airship captain, my lord, not a politician or a military commander. My focus is keeping the *Horizon* in the air and getting your troops what they need to survive this winter and win this war. And if you fine gentleman will excuse me, I'd best be getting back to doing that."

He rose to his feet, his tall frame towering over the seated men. "Much thanks for your hospitality, my Lord. Gentlemen." Roberts nodded around the table at the ten other men and strolled out of the dining room. Topside on the yacht, cold air rushed up from the frigid waters of Balaklava Bay and a handful of icy snowflakes brushed against his face.

The worst of winter is yet to come, he thought grimly. He took a last drag on the cigar before tossing it overboard. The slightest of hisses sounded as the smoking stub hit the dark waters and disappeared below the waves.

Chapter Thirty-Two

Roberts expected some backlash after the dinner party, knowing that Lord Raglan was not pleased with the outcome. However, the next morning dawned and the *Horizon* continued about her work with no repercussions or restrictions. They had cargo to transport, and the cavalry commander's injured pride was not high on Roberts' list of priorities.

He soon pushed the event out of his mind, the demands of his airship corralling all his focus. February was ten days away and the weather was brutal, placing enormous strain on the *Horizon* and severely taxing her men. Her envelope now required two men on the catwalk during flight. Since the envelope was steamy warm, there was no shortage of volunteers. Harding was on constant patrol for signs of frostbite and hypothermia. He paid careful heed to Oboe, who quietly suffered in the cold, and Farrington, whose steamburn scars were particularly sensitive to temperature changes.

Dunlap doggedly kept the *Specter* in Crimea, struggling to lift cargo to and from Balaklava and doing his level best to confound the *Horizon* at every turn. Despite his determination, the *Specter* was visibly floundering, and each passing day further sapped her strength. She was barely holding together and was down for maintenance more than she was in the air. She could only manage a few lifts a day, and Roberts knew that Dunlap couldn't be generating much of a profit, especially with the *Dark Squall* still grounded in the British camp. He suspected that Dunlap would drive his airship and men to their deaths rather than give up.

"He's killing that ship," Barking Jack spoke soberly to Roberts on one crisp, bitterly cold morning. The *Horizon* was waiting at berth in Balaklava for the *Specter* to land, and the other airship was doing a poor job of it. She lurched drunkenly through the air and collapsed heavily on a berth, frozen wood squeaking painfully under her weight.

"He'll kill her and his men as well," Barking Jack continued heavily. "They won't last through the winter."

Roberts said nothing, but it was obvious the *Specter* was struggling heavily. The *Horizon* was having her own difficulties, but she was bearing up admirably under the strain. Her work performance had not dropped significantly when winter hit. In sharp contrast, the *Specter* was obviously flying on little more than sheer, stubborn will.

Big Tom lumbered up to Roberts' side and nodded in respect, then turned his attention to the *Specter*, brow furrowing in thought. Brisk, snow-flecked winds tugged at their clothing and their breaths were clouds of fog in the dry air. Roberts examined Big Tom, noting the streaks of grey in his beard and the sagging lines of his face. The workload was aging them all, dragging them down, and what strength they had to spare was taken by the brutal weather.

Big Tom sucked at his teeth. "She's no cold weather ship," he pronounced, pointing at the *Specter*. "She flew up here with a good envelope but it's falling to bits. Too much strain. Bad maintenance." He shrugged and said no more. After a few more moments of hard contemplation, he respectfully took his leave and disappeared into the envelope.

The object of their scrutiny was downing engines, and the *Horizon* was preparing to lift. Roberts, frowning, saw Dunlap shoot a murderous glance across the wharf at him. He returned it stonily. *You damned, stubborn fool*, he thought with a shake of his head, then called for the *Horizon* to lift.

It wasn't much: only eleven tons lined her hold. Roberts' thoughts were heavy as he directed his airship into the snow-flecked skies. The *Horizon* had worked diligently, and Balaklava was close to empty of supplies. It was never enough; the thronging masses of humanity wintering over in the British camp consumed endlessly, and each load the *Horizon* brought could only stave off death so far.

The *Morning Star* had long departed, hastening back to Constantinople for more cargo from the *Omnia Vincam*. Roberts fervently hoped the merchant marine would return soon, but he wasn't optimistic. With winter, the Black Sea was treacherous to cross and full of enemy ships. Roberts knew it could be weeks before they saw another supply ship. Yet, there wasn't much he could do except get the rest of the cargo moved to camp and wait for another merchant ship to arrive.

As the end of January approached, the sheer force of winter hit with everything it had. Blizzards filled the ground with piles of snow, and bone-biting winds ripped across the landscape with a force that could tear a man's clothing. Days were an endless blitz of cold and unending misery, hardship piling upon hardship. Winter gripped the land fiercely, and ports into the country became nearly inaccessible. Balaklava Bay was choked with ice and almost impossible to enter.

Roberts, struggling to keep his airship together and his men alive, spent nearly every waking minute consumed with worry. The *Horizon* struggled in the nearly uninhabitable climate, fighting against the sharp winds that tore at her canopy and battered her about like a toy, straining her airbags and overtaxing her engines. Jenkins, Sparrowman, and Abelman labored mightily in the engine and boiler room, coaxing miracles out of the airship's valves and cogs, but she still floundered. Her legendary speed and swiftness diminished as her strength waned.

"Never thought I'd say it, but I'd be damned glad to see Halloway back on board," Jenkins admitted to Roberts one frozen afternoon. The engineer ran a hand over his rutted face, liberally smearing it with coal dust. His lean frame was turning gaunt and the hollows around his eyes were deepening. Sparrowman had the glazed, deadened look of a man running on his last dredges of energy. In contrast, Abelman was still relatively sprightly despite his wizened appearance. Roberts had the distinct feeling that the old engineer was going to outlive everyone else on board.

"Will she hold through the winter?" he asked.

"She'll hold, sir," Jenkins pronounced firmly. "By damn, she'll hold. But she won't fly pretty for you and she won't come through it unscathed."

"She'll fly as long as she has cargo to transport, Captain," Sparrowman interjected respectfully. The *Morning Star* was long gone, and the *Horizon* had transported the last load of cargo that morning. Since then, she had sat in Balaklava, her engines silent and her crew catching up on maintenance while their captain paced and worried. She was low on supplies, her crew was exhausted, and it was unclear when another supply ship would arrive with more work for them.

Roberts could hear the unspoken words hovering in the air. Sighing, he asked, "She could make Constantinople?"

Jenkins nodded with bitter determination. "She'll make it, sir." He paused, and added, "I don't know what skies we'll find over the Black Sea, nor what will be in them, but she's got the strength for the journey."

Sparrowman's mouth was a hard, thin line. "We would take a risk, sir, flying alone," he said quietly.

"It's possible Captain Dunlap would sail with us," Roberts offered without much conviction. The other three men did not look any more convinced than Roberts, but he would make the offer anyway. The *Specter* likely needed to return to Constantinople, and it was possible that the extreme weather and brutal hazards would be enough to shake Dunlap out of his obstinacy.

Moving about his airship, Roberts weighed the merits of a trip to Constantinople. They could be weeks at Balaklava with nothing to do. A trip across the Black Sea was risky, but so was staying in Crimea. The *Horizon* needed parts, her larders were near empty, and her crew could use a dose of civilization. If by some miracle, Dunlap agreed to fly with the *Horizon*, they could travel in relative safety.

The *Specter* was down on her berth, boiler silent and air bags deflated, when Roberts arrived at her gangplank, trying not to let his teeth chatter as the wind bit heavily into his flesh. The crew was below decks, and it took some shouting on Roberts' part to draw their attention. Dunlap bided his time, leaving Roberts to stamp his feet and curse irritably until the other captain made an appearance.

"What?" Dunlap demanded, pointedly and abruptly.

Roberts cut to the chase. "My airship is leaving for Constantinople tomorrow. We need supplies and there's nothing left in Balaklava to transport."

"So go then," spat Dunlap, turning his back.

Roberts ran an appraising eye over the *Specter*. "Your ship could likely use a spell in Constantinople, and you need parts for the *Dark Squall*. There's no sense in either of our ships flying alone, not over the Black Sea."

"You want to fly with my ship?" Dunlap growled.

"There's no work and no sense hanging around in Balaklava waiting for it," Roberts stated logically. "A few days in Constantinople will do our ships and our men well. We'll also hear word of other supply ships heading to Balaklava. If none are coming for weeks, we'd best winter over in Constantinople."

Dunlap continued to glower, clinging desperately to his pride, but Roberts could see that the immense strain of the passing months bore heavily down upon him. Not giving Dunlap the chance to answer, Roberts stated bluntly, "My airship flies at sunrise tomorrow to Constantinople. Your ship wants to fly with us, you're welcome to. But she's leaving with or without you. Your choice."

With that, Roberts turned sharply and left the *Specter* and her simmering captain behind him. Back on board the *Horizon*, he discovered that his men was cautiously optimistic. The crew were excited about returning to Constantinople, but sober about the dangerous flight ahead. Roberts didn't need to urge his men into the work of preparation, and they all labored long into the night to ready the airship for her flight.

As if eager to return to civilization, the *Horizon* was surprisingly alert the following morning as her crew prepared her for the flight across the sea. Her boiler and engines sprang to life with little coaxing from her three engineers, and her canopy expanded rapidly under the strong winter sun.

Pacing the decks, Roberts occasionally shot a glance at the *Specter*, wondering if Dunlap's stubbornness would win or if he would concede to reason. Even if Dunlap decided to follow the *Horizon* to Constantinople, Roberts knew that the *Specter* would not come to the *Horizon*'s assistance if she experienced trouble. Still, the *Horizon* was safer traveling in the reluctant company of the *Specter* than attempting the flight on her own.

As the *Horizon* neared takeoff, the *Specter* stirred herself and began starting her engines. Roberts grinned to himself but did not delay the *Horizon's* liftoff. Dunlap would have to catch up on his own if he had a mind to follow the *Horizon* to Constantinople. Soon the *Horizon* was rising up into what promised to be ideal winter flying conditions, with a blue sky and low winds.

Roberts directed her forward in a leisurely flight path, calling for a slow fifteen knots. The *Horizon* frisked a bit as a few gusts of winds off the coast tapped at her gondola. Once over the open sea, she settled down for a sedate journey. She was empty and primed for much higher speeds, but Roberts kept her slow, waiting to see if Dunlap would follow or if the *Specter* had flown in another direction.

They were thirty minutes out of Balaklava when Bloomberg called out into the frozen air, "Well, bless me, I didn't think the old fool would fly with us!"

Roberts looked out to see the dark shape of the *Specter* trailing reluctantly a few miles behind the *Horizon*. He smirked in triumph, then called for the *Horizon* to creep up to twenty knots. She surged forward and held at twenty knots, a snail's pace for her, but one slow enough to keep the *Specter* within visual. As the two airships sailed forward, Dunlap did nothing to close the gap. Instead, he kept the *Specter* well behind the *Horizon* as if wanting to make it seem that the two airships were merely going in the same direction and not actually flying together.

This continued as they crossed the Black Sea. At her best speed, the *Horizon* would have finished the journey in just under ten hours. With the *Specter* following her, it was nearing dawn the next day when the two airships entered Constantinople's air space. Their crossing had been uneventful: good weather and nary an enemy in the skies. With much relief, Roberts directed the *Horizon* into a berth, glad to put the Black Sea behind him.

Dunlap had exchanged no communication with the *Horizon* during the journey and merely followed her lead. Upon entering Constantinople, he directed the *Specter* into a berth far away from the *Horizon* and downed engines in surly silence. Roberts was past caring. The two airships had made the crossing safely, and the *Specter*'s only contribution had been slowing the *Horizon* down. As far as Roberts was concerned, Dunlap could find his own way back to Crimea.

Constantinople was noticeably less bustling, and there were far fewer troops patrolling the dirty streets. Noticing this, Barking Jack and Abelman speculated that there might be more alcohol and better amusements in the city, now that many of the soldiers were gone. The crew of the *Horizon* departed the airship for a day of ground leave, cautiously optimistic about what entertainment they might find and grateful for the warmer weather.

Roberts was exhausted and longing for a rest himself, but his purpose in Constantinople was to find work. The *Morning Star* was nowhere to be found. Roberts could only shrug and look for other merchant ships bound for Crimea. A day of searching and he found one in the form of the *Utopia*, an aging three-master with military cargo and no airship contracts.

"Too rough for airships," stated Captain Harris, master of the *Utopia*. He was a short, villainous-looking fellow with a permanent plug of tobacco in his cheek and little regard for where he spat it. "Couldn't get a bird to fly with us, not to Crimea. Too risky."

He spat again. "Sailed with the merchant marine *Blackwater*, but her captain balked at Crimea. She foundered a bit and he won't risk her on the Black Sea. She'll drop her load here in Constantinople."

Roberts cared little for the sight of the *Utopia*, nor her captain. She was ill-rigged and bore the look of a vessel that had been driven hard with negligent care. Yet, she was headed to Crimea, and Captain Harris was open to the *Horizon* joining his ship.

An hour of sharp negotiation wrangled an agreement that neither captain found satisfactory. Harris was miserly to the core, and Roberts nearly walked away from the deal. Considering the costs of fuel and labor for the trip, he knew he would net only a small profit from the venture. But the *Horizon* would earn it all back once she reached Crimea and was moving supplies for the military. Harris planned to sail the

Utopia to Balaklava, unload her, and return to Constantinople for the *Blackwater*'s cargo. If weather permitted, that meant several weeks of work for the *Horizon*.

Slightly cheered by this but still grumbling over Harris' parsimony, Roberts left the *Utopia* for the airship wharf. It was sparsely populated; only half the berths were full. Dunlap was still sulking at the far end of the wharf, and the *Specter* hadn't moved. All the airships on the wharf were shut down, and the normal drone of engines was silenced.

In the distance behind Roberts' back, an airship hummed its way forward. He paid it little mind. Now that he had arranged work, he had some time on his hands, perhaps enough for a visit to one of Constantinople's famous Arabic baths to steam away the worst of Crimea's cold.

"Captain!" Bloomberg's voice floated over the *Horizon*'s railing. The pilot waved frantically, his face split in a smile. "Captain, look! It's the *Horus*!"

Chapter Thirty-Three

Wulfe had grown slightly more vast in the months since Roberts had last seen him, and no less hearty. He crushed Roberts' hand in his own as the two airship captains greeted each other on the wharf, the *Horus* still humming loudly as she settled down for a rest.

"Damn me, it's good to see you, Roberts!" Wulfe boomed, pounding Roberts' back with enough force to dislocate joints. "All's well on board your ship? You still flying in this fool of a war?"

"Where the hell have you been?" Roberts demanded with a grin. "I could have used you."

"Ahhh, we had almost total engine failure off the coast of France," Wulfe grinned apologetically. "Damn near crashed with all hands on board. We managed a hard landing, but she was nearly broken to bits. Almost scrapped her out, but I didn't have the heart." His beard waggled as his shook his head. "Instead I drained all my money and then some getting her back on her feet."

The *Horus* had grown no prettier in the aftermath of her near crash. In Roberts' private opinion, Wulfe would have been better off abandoning her for another airship. Optimism seemed to be the only thing keeping her together. The aether flyer was battered but alive. Despite her visible scars, she still had the appearance of a happy airship.

Wulfe followed Roberts' gaze and preened a bit. "She's mine now. You're looking at Captain Grey Wulfe."

Roberts thumped his back in congratulations. "Captain Cork had enough of the old tub and sold her to you?" he questioned jovially.

Wulfe's grin disappeared to be replaced with sadness. "Ahh, well, Captain Cork." He paused, then shrugged apologetically. "The madness never quite left him. Sad to say, but he took his own life about a month ago. Never could get right in his head, and the madness was eating him up body and soul. I think he could only see one way out and he took it."

Wulfe shrugged again. "It was after the accident. He got himself pretty banged up in it and with the pain and his madness, well, a bullet was the only medicine he could reach for." More brightly, Wulfe continued. "We were down for weeks putting her back together, but she's flying again."

"You aim to take her back to Crimea?" asked Roberts.

"Molly'll have my head if I don't," Wulfe grinned. "She told me she wouldn't marry me till this damned war's over."

"Well, we'd best get it won," Roberts grinned.

"I've been waiting for two years to marry that woman," Wulfe groused cheerfully. "I'm not letting no war stop me."

Roberts laughed, then turned to business. "I've a contract with the merchant marine *Utopia*, and she should be sailing to Crimea soon. Her captain's tight-fisted enough. I don't know if he would sign on another airship..."

Wulfe waved it away. "I'm taking my ship back to Crimea regardless. You'll need her." He paused thoughtfully. "Your ship's been the only merchant flyer since I left?"

Roberts shook his head darkly. "About two months ago, my ship flew from Constantinople with three other merchant airships commanded by a Captain Dunlap. He took a wrong shining to the *Horizon* from the first meeting, and his ships have done little but aggravate us and get in the way."

He pointed down the wharf to the *Specter*. "Dunlap lost an airship in Crimea, and another's stuck at camp and can't lift. He's down to one working airship, and I convinced him to fly it down to Constantinople with us. As far as I'm concerned, he can damn well stay here."

"Pox on him," Wulfe pronounced cheerfully. "Let's get our ships back to the war and back to work."

    ***   ***   ***   ***

The *Specter* did indeed stay put when the *Horizon* sailed out of Constantinople two days later with the *Horus* at her side and the *Utopia* spreading out her tattered sails below. Roberts had negative interest in whether the *Specter* intended to return to Crimea, for he soon had his hands full with the *Utopia*. Captain Harris eschewed use of technology and the *Utopia* was absent a clicker code machine, making it impossible for the ships to communicate. The navigation skills of the *Utopia*'s pilots left much to be desired, and the ship was sluggish in the dark waves. The journey back to Crimea took twice as long as it should, the *Horizon* and *Horus* drifting slowly in the skies while the *Utopia* plodded through the Black Sea.

At the mouth of Balaklava Bay, the *Utopia* stopped and refused to move forward. Without a clicker code machine, she was unable to express her intentions. Roberts finally called for a quick drop line and slid to the *Utopia's* topdeck, although Harris tried to wave him off.

"You trying to pull my sails down, Roberts?" Harris bellowed as Roberts hit the decks and stormed towards the irate marine captain.

"What are your intentions?" Roberts demanded.

"Not going into Balaklava. It's iced through. I'll never get my ship out." The bay was thickly clustered with ice, and its narrow sides looked capable of crushing a ship. There were three marine ships inside the bay and, from the looks of it, they were staying there until spring. Bringing another ship into the bay would just compound the problem.

There was only one option. "Drop sails," Roberts ordered. "Anchor your ship. My airship will lift cargo and load in air. The rest can be rowed out."

"Are you mad, man?" Harris demanded. "You're not getting your damned airship anywhere near my masts."

"You can keep your ship here for weeks and risk her getting iced in," growled Roberts. "Or my ship can clean her out quick. She's had plenty of practice lifting from marine ships. I'll not harm your sails or masts, that I swear."

Roberts spoke confidently, but he suppressed a groan at the thought of the workload ahead. Harris could bitch and fuss all he wanted, but lifting cargo straight from the *Utopia* was the quickest way to unload her since he would not bring her into the bay. The rest would have to be rowed across the waters, a task that could take days.

Harris scowled furiously, but even he could see that the ship would have to be unloaded offshore at considerable strain and fuss for all parties involved. With angry worry, he cast a hard glance at the *Horizon* hovering steadily in the frozen air, barely moving as a few gusts of wind tapped at her gondola.

"You harm a rope on my ship, Roberts..." Harris warned ominously.

"I won't," Roberts met his eyes firmly. "My airship and my men know their work. They're damned good at getting cargo off a marine ship."

"They damned well be," Harris growled.

With that as permission, Roberts called for the *Horizon* and let himself be pulled back on board. While the airship prepared to lift cargo, Harris anchored his ship in shallow water at the mouth of the bay. In this position, the marine ship was exposed to rough wind and waves, further compounding the problem of unloading her.

Harris was a further hazard, for the irate marine captain did little but stomp and swear and get in Roberts' way. The *Utopia* was badly run, her crew sullen and her master harsh. The task of unloading the merchant marine were severely complicated by Harris' domineering attitude and the lack of unity in her men. Speed was vital, but Harris only slowed the process considerably.

At every step, the sea and winds held them back. Longboats helped with unloading, but it was a long row across the murderously cold waters. Three boats capsized during unloading, sending men and cargo into the waves. One sailor and several hundred pounds of cargo were lost to the sea. Still, the ship had to be unloaded. Harris reluctantly agreed to let both the *Horizon* and the *Horus* lift cargo from his ship while longboats continued to row cargo across the waves.

As the *Utopia* was laboriously unloaded, Roberts was increasingly grateful for the *Horus* at his side. Despite her recent near crash and her battered appearance, the small aether flyer did her work admirably well, carefully lifting supplies from the *Utopia* and transporting them to shore. She wasn't quite as graceful as the *Horizon*, and she came closer to the *Utopia*'s sails far more often than Harris liked, but the *Horus* was a great help to the *Horizon* as the airships struggled to complete the task.

Time was against them. Every day that passed, the *Utopia* risked icing over or foundering on the rocks. Harris swore more loudly by the hour as he bullied his men and snarled at the airships. The shores of the bay quickly turned into a jumbled mess of crates, sacks, and assorted mounds of cargo. Soldiers attempted to inventory and arrange the supplies for transport to camp, but crates froze to the ground and cracked in the cold.

Four days of back-breaking work followed, Harris cursing fluently over the ice and waves and threatening to take his ship back to Constantinople half-emptied. Roberts was close to abandoning the job unfinished, but he stuck to it grimly, knowing that each pound of supplies was precious. When the *Utopia* was finally unloaded, she departed in haste, fleeing the harsh winter. February had just hit and spring was nowhere in sight. Although Harris had stated his intentions to return with the *Blackwater*'s cargo, Roberts' wasn't optimistic. Sailing conditions had steadily deteriorated in Crimea, and the bay continued to be impenetrable. It was highly possibility that no more supply ships would appear until spring.

With that thought heavy on his mind, Roberts turned his attention to moving cargo from the bay to camp. This, at least, was an easier task since *Horizon* could be loaded while she was landed at the wharf. There were plenty of soldiers eager to help, and teams of them quickly filled the *Horizon*'s innards with cargo.

When the *Horizon* brought her first load into camp and landed at the wharf, Roberts wasn't exactly surprised to see the *Dark Squall* still grounded. By the looks of it, she was stuck until spring, taking up valuable landing space and getting in the way. Her topdeck was deserted and heavily coated with snow. Roberts wondered briefly about her crew. They would likely wait a long time for Dunlap to return for them. Roberts hadn't seen the *Specter* since he left the airship in Constantinople.

Soon distracted, Roberts pulled his attention away from the *Dark Squall* and focused on getting the *Horizon* unloaded. Her entry into camp had been warmly received, and plenty of volunteers were on hand to unload her. Indeed, Roberts had to come down hard on the swarm of soldiers pressing forward before eagerness lead to inefficiency. With some yelling and abrupt orders, the *Horizon* was quickly unloaded, soldiers and officers alike crowding the wharf to help.

Roberts dealt with the onslaught of assistance and questions as swiftly as he could. He was primarily concerned with getting his airship unloaded and back to Balaklava. Finally, he extricated himself from the eager interrogation, then moved toward the gangplank, the *Horizon's* engines starting to clang faster in preparation for liftoff.

At the airship's gangplank waited a man, hat in hand and head bowed with respect. Roberts recognized him as Fuller, the first officer of the *Dark Squall*. Despite Dunlap's animosity towards the *Horizon*, Fuller had conducted the *Dark Squall* with a measure of professional courtesy. Of Dunlap's three airships, Roberts had been the least aggravated by the *Dark Squall*. For that reason, he greeted Fuller with a terse nod.

"You'd be First Mate Fuller of the *Dark Squall*?" Roberts questioned, looking the man over.

Fuller nodded, bowing his head again and crushing his hat between his fingers. "Yes, sir, Captain Roberts," he said respectfully. The man had obviously swallowed his pride, and Roberts felt some sympathy toward him.

"You've business to discuss with me?" Roberts questioned, examining Fuller studiously.

"Yes, sir." Fuller set his jaw and stiffened his spine. "I was wondering if you've had any word of Captain Dunlap."

"The *Specter* followed my airship to Constantinople two weeks ago," Roberts responded shortly. "I don't know of Captain Dunlap's plans. We left the *Specter* in Constantinople."

Fuller looked pained but tried to master his worried expression. Sighing, Roberts questioned gruffly, "How's your ship fairing?"

"We can get her off the ground, sir, but barely," Fuller reported. "Her valves are patched but not well, and we can't keep her envelope full. We're losing half our steam, and she's dumping heat like no other, sir." He spread his hands helplessly. "Captain Dunlap was bringing more parts and equipment back from Constantinople, and I can't move her from camp until he does."

Roberts turned this over and finally said, "I'll ground my ship in camp early tonight. You can have my engineers for a time and whatever parts off my ship you need."

Fuller's face widened in surprise, and he looked ready to say something before Roberts interrupted with a question. "The third berth at camp is still broken down, yes?" He didn't need Fuller to nod. The third berth had been out of commission for weeks, and nothing had been done to repair it. Roberts wasn't about to land the *Horizon* on it. This left only two working berths in the camp, and the *Specter* was taking up one of them.

"My ship flew with the airship *Horus* and the merchant marine *Utopia*. Balaklava's now got fresh supplies that need moving, and I need both berths open at camp. Your airship is in the way. The sooner she lifts, the better."

His tone was commanding, but his intent was kindly. Fuller stammered out several thanks, which Roberts waved off. Seeing Fuller on his way, Roberts stomped up the gangplank, moodily chewing over the situation. He expected no thanks from Dunlap who might just very well punish Fuller for accepting help from Roberts. However, with the *Horizon* and *Horus* operating in Crimea, they needed both berths in camp clear. The *Dark Squall* was going to have to relocate to Balaklava where she could take the third berth and stay out of the way.

That evening, Roberts landed the *Horizon* at the camp's wharf before nightfall. When the airship was shut down, Roberts collected Jenkins, Sparrowman, and Abelman and took the men over to assist the *Dark Squall*. Plenty of muttered grumbles accompanied the engineers, but they were eagerly welcomed on board by the *Dark Squall's* crew, desperation having won out over animosity.

Roberts was graciously welcomed by Fuller into a stark captain cabin even more bare than Roberts' own. Stammering and apologizing profusely, Fuller offered Roberts a chair and shakily poured out two tots of what Roberts suspected was brandy reserved for very rare occasions. Accepting a glass, Roberts examined Fuller, looking at his thin face and the blue veins in his hands.

Abruptly, he inquired, "How are your food stores? Did Captain Dunlap leave you with enough?"

Fuller said nothing, but his face told Roberts everything he needed to know. Frowning, Roberts said, "My ship flew up from Constantinople with her larders stocked. We can spare you what you need."

"Captain Roberts, you've done enough..." Fuller feebly protested but Roberts waved him away.

"There's starvation enough in camps, and it may be weeks before you see Captain Dunlap again. No sense in your men going hungry."

Fuller looked down into his glass. "We've no right to ask for your help, sir, and you've no reason to offer it."

Frowning, Roberts finished the brandy in a stiff, determined gulp. It was poor stuff, but it lent heat to his bones. "I've no quarrel with your captain that he didn't pick himself," he stated sharply. "He's a damned, stubborn fool but I'll not see your men starve."

He set the glass down firmly. "We'll get your ship to Balaklava. She'll be safe there and out of the way. With luck, Captain Dunlap will return soon and with supplies enough to get you back to Constantinople."

Fuller was near speechless with humble gratitude, but Roberts had little time for thanks. His offer of assistance was practical: the *Dark Squall* needed to get off the camp wharf and out of the way. To Fuller's sputtering protests, Roberts towed him back to the *Horizon* to claim some food rations while Jenkins, Abelman, and Sparrowman worked diligently with the *Dark Squall*'s sole engineer.

By morning, the *Dark Squall* was heating up on the wharf, her boiler steaming and her engines clanging. An exhausted Jenkins stayed on board to assist while Abelman and Sparrowman blearily returned to the *Horizon* to help prep her for flight. To the collective cheers of both crews, the *Dark Squall* shakily lifted from the wharf and staggered into the sky while the *Horizon* hovered just ahead, leading the way.

The few miles to Balaklava were tense, but the *Dark Squall* kept her altitude and continued to move forward. At last, she landed on the wharf, her engines groaning in protest. Roberts strode over to assess the situation, and Fuller met him on the gangplank, visibly relieved.

"Well, we didn't crash, sir," he said with feeble humor.

Roberts nodded. "Keep her at port. We'll keep an eye out in the skies for Captain Dunlap."

Fuller nodded, but Roberts was already pushing the situation out of his mind. The *Dark Squall* was safe and, more importantly, out of the way. Roberts would keep an eye on her, but the airship would simply have to wait in Balaklava for Dunlap to return.

Fuller looked as if he was going to say something, but he kept it to himself. Roberts, hearing his airship calling to him, took his leave and turned to the gangplank. He was halfway down it when Fuller's hesitant voice paused him.

"Captain Roberts." Roberts looked back at Fuller who was stiff-jawed and determined. "I want to apologize for the actions of my captain and my..." Fuller began but Roberts interrupted him.

"Save your speeches, lad," Roberts responded with gruff kindness. "I've no time for them."

Fuller looked resolute. "I will tell Captain Dunlap what you have done for us, sir," he promised.

Roberts' laugh was hard in the frozen air. "He will give no thanks to you nor myself." He turned again from Fuller, admonishing over his shoulder, "See to your ship. Keep your men alive. Get them out of here as soon as you can."

"I will, sir. Thank you." Fuller's words echoed in the snowflakes as Roberts trod heavily back to the *Horizon*, grim and thoughtful.

Chapter Thirty-Four

"Morning, sir. Cold enough for you?" Farrington quipped tiredly in passing. Roberts stamped his boots on the deck, already forgetting what it felt like to have warm feet. As usual, the *Horizon* had frozen to her berth overnight, and snow heavily crusted her topdeck. It would take the full heat of the boiler and engines to thaw her out enough to lift.

"Cheer up, sir," Carter called out to Roberts while thumping Farrington's shoulder. "It's February. Only another six months of winter."

Blowing on his fingers, Roberts looked out over the frozen bay, silently counting what cargo they had left to transport. It wasn't much. Between the *Horus* and the *Horizon*, the two airships had nearly cleaned out Balaklava of supplies. It was anyone's guess when another supply ship would arrive, and the starvation in camp was nowhere near abating.

Roberts glanced briefly over to the berth where the *Dark Squall* sat. Dunlap still hadn't returned to claim the airship, and it sat frozen on the wharf, waiting for his return. Roberts kept an eye on it, and he knew Fuller was doing his best to keep the airship and his men together. However, if Dunlap didn't show up soon, the *Dark Squall's* crew would have to find a ride down to Constantinople and wait for spring. The airship was stuck in Balaklava, and there was no sense in making her crew suffer. The airship would be safe in Balaklava until spring arrived.

A particularly sharp burst of frozen air skittered across the wharf as Roberts tried not to shiver. However, as he gazed over the bay, he saw the dark shape of a marine ship in the foggy distance. Seizing his spyglass, Roberts trained it through the air and was heartened to see the *Morning Star* approach. With ice blocking her path, she could not enter the bay but she was close enough to see. As Roberts examined her, flashes of clicker code began running across the frozen waters.

"Captain!" Bloomberg called out in alarm, but Roberts was already translating the code. *SOS. Help requested.*

"A ship's floundering, sir, the *Iliad!*" Bloomberg rushed. "The *Morning Star* is sending a position report for it. Permission to respond, sir?"

The *Horizon's* boiler was cold, save for a pilot flame keeping the water from freezing, and her canopy was deflated and flaccid. It would be over an hour before the airship was ready to fly, but her assistance had been requested and she would respond.

"All hands to your stations!" Roberts roared, sending the airship into a frenzy. "We're going to the aid of a foundering marine ship. Double-time *now!*" The crew had been mostly listless and cold with the start of the morning, but Roberts' command broke them out of their drowsiness.

As the crew hurried to get the *Horizon* into the air, Roberts caught sight of a longboat cutting through the icy bay. It was hard going, and the sailors manning the oars labored heavily to bring the boat to shore. At long last, the longboat ran aground on the muddy beach. Instantly, a sailor jumped free and raced towards the air wharf.

Roberts meet him on the ladder. "First Seaman Preston Ives of the *Morning Star*, Captain Roberts!" the sailor gasped out. "We sailed with the *Iliad* and we saw enemy action two days ago. The *Iliad* took the brunt of it, sir. She hit ice along the coast, and is sinking. Captain Fosselweight requests that you go to her aid if you are able."

"We saw your clicker code. We'll lift as soon as we can," Roberts replied quickly.

Seaman Ives nodded. "Per your permission, Captain Roberts, I'm to stay with you and guide you to the *Iliad*. The *Morning Star* is returning to her, but Captain Fosselweight wanted me on board the *Horizon*."

"Permission granted," Roberts conceded. Ives nodded, then flailed his arms at the longboat. The sailors pushed off shore and began rowing back to the *Morning Star*. Glad for another pair of hands, Roberts set the newcomer to work. Ives was no airman, but he was quick and could take orders. His efforts helped the *Horizon* rise into the sky after forty minutes of heroic work.

As the *Horizon's* envelope inflated under the dull sun, Roberts keep scanning the heavens for the *Horus*. The aether flyer had stayed behind at camp the prior night to attend a minor airbag problem. Roberts could have used Wulfe at his side, but with no sign of the *Horus*, the *Horizon* would have to complete the mission on her own.

The *Horizon* lifted and, with the guidance of Ives, exited the bay and flew into gray, cloudy skies. Visibility was poor at best, and thick mist clung to the coastline, masking the sight of pounding waves driving against the beach. Ives spotted the *Iliad* first, and the *Horizon* quickened her pace. As she moved in closer, Roberts saw that there was no saving the *Iliad*. She had wrecked on a jagged patch of rocks, and the ocean was violently pounding her to pieces and sucking her down into its frozen depths.

The *Morning Star* was making valiant efforts to mount a rescue, but the *Iliad* had ran aground on a jagged stretch of rocks. Surging waves tossed longboats around like toys. The sea was murderously cold, and anyone falling into it would succumb within minutes. Hard winds battered the *Horizon*, shivering her in the skies, but she held true as her captain and crew surveyed the catastrophe before them.

Her lift basket dropped toward a cluster of sailors clinging to the railing of the *Iliad*. Frozen, injured, and desperate, they swarmed the lift basket, filling it to the brim. A few began climbing the rope in a desperate attempt to reach safety. Others saw the lift basket and crawled towards it in crazed fear.

"Basket aloft!" Roberts roared. "Bring it up now!" he ordered. Already the lift basket was overloaded, sailors flinging themselves on it as it rose up in the air, its wince creaking under the strain. A scream of terror rose up as a sailor slipped his grasp, his flailing body dropping into the frozen water below. Those safely in the lift basket were trying to assist their comrades, but fear and terror hindered their efforts.

Grimly, Roberts directed his men, shutting his ears to the sound of another sailor losing his grasp. The *Horizon* could not save them all, those who had already slipped under the waves or who were struggling with crushing hypothermia or were being battered to pieces against the rocks. The airship lifted and lowered her basket, bearing those she could to safety.

The *Horizon* deposited her load of shivering sailors on the *Morning Star* and returned to the doomed *Iliad* for more. Back and forth she flew, lifting sailors off the shattered decks of the *Iliad* and plucking them from the dark waves. Longboats rowed across the water, but two of them capsized in the process, adding more victims for the *Horizon* to rescue.

The waves grew fiercer and time ticked passed. As the winds beat more strongly across the *Horizon*'s bow, the crew began to realize that there were no more souls to rescue. Bodies dotted the waves and lay broken on the pounding shore. More had slipped below the waterline, but the living had been harvested from the dead. With that sober thought, the *Horizon* abandoned the wrecked *Iliad* and fell behind the *Morning Star* as the merchant marine turned her prow toward Balaklava.

Thick ice blocked the bay, and the *Morning Star* was forced to make anchor off of Balaklava, well away from the rocky shore. In the frozen, wind-battered conditions, there was little comfort the *Morning Star*'s crew could offer the shipwrecked sailors. Nevertheless, they accepted the additional passengers and ministered to them with care, despite the pressure on space and resources.

In the midst of the chaos, Roberts ordered the *Horizon* to drop him and Harding down on the *Morning Star*. Harding plunged into the swarm of new patients the moment his feet touched topdeck. He left Roberts to greet Fosselweight who was hurrying through the crushing press of bodies.

"Thank God for your airship, Captain Roberts," Fosselweight boomed as he seized Roberts' hand. There was little time for pleasantries for the *Morning Star* was groaning with sailors, many of them injured and all near crazed with cold and fear. Bringing them ashore was pointless. They would be better sheltered and warmed on the *Morning Star* than on Balaklava's frozen mud.

"You didn't have any airships with you?" Roberts yelled over the noise.

Fosselweight shook his head. "None that would come to Crimea." To his immediate right, a sailor rolled over on his knees and began vomiting, blood mixing with his stomach's contents. Fosselweight placed a steadying hand on the sailor's shoulder. The man struggled to rise, but his legs would not hold his weight.

"Sailor Barning, take this man below decks," Fosselweight ordered. A sailor rushed forward to obey, carrying the injured man below decks which was overflowing with casualties.

It was growing late in the afternoon when the chaos on board gave way to order and the initial panic and shock wore off. Captain Jones, master of the *Iliad*, had survived the wreck at the cost of a shattered leg that he was refusing to let Harding amputate until he was assured that his men had been cared for. Thirty-seven of the *Iliad*'s ninety sailors had been lost to the waves, and nine more died of their injuries before night fell. Fosselweight had lost two of his own men in the rescue, and his face was dark with grief as he and Roberts shared a hasty meal in Fosselweight's cabin.

"She should have turned back," Fosselweight stated soberly. "We were a hundred and fifty miles from Crimea when we encountered a Russian fighter. She engaged us both, and the *Iliad* bore the brunt of it. I urged Captain Jones to return to Constantinople, but he was resolute and determined to bring supplies up to Crimea without delay." Fosselweight set his knife down and tiredly rubbed his eyes. "Had she turned back, she might have survived."

"Captain Jones made his decision. He knew the risks," Roberts replied tiredly, knowing that his words were no comfort. Glancing out the cabin window, he saw a line of longboats rowing cargo ashore from the *Morning Star*. Despite the maritime disaster, supplies were urgently needed inland and Balaklava was astir with activity. In the distance, the *Horus* droned loudly as she brought a load to camp. With fresh cargo to transport, there was little time to mourn the dead. They could only concentrate on the living.

Fosselweight followed Roberts' glance. "I dare not risk my ship in the bay."

"She'd be stuck fast until spring," Roberts shook his head. "We'll unload her where she is."

Fosselweight looked strained. "I cannot keep her here long, Gavin. Not exposed to the coast like this, and not with my hold full of injured men."

"The *Horus* is here," Roberts spoke bracingly. "She can lift cargo off your ship almost as well as the *Horizon*. We'll clean you out as quick as we can and get you out of here."

"And yourself?" Fosselweight spoke pointedly. "You intend to keep your ship in Crimea through the winter?"

"Winter's more than half over," Roberts shrugged philosophically. "She's lasted this long and she's commanding better transport fees than I can earn elsewhere."

"At what cost?" Fosselweight's voice was sharp but full of concern.

The comment rankled Roberts but he spoke evenly. "She's strong enough for it. My men are as well."

It was a moment before Fosselweight responded quietly. "I would see you return to Constantinople with us."

"Soldiers would starve then," Roberts shrugged.

"They are starving now," Fosselweight insisted evenly. "This is a fool of a war, Gavin, hastily entered into and even more badly planned." He frowned, then stated carefully, "It perhaps would be wise to consider if the admirable and wholly commendable actions of your airship are inadvertently prolonging a conflict that is best speedily resolved."

"I'm no politician, Archibald," Roberts grunted dismissively. "I flew my ship here to find work and she's found it. I'll keep her here as long as she can earn money."

Fosselweight fixed Roberts with a cool glance which he returned. "You brought your ship back," Roberts stated roughly. "You obviously see profit in it."

"I came back partially for you and your ship, Gavin," Fosselweight spoke with a trace of heat. "You're a good man, and your airship is excellent. I am disinclined to losing either. However," he stated firmly. "I cannot risk bringing the *Morning Star* to Balaklava again before spring. This winter is not nearly spent, and the weather will not improve for months."

"My airship is staying in Crimea," Roberts insisted with dogged stubbornness. "There's too much at stake to leave."

"Resolute to the last, I see," Fosselweight sniffed, but with some admiration. "You dashed stubborn fool."

"The cold can't hold out forever," said Roberts, leaning back heavily in his chair. He tried to will himself into warmth with thoughts of the oncoming spring.

"Hmmm. Can you?" Fosselweight crossed his arms over his narrow chest.

"I don't aim to come out of this a hero," Roberts pronounced. "But I damned well aim to come out on top."

Fosselweight huffed, then leaned over to fill Roberts' glass. "A toast to you, Captain Gavin Roberts," he said wryly. Lifting his glass in a wry salute, he stated, "To your infernal stubbornness and bull-headed will. May it be enough to see you through the winter."

"To yours as well," Robert returned the gesture. "Fair speed to your engines and may your ship get back to Crimea quickly. I could damned well use the cargo."

Fosselweight laughed. The sound of his voice mingled with the shouts of sailors and the cries of the injured below decks as nightfall cast dark shadows across Crimea.

Chapter Thirty-Five

Snow fell, dropping down on the *Horizon*'s wooden decks as she flew through the bitterly cold air. Patrolling topdeck, Roberts sunk his chin into his collar and gazed wearily out over the snow-coated landscape surrounding him. It was early mid-afternoon, but if the snow continued, the *Horizon* would make no more transports for the rest of the day. Visibility was falling, and unknown dangers could lurk in the skies. Since the *Horizon*'s return to Crimea, there had been no reports of Russian airships, but there was no room for carelessness. Roberts wouldn't risk his airship or his men, not when the slightest of mistakes could send them all crashing to the ground.

Shuffling through his thoughts, Roberts pinpointed the day as February 19th. Time had ceased to mean much. Spring seemed as far away as the moon, and winter had not exhausted its store of brutality. Wincing as he stepped, Roberts was fairly certain he was going to lose a toe on his left foot to frostbite. Bloomberg, William, and Oboe also had severe frostbite on various digits. Harding monitored the crew carefully, but Roberts suspected there would be less fingers and toes on the *Horizon* once spring finally arrived.

The airship moved woodenly through the sky as Roberts paced topdeck, impatient to get the transport over and the *Horizon* back to Balaklava. Few of the crew were topdeck, most seeking tasks below out of the elements. Barking Jack was alone at the wheel. Approaching the pilot, Roberts questioned, "Need me to take over?"

"We're switching after the drop, sir," Barking Jack responded briefly, shaking his head. Due to the bitter elements, the pilots rotated every hour to keep from freezing. Bloomberg was currently below decks warming up after his shift. The *Horizon* had a running drop ahead of her, and she needed Barking Jack at the wheel.

They were bound for a winter camp ten miles to the east of Balaklava. Roberts wasn't exactly pleased with their destination, but Prachett had asked him to consider it, and Roberts had conceded. Although most of the soldiers were wintering over in the main camp, there were other camps scattered around Crimea in desperate need of supplies. The camps were effectively stuck where they were until spring, and Roberts knew that the *Horizon* was the only way to get food and supplies to the soldiers. It would mean a long series of running drops, a difficult feat made extremely so by the harsh weather and poor flying conditions.

Roberts scanned the sky, measuring visibility and daylight hours at a glance. There was an edginess in the air that he could not quite identify, and he wished the *Horus* were at his side. Wulfe had kept his airship in Balaklava Bay to attend an engine problem, and the *Horizon* had set out alone.

Glancing ahead, Roberts paused, then turned violently to look again. Swiftly, he yanked his spyglass out and jammed it against his eye.

"Captain?" Barking Jack questioned, following Roberts' gaze. "Oh, shite," the pilot swore.

Roberts didn't waste a moment. "Enemy ships approaching!" he bellowed into the com device. "Man your stations! Gunnery crew to your posts!"

At his word, the decks of the *Horizon* burst into activity. Crew members, formerly preoccupied with staying warm and getting the drop over with as soon as possible, were now racing about the airship on high alert. With few people topdeck, no one but Roberts had spotted three Russian airships sliding through the frozen air, their prows pointed at the *Horizon*

You damned, damned fool, Roberts growled at himself. *You've gone soft.* It was painful but true; the *Horizon* had been months in Crimea with only a few encounters with enemy airships. As time passed and winter grew harsher, Roberts' main focus had been on keeping his airship together and his men from freezing. His vigilance had waned slightly, and his men had grown a trifle lax about keeping their eyes peeled for attackers. But there was no time for Roberts to chastise himself further; the Russian ships were closing in fast.

"Man your posts!" Roberts barked loudly. "Hard to portside and nose in the air, Barking Jack! Engine room! Full power *now!*"

"Not easy with a full load, Captain!" Jenkins hollered back through the com device. Roberts' eyes narrowed. The *Horizon* was carrying twenty-five tons of cargo, her maximum capacity. Each launch was a strain on the airship and, with the hazards she faced, it was preferable for her to carry more and make fewer trips to and from Balaklava. She was currently full to bursting with tents, food, and medical equipment, and the weight made her sluggish.

Jenkins, Sparrowman, and Abelman shouted vigorously in the boiler room as they struggled to get the *Horizon* every last ounce of speed and altitude she could muster. At the wheel, Barking Jack fought to pull the *Horizon* up sharply while Roberts swept his spyglass toward the enemy vessels. One was slow in the air, but the other two were rapidly gaining ground. The *Horizon* was fighting for more speed, straining against the cargo weighing her down.

Roberts shot a quick glance at the speed meter and shouted, "We're only at twenty-two knots! Full power, *now!*"

"Trying, Captain!" Jenkins yelled back. "But she's got too damned much weight in her!"

To compound Roberts' troubles, the snow was falling faster and thicker. Visibility was dropping by the minute, and fog threatened to appear. One of the Russian vessels started to blend into the snowfall. Roberts watched it worriedly, torn between an enemy he could not see and two others that were becoming rapidly clearer. The *Horizon* needed to escape but even if she could reach forty knots, Roberts wouldn't fly her that fast unless visibility dramatically improved.

The sound of cannonfire roared through the white air, but there was no impact on the *Horizon*. She was kicking up more speed and rising in the air, but two of the Russian vessels were very close, well within cannon range. Roberts could just see that both airships had run their guns out and were struggling to target the *Horizon*.

Cannonfire. Not grappling hooks, Roberts thought quickly. This meant that the other airships were aiming to shoot the *Horizon* down, not take her as a prize. Trying to take another airship in the air required a finesse that presented easier defense maneuvers. But it was glaringly clear that the attacking airships wanted to sink the *Horizon*. Three Russian airships spitting out gunfire was a perilous scenario, and flying conditions were too dangerous for fancy defense maneuvers.

The crew of the *Horizon* held back their panic as the first of the three Russian airships surged ahead, close to the *Horizon*'s aft. Roberts, snapping out orders and keeping both eyes in all directions, was nearly knocked off his feet as the *Horizon* juddered sharply. Her Vandenberg had shot off, and the noise of the explosion screeched through the snowy air. Roberts had given no order to fire and was instantly angered that it had happened. As his eyes followed the trail of the rogue fire, all his protests died.

A Russian airship was enveloped in thick curls of hot steam. Screams of agony rose in the air as the steam poured along the topdeck. Roberts jerked his spyglass out and trained it though the almost opaque air, cursing the low visibility. Through the avalanche of steam and crazed panic on the Russian airship, he could just make out that the Vandenberg shot had torn through the other ship's steam valve network, the most vulnerable part of an airship. That one shot had completely crippled the Russian airship, and she was already starting to sink towards the ground. Steam roared across her main deck and engulfed her crew in agonizing waves of boiling heat. She'd be a wreck on the frozen Crimea ground in a few moments, no longer a threat to the *Horizon*.

"Captain!" Carter's voice roared over the com device. "That was a weapons misfire, sir!"

"That was a hell of a shot!" Roberts barked back into the com device. "Fine work! Two more misfires like that, and we're free and clear!" But there was no time for congratulatory celebration. The other two Russian ships had spotted their fallen comrade and were bent on revenge. What once might have been merely an order to kill on sight was now personal.

A quick glance at the controls told Roberts that the *Horizon* was running at twenty-seven knots, not nearly fast enough. "Engine room!" he barked loudly. "You've got one minute to get us up to thirty-five knots!"

"This blasted bird is not going to go much faster, Captain!" Jenkins shouted in exasperation.

"Then make her," Roberts commanded, wishing heartily for Halloway's presence, as he knew Jenkins was also doing. Halloway was the only person capable of wresting every last ounce of effort out of the *Horizon*'s boiler and engine system. At a time like this, an ounce of energy could mean the difference between life and death.

Another cannonball rocketed overhead, missing the *Horizon*'s envelope by mere feet. Barking Jack jerked the wheel, sending the *Horizon* up into the sky. She shimmied through the snow-flecked air, a Russian airship hot on her tail and the other one close behind.

"We'll rise to fifteen hundred feet, then drop as fast and hard as we can!" Roberts ordered loudly. "Mister Jack, you've pulled off more running drops than I can count, and by God you'll do it this time. Get her down low, then porpoise her across the ground. Visibility's piss-poor. We'll ram the Russians into the ground!"

"Too risky, Captain!" Barking Jack shouted.

Roberts shouted him down. "We're better off fighting low!" he commanded. This flew in the face of standard airship battle tactics, but Roberts knew that in this particular case, height was not their friend. The clouds were lying low and thick with no promise of clearer skies up higher. There were plenty of unexpected barriers underfoot, but the *Horizon* was accustomed to hovering a few dozen feet above the ground. Roberts doubted the Russian airships would perform well at low altitude.

Barking Jack looked furious about his orders, but he obeyed, sending the *Horizon* up into the heavens while the engineers sweated to push the airship faster. Roberts would have dumped cargo if he could, but every hand was needed to keep the airship moving forward. There wasn't any time to throw cargo overboard to lessen the weight.

The *Horizon* seemed to find some hidden reserves of strength. Her speed meter quickly pushed up to thirty knots as she raced upward into the air.

At the apex of fifteen hundred feet, Barking Jack hauled painfully at the wheel and sent the *Horizon* plunging towards the ground in a sharp swan dive. The weight in her hull and Barking Jack's hands on the wheel lent the *Horizon* speed as she roared downward. The two Russian airships wheeled and dove after the *Horizon*. They were swift but clumsy, their response time lagging far behind the *Horizon's*. With her increased speed on the downward slant and her superior maneuverability, the *Horizon* quickly surged ahead.

Frozen air bit into the crew as the *Horizon's* decks tilted steeply, setting the airship on a line to plow heavily into the ground below. The cargo in the hull was carefully secured, but the men on board were fighting to keep their balance as the decks tilted underfoot.

"THREE HUNDRED FEET!" Barking Jack called out.

"STAY ON COURSE!" Roberts commanded sternly.

"SHE'LL CRASH, CAPTAIN!" Barking Jack bellowed.

"STAY ON COURSE!" Roberts repeated the order, his eyes trained on the swirling snow around them.

"TWO HUNDRED FEET!" One Russian airship was clinging to the *Horizon's* tail, matching her speed and angle of fall with some accuracy. A cannonball rang out, but it missed the *Horizon* by several yards.

"ONE HUNDRED FEET!" Barking Jack yelled. The ground below was visible, and ragged trees capped with snow whipped past the *Horizon* as she continued to plummet. The Russian airship slowed its fall to avoid crashing into the ground. Its speedy descent was threatening to become an uncontrolled fall.

"FIFTY FEET, CAPTAIN!" Barking Jack screamed with controlled anger.

"LEVEL HER OUT AND HOLD HER RIGHT UNDER THE RUSSIAN SHIP!" Roberts ordered. With superhuman effort, Barking Jack pulled the *Horizon* out of her nosedive and wrestled her level. Abelman and Jenkins shouted fluent curses from the boiler room, and the rest of the crew scrambled to keep the airship from slamming into the ground. For one heart-stopping moment, she seemed poised for a crash. At the last second, she righted herself and her decks leveled. The *Horizon* skimmed through the air, Barking Jack clinging grimly to the wheel and watching intently for any tall obstacles.

At Roberts' orders, Barking Jack quickly inserted the *Horizon* underneath the Russian airship's gondola and kept her there. The Russian airship continued to drop, trying to force the *Horizon* to the ground, but was making a poor job of it. The airship staggered drunkenly through the air, popping jerkily up and down while the *Horizon* flew just under its gondola. Roberts barked out his orders, his men racing to obey even as the ground below beckoned treacherously. The air was thick with the clashing of engines and the stink of anxiety as the white void of snow threatened to consume them all.

Finally Roberts gave the command. The *Horizon* popped out from underneath the Russian airship, her Vandenberg pointing at the enemy a few dozen yards away. Despite the driving snow, Roberts could see some of the Russian airmen. They were panicking as the *Horizon* suddenly loomed in their path, gun at the ready.

The *Horizon* rocked as her Vandenberg loosened a shot. One hundred and fifty-two rounds of metal cut through the white air and blasted a hole through the Russian airship's envelope. Steam gushed from the airbags and shrieks of panic filled the air as the Russian airmen scrambled to attend their damaged vessel. She wasn't fatally wounded, but she had been neutralized and was no longer a threat. Roberts wasted no time calling for his men to climb up into the heavens and away from the battle. The Russian airship was sinking towards the ground, and the *Horizon* was able to flee the scene unchecked.

Without a backwards glance, Roberts turned back his crew, who were suddenly jubilant in the face of two enemies downed. Mindful of the third Russian airship somewhere in their vicinity, Roberts did not allow his men to celebrate their victory. "There's another one of them out there somewhere!" he bellowed. "Keep your wits about you!"

There was no sign of the third vessel as the *Horizon* quickly exited the scene, soon at a thousand feet and rising. Skies were clearer once she topped off at a thousand feet, then hovered in the air so the crew could catch a breather. From the blizzard of reports flying in, Roberts quickly assessed that his little bird had escaped with only minor flesh wounds. Big Tom patched some holes in the envelope while Harding made a quick assessment of the men. There were some bruises and cuts, but the crew was essentially unharmed.

Mindful of the third Russian airship, Roberts kept the *Horizon* at a thousand feet while her crew attended to her injuries and tried not to freeze. Everything below the hull was a blank void of white, but the snowstorm abated not long after the crew completed their assessment of the *Horizon*. That accomplished, they flew to the British Headquarters with paranoid attention to their surroundings.

Sorry, Staff Sergeant, Roberts thought grimly. *I'll not risk my men and my ship again.* He knew it would mean death to the soldiers huddled in smaller camps, but it was too risky for the *Horizon* to fly anywhere but from Balaklava to the British camp. Roberts would keep her strictly on that flight path and stay well away from the rest of Crimea.

The British camp was its normal mess of sagging tents and dying men, but Roberts was exceedingly glad to see it. Carefully, he directed the *Horizon*'s landing and held off the crowd of soldiers waiting on the wharf until he was certain that the airship was settled properly. Only then did he turn his attention to Major Bryson, who stood waiting.

Bryson looked anxious as he examined the *Horizon* critically. "Were you attacked, Captain Roberts?"

"We ran into some trouble in the sky," Roberts reported shortly. "Three Russian birds."

"Three?" Bryson looked shocked. "The Russians can't build a decent airship to save their souls."

"Well, they had a few that were good enough to fight us," Roberts rolled his shoulders tiredly. "We downed one, damaged another, and lost sight of the third."

"Two in ruins? With one gun and a few rifles on board?" Bryson smiled in respectful astonishment. "Captain Roberts, if there isn't a medal waiting for you when you return to London, I'll eat my hat!"

"It was luck and some fancy flying from my pilot," Roberts waved away the officer's praise. "I'd rather not trust to luck again if I can help it."

"You've got a star in your hand, Captain, there's no mistaken," the major said in a voice of wonder. "And, I'm dashed grateful for the tents," he added as swarms of soldiers began carrying rolls of canvas out of the *Horizon*. "We've been stacking men like firewood inside the tents, but that still leaves too many of them sleeping in the snow. I don't want to tell you how many of my men have died from exposure."

Roberts heard the words, but, considering the circumstances, he was more concerned about his airship. He directed the unloading of the *Horizon* and carefully lifted her off the wharf for Balaklava. With luck, the *Horus* would be back on her feet. The *Horizon*'s recent skirmish had rattled Roberts deeply, and he was determined that his ship would fly no more solo missions. She and the *Horus* could perform transports together and watch each other's backs.

As the airship gained altitude, her crew was edgy and alert. Roberts fought to keep his tone level as he tried to reassure his men. The topdeck was full, and Barking Jack had plenty of company: Bloomberg, Carter, Long Tom, and William paced the deck looking for potential enemies. Despite their recent attack, Roberts was slightly more at ease now that his airship was sailing the well-worn flight path from the camp to Balaklava. This area was well away from the Russian-occupied territory and was only a few miles from Balaklava. Although he was cautious, he didn't expect trouble along the way.

The clouds were just shaking loose some more snow when a warning drone of engines sounded. Roberts turned sharply to see a Russian airship drop out of the thick cloud cover and begin making a beeline towards the *Horizon*. It was intent and purposeful, its crew yelling over the frozen air and its cannon pitching heavily towards the *Horizon*.

Dammit, Roberts thought, momentarily more irritated than alarmed. Aggravation burned hot in him as he roared at his men and charged toward the helm, intent on getting rid of the new assailant. The situation was perilous, but the *Horizon* was in a better position to defend herself. She was empty and this time facing only one attacker. If the oncoming Russian vessel was the third of the trio that had attacked prior, the *Horizon* would have little trouble outmaneuvering it.

Roberts' men raced for their posts, alert and determined, but before they could start evasive maneuvers, flames burst in a blaze of orange streaks as cannon fire roared out. There was a split-second where the only sound was of heavy iron streaking its way across the sky, and then the *Horizon* shuddered as if mortally wounded. Splintered bits of wood flew in the air as men were knocked off their feet, their cries of alarm mixing with the scream of belabored engines.

Roberts staggered, grabbed the railing to keep his footing, and yelled a string of orders at Barking Jack. "HARD TO STARBOARD AND CLIMB!" he roared. He could instinctively tell that his little bird had taken a hard blow. Barking Jack jerked the wheel, but the *Horizon's* response time was sluggish and hesitant, even with an empty hull.

The Russian ship approached, a riot of bullets flying from her starboard. Roberts bellowed, "HIT THE DECK!" Bullets sprayed the hull, pebbling it with holes. At his post, Barking Jack got a bullet through his arm, the lead shot punching through the living flesh on his left arm, just above the joint where the construct arm attached. Bloomberg, heedless of the flying lead, hurried forward to take the wheel from the wounded pilot.

From the moment of the attack, the *Horizon's* crew kept their wits about them. Damage reports were beginning to pour in from all fronts, and voices rang out in alarm.

"Captain! Engine One sustained heavy damage!"

"Twenty five knots and falling!"

"Portside damage, sir! A hole about three feet wide blown through her!"

"Airbags stable, sir, no damage to the envelope!"

"She's leaking oil like a stuck pig!"

The *Horizon* was too badly damaged to flee; her only option was to fight back. Cursing the snow which had started to fall again, Roberts spat out a fresh volley of orders.

"Long Tom! Carter! Farrington! Lock on target and fire at will!" he commanded to the gunnery crew that were anxiously waiting orders to fire. After a minute or two, a shot burst from the *Horizon*. It exploded in the air, right off the Russian airship's aft, completely missing its mark.

"FIRE AGAIN!" Roberts barked with increasing volume. The gunnery crew scrambled to reload. While they manhandled the Vandenberg, the Russian airship let loose another cannonball that barely missed the *Horizon*. Roberts swore that he could reach out and touch it as it passed.

The *Horizon* shot off her Vandenberg again, and this shot was better aimed. It punched a hole in the Russian airship's bow forward, not near anything vital, but enough to give the Russians something to worry about while Roberts decided his next move. Despite the snowfall reducing visibility, he knew Balaklava was just a few miles ahead. With luck, the soldiers posted at Balaklava would hear the noise of the air battle coming their way and would be ready to shoot down the Russian airship once they had a clear shot. If the *Horus* happened to be in the air, she would come to the *Horizon*'s aid.

For one moment, Roberts stood silent, intent on his next move, his mind processing information and calculating the circumstances with measured precision. In contrast, his men were a scrum of frenetic activity, the crew attending the airship and shouting information at each other. Bloomberg was struggling with the wheel, Barking Jack hanging on grimly and arguing that he could still fly while Bloomberg insisted on taking over. Eyes turned Roberts' direction and time seemed to slow, his mind vividly registering miniscule details such as a bead of sweat rolling down William's face or a flutter of torn canvas flapping in the wind.

But this slow, intense reverie was broken as engines whined in the distance. Roberts turned his head to see a small, tumbledown pile of flying timbers drop out of the sky. Black smoke poured from the back of the airship, turning the falling snow to ebony as the ship wheeled to face the Russian vessel.

"The *Horus*!" Bloomberg screamed into the air. "Captain, it's the *Horus*!"

Roberts raced to the railing and peered out to see the *Horus* approach, Wulfe just visible topdeck. He called out something completely unreadable to Roberts, who got the message and hurried to get the damaged *Horizon* out of the *Horus'* way. The little aether flyer had come with guns blazing, and she wasn't about to let the Russian airship escape.

Cannon muzzles swung into the frigid air and blasted out their payload in one enormous thunder of noise. Four cannonballs streaked across the snow-drenched sky and thudded into the Russian vessel, two smashing into her gondola, one cutting a channel through her envelope and the fourth skittering across topdeck, flinging men off the ship and sending sharp splinters of wood flying through the air.

Barking a roar of triumph, Roberts waved at the *Horus*, then snaked his head around to see the Russian airship sinking fast. Panicked screams filled the air as she pulled her crew down with her. Steam rushed out of her ruptured envelope, melting the falling snow as her keel sank downwards. With luck, she would manage a hard landing, the snow below cushioning her fall. Controlled crash or no, she was defeated and no longer a threat.

There was no time for jubilation; the *Horizon* was wounded and struggling to keep aloft. She was listing to portside, and her canopy was losing steam. Below decks, Engine One gave up the battle, and the other two engines bore the load of keeping the ship moving. She could still fly, and her crew labored to keep her in the air.

A roar of engines, and the *Horus* skipped up to portside, a few dozen feet from the *Horizon*. Wulfe's bellows closed the gap nicely.

"AHOY, HORIZON!" Wulfe roared. "BALAKLAVA'S A FEW MILES AHEAD. STAY ON OUR TAIL AND KEEP IN THE AIR! WE'LL LEAD THE WAY!"

The aether flyer sailed forward, slowing its pace to keep the *Horizon* within visual. Roberts fought to keep his airship moving. She was hurting, and the driving snow did her no favors. Harding was busy with the wounded, tending to Long Tom who had a concussion from striking his head, Barking

Jack's bullet hole, and other cuts and shrapnel wounds. The few miles to camp seemed like a vast distance, and Roberts was worried that they would not make it.

Not soon enough, both airships spotted Balaklava and dropped down from the sky. Landing the injured *Horizon* was difficult, especially since Barking Jack refused to leave the wheel despite his wounds, and kept hovering over the helm, hindering Bloomberg's every step. The rest of the crew was careless in their anxiety, rushing to get the *Horizon* down safely before gravity overcame engine power and the airship fell to the ground of her own accord.

Painfully, the *Horizon* lurched downward until she finally settled into a berth, snow hissing as it hit the boiling hot steam valves and the airbags already deflating in the frozen air.

Chapter Thirty-Six

The moment the *Horizon*'s gondola hit the berth, Roberts started roaring out orders. He wanted to march over to the *Horus* and heartily thank Wulfe for saving the *Horizon*, but the needs of his damaged airship trumped courtesy. Wulfe would have to wait.

However, it wasn't long before heavy feet stomped across the snow-covered wharf in the direction of the *Horizon*. Wulfe's enormous frame moved toward Roberts like a draft horse plowing through a field, his gigantic boots kicking through the knee-high snow. Around Wulfe were three of his crew members, their slender frames like small moons orbiting a massive planet.

Roberts didn't bother waiting to welcome the four men on board, opting to thunder down the gangplank and meet them head on. Wulfe's face was split by an enormous smile, which Roberts mirrored. When the two men stood face-to-face, a handshake was not sufficient. Not caring that it looked a bit undignified, Roberts grabbed Wulfe in a hearty bear hug and just about got his arms fully around the man. Wulfe returned the embrace, nearly cracking Roberts' ribs in the process and pounding him hard enough to collapse a lung. Both men amiably beat on each other for a few moments, then broke apart still grinning, albeit with Roberts knowing that he would take away some significant bruises.

"My ship would be a wreck without your help. My hearty thanks, Captain Wulfe," Roberts proclaimed with heartfelt relief. "You came through in the nick of time."

"Pff, the *Horizon* had already put a cannonball through that damned Russian. You slowed her down enough for the *Horus* to get her shot in," Wulfe said bracingly, then his face sharpened into worry. "Your men? Your ship?" he questioned.

"My men are alive. The ship was knocked around a bit, but she'll live."

Roberts spoke the words confidently, but there had only been time for a hasty assessment of the *Horizon*. He didn't know the full extent of her damages and was simply grateful that she had made it back to Balaklava. After he returned to his airship for a more thorough evaluation, the full extent of her injuries began to unfold in grim light.

Carter and Farrington were already hard at work nailing boards over the hole in the hull to block out the driving snow. The hull was peppered with smaller holes that, in a milder climate, would simply be ventilation vents. In subzero weather, they filled the airship with freezing cold. The envelope was torn, and two airbags were leaking steam. The men themselves were battered and bruised; Long Tom had suffered a particularly bad blow to the head. Nursing their injuries and trying to keep the cold at bay, the crew set to work assessing the airship and starting repairs.

As afternoon wore away, the crew determined that Engine One had suffered the brunt of the attack. Grease-soaked and filling the engine room with swears, Jenkins, Abelman, and Sparrowman hovered over the engine. The three engineers were grim, and their general consensus was that Halloway's presence was sorely missed.

"I can repair her, Captain, but she won't fly forty knots and she sure as hell won't get the efficiency she had." Jenkins bent down and gestured curtly at a complex network of cogs and delicate wiring. "This is his baby, and only he knows it inside and out. That damned cannonball ripped right through the most complex segment, and it's not getting put right again without Halloway. It would have been one thing if he'd left me the blueprints, but he keeps them all in that head of his."

Jenkins made an unsuccessful attempt to wipe some of the grease off his hands. "With the right supplies and enough time, we can get her back on her feet, but she won't be the airship she was, not without Halloway," he pronounced.

Roberts considered this, then asked, "Would she be able to make it to Constantinople?"

"Slow, but she'll get there," Jenkins said worriedly. The problem is..."

"If we encounter anymore Russians," Roberts said.

Jenkins nodded. "Then we're well nigh finished, Captain," he said with heavy certainty. "She won't be able to outrun them and won't be able to duck them."

Roberts paced restlessly, trying to think logically, but battle fatigue and stress bore down on him heavily, clogging his thoughts. However, one thing was glaringly apparent: they were done in Crimea. The *Horizon* was barely flyable, and she wouldn't be transporting anything more without some serious repair work.

With fatigued resolution, Roberts worked his way through the airship, assessing damages and assuring his men as best he could. They were plagued with exhaustion and injury, and all were consumed with worry about the future. There were precious few resources in Balaklava for airship repair. Unless the *Horizon* could limp her way to Constantinople, her crew would be forced to winter over in Crimea, something Roberts wanted to avoid at all costs.

Wulfe tactfully kept his distance for a few hours to allow Roberts time to assess his airship and crew. Toward nightfall, Wulfe made another trip to the *Horizon* to offer assistance to his colleagues.

"My stores are open to you. Whatever you need is yours for the asking," Wulfe offered generously.

"My thanks," Roberts replied wearily.

Wulfe picked at his beard worriedly and asked, "Will she fly?"

"With luck, she'll make it to Constantinople. There, I have a better chance of getting the parts and supplies I need." Roberts ran his hands through his hair. "Problem is, I left my best engineer in London. The boiler and engines are his design. If I can get her to London, he can put her to rights again."

"There's transport ships in Constantinople. You should be able to find one to follow back to London," Wulfe spoke bracingly. "It's a long flight, but if you've got a marine ship to watch your back, you should come to no harm."

Roberts nodded, but he could not think much past Constantinople. Just getting the *Horizon* there would be a heroic feat. Flying her from Constantinople to London would require more luck and strength than his airship or his men could muster. Nevertheless, the *Horizon* needed Halloway. Somehow, Roberts would find a way of getting her back to London.

With a sigh, he spread his hands in a gesture of defeat. "We're finished here," he stated simply. "The *Dark Squall* is still down, and I don't know if Dunlap intends to return before spring." He paused and looked at Wulfe pointedly. "That leaves the *Horus* as the only transport airship in Crimea."

Wulfe looked pained. "My ship's strong, but these past few weeks have put years on her. This is no place for an airship to fly, Roberts. I know they need us right bad but..." he shrugged helplessly. "I can't risk keeping my ship up here much longer."

Roberts had suspected as much. Both captains fell silent for a moment, digesting the magnitude of the situation. There would be no transport airships left in Crimea, unless another captain wanted to take the risk. If a merchant marine ship arrived in Balaklava, the military would be left dragging goods overland, pushing carts through frozen mud, and lugging supplies on the backs of weary soldiers. Supplies would likely pile up in port, stuck in Balaklava while tens of thousands starved to death in the camp.

Staff sergeant Prachett took the news quietly, as did the handful of officers. Roberts broke the news in a dilapidated supply tent that served as a mobilization base for equipment moving in and out of Balaklava. Prachett and several officers were present, and Roberts faced them squarely, Wulfe at his side. With plain words, the two airship captains gave notice of their imminent departure from Crimea. The *Horizon* was a casualty, no longer able to fight, and the fierce climate had claimed victory both from the *Horizon* and the *Horus*.

"I'm sorry," Roberts spoke honestly to the solemn officers. "If my airship was able to stay, I'd keep her here. But she's damaged and, even empty, it's a struggle keeping her in the air. If I can get her to London and get her repaired, I'll return if I can. Until then..." He wasn't quite sure how to finish the sentence, but the faces of the officers took up the task. *Starvation. Disease. Death. Exposure. Defeat.*

Despite this, there was no admonition in the men facing Roberts. Quietly, a captain whose name Roberts vaguely remembered as Worthington, said, "It is we who have failed you, Captain Roberts and Captain Wulfe. The number of times both your airships have flown unescorted missions, the risks you both have taken without backup." Heads nodded solemnly around the tent, and Worthington cleared his throat. "I fear we have grown far too complacent about Russia's lack of airship power, even when the *Horizon* was harried in the sky months ago. We did not take heed, and the *Horizon* suffered for it."

"I knew the risks." Roberts' voice was hard. "You paid me well for them." The *Horizon* had earned stacks of coins in Crimea, but much of Roberts' profits would now have to be funneled into repairing her instead of paying her off. It would be an expensive flight back to London, and an unknown period of time before the *Horizon* would be able to earn her keep again.

The meeting lurched awkwardly to a close. Many of the officers hurried out of the tent after biding Roberts and Wulfe a hasty goodbye. The two airship captains departed in silence, both mulling over their circumstances as they stepped back into a light snowfall on a bleak, blustery day. On the way back to the wharf, Roberts abruptly broke the silence.

"Seems you'll have to delay your wedding again," he commented with more biting humor than he meant.

Wulfe responded lightly. "Mmm, I might be able to talk her into it anyway. Molly knows this damned fool of a war isn't ending soon. I don't think she'll keep me waiting that long."

Roberts laughed dutifully, but his attempt at humor died away with the residual warmth of the tent. With few words, he and Wulfe parted to return to their airships.

The *Horizon*'s crew was busy when Roberts stepped back on board. Sharp curses emanated from the boiler room as the engineers fought to bend recalcitrant metal and cogs to their will. The rest of the crew was grimly repairing the airship, consumed with getting her into shape to face the hard and dangerous flight across the Black Sea.

Three days of hard work got the *Horizon* shakily back up in the air once again, with all three engineers sweating over her engines and the *Horus* hovering around her protectively. Roberts was wracked with anxiety, knowing his airship's precarious condition and the vast stretch of water between her and Constantinople. A moderate squall at sea or an aggressive enemy airship, and she was done for. Not a man on board the *Horizon* was ignorant of their current predicament, and grim tension filled the airship day and night. All knew that there was a very real chance that they would be forced to abandon ship and have to climb on board the *Horus* while the *Horizon* sunk below the waves. Or she could plummet from the sky and sink quickly, taking them all down with her.

Consuming worry haunted Roberts every moment of their long flight back to Constantinople. It was a long flight indeed. Stiff headwinds lashed at the *Horizon*, slowing her already feeble pace. She did not reach above twenty knots during the eighteen hour journey back to the city. Wulfe did everything he could to ease the *Horizon*'s passage, even flying the *Horus* directly in front to block some of the wind, but the small aether flyer could not fully shield the *Horizon*. The damaged airship struggled as her crew coaxed and prayed for her to keep her place in the sky.

The *Horizon* limped into Constantinople under a heavy shroud of fog and with a thin drizzle of rain pattering down on the city. Despite the weather, no port had ever looked more beautiful nor more welcome. Exhausted, the *Horizon*'s crew landed the airship, finished their tasks, and collapsed into their hammocks with sighs of relief. Numb with complete fatigue, Roberts moved blearily about his ship one last time to assure himself that she was down safe and secure at last. *That's my lady*, he thought, patting the wheel with numb fingers. *Thank you*. With that last semi-coherent thought, he made for his own cabin, barely reaching his bunk before oblivion hit.

Only a small portion of their journey was completed, and the work was just beginning. Now safely in the city and with access to supplies, the crew could make some serious repairs. They all slept late, but when the men finally rose to their feet the next day, Roberts had a long list of tasks for them. He was determined to get his airship back to London as soon as possible.

A week passed, and then another. February passed away, and March arrived damply. Rain and fog continued to press down on the city, chilling bones and hindering repair work on the *Horizon*. Her crew was certainly warmer than they had been in Crimea, but the constant rain and chill humidity were their own brand of misery. There were supplies and equipment in Constantinople, but everything was costly and obtained only at a great struggle.

Wulfe kept the *Horus* in Constantinople for a few days, but he eventually turned his prow out of the city. He had work of his own to seek and a crew bored and restless. The two crews parted company with much handshaking and well-wishing. Roberts watched with a sinking heart as the *Horus* flew away. He could make use of the *Horus'* courage on their journey back to London, but he could not ask that of Wulfe.

Roberts knew it was foolhardy flying the *Horizon* back to London alone, but finding a marine ship to accompany would be a difficult task. He wouldn't fly with another captain unless he was reasonably assured that the other ship would come to the *Horizon's* aid if she ran into trouble. Half-crippled, the *Horizon* could offer little to a partnership except surveillance. The first three marine captains Roberts spoke with didn't want a damaged airship hovering over their masts, even one whose name was well-known.

Luck turned Roberts' way in the form of the *Mauritania*, a steamship bound for London. Upon learning Roberts' name and the name of his vessel, Captain Holland warmly welcomed him aboard.

"Of course, I would be glad to have the *Horizon* accompany the *Mauritania* back to London," Holland said with quiet calmness. "Your name and the name of your airship have been filling the papers for months, Captain Roberts. It would be an honor to sail with her."

"We encountered enemy action in Crimea a few weeks ago, and my ship suffered some damage," Roberts stated honestly. "She flies, but she's weak in the air. I can provide surveillance and navigation, but I'll be honest, Captain Holland. My ship will be of little help to yours in an attack."

Holland's pleasant expression did not change. "Surveillance and navigation from your airship will be much appreciated. My ship has eighteen cannon. She can fight well on her own." He cradled a thin china cup between his long fingers and looked thoughtful. "You are, of course, welcome to borrow any supplies or equipment you need," he offered graciously. "My stores are open to you."

"My thanks," Roberts replied sincerely. "With some repair work, she'll make it to London. Not fast and not gracefully, but she'll get there." With only a tiny pang of guilt, he helped himself to a third cup of coffee from the pot on the table. It had been a long night and a short sleep, and he needed all the energy he could muster.

"My ship will be detained in Constantinople another week, Captain Roberts," Holland stated, gesturing with his hands. "Please, feel free to take what you need to prepare your ship for travel. It will be a long journey back to London."

Roberts was grateful for the offer, and his crew gladly raided the *Mauritania*'s stores for equipment and parts. He protested only feebly when Captain Holland insisted on paying the *Horizon* a daily stipend for what surveillance and navigation assistance she could provide. It was less than the *Horizon* had earned partnering with other merchant marines, but Roberts took it gladly.

The week in Constantinople passed quickly, and Roberts struggled to prepare his airship for the long journey. His men made what repairs they could and labored hard to put the airship to rights again. A week later, the *Horizon* lifted into the damp air, the *Mauritania* sailing below, as both ships set out for London. The *Horizon* flew, but there was no strength in her movements and Engine One was barely functional. In the envelope, Big Tom fought to keep the airbags full with the assistance of Carter. The rest of the crew did their work intently, alert for any slight change that signaled a serious problem rapidly developing.

It was a long, arduous journey across the Mediterranean. The *Mauritania* plowed steadily through the waters while the *Horizon* blundered heavily through the skies, her crew strained to the limit with keeping her in the air. Other airships dotted the heavens, some benign and some potential threats. Roberts kept his men on constant alert; carelessness could easily put the *Horizon* in the cross hairs of an enemy she could neither fight nor outrun. The *Horizon*'s crew kept watch on the water as well, but the airship couldn't help the *Mauritania* in the event of a marine attacker. She could only scout the skies and seas for enemies and steer both ships away from potential conflict.

The two ships stopped briefly in Greece for coal, but there wasn't any anthracite available. The *Horizon* would have to wait for Sicily, although her hoppers were low. Before leaving Constantinople, Roberts had filled the *Horizon* with all the anthracite he could find, which wasn't much. With her constant engine problems, the *Horizon* was burning through twice her normal amount of coal. Roberts could only cross his fingers in hope that Sicily would have anthracite. Otherwise he'd be forced to use bituminous, and the *Horizon*'s performance would further worsen.

When they landed in Palermo, the *Horizon*'s crew was relieved to discover a local mine that had plenty of anthracite. Roberts restocked the *Horizon* with coal and asked Captain Holland to carry a store, to which he agreed. The fuel issue resolved, the *Horizon's* crew was also grateful for the abundant sunshine that filled the city. For the first time in months, everyone on board was finally warm.

They tarried in Sicily only a day, for Captain Holland was anxious to keep moving. As the ships continued their journey to London, the *Horizon*'s movements became more labored. Although Jenkins, Sparrowman, and Abelman did their best to nurse her along as she flew, the strain of travel increased every day.

"The other engines are overstressed, Captain," Jenkins explained tiredly. "She's flying, but it's hard on the old girl."

"We've weeks of flying ahead of us to reach London," Roberts frowned.

"She's not got weeks of flying in her, sir," Abelman stated bluntly. "Not unless you want to see her at the bottom of the ocean. She's raddled as a three-penny whore and ride her as you like, she'll give you no satisfaction."

Roberts glared at Abelman, who shrugged. Sparrowman snorted in amusement, but the rest of the assembled men did not laugh. Farrington, Long Tom, and Oboe were in the engine room with Roberts and the three engineers, and their voices fought to be heard over the clashing engines.

"We should make for Barcelona," Long Tom said. "Patch up there, let her rest up a bit. From Barcelona, we could be home in a day, even flying slow." He leaned against the wall and scowled. "The *Mauritania* will just slow us down now."

"Inland, we've got mountains to climb and there's plenty of brigand airships over Spain," Farrington countered.

"We follow the *Mauritania* back to London and all we'll do is strain the ship," Long Tom pronounced flatly. "She'll never make it home."

"We'll go to Barcelona," Roberts commanded abruptly, silencing the argument. Flying over Spain was risky, but Long Tom was right. Every day in the sky was costing the *Horizon*. Weeks of flying would only increase her damages and result in a longer stretch of repair work, costs piling on top of costs. They would make what repairs they could in Barcelona, then nurse the airship home.

Long Tom's eyes gleamed, and he all but strutted out of the room, making no effort to disguise his gloating. Farrington was visibly angry, Sparrowman seemed lost in his own private world of exhaustion, and Oboe was silent. He fell in behind Roberts as the men exited the engine room.

"If you have input, I'm open to hearing it," Roberts grunted over his shoulder at Oboe.

Oboe's response was quiet, but weighty. "I think neither option is advisable, Captain."

Roberts laughed wearily. "Then what would you have me do?"

"I would have you be the master of the *Horizon*," was Oboe's response. "She will fly for you, and only you. And with that, she will bring us home."

They were working their way up to the topdeck, salt air blowing briskly over the wooden boards as bright sunlight bounced cheerfully off worn canvas and fading paint. Roberts could feel every tremor of his airship reverberating through his body, the movement of her cogs echoing in his blood, kinship twining himself through her. She was battered and weary, aching with pain, strained to her very filaments with the labors he had placed on her.

But she would carry them through, born up on her captain's own strength and the hearts of her crew members. She would not fail them. There was still steam in her canopy and power in her engines. It would be sufficient to see them through the end of the journey.

"She'll hold through to London," Roberts said to Oboe as the two men stood at the railing, wind in their hair and the cries of gulls breaking through the laborious crashing of the engines. "She'll get us home."

"No, Captain." Oboe's enigmatic smile was like a sunrise. "You will."

Chapter Thirty-Seven

It was April 14th on a fine afternoon when the *Horizon* flew into London's airspace, battered but unbowed. Her crew was weary but high-spirited as the city spread itself below their feet. Blue skies were dotted with white clouds drifting lazily among the dark shapes of airships droning across the heavens. The perpetual smoke and gloom of London was pushed away by fresh winds, lending the city a crown of splendor.

The *Horizon* had completed her journey with more strength than Roberts had hoped for. Their stay in Barcelona had been prolonged, but the city sold anything an airship captain could possibly want. With fresh supplies and equipment, the crew had been able to finish some significant repairs. The *Horizon* was still fighting serious trouble in Engine One and still plagued with a multitude of problems. Despite this, she had regained some of her strength and had made the trip from Barcelona to London with far less fuss than Roberts anticipated. His luck held, and the *Horizon* only gave him a moderate amount of trouble on the last leg of their flight.

When the *Horizon* landed at Kingston wharf, Port Master Riester welcomed the crew with all but open arms.

"Ahoy, *Horizon*!" Reister bellowed over the sound of her engines shutting down. He waited impatiently for the gangplank to lower and Roberts to step forward.

"Back from the war, Captain Roberts?" Reister crushed his hand enthusiastically, not waiting for Roberts to respond. "Got my boy home two weeks ago from Crimea. He said he was a passenger on your fine airship, that she brought him and a passel of injured lads from Crimea down to Scutari."

There were visible tears in Reister's eyes. "My boy would have died without you, Captain Roberts. I owe you and your airship more than I can ever pay."

"Hey, you lot!" Reister barked over his shoulder at a collection of dock workers. "Double time it! You get this airship whatever she needs."

"Whatever she needs," Reister repeated, turning to Roberts. "She'll be treated like a queen, sir, and her crew will have the best hospitality in London." He had still not let loose of Roberts' hand, and he continued to crush Roberts' fingers as he examined the *Horizon*. "You run into some action, Captain?"

"A couple of Russian airships," Roberts responded. He barely got the words out before Reister yelled again.

"You! Burbane! Bring me the master shipwright!" A dock worker snapped to attention and hurried off. "We'll have her set to rights soon, Captain Roberts," Reister stated cheerfully. "And don't you worry about cost. You've done enough service to Queen and country that said country can throw in a repair job on the house." He winked roguishly at Roberts. "I'll bury it in the paperwork somewhere."

"There's a mad scientist running around London I need to find so he can rebuild an engine," Roberts rumbled, wondering where Halloway was lurking. He likely had marched back to the burnt remains of his former workshop and stayed there. If not, it was going to be a devil of a time tracking him down. Halloway had likely had enough of human contact during his time on the *Horizon* and was probably hiding somewhere, well away from other people.

Reister bellowed and shouted, and soon the *Horizon* was surrounded by an army of dock workers, carpenters, and ship boys. Her fatigued crew found themselves elbowed out of the way by assiduous souls intent on getting the *Horizon* repaired. Reister meant well, but Roberts had to put a tactful handle on the port master's enthusiasm. Halloway, once he could be found, would have his own plans for repair work. He would likely undo just about everything Reister was trying to get fixed on the *Horizon*.

"We're in London for at least a few weeks," Roberts assured Reister. "My men are exhausted and need some rest and time with their families. She'll hold a few days. Right now, I'm more concerned with my crew."

Reister, however, continued to press his services. Roberts only needed to say the word for a dozen men to spring forward. At last, the airship was bunked down for her stay in London, and Roberts tactfully escorted Reister and his men off the *Horizon*. He then turned his attention to his own men, who were chomping at the bit to depart.

Although the airship hadn't earned anything in two months, Roberts was generous with pay, and every pocket was heavy. At their captain's dismissal, the crew of the *Horizon* gleefully abandoned the airship. Farrington departed in haste, nearly frantic to get back to his family. Bloomberg left with similar promptness, eager to resume his courtship of Ruth. William bore away his earnings with pride, striding tall in the company of Carter. Barking Jack and Abelman swapped dirty jokes and talked loudly about women as they debarked, Jenkins a few feet behind them. The rest of the men dispersed quickly, save Oboe, who seemed in no particular hurry to leave. He moved about the ship easily, smoothly fending off the worst of Reister's offers of help and quietly assisting Roberts with the little tasks that never cease needing done on an airship.

Afternoon burned away and nightfall was approaching, but Oboe remained on board in an unobtrusive, yet decidedly present manner. The two men moved in companionable silence about the airship, Roberts restless and preoccupied, Oboe calm and watchful. Around suppertime, a trio of dock workers arrived with a hot dinner courtesy of Reister, whose generosity had not ebbed.

Roberts and Oboe accepted the meal gratefully and ate it quietly, both intent on their own thoughts. Finally, Roberts commented over the blancmange, "Ground leave applies to you as well. There's not much to be done on board until I can find Halloway, and God knows how long that will take."

Oboe looked thoughtful. "You will be visiting Sir Smothers while we are in London?" he questioned.

"Yes," Roberts replied. The time had come for him to face Sir Smothers and make a payment on the *Horizon*. While it had taken a significant amount of Roberts' savings to nurse her home, he had money waiting for him at Rothschild Bank and more on board the *Horizon*. There was enough for a substantial payment, and he would offer it as proof to Sir Smothers that Roberts would honor their agreement to the letter.

It would be an unpleasant excursion and potentially dangerous. The *Horizon* had not kept a low profile during her months in Crimea, and Smothers had surely read about the airship's exploits, thanks to Miss Pickens. There had been months for him to plot his revenge and devise other ways of making Roberts' life difficult. Nevertheless, Roberts would not shirk from the task at hand.

Oboe tapped the blancmange on his plate, watching the white gelatinous mound shimmer under his spoon. "You will do this alone?" he questioned.

"Some things a man has to do himself," Roberts rumbled with firmness.

Oboe was silent, as if choosing his words. Finally he said quietly, "Are you sure that is the wisest course of action?"

"This is between him and me. I'm not dragging anyone else into this," Roberts grunted.

In truth, he would have appreciated Oboe at his side, but this was a private matter. Roberts had endangered his crew enough. This was something he would face alone.

Oboe opened his mouth, then closed it, worry edging his face. The meal concluded and the men's companionable silence disappeared, to be replaced by thoughtful brooding. Oboe was visibly ill at ease, almost hovering around Roberts as they bore away their plates and tidied the eating area.

Preoccupied and weary, Roberts repaired to his own cabin for a stretch of uninterrupted rest without the sound of engines mixing into his dreams. As he slipped into sleep, Roberts was dimly aware of Oboe's feet pacing lightly across the topdeck of the *Horizon*.

Oboe's silent watchfulness did not abate the following morning as both men stirred to life, Roberts intent on the unpleasant meeting ahead of him. He performed ablutions in a tin bath and shaved thoughtfully, gazing at his reflection in a small mirror propped up on a shelf. There was more gray in the mirror than he recalled, and his face had grown sharp and craggy. Dressing in his one presentable set of clothing, Roberts noticed that the garments hung loose on his frame. Crimea had thinned him. He tightened his belt and set his jaw grimly.

Oboe watched silently as Roberts trundled away in a steam cab weighted down with heavily locked money chests. He was armed and grimly alert for anyone wanting to relieve him of his money, but he met no opponents on the way to Rothschild. The journey was remarkably quick through London's crowded streets. It was a fine spring morning with warmth pouring down from the heavens. Nothing hindered Roberts' passage, and the cab zipped easily across the cobblestones towards an affluent area of London.

At the bank, two bank guards obligingly assisted Roberts with carrying his wealth into the bank, where he immediately attracted the attention of several cashiers. Roberts had cherished private dreams of pouring a river of gold coins onto Smothers' desk in a grandiose show, but he rejected the idea. Coins would take far too long to count, and he did not intend to be in front of Smothers any longer than necessary. Instead, Roberts directed the cashier to count out forty crisp one hundred pound bank notes: easy and unobtrusive to carry yet still impressive in their own right. This left just under a thousand pounds still in the bank. The *Horizon* would need it for repair work and wages while she languished at port waiting to be put back to rights again.

The cab car was waiting, puffing out clouds of steam. Roberts reentered it, the small sack of bank notes carefully hidden away in his jacket. The cab car turned its wheel towards the Smothers empire and bore Roberts through the teeming streets. Horses, pedestrians, and other steam-powered transport systems all jostled for just a little bit more cobblestone space as the noise of the city pressed down hard.

As the cab passed the *Times* building, Roberts glanced up at it. He felt a sharp twist in his stomach as thoughts of Miss Pickens rushed to his mind. He had done his best to forget her, tried his hardest to push her out of his mind. But his thoughts had an uncanny way of swinging back to the dark-eyed reporter, like a tongue returning to worry at a canker sore.

Scowling to himself, Roberts forced Miss Pickens out of his head. The task at hand demanded all his concentration. As the cab pulled up to the gates of Smothers' empire, tension knotted in his stomach. He forced himself to relax. It was enemy territory, but he'd be damned if he would let Smothers see him sweat. Coolly, he stepped out of the cab and paid his fare. The vehicle scuttled away in a steam-powered burst of energy, leaving Roberts to gather his courage and stride forward boldly.

The sprawling workyards were crammed to bursting with activity. The clank of automotons and the groaning squeal of gears clashed loudly with the bellowed orders of men. The familiarity of the place was sharp and poignant in Roberts' gut, but he kept his eyes on the opulent building ahead of him. As he marched boldly through the crowded yards, he made eye contact as he went. There were men he knew, but most were careful to avert their eyes from his gaze. They knew the black mark that Roberts carried on his broad shoulders. Exchanging a word with the captain of the *Horizon* was tantamount to treason against Smothers.

There were two guards posted at the front door of Smothers' office, and they were careful to neither notice Roberts nor prevent him from entering. He returned the favor, striding easily past them and through the gleaming oak doors into the reception area. His worn boots sunk deep into the plush carpet. Roberts wasn't a particularly vindictive man but if he had been carrying a cigar with him at the time, he would have enjoyed tipping ash on the floor just because he could.

The clerks at the front desk rose to their feet the moment Roberts sauntered through the door.

"Mister Roberts, sir!" a reedy, pale young man bobbed his head fretfully. "Sir Smothers is waiting for you. This way."

Warning growled in Roberts' stomach. *Mister*, he thought. *Not Captain.* It didn't bode well. His arrival had clearly been anticipated, but Roberts wasn't surprised by that. The *Horizon* had touched down in London several hours ago, plenty of time for Smothers to arrange a welcome committee.

As Roberts entered Smothers' office with a heavy, measured tread, he saw that the richly papered walls were ringed with seven standing men. Three were roughly dressed heavyweights, and four sported well-cut suits and pale complexions. Roberts ignored them, his eyes fixed on Sir Smothers, seated at his luxurious mahogany desk, hands resting on top of it.

Roberts coolly took in his opponent at a glance. The ensuing months and grief from his son's death had not been kind to Smothers. He had a shrunken, drawn look, and his wrinkles were etched more deeply into his face. His white hair was thinner, and although his eyes still burned with the indomitable stubbornness of his soul, it was clear that mortal flesh was struggling to keep pace with the fire inside.

Behind Roberts, the door shut firmly, the lock drawing shut loudly and precisely. He ignored it, his eyes fastened on Smothers, each trying to outstare the other. There was a new construct limb on Smothers' arm, and this one was eerily elegant and life-like. Roberts watched as it lifted and began tapping the table with the fluid elegance of a living flesh hand, each motion as graceful and smooth as a dance. Only the faintest sound of gears and pistons echoed in the room.

All this Roberts took in at a glance. Without preamble, he strode to Smothers' desk and announced firmly, "Sir Smothers, I'm here to pay some on the debt I owe you." He retrieved the sack of money from his jacket and set it with a thump on the elegant desk. "Here's four thousand pounds." Only then did he notice Smothers' desk was free of the clockwork devices Albert had crafted long ago.

"I see." Smothers made no motion to reach for the money bag. "Well, Mister Roberts, and I will call you *Mister*," he stated, sardonically emphasizing the title. You have brought me four thousand pounds and that is well and fair." He settled back into his chair and looked at Roberts with ice in his soul. "That amounts to twelve and a half percent of your debt against the *Horizon*."

A thousand blinding furies screamed to life in Roberts' veins, but he held them at bay. "Our agreed price was fifteen thousand pounds," he replied evenly.

"Was it now?" Smothers questioned lightly. "And you have paperwork documenting this? Witnesses? Evidence?"

Roberts' fingernails dug into his palms as his fists clenched. "You well know, Sir Smothers, that we had an agreement between us. I was to pay you fifteen thousand pounds for the *Horizon* in three years."

Roberts had carried with him a persistent worry that the lack of official documentation of his agreement with Smothers would eventually cost him dearly. This concern had nagged him ever since the *Horizon* had come under his command. Now, standing in the middle of the office, he knew his worries had been well-grounded.

Smothers folded his hands again, metal fingers resting over flesh. "I do know that I agreed to sell you an airship, the very same airship which has been gaining an extraordinary amount of press coverage in the past several months."

As if on cue, one of the men quickly picked up Roberts' moneybag while others placed a fantail of newspapers on Sir Smothers' desk. Roberts knew instinctively that they contained articles from Miss Pickens' hand.

"Quite remarkable the abilities this airship has," Smothers said with light tones that were ominously like the first flakes before an avalanche. "A top speed of forty knots an hour. An impressive fuel energy percentage rate. An ability to operate in the most extreme conditions and with long distance flying abilities hitherto unseen in an airship of her class."

He gave Roberts a pointed look. "Clearly I vastly underestimated her worth before I allowed her to pass into your hands."

"She was a shattered wreck when you sold her to me," Roberts growled, his temper getting the better of him. "She had a damned big hole blown out of her side and a boiler that was a twisted mess, not to mention that she was twelve years old at the time. Fifteen thousand pounds was too much to pay for an old wreck like that, yet I agreed to that price, Sir Smothers. Whatever claim to fame she has for speed and fuel efficiency is due to..." Roberts stopped himself before he said Halloway's name out loud. "A damned clever inventor who gutted and refurbished her and..."

"Ah yes, your friend Jacob Halloway," Smothers said easily. "We've known about Halloway for years, despite his best efforts to maintain his privacy. In fact, I think he has been waiting for you." Smothers waved a hand at a subordinate and ordered, "Bring him in."

It was taking all of Roberts' strength to maintain his calmness, to keep himself from dissolving into a punching rage of fury that leveled anything in his path. But the sight of Halloway stepping awkwardly into the room was like a physical blow to Roberts' midsection.

"Jacob?" he said in a hollow, baffled voice, gazing at the inventor, who did not meet his eyes. Halloway was emaciated and gaunt, and he shuffled his feet restlessly. His eyes were red-rimmed, evidencing a return to his old habit regarding white powder and hypodermic needles.

Smothers' voice filled the room. "Halloway has been a particularly valuable addition to my research and development division," he stated smoothly.

Halloway said nothing, eyes intent on the floor. "You right *bastard*, Halloway," Roberts said with forceful finality. "I didn't think you'd stoop to *this*."

"That's enough language from you, Roberts," Smothers said crisply. He motioned to a guard. "Halloway has work to do. Bring him back to his workshop."

Roberts watched as the guard escorted Halloway out of the room, a meaty hand clamped down on Halloway's scrawny arm. Reason tried to intervene, tried to make some sense of Halloway's betrayal, but raw emotion had seized control of Roberts. With supreme effort, he turned his blazing eyes on Smothers and demanded, "What the hell did you do to him?"

He could hazard a guess. Halloway was helpless with anything that didn't involve gears and need oil. One too many nights on the streets would probably have been enough to convince Halloway to take an offer of a well-stocked workshop. But for Halloway to march straight into Smothers' arms was a betrayal that cut Roberts to the core.

"Halloway is now exactly where he needs to be, putting his considerable talents to use under the watchful eye of those who will ensure that he does not continue to steal ideas and ignore patents," Smothers said, cruelty edging his voice.

"*What?*" Roberts demanded. As an answer, thick, important-looking papers appeared and landed on the desk in front of him.

"These are eleven of the fourteen patent lawsuits that I currently have pending against Jacob Halloway," Smothers continued calmly. "For the willful and unauthorized use of my company's inventions and the blatant attempt to pass off original, patented work as his own..."

"*That's bullshit!*" Roberts roared. The four thugs stepped forward, and one cracked his knuckles loudly. In his rage, Roberts ignored them. Placing his hands on the desk, he leaned forward into Smothers' gloating face. "You know the whole damned passel of engineers you have in your entire blasted estate isn't worth half of Halloway. You damned well know that Halloway never stole an idea to save his soul. He didn't bloody well *need* to..."

Two pairs of hands appeared on Roberts' shoulders and forced him into a chair with practiced ease. They didn't let up as his posterior slammed into the soft seat cushion.

Smothers' voice rang out coldly. "Restrain yourself, Roberts. If you are in need of something to punch, Charley and Malter here will be happy to oblige you. I will warn you that they will punch back." The taller of the two goons gave Roberts a crooked leer and happily leaned the bulk of his weight on Roberts' shoulder, pressing him deeper into the chair.

The cushion under Roberts was practically burning from his rage, and he struggled to gain a grip on his temper. Some rational thought was floating up out of the boiling sea of his fury. *Think, think!* he demanded, calling up every ounce of common sense he possessed.

Even in his anger, Roberts could clearly see what had happened. Halloway had never taken out a patent in his life and never saw the need to do so. As a result, his inventions were widely pirated, stolen, and copied across Europe. Roberts had a pretty good notion that a nice amount of people had grown rich lifting ideas from Halloway. One of those bastards was currently seated behind the desk facing Roberts and gloating from every pore. Where money or a well-stocked workshop may not have sufficiently tempted Halloway, enough lawyers waving threatening summons could have convinced him to accept Smothers' offer.

Sitting in the chair and being systematically crushed by Charley and Malter, Roberts had a moment of admiration for Smothers. He had pulled it off perfectly, backed Roberts into a corner and cut off all escape routes. And sitting there, observing his victim calmly, it was clear Smothers knew exactly what Roberts was thinking.

Smothers continued, "The airship *Horizon*, of course, will be inspected by the Patent Office to ensure that it does not violate any current patent. If it does, you will be named along with Halloway in the suits and you both will be subject to the full force of the law."

Roberts glared at the four pale-faced men in the room, knowing that they represented only a tiny fraction of the lawyers Smothers had at his disposal. Smothers had not lost a legal battle in over thirty years, and there had been many souls that had attempted to overthrow him at the bar.

"Or..." Smothers let the word hang in the air, then selected a document. "I am prepared to offer you a choice, Gavin Roberts."

A long, stern-looking document slid across the desk towards Roberts. The two thugs on his shoulders let up enough pressure for him to pick it up. "The terms of our original agreement, except modified to represent the true worth of the *Horizon*," stated Smothers. "Pay me fifty thousand by our original date, and you're a free man and the *Horizon* is yours."

Roberts stared at it for several long moments. "Fine," he said tersely. "Then give me another three years to pay her off."

"You misunderstand me," Smothers said with cold heat. "Nothing in this document is negotiable. With the terms as they are, you have exactly two years and one month to pay off the balance you owe."

More harshly, Smothers intoned, "Walk out of this room without signing, Roberts, and you'll have the entire patent office swarming over that God-cursed airship. My lawyers will hound you to the ends of the earth, and every legal entrapment I can devise I will lay at your feet."

He looked pointedly at Roberts. "Sign this document and you have a chance at walking free in two years."

"And if the debt isn't paid by then?" Roberts demanded sharply, knowing the answer.

Smothers didn't blink an eye. *Then you are a dead man,* his expression stated eloquently. Aloud, he said, nothing, merely smiled cruelly at Roberts.

Roberts had never wanted more to draw a weapon on someone. His revolvers were hidden inside his jacket, just waiting for him to pull them free. He had no doubt that Smothers' henchmen were armed. Any move on Roberts' part, and they would shoot without question. Yet, the satisfaction of putting a bullet through Smothers' brain would almost be worth death.

Almost. But instead of reaching for his revolvers, Roberts reached for the document and forced himself to read it carefully. It was neat, legal, and exact, and it held Roberts' soul and body in its papery grasp. There were no loopholes, and the terms were simple but absolute. Grasping a pen with enough force to crush it, he posed it over the parchment. Roberts stopped himself just in time.

"I want a copy. Duplicates," he growled. From now on, he wasn't exchanging a word with Smothers without a paper trail, witnesses, and a lawyer of Roberts' own.

Not that it would do any damned good. Smothers had an entire stable of lawyers to extricate him from any legal difficultly he faced. It was months too late for proper paperwork or legal counsel. It had been so the moment Roberts had walked out of Smothers' office with nothing but a verbal contract and an unfounded expectation that Smothers would honor his end of their agreement.

Smothers didn't object. He snapped a few commands, and two identical copies of the document appeared. Roberts, rage in his soul, signed them all, watching narrowly as a witness mutely added his scrawl. With a flourish, Smothers' arrogant signature filled the pages, his construct arm carefully tracing each letter.

The silence in the room, penetrated by the sound of the pen scratching, was deafened by the roaring in Roberts' ears. Motion was happening around him, papers being lifted up and set down. Suddenly, Roberts was acutely aware of Smothers' insolent, triumphant smile gleaming his direction.

"I believe you were leaving, Roberts," Smothers said, his eyes narrowing. "*Now.*"

Chapter Thirty-Eight

Somehow Roberts made it out of the office, out of the workyards, and out into the streets of London with the legal documents inside his jacket. People fled at his approach, recognizing the stormy rage in his eyes and the set of his shoulders. It was the face of a man ready to unleash seven kinds of hell on the first hapless soul who looked at him the wrong way. He was furious and desperate and locked in the vast storm of emotion, blind instinct leading the way.

Without a plan or goal, Roberts stalked the crowded, dirty streets of London. His feet moved automatically, while his rational sense tried futilely to regain control. He had faced plenty of obstacles before; life had been one hardscrabble situation after another. Roberts had always managed to land on his feet. There had been luck at his hands, too many near-death experiences he'd avoided or bad situations he had worked his way out of, but *this* stood before him like the iron gates of Newgate Prison with the leg chains waiting for him.

Hours passed as Roberts' feet took him on an aimless ramble around the city. In a vague, clinical way, he was aware that he was hungry, thirsty, and exhausted, but the demands of his body were overridden by the all-encompassing finality of the documents in his jacket. He had no plan, no goal, not the faintest inkling of what to do next. Shock remained in control, and he felt a strange dissociation with the world around him.

It was only gradually that Roberts became aware of someone calling his name. He turned slowly to see Miss Pickens hurrying his way, her eyes bright. It was the sapphire blue skirt and jacket again, the color that enriched her eyes and emphasized the creaminess of her skin. A new hat was perched on her dark curls and her lips were curved with the panting effort of hurrying.

Dully, Roberts watched her approach, his inner being too troubled to process Miss Pickens' appearance. It was just one more shock to the system, and he had just about had all he could manage for the day. From the excited smile on her face, Miss Pickens seemed delighted at encountering Roberts in London. Either that, or she wanted something from him.

"Captain Roberts!" Miss Pickens called out. "Captain Roberts! All of London is...what on *earth* is wrong with you?" she exclaimed in surprise. "You look like you've been run over by a steam car!" Her head cocked fetchingly to the side as she examined him critically, her creamy brow knitting.

"Ca...*Gavin*," Miss Pickens said in a softer voice, laying a hand on his arm. "What is wrong?"

Suddenly all vestiges of determination and self-preservation fled Roberts. In a flat, dull voice, he recounted his story to Miss Pickens, sparing none of the details. They stood in the street together, her hand still on his arm, ignoring the endless press of humanity swirling around them. Miss Pickens' eyes went wide with shock and she lifted her other hand to her mouth, saying nothing as Roberts told his tale. By the time he had finished, her eyes had grown hard, and there was a stubborn, determined lift to her chin that he knew so well.

"Smothers cannot get away with this," Miss Pickens said darkly. "He will *not* get away with this, not if I..."

"*Victoria*," Roberts intoned. Without thinking, he reached out and clasped her upper arms gently, giving her the slightest of shakes, then sighed. "Let it go," he said wearily.

"Absolutely not," Miss Pickens responded sharply. "That old...*tyrant* has got to be toppled, and I..."

"*Victoria*," Roberts said in a louder voice, shaking her firmly. Her eyes opened wider. Sighing again, he dropped his head so that it was a few inches from her face. Closing his eyes, he said hollowly, "It's *done*. It's too late. Let it go. *Please*."

His last word was pleading. With his fingers still around her shapely arms, he could feel her sag in defeat. They stood for a moment, almost chest to chest, and Roberts swore he could hear her heart beating before she pulled away and he released her arms.

They both stepped back to a more respectable distance. Miss Pickens' eyes glimmered with tears. "I did this to you," she said softly. "This is all my fault."

"No," Roberts said wearily. "Smothers had it in for me the day his son died in the boiler explosion. I should have written the *Horizon* off as a lost cause."

"I made it worse for you," Miss Pickens interrupted. She twisted her hands together and flashed Roberts a look of genuine remorse. "I'm sorry."

In a better circumstance, Roberts would have welcomed the apology. In light of all that had happened, it was small consolation. Silence fell between them for a few moments as Miss Pickens continued to wring her hands together. "What will you do now?" she questioned hesitantly.

"Repair the *Horizon*," Roberts said gruffly. "Find her work. Figure out how to make forty-six thousand pounds in two years." The thought was so far beyond daunting that it deserved its own category, but he tried to focus on the present.

Repair the ship. Get her back in the air, he told himself sternly, although he knew he could not do so without Halloway's assistance.

Miss Pickens' eyes dropped as she bit her lips again. A deep intake of breath, and she said hesitantly, "I have...I have some bad news for you, Gavin. I mean, more bad news."

Roberts wasn't sure he could stomach more of it. Miss Pickens' eyes lifted to his face. "There is to be a railroad in Crimea," she said softly. "To link Balaklava Bay with the camp and move supplies inland. As soon as spring comes and they can start laying track."

Roberts took the news quietly. Miss Pickens tried to smile, but it faded. "I suppose I have done my work too well," she stated. "There has been far too much public outcry about how poorly our soldiers are equipped for our government to stand by and do nothing."

She sighed deeply. "A fleet of three marine ships left London at the end of January with supplies and parts for the new railroad."

His mind ran a brief calculation, and Roberts assessed that the *Horizon* had most likely just missed the fleet. If she hadn't been attacked by the Russian airships, she would have likely been at Balaklava when the fleet arrived bearing their new train system. With flat humor, Roberts realized that the *Horizon* might have been asked to transport some of the equipment, moving what would put her out of work in Crimea.

Miss Pickens' voice interrupted Roberts' thoughts. "You can thank Mister Samuel Peto for it," she said wryly. "He is the leading railroad contractor in Europe. He and his partners have personally taken on the cost of building the new railroad. They claim they will have it finished in a month."

"I see," Roberts said. *Well, that's that,* he thought with flat finality. The *Horizon* was out of a job in Crimea, even if he could get her fully restored. At her full strength, she would have been of great use in Crimea even when summertime made land transport easier. But now, there was no reason to return.

Miss Pickens lifted a clenched fist to her mouth as silence fell again, deafening and heavy. Roberts had so much to think about that his thoughts pushed together as one, like a crowd of people all trying to exit the same door. His entire body ached as if he had just been pummeled and there was a sharpness hollowing his stomach, as painful as acid.

Miss Pickens watched him with anxious eyes. "What are you going to do next?" she questioned, her hands twisting together again.

Roberts stood immobile for several long moments, Miss Pickens watching him anxiously. At last, he turned to leave, seeking words and finding none to say.

"Gavin. *Wait.*" A soft hand caught his and Roberts found himself staring into a pair of deep brown eyes, a few tears welling up in their soulful depths. Desire and dull warning clanged in his gut as Miss Pickens' head tipped his direction, stepping closer, the scent of her perfume in the air.

"I must go." Roberts turned his head from her, feeling Miss Pickens' fingers drop from his arm. He did not look back as he walked numbly into the thick crowds, leaving her behind to call his name over the sound of the streets. He closed his ears to her voice, his feet taking him through the narrow streets of London back to the wharf where his airship lay.

Overhead, engines whirred as a dozen airships glided in an intricate ballet across the sky.

Author's Note

Authors of historical fiction have the freedom to gleefully plunder the past for interesting tidbits and abandon irksome facts that interfere with the plotline. *Clouds of War* is no exception. In creating this work, I have happily rooted through many books, websites, and articles on the Crimean War and Europe's political situation during this time. I've attempted to bring real history and actual events into this tale, while adapting history to suit my particular ends. War historians will note that I pushed back the Charge of the Light Brigade by several weeks, as well as neglected (or bungled) many important elements of the Crimean War.

However, much of what I have described regarding Crimea's infrastructure and the state of military transport during the war is fairly realistic. Balaklava Bay was a difficult port, and the military had great difficulty moving supplies inland, particularly during winter. Many soldiers lost their lives to famine, disease, exposure, and other conditions brought on by limited supplies. All this lead to the construction of the Grand Crimean Center Railway in 1855, which greatly improved transport during the war.

The process of moving clothing, medicine, and food from one location to another is rarely featured in adventure tales. However, no military maneuver is possible without a long chain of supplies and people willing to transport them. "An army moves on its stomach" is an oft-quoted passage that is no less true now than it was during the Crimean War. Quartermasters and military contract workers may not earn many medals, but moving supplies and equipment through a war theater requires great stores of courage and determination.

Patient transport is another overlooked, yet crucial segment of war, as the *Horizon* demonstrates in her role of medical airship. The history of air medical transport began in World War I and was expanded and developed during the Vietnam War. Today, there are thousands of medical transport aircraft in operation, both civilian and military. Medical air transport is difficult and dangerous: I write this a few days after a medical helicopter crash in New Mexico that killed all three souls on board. Medical air transport during war is even more perilous. Yet battle produces great numbers of wounded patients. They need pilots and medical crews willing to fly through bullets and bombs to get patients to medical facilities.

War maneuvers involve a staggering amount of factors: shelter, communication, transport, leadership, training, weather, and terrain, just to name a few. In this novel, I have attempted to bring the focus away from standard fare in wartime historical fiction (one lone platoon taking a hill under heavy fire, love letters between a homesick soldier and his sweetheart, a maverick squad that breaks through a stronghold). Instead, my interest was drawn behind the lines, back in the camps and bases, and in command centers where the means of war happen. This is no mundane stuff. Within the logistics of war are many possibilities for a writer to explore, and these day-to-day activities deserve recognition.

The old proverb that begins, "For want of a nail" exists in various forms as early as the 14th century. For this steampunk adventure, we shall say that for want of a cog, a war would have been lost. However, the *Horizon* was there, along with other forces, to deliver supplies, transport patients, pass on information, and help win the battle.

About the Author

Melissa Ann Conroy is an Omaha, Nebraska native who has dabbled with words since birth. She earned a Master's in English literature (including a brief stint at Oxford), did freelance writing, and taught college-level writing courses for several years before finally producing her first novel.
Follow Melissa on
www.melissaannconroy.com
www.facebook.com/steamygirlpublishing

37552342R00234

Printed in Great Britain
by Amazon